Tangled Web

by

Tarn Young

Book Three of a Trilogy

Grosvenor House
Publishing Limited

All rights reserved
Copyright © Tarn Young, 2017

The right of Tarn Young to be identified as the author of this
work has been asserted by him in accordance with Section 78
of the Copyright, Designs and Patents Act 1988

The book cover picture is copyright to Tarn Young

This book is published by
Grosvenor House Publishing Ltd
Link House
140 The Broadway, Tolworth, Surrey, KT6 7HT.
www.grosvenorhousepublishing.co.uk

This book is sold subject to the conditions that it shall not, by way of
trade or otherwise, be lent, resold, hired out or otherwise circulated
without the author's or publisher's prior consent in any form of binding or
cover other than that in which it is published and
without a similar condition including this condition being imposed
on the subsequent purchaser.

A CIP record for this book
is available from the British Library

ISBN 978-1-78623-997-6

This book is dedicated to:

*My late mum, Joyce,
(my most avid reader),
who unfortunately died before
I had completed 'Tangled Web'*

My late dad, Charles Henry Hill

*My husband, Alan
My daughter Joanne and husband Mark
My son, Stephen and wife Cathryn
and my grandchildren, James, Matthew,
William and Megan
With much love*

Personal Acknowledgements

My husband, Alan, whose editing skills,
patience, encouragement and nautical knowledge,
proved invaluable

My brother, Garry
and in particular, nephew Christopher Hill for
suggestions and expertise in the production of the book cover

My love and grateful thanks to you all

Acknowledgements

'Google' search engine, a huge time-saver! For the extensive research required to give this book authenticity and credibility.
'Google' - Translate
Main web sites: Nottingham History – nottshistory.org.uk.
Wikipedia – enwikipedia.org.uk.
The Ships List – theshipslist.com.
gregormacgregor.com.
Encyclopedia Britannica – britannica.com
Victorian London – victorianlondon.org.
Middleton Guardian – menmedia.co.uk/middletonguardian.
Salford Hundred – Ancestros,
annals and history BBC –
bbc.co.uk. Jstor –
archives on line parish clerks –lan-opc.org.uk
'Everyday Life in 19th Century Britain' – Tim Lambert
English Victorian Society - kspot.org/holmes/kelsey.htm
'Who discovered it?' - discovery.yukozimo.com/who-discovered-polio

Books: 'The Writer's Guide to Everyday Life in Regency and Victorian England from 1811-1901', Author - Kristine Hughes
'Nottingham - As it is Spoke' - Volume Four, Author - John Beeton
'Nicholls's Seamanship and Nautical Knowledge'
– Brown, Son & Ferguson, Ltd. Glasgow
'Everybody's Pocket Companion' (reference book)
A Mercer, M.R.S.C.
'Great Classic Sailing Ships' – Kenneth Giggal
(paintings by Cornelis de Vries)
'The Encyclopaedia of Ships' – General Editor, Tony Gibbons

BOOK ONE: '**Silent Torment**' *is set in the mid-nineteenth century and follows the physical and psychological journey, of Lizzie Cameron, daughter of Agnes and William Cameron, crofters living in the Highlands of Scotland. The untimely death of Agnes in childbirth leaves William distraught. He shuns his newborn son, Robert and gives him away to his friends, Martha and Donald Stewart, to be brought up as their own child. Years later they are reunited.*

William and Lizzie seek work in Glasgow. Their possessions are few, but include Lizzie's 'keeper' box, a present from her father. Josiah Monks, a local priest, accommodates and secures employment for them.

Lizzie becomes housemaid at Low Wood Hall and befriends Kate, extroverted daughter of the owners. Kate becomes pregnant and draws the reluctant Lizzie into a scheme to keep her baby, which includes another conspirator, Kate's Aunt Jayne.

Lizzie leaves with Kate's baby, without word to anyone, including her brother, Robert and first love, Daniel Lorimer, boarding a steamship to Liverpool. After a brief encounter, with one, Marcus Van der Duim, ends in a proposal, they arrange to meet again, after Lizzie fulfils her promise to Kate.

Lizzie's plans go awry when she misses the Royal Mail Coach. Jack Garrett, an independent coachman, changes her route and, subsequently, her life. She arrives in Nottingham en-route to London and visits the Goose Fair, where stallholders, befriend her. She loses her memory when knocked to the ground by a runaway horse, whilst retuning to an Inn in thick fog. Found by a local family, Lizzie and the baby arrive in the Narrow Marsh slums.

Lizzie assumes the name of Hannah Merchant and rears Rosalie as her own, but her memory remains locked away.

Jack the coachman leaves for the onward journey, without Lizzie, but takes Molly his lover. The coach overturns and Jack is killed. Lizzie's luggage, including the 'keeper' box, containing important documents, are recovered by Molly, who survives, but only Lizzie has the key. The box's secret will remain locked away for five years.

Meanwhile, Kate receives word that Lizzie has failed to reach her destination, which sparks a series of dramatic events at Low Wood Hall.

In Nottingham, Lizzie touches the lives of everyone and encounters significant troubles in the local community. Five years later, after a chance meeting with Daniel Lorimer, her memory partially returns and the 'keeper box' resurfaces. Thereafter, a catalogue of revelations begin, culminating with the final piece of Lizzie's jigsaw falling into place.

BOOK TWO, **'Elusive Shadows'** is set between the months of February and December 1855 - Lizzie Cameron is now thirty-five and Rosalie, thirteen. Lizzie and Marcus Van der Duim live together in Littleborough, Lancashire. They have not been blessed with children, although Lizzie sees Rosalie as her own daughter. Marcus's first wife, Belle, his son, Jack and his best friend, Andries, are missing, presumed dead, after their ship, 'The William Brown' sank off Newfoundland. (Under the command of Captain George Harris, the ship departed from Liverpool on March 18, 1841 for Philadelphia. At about 10 p.m. on the night of April 19, the *William Brown* struck an iceberg 250 miles (400 km) southeast of Cape Race, Newfoundland and sank).

༺❀༻

Robert Cameron, Lizzie's brother, has discovered he is the father of Rosalie and is now actively seeking Kate Hemingway, Rosalie's birth mother. Lizzie's own emotional search for Kate, lies uneasily on her conscience. Their meeting could potentially change her own relationship with Rosalie, an integral element of the plot.

Author's Notes

The 'Second Industrial Revolution', in the transitional period between 1840 and 1870 provides the backdrop for the last book in the Trilogy. Technological and economic progress was gaining momentum with the introduction of steam-powered boats, ships and railway engines, along with large scale manufacturing of machine tools and equipment in steam powered factories.

Letters were still the prime method of communication (Penny Post 1840) – In 1845, the first telegraph service opened in the UK. By the 1850s, the sending and receiving of messages had been dubbed 'Telegrams'. By improving personal mobility, the railways were a significant force for social change. Rail transport had originally been conceived as a way of moving coal and industrial goods, but the railway operators quickly realized the potential market for railway travel, leading to an extremely rapid expansion in passenger services. The number of railway passengers trebled in just eight years between 1842 and 1850: traffic volumes roughly doubled in the 1850s and then doubled again in the 1860s. Land and sea travel still relied on the astute use of a humble compass.

Most of the events depicted in 'Tangled Web' are based on actual historical events, which coincided with the novel's time frame of 1855-1857 (December to December), with the exception of the 'Champion of the Seas' arrival and departure dates. In the Chapter entitled 'The Outing', information with respect to dates, times, specifications and descriptions are accurate. Only the year has been altered to accommodate the story line. These events affect the lives of some of the fictional characters, both rich and poor.

In some chapters, the dialogue has been conducted in the local Nottingham dialect. This is synonymous to an area named 'Narrow Marsh,' where everyday living was a struggle for the unfortunate, but remarkably stoical and optimistic inhabitants. The dialogue has been spelt phonically to assist the reader.

I have continued using footnotes to enhance the reader's enjoyment, which I believe contain many interesting facts and anecdotes. Consequently, my fervent hope is that the conclusion of the Trilogy meets all expectations, in what I believe to be a fascinating period in British History. The Crimean War, which affected overseas travel, ended in February 1856 – a conflict between the Russian Empire and an alliance of the French, British and Ottoman Empire and the Kingdom of Sardinia.

"Oh what a 'tangled web' we weave,
When first we practise to deceive!"

Sir Walter Scott (1771–1832),
Marmion, A Tale of Flodden Field,
Canto vi Stanza 17

Prologue

The principal characters re-emerge in a confusion of loyalty, disloyalty, intrigue, deceit and passion in mid-nineteenth century industrial revolution Britain.

Lizzie Cameron, central to the trilogy, engages with the intricate plot, woven around her family, adopted family and many friends.

Significantly, Rosie, Jimmy, Marcus, Kate, Robert, Jack and Daniel figure prominently in a tangled web of seemingly impossible situations. All are destined to reach climatic conclusions, thus ending the trilogy of exciting sub-stories and plots, sometimes calamitous, sometimes disastrous. Some themes are based on factual historical events.

The saga continues in the December of 1855. Lizzie and Marcus are starting a new phase in their lives, after Marcus is reunited with his long lost son, Jack Bernard. Marcus has proposed to Lizzie and are expected to marry in March the following year.

For Rosie Cameron, there is an uncertainty surrounding Jimmy's apparent loss at sea and her new relationship with Jack.

Ida, Jimmy's mother, also does not know if he is dead or alive. However, she believes in her heart that one day he will return.

CHAPTER ONE

Disbelief
'The Chestnuts' - July, 1856

James Renwick absentmindedly flicked through a pile of letters, left on the hall table. He gathered them together and headed for his study, before placing the stack on the leather bound blotter. His eyes focussed[1] on a small square envelope, of dubious quality, which immediately aroused his curiosity. He was significantly intrigued by the stark brevity of his name, lacking his formal title and address, obviously written by an unsteady hand. Using his ivory letter opener he carefully slit open the envelope and unfolded the single sheet. The content shocked him. The words leapt off the page piercing his brain.

In that blinding instant, his whole world shattered. Despite her earlier indiscretions, the apparent betrayal of his wife, whom he loved deeply, hit him like a thunderbolt. His hands shook in anger and he was visibly stunned. Stony faced and in total disbelief, he stared aghast at the short insidious message, devoid of signature:

---

1 Focussed/focussing – Collins English Dictionary – original spelling

'Your wife, Kate is having an affair with Robert Cameron'

He was totally unaware of the identity of the writer, so stood transfixed, with his hand on the brown leather chair for support, in an effort to evaluate the situation.

It couldn't be true...he refused to believe such blatant lies. It must be a cruel sick joke. He crumpled the paper in his fist, his sharp, white knuckles prominent against the pink flesh of his hand. In his all-consuming anger, he pushed the offending letter deep into his jacket pocket and strode disdainfully out of the study...

CHAPTER TWO

Revelations
December, 1855

Christmas Day promised to be a happy and festive occasion, because Christmas Eve had already heralded the reunion of Marcus and his son, Jack, to the delight of everyone present.

Lizzie and Rosie were both shocked but overjoyed that Jack had been living in their midst, in the unsuspecting guise of John Jamieson, son of Lizzie's cousin, Annabella.

Annabella was, in fact, Marcus's wife, known to him as Belle. He initially believed she had died at sea, together with his son Jack (John) Bernard and her lover, Andries, Marcus's best friend. Later he discovered, both had survived, although Andries had perished. The pieces of the puzzle finally fell into place when Marcus was introduced to John Jamieson for the first time. His resemblance to Belle was striking, confirming his sudden realization that the young man who proffered his hand in friendship was indeed his own son.

༄

Initially, John seemed incredulous. Such a revelation was almost beyond belief. Marcus too was stunned and silence prevailed, as the implication of their relationship slowly penetrated.

Lizzie immediately poured them a brandy, realising they would need a dose of 'Dutch' courage to come to terms with such an incredible chain of events, culminating in this meeting.

Astoundingly, Lizzie realised that she could supply some of the missing information. It transpired that shortly before her untimely death in Berriedale, Annabella exhibited some peculiar behaviour. Many seemingly anomalous events now became clear, particularly her reluctance to talk about her 'husband', Oliver and her total indifference to his death. Unfortunately, Annabella appeared incognizant of the ramifications involved, as she careered along a path of self-destruction. Her only goal was to find some unsuspecting male who would share her ambition to lead an exciting lifestyle of endless parties, travel and the money to fund such aspirations. Inevitably, disappointment followed her conquests and this eventually led to her untimely death.

Morag unearthed more information when she discovered suspect correspondence in Annabella's valise. The letters were addressed to their mother from a gentleman by the name of Andrew 'C'. It was, therefore, logical to deduce that Annabella's assumed surname of Campbell, used when she introduced herself to Marcus, might have been that of her biological father, Andrew 'C'.

Marcus pretended indifference, but Lizzie was saddened that her cousin had become embroiled in a game of deception and lies, which almost destroyed the life of Annabella's sister, Morag. However, now was not the time to dwell on such matters, as both Marcus and Jack were in need of her support.

The joy at discovering each other was immense, though tinged with sadness, as now Jack felt betrayed by his mother. She'd never disclosed anything about his biological father. Oliver, Jack's adoptive father, was also led to believe Jack's father was dead. Indeed, it was Oliver who broke the news to Jack, asking him not to breathe a word of his disclosure to his mother. She had manipulated and lied to him about so many things, which were difficult to forgive.

As the truth emerged, both men relaxed visibly and as the evening wore on, they began to appreciate the remarkable events that brought about their meeting.

The very drinkable 1850 classic Sazerac, Germain-Robin brandy, flowed freely throughout the night, as excited conversation warmed their hearts and minds. They talked, laughed and cried into the early hours, despite being apart for over fourteen years. Their common love for Lizzie and Rosie, who had retired earlier, only enhanced their newfound relationship.

An emotional Marcus reminisced, with memories of the good times they'd shared together. 'It was three months after your second birthday, Jack, on Tuesday 16 March 1841; a day I will never forget. It was the last time I would see you. My heart broke as I kissed and waved you goodbye. Belle walked out holding you in her arms. Her intention was to begin a new life with you and Andries and I was left totally alone—'

Jack frowned as he listened intently to his father's recollection, then quickly interrupted him—'Sorry father, but I think you have that wrong, March 1841 was just after my third birthday.'

Marcus seemed totally bemused and an awkward silence prevailed before he replied. 'No Jack, you were born on 21st December, 1838.'

Jack shook his head disdainfully. He realised that this was just another lie perpetuated by his mother. 'Oh...I see, so I am actually only seventeen?'

'Yes Jack...your mother apparently lied about your age, but why would she do that?'

'Well father, I believe I was becoming a burden to her. She needed to be free of the responsibility and enrolled me at school a year early. Fortuitously, as it turned out, I was able to attend Hull Naval College a year in advance, so I suppose I benefitted in the long run,' said Jack, not totally convinced.

He discovered several interesting facts about his mother and himself as their conversation and the evening progressed. He'd already promised himself that they would never be parted again now that their relationship had been established.

Because they had talked for such a long time, with enthusiasm and some melancholy, they'd hardly noticed the sun rising. It was time to at least attempt some sleep, before celebrating Christmas Day with their family and friends. Marcus reflected that he was looking forward to announcing his engagement to Elizabeth, something he once thought might never happen. The joy of that moment would be doubly poignant. His son would now stand proudly at his side.

CHAPTER THREE

The Reveal
Christmas Day, 1855

Christmas Day disappointed *The Beeches'* younger guests in that it was devoid of snow or even a frost. 1855 was the ninth driest winter ever recorded. However, there had been heavy rain on Christmas Eve, which had saturated the ground, so boots were still the order of the day.

The inspirational sermon at the church, which lifted their spirits, generated an extra element of excitement as they entered the ornately decorated hall of *The Beeches*. It exuded heavenly scents of fir, pine and hemlock; in addition, the sweet smell of spices: cinnamon, cranberry and apple invaded their senses as they observed bunches of mistletoe and holly, hung from the candelabra, which truly enhanced the festive scene.

The three youngest, Victoria, Harriett and Beatrice... much to her annoyance, were dispatched to the nursery to play, while adults enjoyed pre Christmas dinner cocktails.

The bright red berries of the holly provided a vibrant splash of colour, in contrast to the cloudy skies outside, which cast long grey shadowy fingers across the walls of the drawing-room[2]. Another garland of holly bedecked the

---

2 *A nineteenth-century designation for a 'sitting-room'. Often with east-facing exposure, the drawing room was the smartest room in the*

mantle, the berries forming jewels in a thorny crown, framing a glowing fire of crackling logs and pinecones. The smell of roast goose wafted through from the kitchen, titillating the taste buds of all present.

Soon, everyone's eyes were drawn to Lizzie and Marcus, as they walked hand in hand to stand by the large, elaborately decorated tree, which gave an indication that some kind of announcement was in the offing.

Marcus's pride in his son was obvious, as Lizzie and he stood between a smiling Jack and Rosie. A sea of expectant faces met their gaze.

Marcus announced their forthcoming marriage amidst a flurry of congratulations and, as he drew breath, he hinted that another happy disclosure could also be made during dinner.

Daniel Lorimer, standing behind the others, could not disguise his hurt and a feeling of unbearable sadness, as the couple embraced each other. While everyone celebrated, he dejectedly turned away to fill his glass from a convenient brandy decanter, raising it quickly to his lips. The golden liquid slipped easily down his throat, momentarily dulling his senses, until his eyes focussed on his wife, Georgina, who unwittingly smiled encouragingly. He reflected that his journey from Glasgow, following a business meeting on Christmas Eve, had been exhausting. He'd picked up Georgina and Victoria en-route, before continuing by train, to arrive in time for the early morning church service. Georgina was obviously tired herself, so probably appreciated how

---

house, usually used by the adults of the family when entertaining. The dimensions of a large drawing-room were approximately 6 metres x 9 metres.

exhausted he felt. Thankfully, she was blissfully unaware of the real reason behind his anguish.

He quickly regained his composure and tipped the glass in her direction, returning her smile. He needed to exercise some control, before his present turbulent demeanour, not his tiredness, as Georgina imagined, became apparent for all to see. Why did he feel this way after all this time? He had struggled with his emotions from the moment he encountered Lizzie at the Goose Fair. Throughout the ensuing years, his secret had remained locked away and he had tried hard to rekindle his love for Georgina. However, he'd failed miserably and now here he was, being forced to endure the picture of glowing happiness, emanating from the eyes of his friends who had just announced their engagement.

He would never accept that he had lost her forever, how could he? when every bone in his body ached to hold her in his arms again and feel his love reciprocated, as she had once done so willingly.

The combination of drink and the heat rising from the fire made him feel suddenly nauseous and very lightheaded. He placed his hand on the mantle to steady himself, but felt strangely surreal, as he imagined a sea of faces floating towards him, laughing and jeering at his foolishness.

Feeling trapped and in desperate need of air, he rubbed his hand over his eyes and looked wildly around the room. Suddenly, a means of escape came sharply into focus. He moved quickly, weaving his way between the other guests who had formed small groups, eventually reaching the sanctuary of the French doors at the far end of the room.

He breathed a sigh of relief as his hand clasped the brass handle. Unfortunately, fate stepped in. Someone called out his name. *'Damn, damn,'* he murmured under his breath, as beads of sweat appeared on his brow. An invisible force prevented him opening the door. Realizing he could not commit to his bid for freedom, without raising suspicion, he turned resolutely, but was instantly horrified to find himself looking directly into the eyes of the woman he loved. He composed himself and even managed a half smile, before engaging her with trembling voice. 'Oh Lizzie,' I am so happy for you both.' Feeling obliged to explain his intended rapid exit, he continued—'I...I was just going out to the patio to take some air. The long journey here has left me feeling rather tired.'

Oblivious to his heightened state of anxiety, an elated Lizzie moved closer towards him and lay her arm on his. He felt his heart bursting out of his chest as she smiled demurely and kissed him lightly on the cheek. 'Thank you Daniel, I am so glad we have both found happiness again. You will always hold a special place in my heart and it means so much to me that we can still be friends.'

Daniel swallowed hard, hoping she would not detect the tremor in his voice. 'Of course, Lizzie, we will always be that. You have been through so much and deserve to be happy.'

'You too, Daniel. I can see how much Georgina loves you and you her. We must get together again soon. In fact, I intended to invite you both for our New Year celebrations, but haven't yet had the opportunity to speak with you. Marcus and I would love it if you could come over. Robert, Amy, Kate, James, Rosie and Jack have already agreed to join us. Even Aunt Jayne and Howard promised to make an appearance and the New Year wouldn't be complete without you, Georgina and Victoria.'

Daniel viewed the invitation as a double-edged sword. Granted he would have the opportunity to see her again quite soon. However, although Lizzie appeared unaware of how he felt, Marcus wasn't blind and each time he found himself in their presence, it became harder to disguise his lasting feelings towards her.

He needed to offer a suitable excuse, as in his experience, parties often created uncomfortable situations, especially when drink featured heavily on the agenda. He distinctly remembered Kate's dinner party, only last month, when alcohol again loosened the tongues of himself and others, much to the chagrin of Lizzie. He was astonished and surprised that no one even noticed the patently obvious.

For everyone's sake, he should decline and surprised himself by speaking calmly and with conviction. 'We would love to join you, but unfortunately, I believe Georgina has already made arrangements for us to stay with her parents. Maybe we could meet up a little later in the New Year?'

Lizzie hid her disappointment. She hoped that all her friends would be together to celebrate and that 1856 would be the year where everyone would enjoy much happiness, with the dark times banished to the past. 'Of course, that would be lovely, if you are sure you cannot make it?' Lizzie enquired hopefully, before she noticed Marcus beckoning to join him. Daniel's answer was left hanging as she excused herself. 'I am sorry Daniel, but I will have to catch up with you later, after you have spoken with Georgina. Do try and persuade her to change her plans.' Lizzie gave her most disarming smile, squeezing Daniel's hand before scurrying away.

Daniel wavered, contemplating his dilemma. He quickly realized he had little choice but to abandon his exit plan and moved to join Georgina, who was talking animatedly to Kate and Amy. He approached her from behind and encircled his arms around her waist, before kissing her briefly on the neck, in a gesture brought on by an overwhelming sense of guilt.

He focussed, determined for the moment to put his feelings on one side and to ensure Georgina had a memorable Yuletide. After all, none of this was her fault. Taking a deep breath, he summoned up some courage and putting his hand to his mouth, gave a presumptive cough, interrupting the threesome with a teasing opener. 'Now ladies what juicy tit-bits[3] are you sharing? You all seem very guarded and somewhat secretive,' he joked.

Kate looked vaguely amused at Daniel's attempt to include himself in their conversation and, never one to miss an opportunity to flirt with a member of the opposite sex, encouraged his participation. 'Well Daniel, apart from speculating what other announcements we have in store, we were posing several questions involving the topic of 'love'. Amy brought up the rather provocative question of whether there is ever any excuse for an extra marital affair?' She grinned mischievously, sensing his slight embarrassment, but continued unashamed. 'What's your opinion?'

Daniel was shocked and felt his cheeks flush, fortunately unseen by Georgina, standing directly in front of him. 'I er... well—' he stammered—'it's not something I have ever given any thought to,' he offered somewhat lamely, if solicitously. After what seemed an age, he realised the women were waiting expectantly for him to continue. He thereby launched into an opinion, which he hoped would satisfy everyone. 'On the face of it, I would say there wasn't, although some married couples appear to be so unhappy that, perhaps in a moment of madness, they embark on something they may

---

3 *17th Century – British definition - perhaps from dialect 'tid' - tender, of obscure origin. A pleasing scrap of anything, such as scandal. American pronunciation – 'tidbits'*

later regret,' he said with a wry smile, focussing his attention at Kate. He continued—'For my part, I would never betray my beautiful wife,' he assured them and gently squeezed Georgina's waist to reassure her, whilst surveying his audience. He sensed their approval, with a consequence that he was completely satisfied he had answered the question admirably.

However, Kate was a little taken aback and appeared unsure whether his initial comment was purposely directed at her. Had he guessed her secret or was it a plea for her to discontinue her emotive questioning, which had obviously left *him* feeling uncomfortable. She stared intently at both Daniel and Georgina, who was presently gazing lovingly into his eyes. Daniel, she noted, rather worryingly, did not appear to have the conviction or spirit to back up his statement. Something in his demeanour unnerved her, but she could not quite put her finger on it.

Kate, astute as she was, knew only too well the tell tail signs of a marriage bereft of passion. *Did Daniel still harbour unrequited love for Lizzie?* Oh dear, she sincerely hoped not, as Lizzie was totally in love with Marcus. Indeed, with a further announcement expected…a pregnancy maybe! Daniel could not hope for any meaningful relationship between himself and Lizzie, only friendship. Lizzie's future lay firmly at Marcus's side.

She was sympathetic, after all, hadn't she found herself in a similar situation? Why was life so complicated she mused?

Kate had no time to dwell on her thoughts, as she was interrupted by Marcus, who was tapping the side of his glass to attract attention. 'Listen everyone, I have an extra surprise. I wanted this occasion to be remembered by us all and have organised a photographer to capture this precious moment in time. He is waiting in the sitting room, so we should all take our places for a group photograph[4].'

All gathered around Marcus expectantly. He seated the younger ones on the settee with the adults standing at the back. For almost everyone, it would be the first time they had had their picture taken. Kate's family had previously visited a photographer, after the birth of Beatrice, but even she was enthusiastic. Having a photograph of Robert was something she would cherish...to gaze upon without raising any suspicions.

The whole process took around thirty minutes, before they gathered in the dining room after dinner was announced and everyone took their seat at the table.

※

It could be said that an air of anticipation and excitement for some key players existed as they were seated for dinner, but for others the stage was set for a Shakespearian 'Tragedy', destined to play out in dramatic fashion over the coming months.

In her naivety, Lizzie's choice of seating arrangement appeared on the surface to be well considered. She ensured a parent supervised the three youngest guests and partners were sat opposite or together. A quick glance around gave her confidence that the day would be an overwhelming success.

Howard, the family's steadying influence, was seated at the far end of the table, opposite Marcus. He had an uninterrupted view of all the guests, much to his delight. Of

---

[4] *The first partially successful photograph of a camera image was made in approximately 1816 by Nicéphore Niépce.*

particular interest was the dynamic between Kate and Robert Cameron. Her behaviour at the November dinner party troubled him greatly. The heart to heart he had with Kate shortly after, had not allayed his fears, despite his daughter's assurances. Fortunately, she was seated further down the table, with little opportunity to converse with Robert, but Howard knew his daughter only too well and consequently he needed to be vigilant.

༺༻

An air of congeniality prevailed as the first course of boudinettes of lobster was served, a recipe taken from Eliza Acton's[5] cookbook, which was Lizzie's gift to Polly, last Christmas, for just such an occasion. Lizzie knew how much her efficient young cook was always keen to try new recipes. Help for Polly came in the form of a 'maid of all works', named Annie. Kate was still of the opinion that four household staff were no where near sufficient to run *The Beeches* effectively, especially, as the gardener, Jacob, also drove the gig, whenever any of the family needed to travel into the town. She wondered sometimes how Lizzie managed. Lizzie, however, was completely satisfied and, therefore, happy that together with Elspeth, they had an efficient, tight knit family group of staff and managed very well. After all, until Marcus's return, there was only Lizzie and Rosie in residence

---

5 *Acton's best-known work 'Modern Cookery for Private Families' was first published in 1845. It was the result of several years of research, undertaken at the prompting of Longman, who had published her Poems. Many of the recipes came from her friends. 'Modern Cookery' quickly became a very popular work, appearing in several editions and remaining a standard cookery book throughout the rest of the century.*

and now that Rosie was spending a lot more time with Kate, Lizzie was certain extra staff were unwarranted and totally unnecessary.

As the adults savoured the lobster and consumed the Chardonnay with gusto, the youngsters were treated to clear turtle soup with small triangles of thinly sliced brown bread.

Happy chatter and laughter resonated around the table, masking the troubled thoughts of some, including Howard. Sadly, his earlier assumptions would prove correct. He'd noted that Kate was clearly unhappy with the arrangements. Unbeknown to him, she had already decided the distance between herself and Robert was not insurmountable. An orchestrated change, just as the flaming plum pudding ceremony took centre stage, was easily achievable. She would suggest swapping places with Beatrice, on the pretext of liaising with James, sat opposite their daughter, about her upcoming birthday. Her plan needed to be achieved before the women eventually withdrew to the drawing-room[6] and the men remained for the traditional cigars and brandy.

Robert, acutely aware of Kate's ambitions with regard to their relationship had felt a safe enough distance away to relax and enjoy the occasion. He had been troubled with the events of last November, realising his feelings for Kate were growing. His resistance to her barely disguised attempts to orchestrate a meeting were gradually diminishing, even

---

6 *Until the mid-twentieth century, after a dinner party, the ladies withdrew to the drawing room, leaving the gentlemen at table, where the tablecloth was removed. After an interval of conversation, the gentlemen rejoined the ladies in the (with) drawing room.*

though he was devoted to Amy. He wondered whether to enlist the advice of Lizzie. However, today was all about the children and everyone celebrating a year full of surprises and reunions. He determined to shelve his feelings and the consequences of such to another day.

⁂

Lizzie, Marcus and Jack were in jubilant mood and could hardly contain their excitement at the totally unexpected revelation of Jack's parentage. Marcus decided to wait until after the main course, before he revealed all.

Rosie, seated next to Jack, was, however, somewhat disturbed by the Christmas Eve disclosure and pushed the lobster aimlessly around her plate, hoping no one would notice her unusual lack of interest in food. She had spent a restless night ruminating about their future. Would the fact that Marcus was Jack's father, make any difference to their relationship? There wasn't any reason why it should, but she still felt uneasy, the marriage of Lizzie and Marcus, meant that Jack would become her step-brother!

She knew in the eyes of the law that this did not make any difference, if they too eventually wished to marry, but conversely, was she actually looking for an excuse not to continue their relationship? Had she still not given up entirely on Jimmy? These questions remained unanswered and left her in a reflective mood.

⁂

Despite the worries of some of the guests, spirits soared with the arrival of the main course. The goose looked resplendent, amidst a sage and onion dressing, with a port wine sauce and roast potatoes. There were several boxes of Tom Smith's Christmas crackers placed around the table, filled with sugared almonds, Christmas hats and a small gift, which excited the youngest members, who pulled more than their fair share. Marcus carved the 'cooked to perfection' goose, then silence prevailed whilst everyone tucked in to the delicious meal; a sure sign that all was well, at least from a culinary perspective.

After toasting his engagement to Lizzie, Marcus rose once more to chink his glass with a fork. This immediately engaged everyone's attention. A buzz of excitement and anticipation surfaced. Several guests had already speculated on what the second announcement could possibly be. Some concluded the couple might be adding to their family, but others were unconvinced on that particular scenario.

Marcus summoned Jack to stand by his side, before divulging his secret. He placed his hand on Jack's shoulder then turned to his guests. Taking a deep breath he spoke with pride. 'You all know John Jamieson, son of Annabella, who sadly lost her life earlier this year.' The guests nodded and quietly expressed their sorrow, before he continued—'What you don't know is'—and at this juncture he paused for effect—'that John Jamieson is my long lost son, Jack Bernard.'

That statement elicited audible gasps from everyone, followed by whispered conversations to each other.

Marcus grinned. 'I know this will come as a huge surprise to all of you and...well, it was equally a surprise to us, as this unexpected revelation only came to light yesterday.'

More gasps followed as all eyes shifted to Jack, who laughed nervously, a little unsure whether or not to comment.

Marcus immediately came to his rescue. 'The reason this has remained undisclosed for so long is complicated and I will explain everything in due course. Right now, I would like us all to raise our glasses to my son, Jack Bernard and welcome him to the family. I say family, as this is how I see you all, inextricably linked together one way or another and as many of us have discovered; blood relations are not a prerequisite of family union.

Several echoed Marcus's sentiments rising joyously to their feet, applauding the unexpected, but delightful news. There were cries of 'Welcome, Jack', 'Congratulations to you both' and 'Wonderful news'.

Everyone was thrilled that Marcus had finally been reunited with his son. However, one person was more than relieved that it had nothing to do with the union of Lizzie and Marcus. Daniel, seated next to Lizzie, breathed a deep sigh of relief in that there wasn't a baby in the offing. The morning's events had left him drained and the announcement of a pregnancy would have added to his misery.

Before everyone re-seated themselves, Jack finally found his voice. He acknowledged everyone's good wishes by raising his own glass. 'Thank you everyone. I am overwhelmed by the welcome you have given me. As my father' —he paused and smiled warmly at Marcus, repeating the last three words with pride—'as my father explained, it came as a huge shock and we will need time to get to know each other in this new role. What I can say is that it is an honour for me to have such a wonderful man as my father and I intend to make him proud of me.'

Marcus, with a tear in his eye, responded. 'I too feel privileged to have such a fine, upstanding young man as my son. I am already very proud of you Jack and will continue to be so.' Then, after a short pause, he grinned, directing his attention to Harriett, Victoria, and Beatrice. 'Now, I think we have kept our younger guests waiting long enough. I do believe the pudding is ready to be served.'

That was the cue for Kate to move places, which she did very deftly and without fuss. Only Amy, the quiet, unassuming member of the group, who felt uncomfortable seated opposite Kate, frowned at this manoeuvre. Ever since the November dinner party, she had her doubts as to Kate's intentions towards Robert.

⁂

That particularly night, at the November dinner party, she'd retired early, but had not been able to sleep. The raised voices of those downstairs had filtered up to her room. She concluded that they were discussing old times, as she recalled Kate's earlier emotive question—*'Don't any of you wonder what would have happened if we had all married our respective first loves?'*—Amy had been pleased with Robert's reply, which was to agree with Lizzie that there was no point dragging up the past, as they had all moved on. However, Kate's insistence on pushing this topic troubled her.

She had already noticed during that evening, Kate's desire to engage Robert in clandestine conversations. Although Robert, who she trusted implicitly, seemed passive, she felt less sure about Kate's motives, as they were after all, lovers at one time; Rosie being the product of that union.

She once mentioned her fears to Robert, who had immediately reassured her. She had felt foolish and was sure he would now dismiss such fanciful thoughts. She understood their requirement to have parental conversations about Rosie, but Kate's body language exuded sexuality.

Rightly or wrongly, she had interpreted certain gestures as too forward. The way Kate's hand sometimes lingered a little too long on his arm as she sought his attention and also when she leaned inappropriately close during conversations.

Amy had deliberately introduced the question about 'affairs' earlier, to gauge Kate's reaction. It was a pity Daniel interrupted shortly before the call to dinner, but she determined to observe the pair. She would decide later whether to tackle Robert, which may put her mind at rest.

⁂

The long awaited pudding finally arrived, amidst gasps of delight from the youngsters, who could hardly contain their excitement. They were anticipating finding a silver sixpence in their portion, or some other small gift. The flaming pudding, soaked in brandy, was held aloft and perhaps given greater ceremony than even the creation of this grand Victorian tradition itself.

Marcus secretly ensured that the three girls each received a silver gift in their portion. Beatrice discovered a small ring, Victoria a thimble, and Harriett the sixpence. All were delighted with their find.

Georgina gave Victoria a hug, as she proudly held up the thimble for her mother to see. 'Look Mamma, aren't I lucky to have found this in my pudding.'

Georgina smiled understandingly. She thought how lucky they all were and despite her earlier tiredness, found herself enjoying the family occasion immensely. She had dismissed the 'affair' question, put to Kate and herself by Amy, as something that would never happen to her. Indeed, she felt safe in the knowledge that Daniel would never betray her. She assured herself that the only person he could ever possibly be drawn to in that way was Lizzie and she was about to marry Marcus.

The stalwart, Aunt Jayne, away in November, was oblivious to the dynamics of that particular evening. She was, however, very close to Kate, who she thought harboured feelings for Robert. Consequently, Kate's orchestrated move did not go unnoticed by either Jayne or Howard. Fortunately, both were out of earshot and for the time, would remain blissfully unaware of the reasons for Kate's planned manoeuvre.

Kate engaged James in conversation for a short while, before turning her attention to Robert. 'How lovely to see you again Robert.' She smiled, placing her hand directly on Robert's thigh. Robert, embarrassed and taken aback, acknowledged her greeting with disdain and surreptiously removed her hand before anyone noticed, but Kate, undeterred, continued—'Amy, Harriett and yourself, of course, must come to *The Chestnuts* again soon. I am having a celebratory birthday party on Saturday the 2nd February and I would love it if you could join the rest of the family.'

James, able to hear the conversation without difficulty, was surprised at Kate's change of plan, as they had previously agreed to go away together for a short romantic break, so interrupted Robert's reply—'Have you changed your mind, darling? I thought we were taking a holiday[7] in the Lakes that weekend?'

---

[7] *The seaside resort was an eighteenth-century invention. 'Orthodox' medicine put a 'scientific' veneer on popular sea-bathing customs and marketed the result as a supplement or (increasingly) alternative to*

Unabashed, Kate reminded James of an imagined conversation. 'No James, don't you remember, we actually decided to go the following weekend, as Aunt Jayne was unable to look after Beatrice until the 15th, due to a prior engagement. I was very disappointed, of course, until you suggested having family and friends over to celebrate instead.'

James, perplexed by his wife's sound reasoning, shook his head; perhaps he had indeed forgotten that particular conversation. Either way, he knew it was no use arguing and muttered his apologies.

However, Robert knew both he and James had been manipulated. It was obvious that James had no recollection of Kate's new arrangement, but, under the spotlight, Robert was obliged to accept the invitation. 'Of course, Kate, we wouldn't miss it for the world,' he acquiesced, still staggered at the blatant lies.

Robert's embarrassment continued as Kate unnervingly returned her hand to its previous position on his thigh, squeezing it gently. 'Oh good, that's settled then, we will look forward to it, won't we James?'

James nodded in the affirmative leaving Robert powerless under Kate's scrutiny, as she continued to exert pressure on his thigh.

༻✦༺

Participation in the evening's 'Parlour' games was expected and usually enjoyed by the majority. 'Sardines', suggested of

---

'taking the cure' at a spa. New romantic ways of perceiving shoreline, made them attractive where hitherto they had repelled, running parallel with the revolution in taste that drew the fashionable and cultivated to the Lake District and the Alps.

course, by the younger contingent, proved exceptionally exhilarating.

None of the other guests at the party in November were aware of Kate's cleverly orchestrated meeting with Robert and were just eager to play; however, as *The Beeches* was a significantly smaller property to *The Chestnuts,* Kate realized[8] she would be unable to use a similar strategy. She consoled herself with the certainty that there would be other opportunities and parties in which to manipulate the occasion to suit her needs.

Nonetheless, 'Sardines' was in full swing when Robert, a reluctant participant, was chosen as the next to be 'hunted'. He remembered very well the last time the game had been played and worried he might once again be huddled in a cupboard with Kate. He would, therefore, ensure he chose a place where he could be found quite easily.

◈

The Beeches with seven bedrooms and several bathrooms, were all contained in one wing, complemented on the ground floor by a sitting room, dining room, drawing-room,

---

8 *'Realise/realize - Although realize is now regarded by many in the U.K. and Australasia as the American spelling, it is not an Americanism. In fact, the -ize spelling variant is older than –ise—realize predates the United States and Canada by nearly two centuries—and has been the preferred spelling throughout most of the word's history in English. In British books and journals published between 1800 and 2000, realise had a brief ascendancy in British English from the late 19th century through the early 20th, but realize was preferred before around 1875 and is again preferred today—perhaps because of the influence of dictionaries like Oxford, Cambridge, and Collins, which encourage -ize over -ise.*

study, a kitchen and a laundry. All were large and airy. There was also a cellar, mostly used for storing wine.

While everyone gathered in the drawing room, Robert made his way to one of the bedrooms on the first floor. He entered the room, containing a bathroom. It was spacious with a bank of wardrobes on the far side and another small cupboard opposite the bed.

He quickly ruled out hiding in the wardrobes and dismissed the small cupboard, which was filled with shelves from top to bottom. Remembering the house's layout, he exited this room and headed for the linen cupboard, which featured a single door at the end of the landing. He opened the door and discovered there was just enough space between the three sides of shelves for one person to squeeze in if they crouched down. He backed into the cupboard, swiftly closed the door and waited.

Minutes later he detected muffled voices in the vicinity of his cupboard and a woman giggling, whom he thought could be Amy. He breathed a sigh of relief, thinking his ordeal was over. However, Marcus, partnered with Amy, dismissed the idea, explaining that the linen cupboard was too small to hide a man of Robert's stature, as there were shelves on all three sides.

Robert knew he shouldn't open the door, as it would not be in the spirit of the game, so was disappointed when he heard their voices trail off as they crept away. He heard them open the door of the bedroom he'd first chosen and was aware of other voices in the corridor, but could not distinguish them. Then to his horror he heard Marcus say, 'We have searched all the rooms on this floor and we've not found him.'

He waited a further ten minutes, but no one came near, then he opened the door slightly to peer into the darkness. As his eyes adjusted, he found he could almost see to the top of the stairs; there didn't appear to be anyone around. Surely someone would find him soon. Reluctantly, he closed the door again on the cramped space, whilst massaging his legs, which were going numb.

A few more minutes elapsed before he heard footsteps treading lightly along the boarded floor. *'Don't let it be Kate,'* he murmured under his breath, but it appeared fate was not on his side. The door slowly opened and Kate peered inside. 'Goodness Robert, I cannot believe you managed to squeeze into this small space. Everyone else dismissed this cupboard and went off to explore other rooms. What a stroke of luck it was me who found you,' said Kate excitedly and mischievously.

Robert definitely did not share her opinion and immediately stepped outside of the cupboard. 'Oh well, now that you have found me, we could go back to the drawing room,' he said quite loudly.

'But the game doesn't work like that Robert, I have to get in there with you until someone else discovers us…you know that!' Kate grinned as she shimmied up close to him.

'Yes Kate, I am aware of that, but you know that isn't going to happen. Apart from the fact that it would not be a good idea, how on earth do you think two people would manage to crouch inside and shut the door?' Robert spluttered, his heart now beating fast and his breath coming in short bursts.

'I concur, that scenario isn't possible,' she whispered seductively—'but in the true spirit of the game, we should stay together until we are found, don't you agree? We could, of course, sit in the bedroom until the others decide to come back.'

Robert looked beyond Kate to the stairwell in the hope someone would appear, but they were quite alone. *Where the hell is everyone?*

'Robert, you seem like a frightened rabbit, surely I am not such a threat to you?'

Robert looked straight at Kate and tried to make light of the situation. 'No, no of course not, but we both know, that given the circumstances, we should not be alone together.'

Kate softened. 'I am conscious of that Robert, but we knew in November that there was no going back. You know how I feel about you and although I do not want anyone to get hurt, I cannot help my feelings. They have not diminished; in fact they have become stronger. Sometimes, I wish I could wake up and find I feel nothing for you, but so far that hasn't happened'—she paused and looked straight into his deep brown eyes, which had an unnerving affect on him— 'Why are you fighting this Robert?' she said, brushing away an imaginary piece of fluff from his jacket. 'I know you feel the same. Are we to dismiss how we feel and live the rest of our lives with partners who we do not love?'—she paused to gauge his reaction and thought she could perceive a glimmer of uncertainty in his eyes. She was now standing very close to him and could feel him trembling slightly under her touch, so continued—'It's not going to work Robert. Some how we have to sort this out, we—'

Robert cut her short and although he felt defeated, was determined not to submit to what was, in his mind, a selfish act. Holding her by the arms he pushed her gently away and in a firm voice offered an explanation in a last ditch[9] effort to make Kate see sense. 'I am fighting this because I am

---

9 *The 'last ditch' was, in military terms, the last line of defense. The term had begun to be used figuratively by the eighteenth century, when Thomas Jefferson wrote, 'A government driven to the last ditch by the universal call for liberty.' Similarly, to 'die in the last ditch' means to resist to the end; it dates from the early 1700s.*

married to Amy and no matter what *our* feelings are, we have responsibilities to our respective partners. Anyway, this is neither the time nor the place to make decisions. If I promise to meet you in the next few weeks, will you agree to wait until then before doing anything hasty?'

Kate sensed resignation in his voice and felt reassured. 'All right Robert, I agree.'

Robert breathed a sigh of relief. 'I will get word to you somehow, but don't pin your hopes on anything happening between us. We will meet for the sole purpose of sorting out where we go from here, if anywhere?'

'Okay, I will look forward to it.' She smiled, but as they both turned to go, they heard a board creak and saw a shadowy figure disappearing down the stairs.

Both stared into the gloom, but neither could discern who it was. Robert spoke first, 'Oh no, who the hell was that?' he choked, his voice taking on a fearful tone.

Even Kate appeared concerned. 'I...I don't know, it is too dark to see. How long do you think they were standing there?'

Robert sighed. 'I don't know Kate, let's hope not long enough or close enough to hear anything we said.'

A couple of minutes later, several of the 'hunters' appeared. First to look in their direction was Marcus, who peered into the darkness, lifted his candle and spotted the couple at the far end, as they made their way back down the landing. 'Here they are!' he exclaimed chuckling. 'Where were you Robert?' he asked, inquisitively, wondering how they had missed him. 'We looked into these rooms earlier.'

Robert swallowed hard. 'I...I was in the linen cupboard Marcus. Not a very comfortable place to be. I realized when Kate opened the door that both of us could not continue to hide in there, so we were making our way to the bedroom to wait for the next person who came along. Where are the others?' he asked anxiously.

Georgina explained, 'We split up, after we couldn't find you in the bedrooms and I think Rosie, Jack, James and Daniel decided to go down to the kitchens. I am not sure where Amy is. I thought I saw her descending the stairs a few minutes ago, but she seems to have disappeared. Lizzie and Aunt Jayne, Howard and the three girls are back in the drawing room. Harriett was trying to persuade them to go down into the cellar, but Aunt Jayne wasn't keen to negotiate the steps in the dark, even with candles'—she paused to look curiously into the small space that had been occupied by Robert—'How on earth did you manage to squeeze into that space, Robert? That was a really clever idea, as we all dismissed it as impossible.'

Robert, whose mind was on the whereabouts of Amy, did not answer, but stared fixedly in front of him.

Kate, now fully alert, covered for him. 'I said it was an impossible place when I opened the door and saw him crouching there, so, as Robert explained, we thought of waiting in the bedroom, but then you all appeared.'

'Ah well, that's solved the mystery, however, I think the girls will be disappointed not to get the opportunity of exploring the cellar, but now let's return to the drawing room, as I think we've experienced enough excitement for one night. Apparently, Lizzie has plans for a late supper and all this exercise has left me peckish,' Georgina discerned.

A plentiful and delicious supper awaited them in the drawing room, which included Elspeth's famous shortbread. Amy, noticeably absent from the gathering, increased Kate and Robert's growing concerns and, indeed, fears.

CHAPTER FOUR

Consolidation
December, 1855

Jimmy rose early, swung his legs over his hammock, put a comb through his hair and reached for his crutch, now used only for confidence. He sensed today would be a good day; the sun would show its head, despite the sound of torrential rain presently thundering down on the deck above. He made his way to the promenade, which was pretty much deserted and despite the rain lashing his face and trickling down his neck, he felt strangely uplifted.

In his opinion, this was the best time of the day, before anyone else made an appearance. 'Today,' Jimmy said to himself—'I'll meck a decision about which path to choose.' He'd not received word from Rosie or his mam and a few weeks had passed since he'd written to let them know his whereabouts. Maybe Rosie had met someone else...if she believed he had died; perhaps she hadn't received his letter. He did wonder whether Maud, despite her assurances, had indeed posted them. He reflected that he hadn't seen her recently; maybe the rumour was correct in that she had been dismissed, following allegations of drinking on duty. Certainly the lack of a response from his mam threw up a red flag. There were too many uncertainties and he needed to be sure. Instantly, he made up his mind, speaking out loud with feeling and determination. 'Me mind's made up. I'll meck the journey ta see me mam. Me leg is almost healed and a might try walking we'out this pesky crutch, get meself a walking stick instead. A could even ask Lucinda ter come wi me...that's if she'd be interested—' His voice trailed off as he gave consideration to how he would broach the subject.

Several minutes later, he realized the rain had stopped. As he'd predicted, the sun appeared from behind a still cloudy sky. He breathed in deeply, walked to the ship's rails and leant over. His eyes fixed on the *Isle of Dogs*, across the river and the ever-changing landscape of frantic activity, relentless and unforgiving on this particular stretch of river. It strengthened his resolve in his quest to achieve greater things. He realized he was missing the exhilaration of being aboard a clipper ship, sailing to far off lands, experiencing the danger and excitement that never failed to invigorate his senses.

Jimmy's baptism of fire on board the *Lightning*, serving under Captain Forbes and his subsequent brush with death, had not diminished his newly found love of the sea. The sense of abandonment and a certain freedom came with sailing across a vast ocean. The fact that he was only an able seaman and life was hard was infinitely preferable to living in Narrow Marsh with a bully for a father! If he obeyed orders and kept his nose clean, he would not suffer the humiliation and pain of being belted on a daily basis by the man who now lay six feet under. That fact alone made him more determined to aspire to achieve a higher rank, albeit with a bit of help, possibly from John—

He put his thoughts to one side and continued to watch the day's activities. He felt envious as a paddle tug towed a small brig downstream and another came up under sail to his right. A third was moored off near the hospital ship and several pleasure craft drifted lazily by. The view over the bow was of the Observatory in Greenwich Park, the spire of

St Alfege's[10] rising just above the lion figurehead of the *Dreadnought*. Jimmy closed his eyes for a moment, conscious of the pain in his leg today, but it did not diminish his enthusiasm as he imagined where his next trip would take him.

A few minutes later, a loud screeching brought him out of his reverie. His eyes were drawn to a colony[11] of noisy seagulls, amassing around a small fishing boat, fighting over fish waste jettisoned by the crew. 'Look at them lot, still fighting ovver scraps...every day the same...but a suppose they've a purpose, a goal...which is ta survive, I guess'—he paused, still thinking aloud—'Well I've a goal which am go-an ta achieve. No idea 'ow long it'ull teck us, but a will get there,' stated Jimmy, the steely tone in his voice echoing his strength of mind.

'Good for you Jimmy!' voiced a cheerful Lucinda, who always rose early to take some air before her shift started and, unnoticed, had crept quietly up to within a foot or two of Jimmy.

Surprised to see her in such close proximity, he almost lost his footing as he swung awkwardly around to face her. For a moment he felt flummoxed and lowered his head slightly in embarrassment. However, Lucinda's smile quickly restored his confidence and he greeted her with enthusiasm.

---

10 *St Alfege is the Anglican parish church in the centre of Greenwich. There has been a church here for over a thousand years, dedicated to the memory of Alfege, the Archbishop of Canterbury who was martyred on this site in 1012.*

11 *A group of seagulls is called a colony, contrary to the popular belief that it is called a flock. However, the misunderstanding arises when seagulls, not old enough to breed, are termed 'nursery flocks'.*

'Good morning Lucinda, how are you? I wah just thinkin abaht ya. I've something to ask ya,' proclaimed a resolute Jimmy, who had minutes earlier made an all-important decision.

Lucinda's cheeks flushed with anticipation. 'I am well, Jimmy. It's lovely to see you looking so able. Your leg appears to be mending well.'

Jimmy glanced at his leg then back to the face of the woman he had grown closer to since his arrival on the *Dreadnought*. His hesitation was brief and with an air of self-assurance he asked his question. 'Do yer have any time off this Yuletide?'—Jimmy's unwavering voice surprised even him as he felt himself growing in stature—'If so, I'd like yer to accompany me on a visit ter see me mam.'

Lucinda's joyous expression betrayed her feelings. 'Oh Jimmy, I would love to. As it happens, I am off from the 23rd until the day after Boxing Day[12]. Helen, Jane and myself have agreed to split the holiday period between us. Helen opted for the period to include New Year, coinciding with a New Year's Eve ball she will be attending with her cousin. Nursing staff are pared down over Christmas, so visits to family can be made. I was going to my parents in Cambridge, but I could still spend some time with them and visit your mam too.'

---

12 *The holidays* - *The wealth generated by the new factories and industries of the Victorian age, allowed middle class families in England and Wales to take time off work and celebrate over two days, Christmas Day and Boxing Day. Boxing Day, December 26th, earned its name as the day servants and working people opened the boxes in which they had collected gifts of money from the 'rich folk'. Those new fangled inventions, the railways, allowed the country folk, who had moved into the towns and cities in search of work, to return home for a family Christmas.*

Jimmy nodded affably and his confidence soared. 'Aye, well that's good. When would yer want ta see yer parents? I wah hoping to see me mam as a suprise, as close ta Christmas Day itself, but what abaht you?'

Lucinda was so excited, she would have agreed to anything Jimmy asked of her. 'Well, we could go to Cambridge on the 23rd and stay for Christmas Eve, travelling up to your mam's early Christmas morning until Boxing Day. Would that suit you Jimmy?' she smiled adoringly as she gazed into his eyes, hardly daring to believe he wanted to spend Christmas with her.

Jimmy nodded. 'That sounds very generous of ya Lucinda. Are ya sure yer parents would be okay with those arrangements?' he asked, secretly pleased she seemed happy to go along with his plans.

'Oh yes, yes Jimmy. I will send a telegram[13] to them today. They have plenty of room for both of us and they will be pleased I have made a friend.'

Jimmy then surprised himself by spontaneously pulling Lucinda to him and kissing her briefly on the lips. 'Well that's settled then,' he said, pleased with her response.

'I...I have to go now Jimmy, I'll see you later,' Lucinda stuttered, quite shocked but delighted at Jimmy's actions. As she turned to go she saw Helen at the top of the stairwell and hurried to share her good news.

Jimmy watched closely and feeling pleased with the morning's events, ambled over to the ship's rail once more and threw some stale bread to the seagulls, still fighting over scraps. 'See you lot, there's always something turns up when ya least expect it,' he murmured, the euphoria and

---

13 *By the 1850s the sending and receiving of messages using Telegraph had been dubbed 'Telegrams'.*

excitement of the moment sending a shockwave of blood rushing through his veins.

He turned to leave, but reflected on the kiss he had instigated. Grinning in satisfaction, he realized he didn't feel half as guilty about betraying Rosie as he thought he would. However, he dismissed his fleeting conscience immediately, because after all, it was only a kiss...

※

The coach arrived at Liverpool Street Station, half an hour before the train was due to depart for Cambridge. Jimmy barely noticed his recent transition from crutch to cane, as he helped Lucinda to alight. He was in confident mood as he hailed a porter to take their luggage to the platform. There was just enough time for them to linger a while in the station café, where they occupied a table for two in the corner.

Despite his newly found confidence, their conversation became stilted as they sipped their tea and ate the slice of cake he had bought as a treat. This was a new experience for both, being out in public together for the first time.

Apart from discussing minutiae on the short journey from Greenwich Reach, there had been a few awkward silences, both anxious for their time together to be a success. Now as they faced each other across a table, the pressure mounted as they attempted to communicate in a more intimate way, but this became infinitely more difficult with each tripping over their sentences in a bid to keep the conversation flowing. When the time came to board the train, both seemed relieved.

However, after settling into the otherwise unoccupied carriage, Lucinda began to feel more relaxed. The pressure of eating, drinking and simultaneously holding a conversation had proved awkward, but now she began to look forward to the journey. Jimmy, however, appeared decidedly on edge, still inwardly ruminating about the prospect of meeting Lucinda's parents.

Since the decision had been made to spend Christmas together, Jimmy had been practising his speech, which was another thing he needed to focus on. He had lost some of his Nottingham accent during his travels abroad, but still the odd phrase interspersed his conversation. He realised Lucinda's parents may not fully understand him and now felt less confident he could converse with them adequately, so decided to practise on Lucinda. He gave a presumptive cough to attract her attention, then launched awkwardly into a somewhat out of character conversation. 'What do you think to the inclement weather we're experiencing Lucinda?' He had heard the word 'inclement' used on many occasion by the Captain of the *Lightning*, which, within a short time, Jimmy knew to mean a 'storm was brewing'. He also emphasised 'do' and 'you' instead of 'da' and 'ya', which he hoped would also impress her, finally stopping to gaze nonchalantly out of the window at the passing landscape, while he waited for her to reply.

Lucinda, a little bemused, responded with equal regulation. 'Oh, well, I was hoping for a cold crisp Christmas, but it looks as if we might be disappointed.'

Jimmy continued—'Quite...I agree. I expect your parents will be disappointed also?'

Lucinda was now totally mystified. Was Jimmy actually nervous being with her on a one to one basis? *or* was he worried about meeting her parents? She couldn't decide, but intended to find out, so tentatively broached the subject. 'Jimmy, are you all right with this visit, or do you have reservations?'

Jimmy fell silent. He began to wish he hadn't said anything at all. Now he was in danger of making a complete fool of himself and he knew he looked sheepish. 'I...er...I'm not sure,' he said. This was not how he envisaged their trip together. Up to this point he was on top of the relationship and certainly had the impression that she was more keen than he, but now that he had displayed a lack of assurance, the boot would be on the other foot. He decided to come clean about his concerns, as he recalled the last time he tried to cover up something on board the *Dreadnought,* which was embarrassing. He continued—'The fact is, I don't want ta let ya down,' he mumbled, his tentative statement allowing his Nottingham accent to manifest.

Lucinda breathed a sigh of relief. 'Jimmy...Jimmy, you could never let me down. You are a very brave, courageous man. How could you think that?' she questioned, then paused before making a confession—'I will let you into a secret. A few weeks ago, when we were getting to know one another, I wrote to my parents telling them about your exploits and the bravery you exhibited when you tried to save the bosun. They will love'—she broke off, not wanting to reveal her true feelings and adjusted her reply—'like... they will like you just as much as I do,' she announced, hoping he had not heard the word 'love', which might, she imagined, see him 'running for the hills'.

She need not have worried, as Jimmy was too mortified to hear everything she said, knowing he would now have to expand on his true meaning. 'It's noat to do with anything I've done in that way...' he began, studying Lucinda's face for a reaction. Should he have said anything at all? She didn't appear to have noticed his accent, but he had dug himself a hole and there was no way out. He continued, 'It's the way a speak. It isn't the same way you speak, or the way yer parents will speak. It mecks me sound stupid. There I've said it.' He groaned, annoyed that he had embarked on such a ridiculous course.

'Jimmy, oh Jimmy, I am only interested in who you are, not where you come from or how you speak. It's not important.'

Jimmy, extremely relieved, still harboured concerns. 'That's really kind of you ta say, but I feel embarrassed. Ta be honest, I have been practising all week and thought I could reasonably get by. I wonder, do ya think ya could 'elp me?' he pleaded.

'Of course, I'll help you Jimmy, but really, I don't think my parents will even notice,' she said generously.

Jimmy began to see Lucinda in a new light. *There is more to her than meets the eye*.

Lucinda interrupted his silence—'Now can we just enjoy our time together Jimmy. I was so looking forward to being with you over the Yuletide?'

A sheepish grin broke out across Jimmy's face. He was on top again. 'Yes, yes of course we can,' he said squeezing her hand. She really was someone special he decided.

The rest of the journey continued with them in deep conversation, Jimmy practising his speech and Lucinda praising his efforts. As the train drew in to Cambridge station, they at last felt at ease with one another. A close bond had formed as they became co-conspirators in a plot to restore Jimmy's confidence.

༺༻

Light rain danced on the wet pavements of Cambridge High Street as they hurried through the crowds of Christmas shoppers, although Jimmy was slightly hampered by his stick. They were happy and pleased they had decided to spend this festive time together.

Browsing in shop windows was new to Jimmy and so was buying gifts for anyone. Previously he always made the gifts he gave. He remembered how much time it had taken to make the keeper box for Rosie, which he was proud of, but it was disappointing not to have had the opportunity to give it to her. *Where might it be now* he thought absently, until Lucinda brought him back to the present as she pointed excitedly to a stick she spied in the Emporium. 'What do you think to that stick Jimmy? I thought my papa would like it,' she reflected. 'He already has a significant collection, but that particular one will be a great addition.'

Jimmy inspected the stick, still unsure *what* he thought about it. He had never owned such a fine specimen, apart from the old 'Albatross[14]' cane Lucinda had managed to find hidden away in a locker on board the *Dreadnought*. However, the excitement on her face was infectious, so he took the time to study it. 'Well, as you know, this'—he gestured, waving the cane in the air—'is the only *'stick'* I've ever used, but a do know quality when a see it. I think ya papa would love it.'

'You are right, I will buy it for him,' she cried happily.

Jimmy continued inspecting several items displayed in the window, until his eyes alighted on a small snuffbox, which he could probably just afford, if he was careful with

---

14 *Unusual walking canes made by Mariner's, circa 1850, are formed from the beak and skin of the Albatross bird. There has been much of the connection between the Sea Mariner and the Albatross bird, famously in the poem by Samuel Taylor Coleridge written in 1797 – 98 (although a tale of bad luck – these canes were given by mariners for good luck!)*

respect to the other presents he had to buy. 'I will get your papa that snuffbox with the hunting scene engraving on the front. Da ya think it is a suitable gift?'

Lucinda smiled appreciatively, pleased that Jimmy was taking an interest in her family. 'Oh Jimmy that is a lovely idea, shall we go in?'

The bell at the top of the door tinkled as they entered. Jimmy surveyed the scene around him, amazed at the variety of items for sale, which filled every available space. One clearly stood out, a small silk hand held fan, resting on a wooden stand, the centrepiece of a shelf filled with ladies purses and other small objects. The fan's sticks and guards were fabricated from a dark wood. Its black Chantilly lace edging and gold silk leaf hand painted flowers were exquisite. 'Do you like this Lucinda? Would your mamma have use for such an item?'

'Why Jimmy she certainly would. That is really lovely, but can you afford it?' whispered Lucinda, hoping she hadn't embarrassed him.

'Well yes I think I could manage it if we can request the shopkeeper to give a small discount on the purchase of all three items.'

He tentatively approached the shopkeeper and placed the three items on the counter. The shopkeeper raised his eyebrows above his spectacles questioningly and observed as Jimmy embarrassingly 'hemmed' and 'hawed'[15], shuffling from one foot to the other, suddenly dumbstruck at the thought of asking for a discount. He felt completely flustered, deciding he would pay the full price, even if it left him short with the purchase of other gifts.

---

15 *'hem and haw' – when someone hems and haws, they are evasive. Now commonly known 'ummed' and arghed'*

The shopkeeper sensed Jimmy's obvious predicament and smiled inwardly, transported to a time when he was in a similar position. Back then he had hoped a particular assistant would look kindly on him, as he desperately wanted to buy a particular brooch for his wife. Alas, it wasn't to be on that occasion and he left the shop without making the purchase. This young man, he decided, would not leave empty-handed. He had had a particularly profitable day and was feeling benevolent towards these young people, obviously very much in love. They reminded him of his wife and himself when they were young. He always wanted to shower her with gifts. However, money was tight in those days and although he knew he should cut his cloth to his means, he inevitably paid more than he should for quality. He considered it worth it, just to see her eyes light up in pleasure at some overpriced piece of jewellery.

When the couple first entered, his eyes were drawn to Jimmy's unusual cane with the Albatross handle and he could see he had clearly suffered some kind of accident. He was, he thought, probably unable to work, so doubted the young man could afford to purchase all three items. The discount he had in mind would not harm his profits too much, having had a bumper year. He was cruelly reminded that he did not have any family of his own to buy gifts for, since his wife died of Tuberculosis shortly after Christmas last year. He would never again see the pleasure on her face as he presented her with some frivolous item she would have adored...or bestow gifts on any other family members. They had not been blessed with children and the only family left was his sister-in-law, Aileen, who lived in Scotland and she had never visited him after the death of his brother two years previously. The sad fact was, he would be spending Christmas alone...He therefore concluded it would be his last chance to spread a little happiness this Yuletide. They would not, of course, realise the importance or reason for his generosity, but he would derive much satisfaction from his good deed anyway and so it proved.

Jimmy was surprised and delighted when the shopkeeper gave him a generous discount on all three items. Now he could afford a gift for his mam and also Lucinda. 'Thank you, sir, am much obliged to yer.'

The pair left the shop with their parcels, thrilled to have secured a good deal, but totally oblivious to the shopkeeper's small sacrifice that had brought him so much joy.

They were passing Eaden Lilley's department store, when Lucinda asked Jimmy if he would wait whilst she purchased some fabric she had spotted in the window. She also wanted to inspect the extensive array of books in Deighton Bell & Company's shop in Trinity Street, which had opened the previous year. She wanted to purchase 'Westward Ho!' only published this year by Charles Kingsley, and an 1816 publication of Jane Austen's 'Emma' for her mamma, also something for Jimmy, which she hoped he would like…'Robinson Crusoe', by Daniel Defoe[16].

'That's okay Lucinda, I will have a wander inside the small arcade we passed earlier. See if I can spot something for me mam. Let's meet at St Mary's Church at 11 o'clock, which should give us both plenty of time ta make our purchases.'

Jimmy watched Lucinda disappear into the store then manoeuvred himself off to the arcade, with the aid of his cane. He was secretly pleased to have some time to himself, as he intended to buy Lucinda a small item of jewellery. So far, everything he had seen was above his price bracket, but

---

16 *'Robinson Crusoe'* - *a novel by Daniel Defoe, first published on 25 April 1719.*

the arcade was just off the beaten track and he was hopeful of making a purchase. He became a little despondent when he found the shops immediately inside the entrance didn't have anything suitable. He was about to re-join the main thoroughfare, when he noticed an interesting shop, tucked away at the far end of the arcade. It was dark and a bit shabby from the outside, but the bull's eye windows revealed a few items carefully laid out on shelves covered in velvet. Unfortunately for Jimmy, all minus a price tag. Time was running out, but with nothing to lose, he ventured inside.

The sound of the bell alerted George Higgins, the shopkeeper and owner, who looked up from his ledger, peered over his C-bridge[17] pince-nez and pondered for a moment on the young man's noticeable disability, before resuming his book keeping.

The shop was small, only big enough for a maximum of two or three customers and Jimmy was his first customer in two hours. It had only just reopened after George finished negotiating with a lady who wished him to resell some items for her.

George stood silently while Jimmy inspected the contents of a small glass topped cabinet, with a limited display of rings, bracelets, necklaces and brooches, hoping to find something he could afford. Ten minutes later, he was still looking.

George's curiosity concerning Jimmy's disability increased. He studied the young man from his position

---

17 *C-bridge – These pince-nez, as their name would suggest, possess a C-shaped bridge, which was composed of a curved, flexible piece of metal, which would provide the tension needed to stay on the nose. This variety is the earliest style of true pince-nez. They existed from the 1820s through to the 1940s, and were available in a tremendous variety of styles*

behind the small carved oak counter, only feet away from where Jimmy stood. He deduced from his attire that he had served aboard a ship. He was wearing a black wool 'reefer'[18] jacket, sitting just above the top of his thighs, its brass buttons engraved with anchors, a white sailor style shirt and black trousers completed the ensemble. Two rather *odd* items, however, intrigued him. His highly polished shoes; not the usual buckled style worn by sailors but also the 'Albatross' handled stick.

He could not have known that the jacket had been given to Jimmy by a fellow seaman on the *Dreadnought* and was nearly new. That midshipman had been discharged from the navy, to start a new life with his brother in Covent Garden, as a purveyor of fruit and veg. He'd lost the lower half of his leg in a rigging accident and wanted desperately to put his navy years behind him, so contributed an additional shirt and trousers to Jimmy's meagre wardrobe. Dr Berredo had kindly donated the smart pair of shoes at the hospital in Natal, Brazil, because at that time, he had very little in the way of anything.

Consequently, the whole ensemble gave Jimmy, who stood five feet ten and a half inches in his stockinged feet, a fashionable bearing, but perhaps not comparable with George's usual smart chic and elegant clientele.

More minutes passed. The young man still appeared to be in a quandary with what to purchase, so at this point George decided to break the silence. 'Was it something in particular you were looking for sir?' he asked, peering closely at his captive audience, who was clearly ill at ease.

---

18 *The 'Reefer' coat, or jacket, was originally used by 'reefers' in the British Navy. It has been around since the 19th Century. They were the sailors who worked 'midships' (if you're a landlubber, that means in the middle of the deck) and whose job it was to 'reef' the sails.*

George was very proud of the family business, which had occupied this spot for the last one hundred years. The family valued their customers' repeat business, anchored on their renowned reputation of providing good value for money.

A little embarrassed, Jimmy pretended to look intently into the glass cabinet again. 'I...I'm not too sure,' he murmured, unable to think of a reason to leave. The prices were much more reasonable than the High Street shops, but still too steep for Jimmy, who was surreptitiously fiddling in his pocket, counting out his loose coinage. 'I was wanting a smaller brooch than those displayed,' he explained, looking down at the floor to avoid facing the shopkeeper.

George felt sorry for the young man. A seaman with a disability probably meant that he could not work until fully recovered. Therefore, he would have a limited budget.

It was then he recalled the elderly lady's items. 'I happen to have some items that might interest you, brought in this morning by a lady who wanted me to sell them for her. I don't usually deal in second-hand jewellery, but she was so persuasive that I said 'yes'. I do hope you are not offended by my suggestion?' he asked tentatively.

'No...not at all. Could I see them?' said Jimmy instantly relieved.

George disappeared from view and returned moments later with two small green velvet covered boxes, which he placed on the counter. He opened the lids to reveal a brooch crafted with semi-precious stones to resemble a bouquet and a small delicate Marcasite[19] bracelet. George pointed to

---

19 *Marcasite jewellery is made from pyrite (fool's gold, not, as the name suggests, from marcasite). It was a popular stand-in for diamonds. Pyrite is similar to marcasite, but more stable and less brittle. Marcasite jewellery has been made since the time of the Ancient*

the brooch, which Jimmy felt must be way above anything he could possibly afford. 'Is this more what you have in mind, sir?' asked George encouragingly. 'Might I ask your name by the way?'

Jimmy still thought he wouldn't be able to afford either item, so shifted uncomfortably from one foot to the other, as he revealed his name. 'Jimmy...me name is Jimmy Mitchell, sir,' said Jimmy nervously looking around the shop, hoping he could conjure up some excuse to leave, before he foolishly committed to making a purchase without sufficient funds.

George endeavoured to help Jimmy with his decision, giving an individual price for each, then one price for both items. He knew he would be selling the jewellery at a loss, but there was something about Jimmy's unpretentious demeanour that struck a chord and he still wanted to discover the story behind Jimmy's injury. 'While you are making up your mind,' he began, 'Tell me, how did you injure your leg?'

Jimmy, aware that time was passing and not wanting to keep Lucinda waiting, gave George a brief account of his unfortunate accident.

'I knew it,' said George, vindicated by his initial judgement of the young man. 'I knew you'd done something really brave, without concern for your own welfare. I pride myself on being insightful when it comes to judging a person's character. I see many people in my line of business, mark my words. I recognise instantly those full of bravado, those who are spineless and then, occasionally, those like yourself,

---

Greeks. It was particularly popular in the eighteenth century and enjoyed another surge of popularity during the mid to late nineteenth century – the Victorian era.

courageous in the face of adversity. Anyway, Jimmy, what reward did you receive for attempting to save a fellow seaman's life?' A question George believed he already knew the answer to.

Jimmy, totally perplexed, remained silent for a few seconds before giving what he hoped was a suitable reply. 'I didn't receive any reward, sir. As I said, the bosun lost his life because I couldn't save him.'

George shook his head, impressed with Jimmy's self effacing attitude. 'Listen to me Jimmy. What you did was very brave and I am honoured to have met you,' he smiled, whilst noting the fact that Jimmy appeared anxious to leave without making a purchase. In an instant, he made his decision, which was the second time that day Jimmy's fortune changed dramatically. 'In fact, if you would not be too embarrassed, I would like you to have both these pieces free gratis![20] Call it a fitting reward for your bravery in trying to save the bosun, one that is wholeheartedly deserved. Anyway, I didn't pay much for them and would have difficulty selling second hand goods. A pawnbroker usually deals with such transactions. This shop prides itself in offering a good deal, but my clientele are only interested in new items and one has to be very careful whom one offers second hand items to, for fear of offence. So Jimmy, I insist. Now who would they be for?'

Jimmy, speechless for a moment, understood the word 'free' but not 'gratis'. Either way, he realised he was being given the items without charge. This sort of thing never happened to him and now it was happening for the second

---

20 *Mid-15 century: 'for nothing, freely', from Latin 'gratis', contraction of gratiis 'for thanks', hence, 'without recompense', ablative of 'gratiae' 'thanks', plural of 'gratia' 'favour'. Meaning 'free of charge' - 1540s.*

time in an hour. He was astonished that anyone could make such a grand gesture and decided to accept before the shopkeeper changed his mind. 'I...well, the brooch would be fer me mam and a would really like the bracelet fer me young lady. She's waiting fer me at St Mary's.' There he'd said it...he admitted he was 'walking out' with Lucinda. He surprised himself but felt a glow of happiness, despite a very small niggle at the back of his mind, which he immediately dismissed.

George searched in his drawer for wrapping paper, carefully cutting a red sheet in half, while Jimmy waited patiently, still unable to believe his luck.

'Shall I put these in a bag for you Jimmy? We don't want your young lady seeing the gift before Christmas do we?' George smiled to himself, knowing he had probably lost all the profit he had made today, but he felt good inside...it was worth it he considered. This young man probably hadn't had a lot of luck in his life thus far and he was deserving of a change in his fortunes.

Jimmy grinned at George. 'Thank you very much, sir. I know they will both treasure these items. I'll not forget your kindness.'

'And I'll not forget you, Jimmy! Please drop in on me if you are in the area again. Now you had better get a move on, you don't want to keep your young lady waiting.'

Jimmy exited the shop and hurried as quick as he could towards the market square. Amazingly, he still had money in his pocket, maybe just enough to purchase some sort of necktie. He didn't own one, but thought he probably should to impress Lucinda's parents. He quickly deviated into a men's outfitters. After establishing the cost and on the advice of the owner, he bought a stiff, two-inch wide silk tie. Feeling rather foolish, he allowed the insistent Mr Bennett Pollykoff, to tie the item horizontally around his neck into a flat half-bow. Mr Pollykoff assured him it would be the optimum dress item for a first meeting of a young lady's parents. Either way, he did not have time for procrastinations and taking his purchase, made haste to St Mary's where he could see Lucinda anxiously scanning the crowded street for him.

She smiled, relieved that he had not decided to leave her there. 'Oh Jimmy, I thought you weren't coming,' Lucinda blushed as Jimmy put his arm around her.

'Don't be daft. Where did you imagine I would go? I just got delayed in the shop. Wait 'til you see the brooch I managed to get fer me mam. I'd value yer opinion.' Jimmy grinned, as he guided Lucinda toward a tea shop, where, he decided, they could sit and have a bite to eat. It would be his treat. This day was going really well, really very well indeed.

༺࿇༻

Grace and Charles Palmerston were delighted their daughter was able to join them for Christmas. They welcomed Jimmy wholeheartedly and he began to feel relaxed as Grace indicated a comfortable seat on the sofa next to Lucinda. He felt slightly less so when offered canapés and a glass of Vermouth, double dipping his sizeable anchovy and olive Palmier into a delectable sauce. *What on earth do I do with this wooden stick?* he thought, hastily pushing it into his jacket pocket.

Lucinda came to his rescue, as she purposefully placed her stick into the small white porcelain dish provided. Jimmy smiled appreciatively and followed her lead, after eating another of the delicious canapés, later using the finger bowl as if he regularly used one on a daily basis.

༺࿇༻

For the second time that day, Jimmy found himself relaying his exploits. Despite Lucinda already giving her parents a brief insight into Jimmy's achievements, they'd determined to include their guest in the conversation. They were particularly interested in his time in Fernando de Noronah, when he was found stranded and unconscious on the shore. Eager to impress, Jimmy gave an embellished account of his time there, careful not to go into too much detail about Renata, who he portrayed as a simple village girl, anxious to practise her nursing skills.

~~~

To Jimmy's relief, the evening meal was a very relaxed affair and he managed to conduct himself admirably, learning the skills of etiquette as he progressed.

After dinner, the couple were left alone for a short while and Lucinda didn't waste any time telling Jimmy how proud she was, adding that her parents were particularly impressed.

Later, Grace and Lucinda retired to the drawing room, leaving Charles and Jimmy smoking cigars and drinking brandy. Jimmy thought he could get very used to this lifestyle as both Lucinda's parents ensured he felt comfortable in their presence. Charles was astute enough to know Jimmy was out of his depth and unused to formal dining, so made sure he did not feel ill at ease by covertly guiding him through the protocols of after dinner etiquette. He determined his guest would enjoy his stay, which would please his daughter, whom he missed hugely and she was his top priority. Charles had quickly realised Lucinda had strong feelings for Jimmy and that was good enough for the young man to be welcomed into the family.

CHAPTER FIVE

Secrets & Regrets
December, 1855

Jimmy's bedroom at the Palmerston's was on the same floor as Lucinda's, but at the opposite end of the landing. *Was this a good thing* he pondered? *Probably so*, he concluded.

Jimmy suffered a restless night. Several diverse thoughts peppered his brain as if fired from a *Puckle Gun*[21]. There were many questions but few answers and all centred around Rosie and Lucinda. The night seemed interminable as sleep evaded him.

Lucinda also lay awake. Similar thoughts invaded her consciousness. *Did she love Jimmy?* She believed so. *Would he love her if he discovered her secret*...Oh dear, the one fly in the ointment...she was regrettably no longer a virgin! She gazed mournfully at the ceiling; reluctantly she decided to relive, in every detail, her encounter with Harry Benfield. Painful though it may be, she could lay this particular ghost to rest and rid herself of ever thinking about him again.

---

21 *The Puckle gun (also known as the Defence gun) was a primitive revolver, invented in 1718 by James Puckle (1667–1724) a British inventor, lawyer and writer. It is a tripod-mounted, single-barrelled flintlock weapon fitted with a multi-shot revolving cylinder.*

She took a deep breath, as she began her regression,[22] as if she were telling the story to an attentive listener who would not judge, but perhaps, agree that she had just made a terrible mistake.

> *'I remember it as if it was yesterday. It all began one wet Saturday afternoon. After shopping in the local food market, off Columbia Road, I returned to my apartment in Shoreditch, which I rented for a brief period, before joining the Dreadnought.*
>
> *The market was only a short distance away, but the rain slowed my progress as it lashed across my face, making me feel wet and uncomfortable. My arms ached with the weight of my bags, but the thought of a refreshing cup of tea encouraged me to quicken my pace. Finally I reached the welcome sight of the front entrance to the Victorian building. My apartment was on the first floor.*
>
> *I remember looking up at the stairs, focussing on the one flight, which stood between me and the haven of my front door. I turned on to the small landing, oblivious of the young man descending at a rate of knots from the second floor.*
>
> *In my attempt to avoid contact, I carelessly dropped one of my bags, the contents of which spilled out on to the landing. The young man came to my assistance, retrieving several potatoes, which had bobbled away down the stairs. In my mind's eye I can see him laughing, as he confidently juggled them in the air before placing them into my bag.*

---

22 *Regression - The act of reasoning backward from an effect to a cause or of continually applying a process of reasoning to its own results.*

It was then I found myself looking up into the once familiar face of Harry Benfield...someone I had not seen for a while. I blushed profusely, feeling the heat rise into my neck as I was instantly transported back to my nurse training days. I had worshipped Harry from afar. The University he attended was only a short walk from the college.

Sadly I was envious of my best friend, Anne, who had become one of Harry's conquests. In the ensuing weeks, I often walked with them, at the request of Anne, to preserve her reputation. Harry barely noticed me and much to my disappointment, excluded me from his conversations. I felt rejected and began to lose my self-esteem.

I knew Harry Benfield was an egotistical young man, but despite this, I felt he had a certain charisma. He was undeniably good looking, but had I viewed the situation more objectively, I would have seen him for what he was...a cad[23]...which in my mind was a man who lacked moral fibre and sensitivity and always 'used' women, casting them aside with indifference.

He walked with a confident swagger, being taller than most of his counterparts. He would brag to Anne that his father was a chauvinist and he much admired the control he held over women, who seemed attracted to him. Everyone recognised that Harry's looks and social standing virtually guaranteed his pick of several young ladies, eager to be seen in his company. I knew,

---

23 *'Cad' - 1730, shortening of cadet (q.v.); originally used of servants, then (1831) of town boys, by students at British universities and public schools (though at Cambridge it meant 'snob'). From 1838 - Meaning 'person lacking in finer feelings'.*

of course, that I was considered too shy and plain for him to pay any attention to, or even notice.

Why I continued to be in awe of him and couldn't see the patently obvious, I'll never know.

That day on the landing, he'd faced a bedraggled figure, whom he failed to recognise. I imagined he felt nothing but contempt. However, later that evening, I began to believe I had misjudged him when, he told me he found me strangely attractive. My wet hair, hanging loose around my shoulders and my vulnerability, obviously sparked a sudden desire to get to know me better. It was, of course, all part of his bigger plan, which he took great pleasure in revealing to me one day later. His parting shot left me more humiliated than I had ever felt, when he informed me of his real reason for feigning friendship that day.

His morning had not gone to plan. He was annoyed that his latest conquest had finally walked out on him, after discovering his true colours. However, the opportunity to salvage the weekend presented itself when he bumped into me right on his own doorstep. Apparently, I looked naive in the extreme and thoughts of easy pickings were too easy to ignore.

He followed me along the corridor to my room, carrying both bags and making polite, friendly conversation. His reputation with women was well known to me, but, of course, I believed I would be the one to change him. At least I knew he was trustworthy, in that he would not have need to force himself upon me. Harry could never be accused of desperation in that respect.

I remember feeling nervous excitement as I fumbled for my key. After several attempts, I managed to unlock the door and, inexplicably, invited him in. My idea was to repay him for his kindness. He must have inwardly sniggered at my offer of a cup of tea, as a tot of brandy would probably have been more appropriate. I was surprised when he accepted and wondered if he had changed over the years and now appreciated a woman's worth. Of course, I realised too late his acceptance was all part of his planned seduction.

We sat close together on the small sofa and chatted. After a short while, he put his arm around me and began showering me with compliments. I became a little nervous and was shocked at his boldness. This wasn't the way I expected him to behave after such a short acquaintance. However, my naivety and lack of experience meant, although I felt uneasy, I did not want to give him the impression I was prudish. I also found him physically attractive, but was afraid everything was happening too quickly and moving in the wrong direction.

My mixed emotions left me unsure where to draw the line. I realised I was out of my depth, but did not want to miss the opportunity of another meeting. I decided to give him a limited amount of encouragement and remember trying to impress him with my exploits in Australia. After all, not many young women had travelled so far unaccompanied.

Unfortunately, this information must have led him to believe I was worldly-wise. He took it as an invitation, cupping his hand around my breast. Surprised by this development, I gave a nervous laugh and immediately pushed him away.

I think he realised he had misinterpreted the signs. He must have concluded I wasn't sexually experienced and I was relieved when he made an apology, telling me he didn't know what came over him and pleading forgiveness for his overzealous enthusiasm. He claimed he found me irresistible...a very sensual woman. He explained it was easy to be carried away by the moment. I don't know why I found his explanation so plausible, but admit to being flattered by all the attention.

He smiled persuasively as he lightly stroked my face, so I smiled in return as I still hoped to convince him that he'd want to see me again. I resisted moving away from his touch, but explained that as we had only just met, I didn't want him to think I would give myself so easily to a relative stranger. I pointed out that I wasn't that kind of girl.

He assured me he had realised immediately I was a woman of high morals and he would not want me to suffer regrets; adding with sincerity that he enjoyed my company and wanted to see me again. I believed him. It appeared Harry was happy to go at my pace. The simple truth was, I had inadvertently given him the impression that sooner or later, I would succumb to his charms.

I began to relax, confident this would not be our only encounter. I admitted to liking him enough to see him again and looked around for an excuse to stretch the evening out in his company. I remember catching sight of the shopping bag containing ingredients for a meal, which gave me the idea to invite him to stay for dinner. Harry accepted.

Later, we sat down again on the sofa. Harry moved closer towards me and asked if there was any brandy in the house. I remembered there was half a bottle left by the previous tenant and poured us both a glass. My confidence grew as I thought Harry really seemed to like me.

After two glasses of the liquor, which I had never tasted before, I began to feel warm, happy and relaxed. Harry made no further advances and seemed more interested in finding out about my life. I was flattered and decided to admit we had known each other previously.

He was noticeably surprised, but with hindsight, he probably used the information to exploit the situation, suggesting that he would surely have remembered. I told him we lived in the same area as students and some of the nurses from St John's House met with Graduates from the University in the gardens near Russell Square. I sought to remind him that Anne Brooks was our mutual friend.

At first, Harry appeared to have no clue who Anne was, but after searching back in his memory he announced he did remember her. He suggested that if I was Anne's friend, he couldn't believe he had chosen her over me.

I explained to him that I would not have been his type. I wasn't pretty enough and Anne was stunning with long dark hair, much more the sort of girl that would appeal to him.

I remember his wry smile as he told me I should not put myself down, that I was very attractive and had lovely hair. He also told me that as we had met previously, he considered us friends already, not strangers; another ploy no doubt. He then moved my fringe gently away from my forehead before stroking my face again and placing one arm around my shoulders. His other hand rested gently on my covered thigh. At this point, I felt my resistance slowing fading and at his suggestion, took another sip of brandy.

Significantly, at that moment, I wanted nothing more than for Harry Benfield to kiss me and told him so. Harry did not need a second invitation, he leant forward and began planting little kisses on my neck and whispering endearments in my ear. My heart beat faster and I found myself responding as he kissed me softly on the lips. I was powerless to resist. Suddenly he released me from his hold and stood up to go, explaining that he was having difficulty controlling himself. As he moved towards the door, he said if I wanted, he would call for me the next day.

Still reeling from the kiss, I readily agreed. He said we could take tea at Fortnum's, in Piccadilly, then we could 'finish the evening off' back at my flat. I wasn't entirely sure what he meant by that phrase, but at that moment I definitely felt in control. Unfortunately, that feeling was short lived.

※

The following afternoon, as we took tea at a secluded table in Fortnum's, I felt on top of the world. Harry treated me like a queen and I couldn't wait for us to be alone later that evening and for many more evenings. However, back at the flat, the situation very quickly deteriorated. Harry poured us drinks, insisting that we should indulge ourselves. He told me not to worry, as alcohol would make me lose my inhibitions and create a relaxing atmosphere. He said he had already decided to take me out again later in the week and that he really enjoyed my company. Once more I was taken in by his apparent sincerity. How could I have been so gullible?

Unfortunately, I was lulled into a false sense of security by the warmth of the fire and the brandy we'd consumed. It was then that Harry made his move. This time he did not hold back. He seduced me with promises and used his experience to exploit my vulnerability. His first kisses were soft and sensual as he stroked my hair and moved his hands over my body. Even then, I believed he would stop short of penetration, as I thought he respected my wishes. I was mistaken. Before I could catch breath, his kisses became urgent and without tenderness. He pushed me unceremoniously on to the floor, pulling up my skirts and petticoat. He said I had led him to believe I wanted to make love as much as he did and I should prove it by allowing him to enter me. Before I could protest, he covered my mouth again with his harsh kisses and began having sexual intercourse with me. The whole sordid affair took less than five minutes. With a smirk he headed for the door, leaving me lying on the floor with my clothes in a state of disarray. His parting shot was that he had never before had sex with anyone quite so frigid.

The following day, a whole raft of emotions tore away at me and I realised our brief encounter had ended as swiftly as it began. I felt violated, humiliated, foolish and heartbroken. I was too ashamed to tell anyone and suffered in silence. It was the last time I saw him. I moved out the following week to take up my nursing assignment on the Dreadnought and there was Jimmy to pick up the pieces. I wish with all my heart I had never set eyes on Harry Benfield.

As her regression ended, Lucinda lay exhausted and motionless, staring at the ceiling, until a sense of calm washed over her. Realisation dawned that the ghost of Harry Benfield had finally been laid to rest. She thought only of Jimmy and the future they might share together. She was certain of her love for him and hoped it would be reciprocated, if not now…some time in the future. One thing was irrefutable; Jimmy was an honourable man who would never hurt her. With Jimmy she felt safe, but he also set her pulse racing. If Jimmy wanted to make love, she knew she would give herself wholeheartedly to him. Jimmy was the one with who she wanted to spend the rest of her life. Suddenly the future seemed very bright. Her nightmare had been swept away with the breaking of a new dawn. Harry Benfield was dead and buried. Now nothing, she determined, nothing would ever come between herself and Jimmy.

CHAPTER SIX

New Beginnings
24-25th December 1855

The Palmerstons and Jimmy rose early on Christmas Eve morning. Jimmy and Lucinda, despite their late night, were excited at the prospect of spending Christmas together.

Jimmy dressed quickly, then waited patiently behind his bedroom door, listening for Lucinda's footsteps. His intention was to 'accidentally' bump into her on her way down to breakfast. It wasn't long before he heard her melodious humming as she made her way along the landing. He opened his door in one rapid movement, feigning surprise, whilst simultaneously adjusting his recently acquired, but unfamiliar silk necktie. 'Oh Lucinda...you're up early. We'll be able to go down for breakfast together,' said a grinning Jimmy.

Lucinda, impressed with Jimmy's attire, gave him an admiring glance, but at the same time noted his discomfort in the stiff shirt and necktie. Her papa would most certainly wear a similar outfit but it was obvious that Jimmy had gone to great lengths to please her.

Lucinda looked stunning in a simple dress of pale blue silk taffeta. The effect was not lost on an appreciative Jimmy, more used to seeing her in formal nurses uniform. On their journey to Cambridge, she wore a smart wool day dress, but the blue silk elevated her to another level, which complemented the smooth creamy softness of her skin.

'You look lovely Lucinda. Am pleased yer accepted me invitation to spend Christmas together.' Jimmy smiled but was still nervous at meeting her parents again and mildly reverted to a Nottingham accent. Instantly, he remonstrated with himself to try harder with his speech.

Jimmy took Lucinda by the hand as they descended the stairs. As they entered the dining room, he noticed the elaborately decorated tree. It was obvious that someone, very early that morning, had placed *his* gifts alongside the rest of the family's presents, which were evenly distributed around its base.

Charles acknowledged their arrival by shaking Jimmy's hand to wish him greetings of the season, as Grace suggested they take a cup of 'Grey's Tea[24]' before they sat at table. Betsy, their cook, would serve breakfast. She was one of only three staff employed by the Palmerstons, together with a maid of all works and a gardener, who doubled as a chauffer. Betsy had surpassed herself by laying out an impressive buffet and soon bustled in with a tea tray, setting it down on a French Provincial walnut coffee table, with barley twist legs and stretcher. Grace poured Jimmy a cup, which he accepted gracefully, although his hand shook as he lifted the elegant china cup to his lips, hoping the contents would not spill on to the highly polished table-top.

Eventually, Jimmy relaxed as he gazed into the blazing fire, laid promptly at 5.30 that morning by the maid. He

---

24 *'Grey's Tea' – Drunk in the 1850s - the precursor to 'Earl Grey' - Jacksons of Piccadilly claim they originated Earl Grey's Tea, Lord Grey having given the recipe to Robert Jackson & Company's partner, George Charlton in 1830. According to Jacksons, the original recipe has been in constant production and has never left their hands.*

noticed the small curls of smoke whipping over the coals as the flames danced up the chimney and he began to reminisce. He remembered it was but a short while since he and Rosie had sat together in front of such a fire. She had laughed at his woeful attempts to dry his hair, which only resulted in producing a 'head of steam'. They were good times, but, he reminded himself, he was with Lucinda now, so there was no time for regrets.

Grace interrupted his thoughts, which brought him swiftly back to the present. 'Jimmy, are you all right? You seem miles away. Would you like another cup of tea?' she queried, smiling caringly.

Jimmy had never sampled Grey's tea before and didn't much care for the taste, but felt obliged to acquiesce. 'Oh, yes thank you…I am fine and happy to be here. The blazing fire made me think of Christmases past…back home in Nottingham'— he fibbed, before continuing—'I was wondering what me mam was doing now.' He didn't like telling 'fibs'[25], but it was true that when he woke this morning, he had thought about his mam and although he was enjoying his time with the Palmerstons, he couldn't wait to see her again. It made him sad to think she may not know whether he was dead or alive and he wondered what her reaction would be when she opened the door on Christmas Day to see him standing there.

Grace was sympathetic. 'Oh Jimmy, of course you are thinking of your mam, especially this Christmas. Consequently, I have already arranged for cook to pack

---

25 *Derived from the word 'Fable' (also fibble-fable) - from the earliest appearance of the word in English, six hundred years ago; not only meant a pleasant narrative, but also meant a downright lie, and we still use the word in either sense.*

some items for you to take, as your mam probably won't have enough food in for two more hungry mouths. We will breakfast at 7 o'clock tomorrow and Alfred, our driver, can take you to the station to catch the early train to Derby[26]. You should hopefully be in Darley Abbey around lunchtime.'

'Thank you very much. Me mam will, I know, appreciate your kindness,' stated a relieved Jimmy, who had worried how he could propose they leave directly after breakfast, in order to arrive in Derby as early as possible.

'You are very welcome Jimmy. Now why don't we open our presents today, to save time tomorrow? We are all grown ups,' she said smiling, 'so we don't need to wait. There's actually quite a collection on and around the tree.'

Charles was delegated the task of distributing the gifts.

Jimmy was surprised to receive four presents, two from Grace and Charles, one of which was very large and an irregular shape. The other two gifts were from Lucinda.

Nothing about this occasion resembled Jimmy's Christmases past. The tree, elaborately draped with tinsel, ribbon, cookies, candies and lighted candles, was a sight to behold. He couldn't remember ever having a tree at Christmas before, except for the one spent with Rosie when they were young and that was the best Christmas he had ever experienced. Prior to that, he only remembered the occasion when his father came home drunk, slapped his mother and beat him with a belt. There was always a noticeable absence of presents, although his mam did her best with dinner.

In comparison with the Palmerstons' Christmas, their occasion paled into insignificance. Even now, he would love

---

26 *The running of Sunday services on Christmas Day was normal across the railway industry in the mid nineteenth century, even offering reduced fares!*

to get his mam a tree and would dress it magnificently to take pride of place in her parlour.

Lucinda interrupted his thoughts, 'Jimmy why don't you open Mamma and Papa's unusually shaped gift. I am so excited for you to see what is inside.' She grinned, glancing conspiratorially at her parents.

Embarrassed, Jimmy started to peel the paper, amid shouts of 'carefully does it Jimmy' and 'look out for the needles'.

Casting caution to the wind, he tore at the carefully wrapped item and was astonished to discover it was a perfectly formed rooted fir tree, planted in an earthenware pot. His face displayed utter delight. It was as though they had read his mind and in an instant, granted his wish. Unbeknown to Jimmy, of course, the truth was, it had actually been bought by Charles a couple of days ago and planted in their garden by Alfred, the gardener. He had dug it up very early that morning to keep the needles fresh and intact.

A bewildered Jimmy quickly wiped a tear from his eye. 'Thank you, thank you so much'—he paused, anxious about his forthcoming question. Would he sound ungrateful he wondered? Either way, he summoned the courage—'Do yer mind if a give it me mam?'

The Palmerstons answered in unison. 'Of course not Jimmy!'

Grace stepped forward, putting her arm around his shoulder. 'We expected you to make that request. We wish it was a full sized tree, but this one is just about transportable. Betsy has put aside some candles, tinsel, ribbons and cookies, for decoration. Please let us know your mam's reaction when she sees it. It is an unusual gift, but we hope she likes it.'

'A cannot repay you for yer kindness, but me mam will love it,' replied Jimmy in a faltering voice.

Charles took the tree from Jimmy. 'I'll make sure Alfred keeps it well watered and sprayed before it is packaged tomorrow morning ready for your journey.'

His second gift was also from Grace and Charles. He was overwhelmed to find an intricately carved deck knife, encased in a leather sheaf.

Next came Lucinda's gifts, which were equally well received.

'I thought you would like to read the adventures of *Robinson Crusoe*, as he too was shipwrecked on an island.' Lucinda looked expectantly at Jimmy, who thanked her by placing a chaste kiss on her cheek.

Her second gift was a warm woollen scarf, to keep out the wind and rain when he was aboard ship.

'Now Lucinda it is your turn to open something. What about that small parcel wrapped in red tissue?' Charles pointed to the gift he knew was from Jimmy.

Jimmy held his breath as Lucinda carefully unwrapped the box containing the bracelet. 'Oh Jimmy it's beautiful,' she said, planting a kiss on his cheek in return. 'I will treasure it always.'

Jimmy blushed, as all eyes focussed on him. 'Am glad yer like it. A wasn't too sure if yer would. Shall I fasten it for you?' he asked, taking the intricate bracelet and wrapping it around her wrist.

Lucinda, delighted Jimmy had bought her something so personal, would not have minded if it had been made from string.

She also received an exquisite silk evening bag from her parents. Her stocking fillers, included a magazine entitled *The Pocket Magazine of Classic and Polite Literature 1832*, containing several useful phrases. Lucinda, intrigued, couldn't wait to practise some on her friend Helen, who often quoted interesting or appropriate idioms.

Grace, next to unwrap a gift, gazed happily on the fan bought by Jimmy. 'Oh Jimmy this really is lovely. How very kind of you. It's most appropriate for the New Year Ball. I'll be the envy of everyone,' enthused Grace, kissing Jimmy on the cheek.

Charles then spiritedly accepted the snuff-box. 'Good choice, Jimmy, the hinge recently came off my old one and this is the perfect size to tuck into my pocket. Thank you very much,' he said shaking Jimmy's hand.

Other smaller hand made gifts were appreciatively received and shown around, while Betsy gathered up the discarded ribbons and wrapping paper. The Palmerstons knew she would smooth it out to use on her own family's gifts next Christmas, hence their careful unwrapping to ensure that the paper remained intact.

'Actually, there are two more gifts,' exclaimed Grace. 'They are both for your mam, Jimmy. One is from Charles and myself and I believe the other is from Lucinda.' She smiled as Charles handed Jimmy a large tin of shortbread biscuits, the lid decorated by a Christmas scene, to complement Lucinda's gift of a trio of homemade jams.

Jimmy was in awe of the generosity of Lucinda's family. *After all, they hardly know me* he thought. 'I don't know what to say,' he exclaimed. 'I just hope me mam is well and it won't be too much of a shock seeing me again. How can I thank you all?' he asked.

Grace felt humbled. Their gifts weren't overly expensive and Jimmy was sincere in his acceptance. She hugely admired the young man for his humility. 'Jimmy, you have repaid us already by befriending our daughter and we are pleased you could join us this Yuletide. We hope you are enjoying your stay and try not to worry too much about your mam. If it is a shock at first, she will recover quickly, knowing you are alive and well.'

'Do you think so?'—Jimmy paused to look at Lucinda—'And by the way, I am very lucky to have met your daughter and will do my best to make her happy.'

⁂

After a delicious lunch, Lucinda and Jimmy spent a relaxing day, talking with Grace and Charles, who took an interest in the sometimes harrowing tales of Jimmy's early life in Narrow Marsh. Some saddened them, but others made them laugh, especially the ones, which Jimmy described as 'eventful'. He was careful not to mention Rosie too often, but as she was a big part of his childhood, it was inevitable she was included.

By the time the evening came to a close, everyone seemed at ease with one another and Jimmy's accent diminished as he became more confident.

When Grace and Charles retired at 11 p.m., Lucinda and Jimmy discussed his mam and her probable reaction to their visit, until Betsy interrupted their conversation. She bustled in with mugs of hot chocolate and homemade biscuits, complemented with an enthusiastic smile.

Jimmy thanked Betsy then sipped his chocolate as he settled comfortably into the armchair with his feet close to the hearth. He thought life could not get much better than this. His fascinated gaze took in the hot coals and his imagination ran riot, as it created a host of mythical beasts amongst dancing flames, burning fiercely in the cast iron dog grate.

As a child, when his dad was at the alehouse, he would sit on his mam's knee with a mug of hot milk and sugar and watch as she pointed out unusual but sometimes familiar shapes in the flaming coals. He remembered how happy and content he felt, until the front door flew open and his dad staggered in, belt in hand...Strangely, this memory once more reminded him that his mam had no idea if he was dead or alive. He felt her pain and his worried brow knitted in anguish. What he wouldn't give for her to be here, right now, sharing the hospitality afforded by Grace and Charles. He would give anything for his mam to see what a real Christmas could be like...full of laughter and cheer, with loved ones sitting in front of a roaring fire and a majestic tree, twinkling with tinsel[27] and candles, just like the one he was looking at now.

He recalled his recent conversation with his hosts about life in the Marsh, which evoked old childhood memories, particularly the one on Christmas Eve, when his dad fell asleep on the settle in the parlour. He visualised him lying there, relieved of his belt and braces; the stench of his beer soaked trousers mingling with the smell of sweat, permeating the very fabric of the room...What a complete contrast to the aromas of fir, pine and cinnamon that wafted throughout the Palmerstons' home.

His mam would damp down the dying embers of their fire, before she took him to bed. He remembered shivering

---

27 *Tinsel was invented in Nuremberg around 1610. Tinsel was originally made from extruded strands of silver. Because silver tarnishes quickly, other shiny metals were substituted. Before the 16th century, tinsel was used for adorning sculptures rather than Christmas trees. It was added to Christmas trees to enhance the flickering of the candles on the tree.*

and feeling icy cold as they ascended the wooden stairs, treading carefully on each step for fear of waking his dad. Thankfully, more often than not, his loud, unrelenting snoring assured them he remained asleep.

In the relatively safe but cold, dark, attic room, a small candle flickered and burned slowly. Their nightly ritual began with prayers. Jimmy knelt on the well-worn pegged rug by his bed and asked God to look after his mam and, very reluctantly, his dad, then promised to be good. His mam tucked him in, so only his eyes and nose showed above the rough grey blanket. She kissed him goodnight and told him everything would seem better in the morning…but it never was! However, Christmas Eve did differ from other nights, because his mam hung a stocking up at the end of the bed. Jimmy would be really excited just seeing it hanging there. Invariably, on Christmas morning, the only items to be found were an apple, a few sweets and a farthing. If he was lucky there might be a small toy, possibly a 'hand me down', which his mam had been given by someone 'better off' in the Marsh, whose child was now too old to play with it.

Before she closed the door on Christmas Eve, she always whispered, 'Close your eyes and make a wish Jimmy'. All the years he had made the same wish, which never came true… until the day his dad met his demise. If only she'd known his secret wish was for his dad to disappear, which meant he and his mam could live safely and happily together.

His life then took a dramatic turn. He'd been beaten once too often, so retaliated, pushing his dad in anger. His head hit the tiled hearth, rendering him bleeding and unconscious, or so he thought. His mother, realising the enormity of the situation had immediately packed him off, before the authorities became involved. Tragically, he was unaware that his father had died that night and only found out when Rosie told him of the circumstances much later.

Reluctantly, Jimmy left his mam alone to fend for herself. When he found a job, he would send money for rent, coal, food and candles, which meant her not having to rely on the light from the fire during the winter evenings to knit. His financial support would ensure she had enough to eat and never go hungry.

What, he thought, *would she make of some of the food he had enjoyed here?* He gave a little laugh, imagining how she would ever cope with table etiquette. She'd muddle through of course and he knew Grace and Charles would graciously and diplomatically turn a blind eye.

Lucinda, just finishing her hot chocolate, interrupted his thoughts, 'Jimmy, we need to go to bed now as we have to be up early tomorrow.'

Jimmy reluctantly agreed, relinquishing his comfortable chair. 'Yes I think we should, as you say, we need an early start.'

They ascended the stairs to the first floor and stood for a few moments outside Lucinda's door, feeling a little awkward. Jimmy bent down and kissed Lucinda softly on the lips, whilst looking furtively along the landing to see if anyone was around. He pulled her close and the kiss continued in its intensity. Jimmy's feelings were aroused, although his intentions were honourable. He was terrified of being caught and did not think that moving into her bedroom was appropriate under the circumstances. He was, after all, a guest of Lucinda's parents. He pulled gently away. 'Goodnight Lucinda, I'll see you tomorrow morning,' acknowledged a reluctant Jimmy.

'Goodnight Jimmy,' said Lucinda, disappointed that he didn't linger at least a little while longer. 'We'd better be ready by 7 o'clock tomorrow, as it's going to be a long day.'

Jimmy knew he had become closer to Lucinda and even considered they might have a future together. Surprisingly, he only gave a passing thought to Rosie. Lucinda was ecstatic that Jimmy held their kiss for a long time and enjoyed holding her close. Harry Benfield was no longer a factor in her life, no more than a distant and fleeting memory. They slept well, dreaming happy thoughts of one another.

The following morning everyone rose early again and met in the dining room for breakfast. Their luggage was packed and ready waiting in the hall, along with the all-important tree and Alfred was on hand to take them in the carriage to the station. It wasn't long before their goodbyes were said and promises made to visit as soon as they could. Grace and Charles watched as the horse and carriage made its way down the drive and through the gates. Lucinda and Jimmy's Christmas break was already a huge success and it still wasn't over.

CHAPTER SEVEN

Homeward Bound
24-25th December 1855

Ida Mitchell knelt by her bed deep in silent prayer on Christmas Eve. God willing, her prayers would be answered and Jimmy would knock on her door on Christmas morning, banishing to the past the months of worry and uncertainty she had suffered.

Several months ago, Lizzie delivered the devastating news that Jimmy was missing. In spite of this, Ida refused to believe he was dead, trusting he would return home. Christmas, after all, was a time for families and Jimmy would not let her down. Such was her belief that she slept soundly for the first time in months.

༺༻

Ida rose early at 5 a.m., feeling refreshed. Her first job was to light the fire and put the porridge on the hob. She shivered, but barely noticed the cold as she hummed 'Homeward Bound'[28]. She grinned, imagining Jimmy might also be whistling the shanty on his journey home.

---

28 *Said to be 'the most popular homeward-bound shanty of them all'. It was sung at the capstan or the windlass. We're homeward bound, to Liverpool Town, Goodbye, fare-ye-well, Goodbye, fare-ye-well, And*

She returned to her bedroom to plump up her pillows and smooth down the coverlet. Her next task was to put clean sheets, blankets and her best eiderdown on 'Jimmy's' bed. She arranged sprigs of holly, adorned with bright red berries in a pot vase, but it seemed incongruous in the 'Spartan'[29] room. Nevertheless, she stood back to admire her handiwork, before descending the stairs once more to the kitchen and its cobbled floor. She ladled out a bowl of porridge and poured herself a cup of tea. It was still only 6.30, when she washed and then dressed herself in a smart blouse, complemented by a shawl and a new skirt, bought for the occasion. Last night she had tied her greying hair in rags and now lightly brushed through the curls, which fell haphazardly around her face.

Ida's life had been harsh, living with a drunk of a husband. He'd kept her short of money, which meant living frugally, virtually from hand to mouth. She was only forty-four years old, but her lined face gave her the look of a much older woman. The damp conditions in the Marsh contributed to her severe rheumatism. However, this condition did not weaken her determination and resolve; she would not 'give up the ghost'. Always rising at dawn, she took pride in her home, busying herself from morning until night, never taking to her bed before 10.30 p.m. Today, she looked younger and felt sprightlier. Her obvious happiness shone from within as she accomplished her many tasks with a spring in her step.

Satisfied she looked presentable, she took another cup out of the cupboard and set it down on the table, then

---

over the water, To England must go, Hurrah, my boys, we're homeward bound.

29 *Mid 17th century: from Spartan, because the inhabitants of Sparta were traditionally held to be indifferent to comfort or luxury.*

looked out of the window at the deserted lane. Lights twinkled in her neighbours' houses, their children rising early in expectation of the day's festivities.

The hours passed excruciatingly slowly. Eight o'clock came and went, but there was no sign of Jimmy. Ida's belief was beginning to waver as she forlornly turned away from her window, but she consoled herself with the thought that he might come later, depending on how far he would have to travel. Then hope and expectation gave way to common sense - if she was honest with herself, it was indeed possible he may never come at all. Was her absolute conviction merely just wishful thinking?

Her earlier euphoria began to evaporate, as she took one more look out of the window on the still deserted lane. Dejectedly she drew the curtains to keep in the heat. Her rocking chair beckoned and she sat down wearily. Two more hours passed slowly. A faraway look betrayed her anguish as she stared blankly into the fire. She watched the diminishing flames flick staccato fashion around the hob and up the chimney, barely noticing that the large black cast iron kettle had almost boiled dry. Even the drab grey walls appeared more damp and depressing, in the pale orange glow of the fading fire. With a heavy heart, she removed the kettle and placed it on the hearth next to her empty cup; its contents long since gone. Sadly, she hadn't the energy or the inclination to stoke up the dwindling coals, with the consequence that the room temperature dropped sharply over the next hour.

※

Ida's sisters, Nancy and Gertie and her husband George were celebrating Christmas at Gertie's house in Wirksworth. Nancy encouraged Ida to visit but she was adamant that she wanted to be at home, just in case Jimmy came. Until that happened, there was nothing to celebrate. She rocked to and fro in her chair and dreamed of better times. Thoughts of Jimmy provoked a stream of tears, which cascaded down her cheeks. Suddenly she felt very tired; a frail old woman, without a future. Another hour passed, in which the dying embers glowed fleetingly before surrendering their existence. The room temperature deteriorated rapidly and Ida began to shiver, as she fell into a fitful sleep.

※

Meanwhile, Lucinda and Jimmy were nearing their destination. Jimmy, staring introspectively out of the window, shared his thoughts. 'Am still a bit nervous, me turning up out of the blue so to speak. It's bound to shock her. Am not sure whether ter knock on her door or wait a little way down the lane while *you* break the news to her. What do yer think?'

Lucinda had also given thought to Jimmy's predicament, having discussed it the previous evening. 'Well, Jimmy, perhaps it would be better if I do break the news. I don't want to frighten her, but I thought I could say something about being your friend, then tell her I've brought good news. That way, she won't be too alarmed.'

Jimmy brightened. 'Yes, that's a really good plan. That would work,' agreed Jimmy, pleased that Lucinda had considered Ida's probable reaction. 'That is what we will do. I will leave it ta you ta give me the nod when yer think the moment is right.'

Their train pulled slowly into Derby station at midday. Jimmy beckoned a porter to take their luggage along with the Christmas tree to a waiting coach, bound for Darley Abbey. This journey was rickety, but otherwise uneventful.

TANGLED WEB

The coachman dropped them close to 9 Mile Ash Lane, but out of sight of Ida's cottage. Jimmy quickly disembarked and set their luggage down. He surveyed the area and felt pleased his mam had settled here. It was a far cry from the 'back to back' terraces of Nottingham and the air felt clean and fresh. The only downside it seemed was the steep hill. Carrying her shopping from the bottom was bound to be an arduous and unforgiving task.

On reaching her cottage, Lucinda tapped on the door, but Ida was oblivious to her knocking. She tried again a little louder this time, but still Ida did not stir. Lucinda began to think there wasn't anyone home. The curtains were drawn and she began to wonder if all was well. She beckoned to Jimmy to join her, whereupon he struggled the last few yards with the tree, leaving the luggage behind. 'What's up? Isn't she at home?' Jimmy queried, concerned and perplexed that his mam's door remained firmly shut.

'I'm not sure. I have knocked a couple of times, but there is no reply. Could she have gone away for Christmas? Look the curtains are drawn. Would your mam draw the curtains if she was out?' Lucinda questioned.

'Mmm...I suppose she might, but me mam usually drew her curtains back first thing in the morning, sometimes as early as 4.30 when me dad was alive, as she had a lot ter do before he went ta work or, more often, a beer-house[30],' mused Jimmy as he reflected on the harsh times his mam endured. A deep quizzical frown appeared on his forehead

---

[30] *The Beerhouse Act of 1830, enabled anyone to brew and sell beer on payment of a license costing two guineas. The intention was to increase competition between brewers and it resulted in the opening of hundreds of new beerhouses, public houses and breweries throughout the country.*

as he looked up at the bedroom windows. Upstairs the curtains were drawn back, which indicated that she was not in bed. Still concerned, he turned to walk the few yards to her next but one neighbour. 'Think I'll give me Aunt Nancy a knock. Rosie told me, Mam stayed with Nancy after me dad died, so she could be there,' he said, hoping to resolve the mystery.

Jimmy knocked hard on Aunt Nancy's door and was again disappointed not to receive a response. He turned to Lucinda. 'Well, that's odd, she's not at home either. Perhaps as you suggest, they've both gone away fer Christmas.'

Jimmy dejected, looked apprehensively down the hill to the village, as he continued to ruminate as to her whereabouts. *One thing is for sure, she couldn't be shopping on Christmas Day*...then like a mist suddenly clearing, the word 'shopping' evoked a distant memory. 'I wonder if she's left a key under the mat? Me mam always left me one when we lived in Narrow Marsh, especially if she was going to the shops.'

Excitedly, Jimmy returned to number nine and lifted up the core matting. Delight enveloped his face as his hand brushed against a solid metal object. Triumphantly, he withdrew the key and held it aloft. 'Right, let's gain entry, but quietly. If she is in, I still want to surprise her.' Immediately he inserted the well-worn key into the hole and turned it. The door sprang open and Lucinda followed him into the parlour. He was relieved to see the back of his mam's head, tilted to one side and just visible above the top of the chair. Grinning from ear to ear, he placed his finger on his lips to maintain silence. He then crept around to face her. She was asleep, but he was still overwhelmingly pleased to see her again. 'I'll bet she's bin up since dawn beavering away and now she has nodded off,' whispered Jimmy. 'Tell you what,' he pronounced, 'I'll put some coal on the fire and place the tree by the far wall, while you make a cup of tea.'

'Okay Jimmy, is the kitchen through here?'

'Yes, I would imagine so. Me mam is very organised, so you should find everything you need. I'll also fill the kettle and fetch in the luggage, before we wake her,' asserted Jimmy.

After accomplishing the tasks he set himself, he quietly placed the tree in the corner of the room and dressed it with tinsel and candles, then lay the gifts from the Palmerstons, Lucinda and himself at its base. The glow from the candles and the fire, now well ablaze, reflected on Ida's peaceful face.

At that point, Lucinda, who had brought the tea through and was admiring the tree, turned to study Ida for the first time. Instantly she recognised that all was not well. Ida seemed pale. Quickly she shouted, 'Jimmy, I think your mam is suffering from hyperthermia; she's unconscious, not asleep and cold to the touch. We didn't notice how chilly it was in here, as we haven't taken off our coats. Bring some blankets, we need to get her warmed up.' The urgency in her voice galvanised Jimmy into action. He rushed upstairs and returned with two thick grey blankets. Lucinda gave rapid instructions. 'Fill up a water bottle,' she said, whilst carefully wrapping the blankets around Ida and gently rubbing her arms.

Several minutes elapsed before Ida began to stir. Shaken and surprised, she stared incomprehensibly at the young woman who was kneeling beside her, offering her hot sweet tea. 'Who are yo?' she asked weakly and without waiting for a reply, 'Where am a?'

Jimmy didn't hold back any longer, he rushed to her side speaking softly, 'Mam, it's me, Jimmy. I've come back to see you.' He cradled her head in his arm and kissed her cheek then gently squeezed her hand.

Ida scrunched up her eyes to peer at Jimmy's smiling face. 'Am a dreaming or is it really yo our Jimmy?' she asked, hardly daring to believe he'd come home at last.

Jimmy, holding back his tears confirmed that it was indeed him. 'It is me Mam. I've been on a hospital ship, but I'm home now. I did write a letter to let you know I was all right, but I guess you didn't receive it. Anyway, how are yer feeling Mam, yer look a bit pale.' Which seemed to Lucinda, who raised her eyebrow, to be the understatement of their visit thus far.

'Don't rightly know Jimmy. A feel a bit coad, but now yer 'ere, everything seems as right as rain. Hold me agen Jimmy and tell me it is you. I still think I'm dreaming, but a knew yu'd come back one day. They said yer were dead, but in here'—Ida patted her chest—'a knew yer weren't. A din't receive yer letter Jimmy, probably it wah lost in the post, but that don't matter now.'

Jimmy held his mam as tight as he dare, given her present condition and this time he allowed the tears to flow. 'It really is me Mam. I've come to spend Christmas with yer. Look over in the corner; it's a real tree with candles and tinsel. Something we never had when we lived in the Marsh. Do yer like it Mam?' he asked, regaining his enthusiasm at seeing his mam again.

Ida's eyes focussed on the once gloomy corner, now bathed in a bright orange glow. 'Ee Jimmy, what a sight that is'—she paused, a long distant memory creeping back into her mind—'A once got us a tree Jimmy. Ad done some sewing fer one of them grand ladies up St James Street. Wokked through the night ta get it finished and she gev me a tree...it wah about same size as yer one, but we never even got ta dress it, afore it wah gone. Yer were abaht three, but yer dad said it wah a waste a money, even though we hadn't paid forrit and he flogged it fer some baccy and beer.' Ida sad and angry for a second, quickly regained her joy when she focussed on Jimmy.

Lucinda, who had watched the scene unfold, offered Ida another cup of tea. Ida turned quickly, suddenly remembering there was someone else in the room. 'Thanks, nurse, a would like one. Did ow Jimmy send fer yer?' she asked, perplexed that he could afford to send for anyone in the medical profession.

Jimmy laughed. 'Well Mam, in a manner of speaking, I did and you are right, she is a nurse. Her name is Lucinda and she is a nurse on the hospital ship.'

Lucinda took Ida's hand. 'I am really pleased to meet you Mrs Mitchell. I am a friend of Jimmy's and very happy to be spending Christmas with you.' Apprehensively, Lucinda waited for Ida to speak. She really hoped they would get along.

'Oh, a see...well any friend of Jimmy's is a friend of mine. Am pleased ter meet yer too, but I'd like yer ter call me Ida if that's a'right,' she said, winking at Jimmy.

'Yes, yes it is Ida and I hope we can become good friends. I am very fond of Jimmy, he is a very courageous and thoughtful person. Anyone who Jimmy befriends is lucky indeed.' Lucinda blushed as she caught Jimmy looking at her in a way he hadn't before.

༄

A little while later, Jimmy again stoked up the well-established fire. Ida, feeling much better, was anxious to prepare a meal for her guests. ''elp me up Jimmy, me rheumatism is playing up today. A need ter get a pan of spuds on. A did buy some chicken...just in case yer turned up. It's on the cold slab in the pantreh'—Ida nodded her head towards the kitchen, then turned to Lucinda before continuing—'It not be much me duck, but a cook a good, crispy roast tata.'

'Mrs'—she corrected herself—'Ida, that is really good of you. I can see where Jimmy gets his kind heart. I would like to help you, if that is all right?' offered Lucinda.

'Oh, no a can't let yer da that. Yer me guest and it's my way of thanking yer fer saving me life—'

Ida was cut short, as Jimmy stepped in. 'Listen Mam, there'll be no arguments, you've always done the cooking for me and considering you are recovering from a chill, Lucinda and me will make dinner. You sit here a while and enjoy the warmth of the fire and we'll get cracking.'

Ida's protests were lost on the couple, as they wandered off to the kitchen. She was left staring cheerfully at the bright flames darting up the chimney, as she settled into her thoughts. *Well, he talks a bit funny, more posh like, but he's still my Jimmy…my Jimmy…and he is home safe and well.* She smiled, as a warm glow enveloped her. Within seconds her eyes closed and she drifted into a contented sleep.

⁂

Some while later, as a delicious aroma filled the room, Ida began to stir. She felt comfortable and much like her old self, as the heat from the fire warmed her small frame. Her eyes focussed on the Christmas tree and to the beautifully wrapped gifts placed around it, but best of all, Jimmy stood alongside Lucinda. Joyously, she noted plated meals, the extra dish of roast potatoes and vegetables and the small gravy boat, on the table. Lucinda had also managed to find space for a candle, some sprigs of holly and three crackers. In addition, Jimmy's paper chains with mistletoe and red-berried holly on the mantle transformed the parlour. Lucinda and Jimmy, noticeably affected by Ida's obvious delight and tears of happiness, nearly succumbed themselves, surreptitiously dabbing their own eyes.

'Oh Jimmy,' Ida exclaimed in a faltering voice—'me prayers 'ave been answered, but even now a feel am still dreaming, so come ovver 'ere and sit wi me.'

Jimmy dutifully obeyed and sat on the arm of the chair. He kissed her on the cheek, as they held each other tight. Ida hardly dare release him in case he vanished. Lucinda watched and this time, a tear slid down her cheek. She realised how lucky she was to have a friend like Jimmy.

'Right Mam, let's get you seated afore it gets cold,' urged Jimmy as he helped Ida out of her chair. In joyous mood, they toasted their good fortune with a glass of Chardonnay, 'courtesy of Charles'. After they had eaten their Christmas dinner, Lucinda retreated to bring in the pudding and Jimmy seized the opportunity of a quick word. 'What do yer think of Lucinda Mam?' he asked tentatively.

'Why Jimmy she's a lovely gel,' she exclaimed, nodding her approval. 'A took to 'er straight away…and, well, she probbly did save me life. Wi'out 'er a might 'ave…ooh it dun't bear thinking abaht,' she whispered sombrely.

'Well I suppose you're right about her quick thinking. Her training came in handy and she's a really good nurse. I'm glad yer like her Mam, cos am thinking of walking out wi her, so ter speak,' said Jimmy, matter of factly lowering his gaze, as Lucinda reappeared holding the flaming pudding aloft.

'Let me take that,' he suggested. 'I'll clear the sideboard of the crockery and make room for it and the brandy sauce. There's dishes in the cupboard by the way.'

Ida's eyes widened as Jimmy placed the biggest pudding she had ever seen on the table. 'I'll serve it and you can put your own sauce on Mam.' Jimmy smiled as he spooned a large portion into a dish.

'Ooh Jimmy, I'll never manage all that,' Ida exclaimed.

'Well Mam, do your best but be careful not to swallow any silver sixpences,' he said laughing.

After they'd finished, the tree became the focus of attention, with Jimmy doing the honour of distributing gifts.

He waited in anticipation as Ida carefully unwrapped his present. Her eyes glistened with tears as she held the brooch against her blouse. 'Why Jimmy, you shunt 'ave bought me oat.' She grinned mischievously. 'Yer will need all yer money if you're go-an ter be courting.'

Jimmy blushed. 'Aw Mam, I have enough put by,' he mumbled, glancing surreptiously at Lucinda, who was smiling modestly at Ida's veiled suggestion. 'Anyway, da you like it Mam? I chose it myself,' Jimmy added, raising his eyes to the ceiling as he silently asked God to forgive him, acutely aware of the fact that he hadn't actually paid anything for it.

'It's beautiful Jimmy. No one 'as ever given me oat as lovely as this. A will cherish it always.' She smiled in contentment as Jimmy pinned it securely to her blouse.

The presents from Lucinda and her parents were unexpected, but gratefully received. 'This is the best Christmas ever, Jimmy,' she exclaimed, suddenly remembering the gifts she had knitted for her son. 'Ave summat fer yo too,' she said pausing—'but I din't expect yer ta arrive wi a young lady,' she exclaimed, chuckling with embarrassment. Her eyebrows knitted into a frown and her mind whirred with thoughts on what she could possibly give to Lucinda. Several moments elapsed, before a past memory leapt into her head. 'Ave bin chewing ovver 'ow a could repay yer kindness me duck and, as luck would 'ave it, 'av just suddenly remembered summat—' Without further explanation, Ida disappeared up the stairs, leaving a puzzled Jimmy to ponder on what on earth his mam had in mind for a thank you gift.

A few minutes elapsed before Ida reappeared with a wrapped present for Jimmy and a small box for Lucinda.

Jimmy unwrapped his gift of a hand knitted blue scarf and gloves, which Ida had worked on for months, praying that he would return to receive it. 'Thanks Mam, you can bet I will make good use of these.' He grinned, kissing her lightly on the cheek.

'Good, good Jimmy. They'll keep yer warm when yer on board a ship. They're made from best wool. Yer remember Flo Baker Jimmy? Well 'er sister, Ada gev me some blue wool she had left ovver. It came straight from Gnathole Mill and it is real quality. She smiled to herself as she recalled the tale told by Flo on the journey back to Nottingham, after Lizzie confirmed Jimmy had joined the Navy. Almost lost in her memories for a moment, she recovered her momentum. 'Now then oppen yours Lucinda. It in't new, but it's bin in the family a while, a 'ope yer like it,' she said expectantly as she proffered the small box.

Lucinda carefully opened the box, to reveal a small gold posy ring[31], encircled with stars. 'Oh dear, it's beautiful, but I cannot accept it. How long as it been in your family Ida?'

Jimmy, equally surprised waited expectantly for her reply. 'Well, it belonged to me great grandma, Esther. She wah given it by a lady named Isabella, mistress of a large house where Esther wah a maid. It finally got passed down the family ter me. Lady Isabella wah given it by 'er beloved

---

31 *'Posy' rings. The practice of giving gold hoop rings engraved with mottoes at betrothals or weddings was common in England from the sixteenth century onwards. 'Posy' rings could, however, be given on many other occasions as tokens of friendship or loyalty.*

husband, who worshipped 'er. They wah childless and when 'er husband died, she too fell ill. Esther 'elped nurse 'er in 'er final months…sat wi 'er fer hours through the long nights. She wah very poorly wi consumption you see. Isabella and 'er would count the stars in the night sky. One such night she asked Esther ta seek out a box in the drawer of 'er dressing table, which contained the ring inscribed with the words, *'Many are the stars I see, but in my eye no star like thee'*. She told Esther she wanted 'er ta have it, as she had bin a loyal and kind servant ovver the years. I could never wear it of course, as Bill 'ud a flogged it wi'out a doubt, if he'd seen it, so I kept it 'idden under the floorboards, covered ovver wi' a pegged rug. It's Jimmy's be rights, but as he's a man, am sure he wun't mind me giving it ter you, as a thank you fer saving me life. I can't get it ovver me knuckle now anyrode and it's abaht time it saw the light of day.'

Lucinda was touched with Ida's gesture, as they had only just met, but humbly accepted the gift with one proviso. 'It is really very kind Ida and I thank you, but if Jimmy and I part, I will return the ring to him.'

Jimmy, amazed at his mam's story, butted in—'If me mam wants you to have the ring Lucinda, you should keep it whatever happens in the future.'

Reluctantly Lucinda agreed then kissed Ida on the cheek in heartfelt gratitude. 'Can I get you another cup of tea Ida or would you prefer something stronger?'

'Well, as we're having such a lovely time, a think we should raise a glass of summat stronger, ta the future.'

Glasses filled, Jimmy proposed a toast. 'To the future and a new start for us all.'

As the eventful day drew to a close, Lucinda made an excuse to retire, so that Jimmy could spend some time alone with Ida. *After all, they have a lot of catching up to do,* she surmised.

Ida immediately made a proposal. 'A made a bed up fer Jimmy in the second bedroom, but you should sleep there instead, he'll be all right 'ere on the sofa. Would yer fill a water bottle fer Lucinda, Jimmy? There's a stone one in the kitchen under the sink.'

Jimmy and Lucinda exchanged knowing glances, as she left for Jimmy's bedroom, then Jimmy made his mam a hot mug of milk with a spoonful of sugar, just like she used to make for him when he was small. He put another shovelful of coal on the fire and settled down on the sofa, observing the flames as they whipped around the coals and flickered up the chimney. 'Can you see any shapes in the fire Mam?' he prompted, a question that she sometimes asked him as a boy.

'Ee Jimmy, I *can* see summat...there in the centre, looks like an angel. Do ya see it?'

Jimmy couldn't for the life of him make out an angel but knew she was entering into the spirit of things and the bond they shared, so agreed. 'You're right Mam. Perhaps it is the angel that watched over me and brought me back home to you.'

'Yes, that 'ull be it Jimmy and I thank the Lord you're back safe and well. Now tell me all about yer escapades,' Ida begged, 'before I ga ta me bed.'

Despite her overwhelming tiredness, Ida, eager to know what had happened to Jimmy, listened intently to his adventures while sipping her milk. Her close proximity to the fire meant she acquired a red mottled look to her feet, which extended up to her ankles. Long ago, a young Jimmy entering the scullery after playing in the snow, would discard his boots and stand too close to the fire, mottling his legs from knee to foot. Ida would gently admonish him, explaining that he would get chilblains if he stood there too long.

Another hour passed in which they laughed and reminisced about the good and bad times in the Marsh, but Ida, barely able to keep her eyes open, still needed to tell Jimmy some news of her own.

'There's summat I think ya should know Jimmy,' she whispered quietly. 'It's abaht Rosie...I've dreaded telling yer, but yu'd eventually find out. She's courting Jimmy...it wah a long time after she'd received news that yo were missing, but eventually a think she had ta admit yer weren't coming home. In fact, she still won't know yer alive...It's yer friend, John Jamieson'—she paused, as she acknowledged Jimmy's reaction, which conveyed solemnity and sadness. Her voice wavered as she struggled to impart some comfort—'Try ter understand the way things were Jimmy.

'For a long time she held out, hoping yer would return, but she had ter let go. She couldn't go on.' Ida frowned, anxious that Jimmy would not be too distraught, but her fears were realised as Jimmy's furrowed brow betrayed his emotions. He appeared shaken as he experienced an unexpected sinking feeling in the pit of his stomach.

He stared silently into the fire. Why had this news affected him at all? He knew in his heart she wouldn't wait for him forever; consequently, he didn't blame John, who must have presumed he'd died that night attempting to rescue the bosun. Perhaps they both needed to move on, realising he had actually done that with Lucinda. His life was happier these last few weeks, especially since Lucinda had agreed to share Christmas with him. Naturally he was sad, because Rosie and him had grown up together. *That is it, I'm bound to be a bit sad, she was my first love.* He would get over it. He studied his mam's worried face before seeking to reassure her. 'It was to be expected Mam and I understand why Rosie would turn to John, at first for friendship then later for...for something more, but I am with Lucinda now, so don't worry about me.'

Ida nodded. 'Good Jimmy, so long as yer all right, then I won't worry. I like Lucinda Jimmy, she seems like a good gel. Me only advice would be not ta rush inta marriage Jimmy. Teck yer time and get ta know each other first.'

Jimmy grinned. 'You're putting the cart before the horse[32] there Mam, I don't have any intention of getting married yet, but I thought I might meck it a bit more official that we are courting. I intend seeing Rosie at some point to assure her that I don't blame her for finding someone else. When that will be I'm not sure, because I hoped to find a berth on a short passage vessel to get me back in the swing of things.'

Ida nodded and breathed a sigh of relief...relief that he had not taken the news of Rosie's new relationship too badly and that he intended to continue going to sea. She wanted a better life for her son than coalmining or a job in a factory. A sailor's occupation was dangerous, but much better than spending days underground, deep in the earth, risking his life as a pit worker and not seeing the light of day for most of the time. She felt content that he too wanted to enrich his life. At least his rough upbringing had taught him one thing: *Not to walk in his father's footsteps!*

Ida finished her mug of hot milk and stifled a yawn. 'Well Jimmy, we've 'ad a wonderful day, the best ever. Would yer come ta me room and we'll both say a prayer, like we used to, thanking God fer our good fortune.'

---

32 *The earliest recorded use of the proverb was in the early 16th century. The idiom is used in a context, which reverses the usual chronological order of A and B.*

'That'ull be perfect Mam. Let me help you up the stairs.' Jimmy smiled, grateful his mam was well and back to her old self.

'Will yer be okay dahn 'ere me duck? Yer cun 'ave them two thick blankets ta keep yer warm,' suggested Ida struggling to her feet. The two glasses of Chardonnay, coupled with her rheumatism, were beginning to affect her co-ordination and mobility, which she found vaguely amusing.

'Course Mam, I'll pull the sofa closer to the fire, it'ull be right cosy.'

Satisfied that all was well, she ascended the stairs with a helping hand from Jimmy.

They knelt by the bed, hands placed together in prayer and thanked God for each other, before Ida insisted they make a wish. Her wish was to keep her son safe from harm in the future, but Jimmy's wish was two-fold, for God to look after his mam while he was away at sea and for his own future to bring health, happiness and luck, with the emphasis on 'luck'. He knew he'd need a lot of that in the coming months.

※

Lucinda lay awake for some time in Jimmy's bed. She reflected that the day had gone really well and was happy and content, but sleep eluded her, as a niggling doubt crept into her mind. She was sure Jimmy was the man for her, but she hated keeping secrets and wondered whether she should tell Jimmy about her past, in particular, her encounter with Harry Benfield.

Jimmy was also awake. He was considering going to Lucinda's room and telling her he would like them to become more than friends. Would he be rebuffed or would she be equally keen? For the next few minutes he gazed intently into the glowing coals of the fire, hoping the answer would manifest in two foot high letters and rise up from the dwindling flames...it didn't.

Suddenly deciding, he threw back the blankets, put on his dressing gown, pulled a comb through his hair and gingerly exited the room, mounting the stairs. Each step creaked alarmingly, loud enough to wake the dead, no matter where he trod or lightly placed his feet. 'Blast!' he said to himself. 'Me mam will surely waken,' but as he drew level with both bedrooms, he could hear the feint sound of rhythmic snoring emanating from his mam's room. He placed his hand to his mouth to stifle a sudden urge to laugh, but reassured himself that the two glasses of wine would surely ensure she slept soundly.

He was only inches away from Lucinda's door and poised to knock, but he hesitated, debating whether to follow through with his plan. However, fate intervened as his trembling hand involuntary made contact with the wood and the decision to retreat was taken away. There was no going back.

He coughed self consciously, before announcing his presence. 'Lucinda...it's me, Jimmy. Can I come in?' he asked tentatively, as he shuffled from one foot to the other, hoping the floor would swallow him up.

Lucinda hesitated, then quickly discarded her thick winter robe and woollen socks and slipped into a silk gown, from their shopping trip to Cambridge. She hoped Jimmy might want something more than a polite conversation and that time had come. She sat nervously on the edge of the bed and whispered encouragingly, 'Of course, Jimmy, the door is unlocked.'

He clasped the round brass knob and turned it anticlockwise, half regretting his possible folly. The door opened with a loud creak and his heart missed a beat. He closed it silently and gasped in astonishment as Lucinda moved from the bed and stood before him. He held out his arms in a welcoming embrace. The flickering candle revealed she was bare foot and clad only in a long, pale blue silk nightgown; her dark hair falling loosely around her shoulders. In that instant, her smile melted Jimmy's heart.

'I...I'—Jimmy hesitated, feeling really foolish—'I just thought...I wondered if you might like to become'—he coughed again before completing his sentence—'like to become more than a friend?' Jimmy lowered his head, so she wouldn't notice the red flush, which was rising up from his neck. His hands felt clammy as he clasped them together in front of him. *Well, you don't have the upper hand now... what the hell were you thinking?* He need not have worried about blushing, as the semi-darkened room, cloaked his embarrassment.

Lucinda moved closer, almost touching his masculine frame. 'Oh Jimmy, I have wanted so long for us to be together. Are you sure it is what you want?'

Her remark boosted his confidence. 'Yes, it is.' He smiled, tenderly holding her face in his hands, as he kissed her softly on the mouth. Then with more urgency he kissed her neck and shoulders, whilst carefully releasing the straps of her nightgown. It slipped effortlessly to the floor. Jimmy gazed unabashed at her nakedness, delighting in the curves of her body, before boldly discarding his own robe, as he lowered her gently to the bed.

Uninitiated in the art of seduction, Jimmy let his emotions take over, realising Lucinda was as keen as he to consummate their relationship. Their eyes locked together as his hands glided sensuously over her body; first circling her breasts then moving down over her hips. Lucinda quivered as Jimmy's fingers softly and slowly caressed the wet sensitive softness of her most sensual place. Her breathing became frantic as she thrust her hips seductively, inviting him to begin their lovemaking in a passion that became overwhelming.

Jimmy entered her and they were swept away on a tide of ecstasy. Much later, they lay in each other's arms, their bodies spent physically and emotionally. Sadly, they realised they could not spend the whole night together, but still lay for several hours talking and embracing each other. Both wondered how the other was feeling, but neither was brave enough to ask. After a final goodnight kiss, Jimmy returned to his makeshift bed by the fire, while Lucinda was left wondering whether he realised she had already lost her virginity.

※

At 6 o'clock the following morning, a refreshed Ida descended the stairs and was surprised to find that Jimmy already had the fire blazing. The Christmas candles were lit and the room felt warm and cosy. Inevitably, a pan of porridge bubbled on the hob. 'Hello Mam, come and sit here,' he said, indicating her rocking chair, next to the fire. 'I've mashed yer a cup of tea and the porridge will soon be ready.' He disappeared into the kitchen, whistling as he poured out two cups of tea.

'There we are Mam. I hope yer slept well?' enquired Jimmy sheepishly, hoping she wouldn't detect even a slight hint of guilt in his voice.

'I did Jimmy. Best sleep 'ave 'ad fer a long time. Couldn't believe it wah 6 o'clock. A never sleep in normally, up at five most days.'

'Ah well, there's no need ter rise that early now Mam. Yer've no one to please but yourself,' asserted Jimmy before continuing, 'I think I will put some bacon on when Lucinda joins us, I saw some rashers on the cold slab and we brought some eggs and mushrooms, courtesy of Grace and Charles.'

'That'ull be lovely Jimmy. There's some dripping as well, noat better than a slice of bread fried in dripping.'

'I agree with you there Mam and after breakfast, we could all go out for a walk…what do ya say?' Jimmy, full of enthusiasm, felt all was well with the world.

Lucinda rose at 7 o'clock and brushed her hair before apprehensively descending the stairs. She hoped Jimmy did not regret last night's encounter, but immediately realised her worries were unfounded. Jimmy and Ida were, in fact, happy and content. Jimmy had already anticipated her imminent arrival, when he heard her moving around upstairs, so poured a cup of tea and ladled some porridge out in readiness. Lucinda was used to bathing before breakfast, but accepted their practice of eating in their dressing gowns without question.

'I hope yer don't mind Lucinda, but me mam doesn't have the same washing facilities as your parents. We thought we would have breakfast first, before providing a kettle of hot water for your bedroom, so you can wash and dress in private.

'Thank you Jimmy. Is there anything I can do to help?' she added.

'No it's all prepared…there's a cooked breakfast keeping warm, so just sit and enjoy it,' urged Jimmy with a cheeky wink.

※

Later, excitedly donning hats, coats, mufflers and boots, they set out on a steady walk to the top of the lane. Ida, still not fully recovered, leant on Jimmy for support. He was amazed how clean and refreshing the air seemed as he admired the beautiful countryside spread out in the valley below. 'I'm really glad you moved to Darley Abbey Mam, although I do worry about the long haul up the hill you have to make with your shopping,' observed Jimmy.

'It's not sa bad son, the *The Boar's Head* mill owners deliver us groceries like flour, oatmeal, cheese and coal very cheaply. They even sell us beer, but 'ave no need fer that! The tenants of Evans farm in Darley Abbey deliver us milk at tuppence ha'penny a quart and there's also a delivery of fish and bread, so a don't 'ave much ta carry and…am not done fer yet. Me lungs 'ave improved since a came 'ere. The smoke billowing out from Narrow Marsh's chimneys' can't harm me now and a don't cough any more. I also meck a bit of money 'drawing' lace, as there's only me to feed and clothe, so a manage quite well Jimmy,' Ida emphasized with pride and conviction.

Jimmy, however, wasn't at all convinced. He'd ventured down to the cellar earlier that morning and struggled to find large lumps of coal, only a thin layer of nutty slack covered the cellar floor. He'd already planned to call at the mill on the way back and slip a note to the owners. He'd ask them to deliver some 'good stuff' to see her comfortably through the winter. He also intended to put some cash into the money tin his mam kept in the kitchen for groceries and other necessities. When he joined his next ship, he could send money to her on a regular basis, to secure her wellbeing and financial future.

'Aye well Mam, yer certainly have roses in your cheeks now and there is a spring in your step, even though you leant on me for support,' Jimmy joked, grateful that everything had actually turned out so well.

Before they left, Jimmy managed a quiet word with his mam, to request that she write to Rosie, to let her know he was alive and well and would visit in the near future.

Ida had enjoyed Jimmy and Lucinda's visit, but as she prepared to wave the pair off, she became saddened, aware of her forthcoming loneliness. She tried desperately to smile, but a tear formed in her eye as she said her goodbyes, wondering when she would see her son again. Inevitably, the coach in which Lucinda and Jimmy travelled, disappeared from view, leaving her alone once more.

She re-entered her warm living room and her eyes alighted on the decorations Jimmy had brought with him. The tree, proud with its candles still burning, was a reminder of the wonderful time they'd spent together. Her melancholy returned momentarily, but after making herself a cup of tea, she knew what she must do. She would join her sisters Nancy and Gertie in Wirksworth for the rest of the holiday; after all, she had some wonderful news. Her sister Gertie and husband George were always asking her to stay whenever the fancy took her. She might stay longer, even until spring, especially as it was likely to turn colder. With renewed vigour and sense of purpose, she jubilantly packed her valise and was soon locking the door behind her. It was then she suddenly remembered Jimmy asking her to write a letter to Rosie and considered going back inside. On reflection, she decided that Jimmy should write to her himself, as she needed to hurry to catch the regular coachman, who stopped in the village centre at 6 o'clock. It would take her half an hour at a slow pace, carrying a valise, to reach the bottom of the hill, where she'd catch the coach for the three mile journey to Wirksworth. Consequently, a letter from herself would make little difference, she argued, if Jimmy planned to visit Rosie anyway.

Unbeknown to Ida, now in Wirksworth, her son had already boarded a ship for Australia. His planned visit to Rosie shelved for several months.

CHAPTER EIGHT

The Letter
Christmas Day 1855

Robert's much vaunted small 'sardine' hiding place galvanised their excited chatter, as they gathered in the dining room for supper; apart from Amy. Her worried frown was concealed from view as she hid in the shadow of an alcove off the main hall.

Her initial intention to seek refuge in the bedroom, allocated to Robert and herself, was almost thwarted by the sudden appearance of Lizzie. She'd spotted Amy's apparently forlorn and solitary figure. 'Oh, there you are Amy! Everyone wondered where you'd disappeared. Are you all right?' she asked.

Amy quickly pulled herself together. 'Why yes, Lizzie, I was just about to look for Harriett, but I had a sudden headache and thought I might lie down for half an hour.'

'Probably a good idea,' offered a puzzled Lizzie. 'Harriett, Beatrice and Victoria are amusing themselves in the playroom with the dolls house. Beatrice is being somewhat laborious in her efforts to explain how playing with the house can help young ladies run a home, but she is losing the battle. I think the logic has been lost on the other two.' She grinned as she recollected Rosie not really seeing the rationale behind the teaching when she was younger. 'Anyway, I'll let Robert know your intention, so you won't be disturbed. If you feel better why not join us for supper?'

'Thank you, Lizzie. I am sure half an hour will see me fully recovered. I don't want to miss all the fun,' she called back, as she ascended the stairs.

Safe in the privacy of her bedroom, Amy sat dejectedly at the writing desk fronting the window. In her heightened state of anxiety, she frantically jerked the middle drawer open and extracted a single sheet of paper. In an instant, she knew exactly what must be done, although, minutes later, she realised that there was a deep chasm between 'knowing' what to do and what was required to 'accomplish' such a task. Consequently, the virgin paper lay devoid of commitment, as her pen hovered above it.

Her ordeal became unbearable in the extreme. She leant forward and buried her head in her hands, powerless to prevent hot salty tears cascading unchecked down her cheeks in her angst. A quarter of an hour passed, which seemed endless. The second 'tear stained' sheet of plain writing paper, suffered the same fate as the first. She crumpled it tightly in her hand and threw it in the basket, atop the original discarded attempt, then stared wide-eyed at the third sheet. She hunched forward, once more dipping the pen into the pot of indigo ink. Her hand shook uncontrollably as several more attempts failed to produce a single word, although small globules of ink had dropped on to the leather-topped desk. These she subconsciously mopped up with her handkerchief, before reluctantly repositioning the pen on its stand. Consumed with guilt and unsure of the consequences such a deliberate act might evoke, she sat back, absently gazing out of the window. Her vacant eyes belied the silent torment she was suffering.

Soon Robert would surely come looking for her...Robert her rock, her confidante and her husband, who she loved dearly.

She knew she wasn't his first choice, as that particular accolade belonged to Kate. When she first met Robert, he was consumed with sorrow at losing Kate, who had left him without a word of explanation. She was, of course, instrumental in him coming to terms with this loss and so they became good friends. Several months later, their relationship changed irrevocably. They became lovers, although she could never be sure he had really got over his first love. Robert *told* her he loved her, but was it passionate love or safe, familiar love, drifted into? She did not have an answer, but did it really matter? They were happy weren't they? They had their own little family, of which Robert was fiercely protective. Their marriage would flourish in a wonderful future, if it were not for Kate's constant selfish interference.

The answers to the rights and wrongs of pursuing such a dangerous path eluded her, but in her heart, she knew she wasn't about to hand her husband over to someone else and destroy her own happiness. She would fight for him!

This minor betrayal, which is what she perceived it to be, was the sacrifice she must make to keep him; conversely, she didn't really have the heart to carry through with her plan… to expose Robert as a willing participant in an illicit affair. There was, after all, the possibility that he may not have actually done anything wrong and, consequently, had no reason to leave her for Kate! But was that enough? She wanted him to be hers and hers alone and could not bear the thought of the two of them indulging in any clandestine meetings, with the inevitable consequences. Even if he wasn't the instigator, it would be, nevertheless, an ultimate betrayal of herself.

Even now, she trusted Robert implicitly, but Kate? Kate was another matter entirely. Amy had witnessed her in action on several occasions. Her suspicions were initially aroused at the November dinner party at *The Chestnuts*. Drink induced reminiscences, resulted in hypothetical questions being bandied around. Most were instigated by Kate, on the 'what if' scenario of relationships between first loves.

Their recent whispered conversation, confirmed her worst fears. They planned to meet, each for their own reasons. Kate to lure Robert into an affair and Robert seemingly to find a solution to Kate's obsessive behaviour. Would his emotions take over, to rekindle a lost passion? Did he secretly want to hold her and make love to her again? She couldn't be sure.

Her thoughts on the consequences of such an exposition were confusing and her options few. It was hopeless to approach Robert directly, having tried that already. Indeed, he had assured her, that the only relationship he shared with Kate was one of mutual interest as parents of Rosie. At that time, she had wholeheartedly believed him, so to ask again would create distrust.

If she wrote the anonymous letter, James would have to confront Kate. He would not tolerate his wife seeing another man right under his nose. He had his pride, so if he could put a stop to their possible affair, he too would save face. A promise by Kate to end any relationship with Robert would restore equilibrium and negate the need to actually confront Robert. Kate, for her part, would undoubtedly vehemently deny any accusation and fear might see her abandon her plan to seduce Robert. Their conversation on the landing was evidence that he needed persuasion. She acknowledged Kate was equally determined and would never give up, but if Kate tried to back Robert into a corner, it would anger him. Might *that* be her trump card?

A few more minutes elapsed before she made her momentous decision…there were no viable alternatives.

Determined, she wrote a brief note with an unsteady hand, then read it through several times. She hastily scribbled the recipient's name and address on the envelope. The date of posting she would decide later.

A staccato knock on the bedroom door abruptly interrupted her thoughts. In a panic, she quickly pushed the letter into her handbag, then opened the door to Robert.

CHAPTER NINE

Indecisions
New Year's Eve 1855

Early on New Year's Eve morning, Rosie sought out Lizzie, eventually finding her in the sitting room. She wanted advice concerning her future with Jack, who she wouldn't be seeing until late that evening.

'Hello Mam, might I have a word?' Rosie began rather sombrely, which reflected her present mood.

'Of course Rosie, Marcus has gone into Manchester to buy some essential items for this evening. Jack left with him; he's meeting a captain of a ship in Liverpool, so he will catch the train from Manchester to the port later and, apparently, might only just manage to get back to see in the New Year. Didn't he tell you?'

'Oh yes Mam, I knew about the meeting, but I didn't think he would have time for shopping, before he caught the train.'

'I expect he wanted some time with his father in Manchester, especially if he might miss the New Year, which would be disappointing for Marcus. Anyway, what exactly is bothering *you* Rosie?' Lizzie queried, aware of Rosie's unease.

'I am confused Mam, but it's complicated. I'm not sure how I feel about Jack.'

Lizzie sighed, then patted the seat next to her on the sofa. 'I will send for coffee and then you can begin. I hate to see you so sad. Has something happened to make you feel unsure Rosie?'

Rosie hesitated, wondering if her mam would understand. 'Well, sort of. I thought I had moved on since Jimmy disappeared, but I have this strange feeling that he is still alive. I don't think I love Jack in the same way as I loved Jimmy. It scares me Mam. I know I am holding back from committing to Jack and wonder whether it is fair to give him a false impression, but he is a good man and maybe I could grow to love him.'

At that moment they were interrupted by Elspeth, who placed a coffee tray on the table. She too had noticed how troubled Rosie was over the last few days, so compensated by adding a plate of shortbread. She winked conspiratorially at Rosie before closing the door behind her.

Lizzie poured the coffee and offered Rosie a biscuit. 'Perhaps Elspeth's shortbread will alleviate your misgivings,' she said optimistically.

'No Mam, I'm afraid not. I don't know what will, because I am in such a quandary.'

Surprised as Rosie's response, Lizzie began to realise the severity of her daughter's anxiety. 'Well Rosie, you are still very young. A commitment of this nature should not be taken lightly, especially at your age, so you should take as much time as you need and not rush into anything,' advised Lizzie.

'But Mam, I will be *fifteen* this year,' argued Rosie. 'How old were you when you fell in love with Daniel?' she added, hoping to draw a comparison.

'I was over eighteen Rosie and we weren't promised to each other even then,' emphasised an increasingly alarmed Lizzie, who considered that her daughter's relationships, initially with Jimmy and now with Jack should be platonic, at least for the foreseeable future.

Rosie became thoughtful; her mam might have a point.

Lizzie continued—'Most young girls dream of falling in love and getting married, but you shouldn't be hasty Rosie. It is so much better to be friends and to get to know one another, before you consider a commitment. Sometimes at your age, you imagine you are in love, but usually it is just infatuation, a first flush of young love, which usually doesn't last.'

Rosie remained pensive. If she wasn't in love with either, perhaps it *was* just infatuation. 'Mmm...I suppose you might be right Mam, but should I just forget Jimmy? How long should I wait, in the hope he returns?'

Lizzie smiled compassionately, pleased that Rosie had confided in her, consciously relieved that she still valued her opinions. She took a sip of coffee while she contemplated a response to Rosie's last question, which was emotive and difficult to answer—'I know how much Jimmy meant to you, but we would have heard from him if he was alive and there isn't any evidence to suggest he might be. You should continue your friendship with Jack, but keep Jimmy's memory alive. It may help you to come to terms with the fact that he might never return. Time is a great healer, I know that from my own experience and, in the months ahead, the pain of his loss will fade. You will always have the memories of the time you spent together to comfort you.'

'All right Mam, I'll do my best not to let my thoughts run away with me and I will tell Jack we should remain friends and see where it goes,' smiled a rejuvenated Rosie. 'I am so glad you are my mam. I can always rely on you to give me the best advice,' exclaimed Rosie giving Lizzie a big hug.

Lizzie wiped away a tear as she realised, despite her concern, that her daughter was growing up very fast. In the not too distant future, rightly or wrongly, Rosie would make her own, life changing decisions. Lizzie just hoped there wasn't heartache ahead for her.

※

The continuing mild weather meant that Lizzie's family and friends would have little difficulty travelling to *The Beeches* for the New Year celebrations. Aunt Jayne and Howard weren't coming with Kate and family, as Howard wasn't well enough to travel. Aunt Jayne agreed to see in the New Year with him, as Aubrey was, as usual, away on business. Lizzie's open invitation to Georgina, Daniel and Victoria was dependent on them cancelling plans to stay with Georgina's parents. Lizzie was, of course, unaware that Daniel had used this excuse in order to preserve his own sanity over his desire to rekindle his relationship with her. Realising his love was unrequited, he determined to try and salvage his marriage to Georgina.

※

Annie, the maid of all works, overseen by Elspeth, had worked especially hard to ensure *The Beeches* looked resplendent. A traditional 'clean'[33] was accomplished befitting the occasion. Bedrooms were aired and the main rooms made 'spick and span'[34]. The fading Christmas

---

33 *For some, New Year's Eve meant thoroughly cleaning the house to start the New Year clean. Old superstitions required ashes, rags, scraps and anything perishable to be removed from the house, so that nothing carried over from one year to the next. In this way, the family would preserve their good luck and banish the bad.*
34 *Origin late 16th century (in the sense 'brand new'): from spick and span new, emphatic extension of dialect - span new, from Old Norse*

garlands were replenished with fresh holly and mistletoe and Polly intended to cook a special meal for the guests, with a recipe she found in Eliza Acton's cookbook once again.

Although the weather was mild, Lizzie insisted the fires be lit to give the drawing and dining rooms a cosy glow. Lizzie and Marcus expected the evening to be a huge success because they'd gone to such great lengths in ensuring the evening ran smoothly.

Their intention to keep the fires burning all evening was necessary to ensure an enthusiastic welcome for the 'first footer's' traditional lump of coal.

On the stroke of twelve, Marcus, as head of the family, intended to open the back door to usher out the old year and then open the front door to welcome in the New Year. Marcus's 'first footer', of course, would be kept secret.

By mid-afternoon, Amy, Robert and Harriett arrived, along with Kate, James and Beatrice and were busily chatting in the drawing room.

Eventually, Harriett took herself off to the playroom, where the lure of the dolls house[35] once again beckoned. The elaborate house constructed by Silber & Fleming, was a gift from Kate to Rosie.

---

spán-nýr, from spánn 'chip' + nýr 'new'; spick influenced by Dutch spiksplinternieuw, literally 'splinter new'.

35 *According to Gaston Bachelard (French Philosopher 1884-1962) 'one is able to possess the world by miniaturizing it'. Likewise, the presence of a doll's house in the home symbolised that a family was wealthy and privileged and able to educate girls, through play, in the rules of housekeeping, and engage with fashions and trends, through the miniaturization of houses and their contents.*

Beatrice lingered, waiting patiently for an opportunity to speak with her mother to request an extension to her usual bedtime. Unable to attract her attention, she too reluctantly, wandered off to the playroom.

When Beatrice eventually went in search of her mother again, she found everyone had vacated the drawing room, with the exception of her father. He usually gave in to her demands, but certain requests were overruled by her mother. Unfortunately, that included strict rules on bedtimes.

She walked down the hall and approached the study. The door was partly ajar, which enabled her to glimpse her mother looking out of the window. Pleased to have found her, she was about to enter the room, when she realised her mother was not alone. Kate was speaking in hushed tones to someone seated in a high backed chair, partly concealed by the open door. The secretive nature of the conversation seemed intriguing. *Maybe, the person is helping Mamma plan my birthday party*! she thought. She knew that her twelfth birthday promised to be special, with the whole family present and a proposal to visit the Glaciarium[36] in London.

---

36 *A Glaciarium was an artificial skating rink, invented in 1853. The rink has an area of more than one hundred square yards, and the ice is about two inches thick. The ice is produced and its solidity maintained by the constant circulation of an aqueous solution of glycerine through a series of copper tubes of a flat, oval section, which are embedded in the ice. The glycerine solution is kept at a low temperature by means of liquid sulphurous acid, which is constantly circulated, between a refrigerator on the one side and a condenser on the other, by means of an air-pump placed between the two and driven by a steam-engine.*

Beatrice strained to hear, flattening herself against the door to ensure she could not be seen, then someone tapped her on the shoulder. She turned around and encountered Amy, frowning and looking rather serious.

'Beatrice, what on earth are you doing? Come away from the door, it is really rude to eavesdrop,' she chided.

Beatrice hung her head as they walked back along the hallway. 'I'm sorry Aunt Amy, I was only listening to see if my mother was discussing my birthday party; she was whispering, so I thought it was secret.'

Amy, surprised that the occupants were obviously having a private conversation, felt obliged to admonish the little girl. 'Well Beatrice, you really shouldn't be listening at doors, I think your mother would be quite cross. Why don't you go and find Harriett, I think she is upstairs in the playroom.'

'All right, I will,' murmured a contrite Beatrice, who was really annoyed that she would have to settle for playing with Harriett, who she considered to be very young and silly.

Amy watched Beatrice climb the stairs, before retracing her steps along the hall. She too was curious as to the identity of the other person in the room. She approached the study, her attention concentrated on the raised voices. She paused nearer the door and despite chiding Beatrice about eavesdropping, froze to the spot in the instant she recognised the voice of Robert. Moments later, he rose from the chair and walked over to the window, pulling his fingers through his hair in exasperation. He spun around to face Kate; muttering something inaudible under his breath. Amy summed up the situation; whatever had annoyed Robert, was obviously connected with Kate's ongoing obsession. *I was right to pen that letter to James*, she determined, then instantly reacted by knocking on the door and making her presence known.

Kate and Robert were startled and surprised to see her there, believing her to be engaged in the drawing room.

Kate, usually adept at quick-change conversation, attempted an explanation. 'Hello Amy, do come in. Robert and I were discussing'—Kate's eyes darted from one to the other then quickly resumed—'Beatrice's birthday party and'—she frowned, focussing on Robert, flashing him a beseeching look, which did not go unnoticed by Amy. She continued—'I think I may have upset him by suggesting we all go ice-skating. He's of the opinion that possibly Victoria and Harriett would feel left out, as neither can skate. What would you suggest Amy?'

Robert, staggered at Kate's ability to turn a conversation on its head, gave a nervous cough and before Amy could reply, launched into an unnecessarily protracted explanation, as to why they were there at all. 'I came to find you Amy, but you weren't anywhere around. I encountered Kate in the study, who, as she explained, asked my opinion on a visit to the Glaciarium for Beatrice's birthday, but I wasn't sure it would be suitable for everyone. On that point, I think you would agree with me?'

An awkward silence prevailed until Lizzie suddenly entered the room. 'Here you all are! Everyone else is gathered in the drawing room for afternoon tea. Do come and join us,' suggested Lizzie, who'd obviously sensed the tension, concluding that Kate was probably responsible.

Robert breathed an inaudible sigh of relief. 'Thanks, Lizzie,' he exclaimed, taking hold of Amy's waist to guide her through the door, while Lizzie engaged Kate in conversation. 'James wondered where you were,' she stated pointedly, trying to elicit an explanation from Kate.

'Oh, did he? Well I was going to discuss the party with him earlier, but decided to run it past Robert when

I fortuitously bumped into him in the study. My idea was to take everyone to the Glaciarium on Beatrice's birthday, but Robert informed me that Harriett and Victoria couldn't skate; so, in retrospect, it may be that a visit to the zoo might be a better option.'

Lizzie was indeed sceptical, but as they'd already reached the drawing room, there wasn't time to pursue Kate's explanation, but she did wonder what had actually transpired.

༻◈༺

For the rest of the afternoon and evening, Robert ensured he stayed well clear of Kate and gave all his attention to Amy. Despite drinking too many glasses of red wine, Kate behaved impeccably, circulating and chatting amicably, in an effort to make amends. Lizzie's intervention and apparent disapproval had, momentarily, had a sobering effect on her and acknowledged that she probably wasn't Robert's favourite person at the moment...or indeed Amy's.

༻◈༺

When the clock struck midnight, with the celebrations in full swing, Kate's desire to get close to Robert superseded her need for restraint. A quick glance confirmed that an opportunity might present itself whilst everyone hugged and kissed, as the New Year demanded, to manoeuvre Robert into an alcove and she succeeded in kissing him. Robert, again staggered at Kate's foolhardy performance, pulled away, in the hope that Amy had not witnessed their embrace. To his relief, he realised that she was also caught up in the round of greetings and was thankfully oblivious to Kate's audacious actions. Sadly, he didn't realise that Lizzie had witnessed all. She decided to have words with her brother, but not before bestowing a withering look of disapproval on Kate. She realised Robert had, in fact, tried to break off the embrace. He'd actually looked stunned and seemingly annoyed, which confirmed that Kate was probably more keen than he to play such a dangerous game.

Fortunately, Auld Lang Syne[37] saved their blushes, as Marcus opened the back and front doors. This was the cue for Jack to make his grand, unexpected entrance. As 'first footer', he breezed cheerily through the door carrying a piece of coal, a bottle of single malt and a Christmas Rose. Shouts of 'glad you could make it Jack' and 'Happy New Year Jack,' produced a round of welcome embraces for their 'first footer'. After the coal was placed on the fire and the traditional cheese and cake distributed, chairs were placed around the edge of the room, leaving enough space in the centre for those who wished to dance.

While some enjoyed a glass of fine malt whisky, Jack presented Rosie with the Christmas Flower under the mistletoe. He held her close, then kissed her softly on the lips. Rosie, although embarrassed at Jack's forwardness, reciprocated, but knew instinctively that he was not the man she loved. She felt awkward, but allowed herself to be led in a traditional waltz[38].

---

37 *'Auld Lang Syne' is an old Scottish song that was first published by the poet Robert Burns in the 1796 edition of the book, 'Scots Musical Museum'. Burns transcribed it (and made some refinements to the lyrics) after he heard it sung by an old man from the Ayrshire area of Scotland, Burns's homeland.*

38 *Waltz in the 1850s - The Demi Sautien or the Half support: The Gentleman puts his right hand round the lady's waist, and holds her right hand with his left, whilst she rests her left hand on his shoulder.*

For most, the evening had been an overwhelming success, but others found themselves facing dilemmas, which seemed destined to lead them to heartache and unhappiness.

Courageously, Amy had kept her dignity throughout the night and did not witness Kate and Robert's brief embrace, believing she held the overall trump card. How long would it be before she played it?

CHAPTER TEN

Crossroads
December 1855/January1856

Jimmy's return to the *Dreadnought,* just a few days before the New Year, brought news that he had secured a berth on a coaster to Hamburg, scheduled to depart around the middle of January. His leg had mended well. Very soon he would leave the *Dreadnought* for good. The *Dreadnought's* physical therapist spent long hours ensuring Jimmy's leg was strong and that he was fully fit. His progress was that good that he'd try and visit Rosie en-route to the coastal vessel. He expected his mam had written to tell her he was alive. Consequently, he could delay the unenviable task of telling Rosie about Lucinda a while longer. His new relationship with Lucinda was going well and he considered her his girlfriend. Although they hadn't seen much of each other this week, they planned to see in the New Year together.

※

However, in the early part of January, Jimmy realised he'd come to a crossroads in his life. Surprisingly, he'd been recommended by the captain of the *Dreadnought* for a berth on the *Champion of the Seas*,[39] (built for the Blackball line), under Captain John McKirdy. He felt Jimmy deserved some good fortune for his bravery in attempting to save the Bosun aboard the *Lightning*. Captain McKirdy agreed that Jimmy was just the right kind of seaman for the demanding voyage to Australia, where initiative was paramount.

This latest development meant he wouldn't now 'sign on' the coaster, which might have given him more time with Lucinda, but he knew he must seize this great opportunity. It would mean not setting foot on English soil for another six months. He would obviously miss Lucinda and his mam.

Jimmy reluctantly broke the news to Lucinda, but softened the blow by making a grand gesture. 'Give me your hands,' Jimmy instructed a bemused Lucinda, who dutifully raised them for Jimmy to hold. 'We will be apart for some while,' he began, 'but you could wear the posy ring on your left hand, to cement our relationship…if you agree of course?'

'Oh Jimmy, only if you are sure?' replied an ecstatic Lucinda.

'Yes, I'm sure. So will you wait until I return?' Jimmy asked, fairly confident of a positive reply.

'Of course, I will Jimmy. I will miss you but will look forward to our reunion.'

Jimmy held her close and kissed her softly, before pulling away. 'I have to go now as I have a lot to do. I'll see you later.'

Lucinda released him reluctantly then hurried to share her news with Helen. Her reaction was not what Lucinda expected.

---

39 *Extreme clipper, built in 1854 by Donald McKay, East Boston, for the Blackball Line of Liverpool. Dimensions: 252' x 45'7" x 29' and tonnage 2448. Built with three decks. The figurehead was a sailor with a hat in the right hand and the left extended. The ship was painted black outside and white inside, with blue water-ways.*

Helen listened to her announcement with mixed emotions, after plucking up the courage to reveal her own plans before their shift started. Now, with some relief, it became clear that Lucinda's news was a blessing in disguise. Her excitement grew as an alternative plan surfaced in her mind. She couldn't hold back any longer. 'Oh gosh Lucinda, that really is the best news but you aren't going to believe what I am about to tell you. I've a most wonderful idea'—she hesitated momentarily, briefly considering the implications, then went full speed ahead with her proposal—'My parents want me to return to Australia for a few months and I didn't know how to tell you, but I've solved that problem. We could reserve a cabin each on the *Champion of the Seas*, then you could see Jimmy every day!' exclaimed Helen.

'Oh, what a lovely idea!' A delighted Lucinda acknowledged, as she realised the benefits of a voyage to Australia.

However, moments later, her happy countenance was quickly replaced with a frown, when she realised Helen had not told her previously that she would be leaving her job on the *Dreadnought*. 'When did you decide to go?' she queried.

'Only yesterday, I made up my mind and was going to tell you before we went on duty this morning. I thought you would understand my dilemma, as I do miss my parents.' Helen sighed, looking to Lucinda for a gesture or word of understanding, but Lucinda remained subdued. Helen became worried and continued with her explanation. 'Please don't be cross, it would only have been for six months and I had every intention of returning to the *Dreadnought*. I have already spoken to Matron and she assured me my job will be kept open.'

Lucinda was placated. Her own concerns were perhaps selfishly motivated, so, in turn, she reassured Helen, 'Oh I do understand...Of course you miss your parents, but what would Matron say if we both decided to go?'

'Well, they will always need nurses to treat the wounded returning from the war, so I am sure they would take us both back. I must speak to matron again and explain the circumstances. You are such a good nurse, Lucinda, I cannot imagine her not wanting you to take up your post again, even with the war seemingly coming to an end. There are still many soldiers requiring nursing back to health, so what do you say?' urged Helen, barely able to contain her excitement.

The more Lucinda considered the proposal, the more it seemed like the perfect solution. The idea of seeing Jimmy every day certainly appealed. 'Okay, I'll go, subject to matron's approval,' she said assertively, in the realisation they would be leaving very soon. 'Oh gosh, we don't have much time. I need to pack and get myself organised. Do you think Jimmy will be pleased?'

'Of course he will be pleased. You said you are a couple and had a wonderful time over Christmas, so you should trust Jimmy. He is a good man.'

'Of course Helen. Oh, I can't wait. I'm sure Jimmy won't mind if I'm a passenger on the ship.'

༄

The following day, Jimmy scribbled a hasty letter to his mam, to let her know he would be away for six months and she wasn't to worry. He then left to join his ship, a couple of days before Lucinda and Helen would be allowed to board. Time was short, so he wouldn't be able to visit Rosie.

Later, as he walked along the dockside, his eyes scanned the other sailors' preparing to embark. He desperately wanted to catch sight of one particular seaman, his friend *John Jamieson*. He fervently hoped *John* would also be joining this relatively new ship. He believed the chances were quite high, considering it belonged to the Blackball Line.

Delaying his embarkation for half an hour, whilst perched on a bollard, he reluctantly climbed the gangway. Maybe *John* was already aboard, he thought hopefully, as he scanned the dock once more, but on reaching the deck, Jimmy felt a hand pressed to his shoulder. He turned around to find Jack staring straight at him. Jack's incredulous raised eyebrows emphasised his astonishment in the realisation that Jimmy was indeed alive. The two men immediately embraced, slapping each other on the back. 'My God Jimmy I cannot believe it's you! I thought I spotted someone who looked like you on the dockside, but thought it couldn't be. You were lost to us, or so we believed, as we'd heard nothing since that awful day. Where've you been Jimmy and why didn't you get in touch?' asked Jack, genuinely delighted to have been reunited with his old buddy.

An elated Jimmy responded eagerly. 'Good to see you too, *John*, it's a long story. We need to catch up. I cannot believe we will be sailing together on this magnificent vessel.'

An equally excited Jack decided not to reveal his birth name at this point; that could wait, so picked up on Jimmy's statement. 'She's certainly that Jimmy. At 2447 tons, she is the largest merchant ship in the world. How did you manage to get a berth?'

'I struck lucky. The captain of the *Dreadnought*, that's a hospital ship by the way, recommended me to Captain John McKirdy. He felt I deserved a chance at reviving my career after the bad luck on the *Lightning*. Mind, I was surprised Captain McKirdy agreed...said I was just the kind of seaman he wanted in his crew,' Jimmy pronounced proudly. 'So here I am.'

Their conversation flowed as Jack steered Jimmy towards the privacy of his cabin. 'It's amazing, just wait until Rosie knows, she's coming to see me before we set sail,' informed Jack, still shaking his head in disbelief.

Jimmy was unsurprised by this statement. 'That's good *John,* I'll look forward to meeting her again. Me mam told me you were together. I wrote to her a while ago, but she obviously didn't receive it? Consequently, I asked me mam to write after we left Darley Abbey on Boxing Day. It looks likely that she didn't receive that letter either?'

'Not as far as I am aware Jimmy, but I haven't seen Rosie since New Year's Day; however, she will be overjoyed,' Jack emphasised, slightly embarrassed that Jimmy had been forewarned about him and Rosie. He cleared his throat before attempting to justify their relationship. 'I want you to understand that we didn't get together until long after you went missing Jimmy. Rosie refused to believe you wouldn't return, but eventually, she felt she should move on, as it seemed less and less likely she would ever see you again,' he explained, feeling a tinge of guilt that Rosie was right after all. Jimmy had survived!

They fell silent, but the lull in conversation presented Jack with the perfect moment to impart his own news. 'Jimmy, before we talk further, I have something to tell you about myself. It's a long story, which I will relate to you later, but you should know that my name is not actually John Jamieson. It's Jack Bernard Van der Duim, the name by which I am now known. It is very complicated Jimmy, but I did not know myself until Christmas Eve, when I discovered Marcus was my real father.'

Although a trifle confused, Jimmy acknowledged Jack's explanation without question. He knew his friend would explain everything in the fullness of time. 'Okay, Jack it is!' he stated, shaking his hand vigorously; knowing it was his turn to impart his news. He wondered fleetingly how Jack would react. 'While I was aboard the *Dreadnought*, I met up with Lucinda and Helen. You remember the nurses from Melbourne?'

'Ha, indeed I do'—Jack grinned—'How are they?'

'They're very well,' informed Jimmy. 'In actual fact, they've booked a cabin on this ship, as Helen's visiting her parents and she's asked Lucinda ter go with her. That suits me, as Lucinda and me are seeing each other. In fact we spent Christmas together,' boasted Jimmy, wishing to prove to Jack that he no longer had designs on Rosie and was now a man of the world. The last months had seen him grow in stature. He was no longer unsure of himself and had expanded his circle of friends, which he communicated to Jack. 'We went down to Lucinda's parents in Cambridge, then spent Christmas Day and Boxing Day with me mam.'

Inwardly, Jack breathed a sigh of relief. It also hadn't gone unnoticed that Jimmy had almost lost his Nottingham accent. 'My Jimmy, things are certainly looking up for you. I'm glad and wish you well'—he paused, unsure whether Jimmy would still wish to share any intimate thoughts with him on anything, given their changed situation. He decided to test the water—'How close *are* you then?' Jack enquired audaciously, hoping Jimmy had permanently closed the door on his relationship with Rosie.

'Well let's just say, as close as you can be.' Jimmy winked and the two men laughed irreverently.

Significantly, Jack observed a very different Jimmy, as he remembered the last time they had a conversation about women. 'So you took my advice and decided to spread your wings a bit before settling down?' continued Jack.

'Yes indeed, but we'll see how it goes. I do like her though. Anyway, how *are* things with you and Rosie?' Jimmy asked with equal boldness.

The question left Jack with a dilemma. Should he tell Jimmy the reality, that they had not yet slept together, or be economical with the truth, thus avoiding a direct answer. He decided on the latter. 'Good, good Jimmy, we are very close and get on really well.'

Jimmy's eyebrows arched questioningly, which forced Jack to qualify his statement further. Once again, he was non-committal. 'We are moving at Rosie's own pace,' he added, hoping Jimmy would not continue to press him. In the event, Jimmy didn't, although Jack assumed he would find out soon enough anyway.

Jimmy still had to 'sign on' and catching up would have to wait. They had plenty to think about before meeting with their respective partners two days later.

※

Early on the morning of 7th January, the Albert Dock bustled with people waiting to board the *Champion of the Seas*. Jimmy and Jack organised special dispensation to spend time with Rosie, Lucinda and Helen. They would be among the throngs of passengers and loved ones, gathering to wave goodbye to husbands and sweethearts, before the ship sailed later that day. Jack quickly spotted Rosie standing alone in the midst of the crowds. She wore a long thick red coat, muffler and boots and her cheeks glowed in the cold wind that whipped across the dockside.

He hurried to her side, hugged her close and kissed her on the cheek. 'Hello Rosie, I thought I might struggle to find you among all these people.'

'Oh it's good to see you again Jack,' responded Rosie. 'Will we have time for a hot drink before departure? It's quite chilly standing around on the dockside.'

'Yes, of course! I've permission to spend a couple of hours with you before we sail, but first there's someone who wants to see you.' Jack grinned taking her by the arm.

'Who's that? It does sound mysterious!'

'It's a surprise, but hopefully a pleasant one.'

Meanwhile, Jimmy found Lucinda and Helen and organised stowage of their portmanteau, but hadn't a chance to tell them he had met with Jack. When Jimmy spotted him he gave him a wave. 'Jack,' he called, 'over here'.

'Who is that?' asked Helen, unable to get a clear view of Jack's face as he moved swiftly through the crowds, with Rosie hanging on his arm. Before Jimmy could reply, they were facing each other. In that instant, Rosie rushed up to Jimmy. 'Jimmmmmmy, Oh Jimmy you are alive,' she shouted, kissing him on the cheek and giving him a hug. 'I am astonished, but so very pleased to see you alive and well. Where have you been and why didn't you get in touch?' she asked, unable to prevent her tears of happiness.

For a moment, Jimmy was stunned into silence by the powerful feeling he was experiencing being so close to Rosie again. It left him confused and transparently scared. This wasn't supposed to happen and he had difficulty hiding his emotions. Thankfully Lucinda quickly stepped in, addressing Rosie directly and producing her most disarming smile. 'Hello Rosie, I am Lucinda, Jimmy's friend. I'm really pleased to meet you.'

Rosie, taken aback that the two women appeared to be with Jimmy, was also experiencing strong emotional feelings. Jimmy was very much alive and well. She suddenly found difficulty responding, but stammered a reply. 'I'm pleased to meet you too, Lucinda,' she said with reluctant enthusiasm, surprised to see Lucinda's gloveless left hand, sported a gold ring.

The introductions continued, as Helen greeted Rosie, then Jack, who she'd recognised instantly. 'It's been a long while, *John*, how are you?' she asked, planting a kiss on his cheek.

Without informing Helen of his name change, Jack responded. 'I'm good, Helen and it is really lovely to see you again. Jimmy told me you and Lucinda have cabins on board and that you are going to Melbourne to stay with your parents for a while.'

'Yes, we are so excited, especially Lucinda, who will be able to see Jimmy every day.'

Rosie, on hearing this became more subdued; it appeared she was the last to know that Jimmy and Lucinda were a couple. She was cross that Jack had not forewarned her, but now was not the time to kick up a fuss. All four would soon be boarding and she would be left alone.

Her thoughts were interrupted by Jack, who, oblivious to the dynamics happening around him, glanced briefly at his watch before making a suggestion. 'Shall we find a cafe, so we can all do some catching up? We still have more than an hour before we have to be on board.'

With everyone in agreement, they walked the short distance to the Kardomah[40] café on Bold Street.

Jimmy took charge and ordered hot drinks for them all. He wanted to prove to Rosie and Jack how assertive he had become during his time away.

They settled in a benched booth by the window and Jimmy launched uncharacteristically into a brief account of his exploits, post his rescue in Brazil. 'I have been convalescing at Greenwich on the hospital ship, the *Dreadnought*.

---

40 *1844/45 – Kardomah Coffee Company founded in Pudsey Street. Cafes opened in Bold Street and Church Street.*

That's where I met up with Lucinda and Helen again.' He added the word 'again'; there was no use denying he had met with them before, as it was obvious that everyone knew each other, attested by Jack and Helen's reunion. Jimmy locked eyes with Rosie, addressing her specifically. 'I did write to you and me mam, but as Mam didn't receive her letter, I suppose you didn't receive yours either? Then Mam said she would write to you after Christmas, but I guess she might have forgotten,' he suggested. 'She's not been well,' he added as an afterthought.

'No…no I didn't receive any letters, Jimmy,' she said, saddened by the non-deliveries. It could have changed the decision she'd made about her future with Jack, but there was nothing she could do about it now. The men were about to board a ship and would not return for six months and there was also the question of *that* ring.

Their eyes, irrationally locked together, suggested to both of them that many questions still needed answering.

Conscious that everyone was looking at him expectantly, Jimmy broke contact then continued with his story. 'You see, I was incapacitated, still recovering from a broken leg. Consequently, I was reliant on others to ensure my letters were posted. Unfortunately, it seems highly likely that a nurse, who promised she would post them, may not have done so, for whatever reason and that is why neither Rosie nor me mam received them,' he finished, having addressed them all.

'Yes, of course, Jimmy, I see that now,' Rosie acknowledged, deciding to lighten the conversation, before the others noticed the obvious chemistry that was building between them. 'Well you are here now and we are both delighted to have found you, aren't we Jack?'

The all but too brief hour saw them catching up on events. Jack recounted the story of his birth father to Lucinda and Helen. Rosie and Jimmy fell relatively silent, only contributing briefly to the conversation. Every now and then their eyes fixed on each other, seemingly oblivious to their companions. Fortunately, everyone was too engrossed in conversation to notice.

Lucinda was firmly convinced by recent events, that Jimmy only wanted her. Jack was euphoric. He was sailing with his old friend and was more confident of Rosie because Jimmy seemed committed to Lucinda. Unbeknownst to all, Helen was still harbouring unrequited feelings for Jack and was pleased that she would be seeing a lot more of him over the coming weeks.

It was soon time for them to return to the ship, but as they rose from the booth, Jimmy's hand brushed against Rosie's. It confirmed their innermost thoughts, that their strong sexual feelings towards each other were undeniable. Jimmy was the most affected, as he realised the depth of his feelings could not be ignored. The ramifications, therefore, were immense. It was undeniably disastrous that he would not have the opportunity to talk to Rosie for another six months. However, without anyone else noticing, she whispered some meaningful words in his ear as they exited the café. 'I'll wait for you Jimmy,' she said, pressing her hand into his.

Jimmy nodded.

CHAPTER ELEVEN

The Journey
January 1856

A raft of emotions overwhelmed Rosie as she waved her handkerchief to the four aboard the *Champion of the Seas*. Realisation dawned that she would be alone for the next six months, unable to resolve her dilemma. Strangely, however and paradoxically, she truly believed that maybe, just maybe, the future could be all she hoped for.

The four returned her wave, each she believed, retained a differing perspective of herself, her character and their own future. Jack believed she would be eagerly waiting his return. Lucinda would be confident that Rosie no longer posed a threat, as she had the opportunity to consolidate her relationship with Jimmy on the long journey to Australia. She also noted that Jack's re-acquaintance with Helen may prove fortuitous, as it might reignite his interest. There was a distinct possibility that anything could happen on this voyage. Helen was older and more experienced than herself, which indicated there was every chance they could rekindle their attraction.

Jimmy's dilemma would not be resolved until he set foot back on English soil. The familiar feelings he felt when he encountered Rosie once more, shook him to the core. He had no clue how the months stretching out in front of him would evolve. How would he cope with such an uncertain future?

As the ship pulled off the berth, Rosie's eyes locked with Jimmy's. In that brief moment, her heart beat faster, in parallel with an overwhelming sense of optimism for the future. Even at this distance, she felt the connection and realised that he too felt the same way. She remained transfixed to the spot while the ship made its way slowly from the berth to the breakwater, until it reached the open sea and became a mere spec on the horizon.

Rosie, alone in the carriage for the return journey, reflected on the extraordinary events, which had unfolded a short time earlier. *Jimmy wasn't dead!* She felt elated and a contented smile spread across her face, knowing the chemistry between them still existed! There was just the little matter of the ring worn by Lucinda and also the heartbreak Jack might suffer if she and Jimmy renewed their love for each other.

She considered her mam's advice, now redundant, because Jimmy was alive…he was alive! On Jimmy's return, she would be fifteen, old enough, she believed, to be sure of her own feelings. How did she ever doubt her love for him? She knew he would come back didn't she? It was others who'd tried to persuade her otherwise.

Happy and undaunted, she slept the rest of the journey, until the train pulled in to Manchester. She couldn't wait to return home and share her good news.

On board *The Champion*, Jack escorted the two excited girls to their spacious state-room, secured for them earlier that morning, after the original occupants had been informed of a close family bereavement. They'd reluctantly cancelled their booking and disembarked an hour before the ship sailed.

The three entered the vestibule and walked through to the opulent main cabin, where Jack launched into a dialogue extolling the finer points of *The Champion of the Seas.* 'She was built with three decks and is the largest sailing merchant ship in the world,' he enthused, addressing Helen, who, dazzled by his knowledge, afforded him her full attention. He continued—'The double staircase we passed leads to a spacious open area below and also the dining saloon. That's an impressive forty feet in length, painted white, but relieved with gilding, and beautifully finished and furnished. She really is a luxurious ship and we are lucky to have the opportunity to sail on her,' said Jack proudly. 'Anyway, I will leave you to unpack and, hopefully, Jimmy and I might get the opportunity to show you the rest of the ship later.'

'Thank you Jack, that would be lovely,' said Helen, colouring imperceptively. She couldn't wait to re-acquaint herself with the handsome young officer.

Lucinda noticed Helen's sudden desire to impress Jack again, before she resumed her unpacking. She selected the smaller valise in her luggage and proceeded in a somewhat pensive state to hang her dresses in the spacious closet provided in the cabin area of the state-room. All in all, she was extremely curious as to Helen's intentions and couldn't resist commenting on her flirtatious demeanour. Consequently, she abandoned the rest of her unpacking and deliberately asked Helen a direct question. 'So, what do you think to Jack then Helen. Is he as irresistible as you found him when you last met?'

Helen, slightly embarrassed, flippantly replied, 'Oh, he's nice enough, of course, but he does have a girlfriend already,' she stated, hoping that Lucinda might suggest that Jack's friendship wasn't serious.

'You mean Rosie?' queried Lucinda.

'Indeed, that *young* girl,' emphasized Helen. 'Although from what I can gather, their relationship is pretty much platonic.'

Lucinda had mixed feelings about Jack's relationship with Rosie, but hoped they were much closer than Helen was suggesting. 'Mmm, maybe at the moment, but I would suggest that the situation could change when we return. What do they say, 'Tis absense, however, that makes the heart grow fonder,' she recalled. 'I read that in the *Pocket Magazine of Classic and Polite Literature 1832*[41], which Mamma gave to me at Christmas. Do you think it is true?'

'Well it's very prophetic, but there is another phrase I can think of, which is 'Out of sight, out of mind' – 'John Heywood's Works' 1562*[42]* I believe,' quoted Helen laughingly.

The two girls appreciated one another's knowledge and mutual sense of humour. 'I think the latter suits both of our needs, as Jimmy and Jack won't be seeing Rosie for six months. She seems a lovely girl, but I want Jimmy for myself,' Lucinda added candidly.

Helen frowned, surprised by her friend's statement. 'You're not still worried about Jimmy falling for Rosie are you?' she admonished. 'I thought you two were rock solid now. He has even given you a ring.'

---

41 '*The Pocket Magazine of Classic and Polite Literature, 1832, in a piece by a Miss Stickland*' - 'Tis absense, [sic] however, that makes the heart grow fonder'.

42 *Famous Epigraph by John Heywood 1562*

Lucinda was silent for a few moments and twiddled the ring around her finger, before replying. 'Yes, you are right, I do have a ring and Jimmy assured me we were a couple. He told me he would make our union permanent on our return to England,' confirmed Lucinda. However, a persistent, niggling doubt still flooded her consciousness, after she'd witnessed Rosie and Jimmy's reunion on the dockside. Rosie seemed more focussed on Jimmy than Jack as she waved goodbye, but she would keep that to herself, in the hope that she was mistaken. She considered that Helen would think she was paranoid anyway.

'Well then, I think you should trust Jimmy and forget all about Rosie. Don't forget, we will see Jimmy and Jack most days in the coming months; whereas Rosie will be back in England without any means of communication. A lot can happen in that time. Now let's finish unpacking so we can take that tour of the ship with Jack,' enthused Helen, hanging the last of her clothes in the closet. 'I think we are going to really enjoy this voyage.'

Unfortunately, however, Helen and Lucinda did not see either Jimmy or Jack for twenty-four hours after their tour, as both were seasick and the men busy with their duties.

The ship had a spacious topgallant forecastle[43] to accommodate the crew. Abaft the foremast, a robust housing, measuring fifty feet by eighteen and six and a half feet high, was constructed. It contained the galleys, a cabin for

---

43 *Commonly abbreviated 'fo'c's'le' refers to the upper deck of a sailing ship, forward of the foremast, or the forward part of a ship with the sailors' living quarters.*

second-class passengers and staterooms for the forward officers. One such room was occupied by Jack. He had never been afforded this luxury before, but intended to make the most of it. In contrast, Jimmy's accommodation consisted of shared space, occupied by several members of the crew sleeping in hammocks, similar to the 'Lightning'.

Both men were looking forward to the voyage, despite the hardships expected on the 85-day passage to Australia. Jimmy, however, had a lot on his mind, so was pleased to be busy, especially when they entered the Bay of Biscay, a day out after leaving port, notorious for rough weather and the rolling swells of the continental shelf.

Lucinda and Helen's seasickness seemed interminable as they spent a very long time indeed in their cabin, staring at the deck head. Neither remotely considered venturing to the dining room. Their fervent hope was that the ship would cease rolling so violently as they neared the Portuguese coast.

The following day, Lucinda still felt queasy, despite the relatively calmer sea and swell. Conversely, Helen felt much better, so after washing, she slipped into a blue cotton day dress before winding her hair into a chignon, ready to face the world. 'I'm actually feeling hungry now. Shall we go down for some lunch Lucinda?' she suggested.

Lucinda, however, lay motionless on the bed, feeling tired and not a bit like eating. 'Oh, I'm not sure, I think I will lie here a while longer. You should go and report back to me, who you have seen and what the food is like.' She groaned, wondering if she would ever gain her sea legs.

'Okay, I won't be too long, although I might have a wander on deck and see if Jack or Jimmy are around. I'll see you later.' Helen smiled as she breezed out of the cabin in buoyant mood.

Just as Helen was leaving the dining room, after a delicious lunch of soup, followed by crayfish salad, she 'bumped' into Jack, who was walking in the direction of their state-room. 'Hello Helen, how are you getting on? We have been so busy we have not had the chance to sneak off,' Jack said, winking at her conspiratorially.

Helen brightened. She was delighted to have 'run into' Jack. 'We haven't got off to a good start,' she admitted. 'We've spent most of the last twenty-four hours suffering from awful seasickness. I am feeling much better now, but Lucinda has still not recovered. She's also missing Jimmy, although she knows he is working and won't be able to spend a lot of time with her, perhaps some snatched moments between watches,' advised Helen, whilst admiring Jack, standing tall in his officer's uniform.

'Well, as far as I know, Jimmy's watch ends soon. I'm off duty now, so I'll accompany you back to your cabin if you like,' suggested Jack, taking her arm and propelling her along the companionway.

Outside the stateroom, Helen gave a light tap on the door, whilst listening for any sign that Lucinda was awake. Satisfyingly, she could hear her humming cheerfully so they entered the cabin. Lucinda was seated at a dressing table, brushing her hair. She had changed into a day dress and was now looking a picture of health.

'Well, that's better! A far cry from earlier. You seem to have made a miraculous recovery,' exclaimed Helen, pleased that her friend was obviously feeling much better. 'When I left, you were awfully pale and I didn't expect you to be up and about.'

Lucinda smiled. 'Neither did I, but the sickness suddenly disappeared and I feel much, much better. I was going to join you for lunch, but you must have eaten already I think and brought a guest back with you,' she said teasingly.

Helen blushed turning her face away from Jack, so as not to give her emotions away. 'Yes, I bumped into Jack on the way back from the dining room, which, incidentally, serves the most delicious food.'

Jack, acknowledged the comment then made a suggestion. 'If you are hungry Lucinda, I could arrange for some sandwiches to be brought to the cabin. That way, when Jimmy's watch finishes, he could sneak in here. The crew don't eat in the dining room with passengers,' informed Jack.

'That's a good idea. I'd be really grateful Jack. Perhaps I might ask for a pot of coffee and a piece of cake too?' Lucinda hedged coquettishly.

'Very well ma'am, I will see what I can conjure up,' chortled Jack, then turned to Helen, continuing in a mock subservient voice. 'Will there be anything I can get for you, m'lady? A glass of wine perhaps, if it's not too early?' he asked, beaming.

Helen, laughing behind a fan she picked up from the dressing table, responded. 'Yes, young man, it is far too early for alcohol, but I would appreciate a fruit juice and perhaps a plate of Basler Brunsli[44] cookies. Thank you.'

'Very well ma'am, I will see to that for you,' said Jack as he winked and bowed then exited backwards out of the cabin.

Helen was in fits of giggles, ecstatic that Jack had been so flirtatious, albeit Lucinda felt obliged to give her some

---

44 *Basler Brunsli (chocolate, almond spiced cookies) originally from 16th century Switzerland. Ingredients, almond flour, coconut, sugar, chocolate, ground cinnamon, ground cloves and egg whites.*

realistic advice, as a consequence. 'You shouldn't read too much into Jack's teasing. You remember he was the same when we last spent time with him in Melbourne, but he didn't contact you on his return,' reminded Lucinda.

'Oh, don't spoil the moment, I am quite capable of holding my own with Jack. I know he is an outrageous flirt, but I am not going to discourage him,' Helen advised, as she applied more makeup and sprayed perfume lightly over her hair.

'I didn't mean to spoil your fun, but I just don't want you to get hurt that's all,' Lucinda assured her. 'I really only have your best interest at heart. Anyway, I don't suppose there is anything wrong with a bit of harmless flirting...?' Lucinda tailed off, leaving the question hanging, then gave her hair another brush before smoothing down the simple light green slub cotton dress, which skimmed over the curves of her hips. 'Do you know, I feel so much better, as if I never had motion sickness at all.'

'Yes, it's funny how one minute you can feel so ill and the next you cannot remember how bad it was'—Helen paused, suddenly noticing how attractive Lucinda looked—'Your hair really suits you hanging loose like that. I'm sure Jimmy will appreciate what a lovely lady he has.'

'I do hope so!' sighed an enthusiastic Lucinda, as she pulled a crisp white cotton cloth out of a drawer. 'Let's put this on the table and pull up some chairs, in readiness to greet that handsome waiter when he returns.'

True to his word, Jack arrived with coffee, a plate of sandwiches and some shortbread, prepared by the cook, who'd muttered, 'Bloody passengers,' under his breath, as he substituted the shortbread for the cookies. Apparently, he did not have a supply of Brunsli cookies to hand! Jack placed them on the table and without waiting for an invitation, sat on a chair and helped himself to one of the array of sandwiches.

Within a few minutes a knock on the door announced Jimmy's arrival. 'You look lovely Lucinda,' complimented Jimmy, as he remembered Christmas, when he'd first seen her dressed for that occasion in the blue silk dress.

'Thank you Jimmy and you look very handsome,' smiled Lucinda, eagerly returning the compliment.

They chatted for an hour about how lucky they were to be sailing to Australia on such a splendid ship, until Jack felt he should remind them that only two of them were passengers, which brought them down to earth. He and Jimmy would spend most of their time on duty, or asleep, so consequently, the girls would have to amuse themselves for much of the voyage. 'There's plenty for you to do,' he assured. 'Wining and dining will take up a good part of the time you spend on board. Dinner with Captain John McKirdy is a grand affair. He loves entertaining the ladies at his table. Walks on deck, weather permitting, can be very exhilarating. You can also sit out and read the '*The Champion of the Seas Times*'[45], it's published weekly, which should keep you amused, or you could write a journal of your journey. Jimmy and I will sneak back to your cabin as often as we can, of course, but we can't promise it will be every day.'

Lucinda and Helen were a little deflated at this scenario. 'Oh dear, we thought we would see you whenever you were off duty,' commented Lucinda, who was beginning to wonder if she would get as much time alone with Jimmy as she wanted.

---

[45] *Handwritten shipboard newspaper, which included items about progress of the journey, the weather, accommodation and food, as well as an obituary column and other items of interest.*

'Well, we can see you for brief periods, but we have to catch up on our sleep in our 'off watch' time,' explained Jack. 'Anyway, Helen, let's leave these two lovebirds alone for a while and, as the sea is relatively calm, we can take a walk on deck?'

Helen, ecstatic at Jack's suggestion, followed him meekly out of the cabin.

On deck, the sky was blue and the sun shone, just the day to take a leisurely stroll. Jack was the perfect gentleman and walked closest to the ship's rails. He was already missing Rosie so it was nice to have a conversation with someone other than a fellow crewman. 'It's really good to see you again Helen. You must tell me about your time on the *Dreadnought*, I bet it kept you busy. From what I understand there are many injured sailors requiring nursing.'

'Yes, yes there are. Lucinda and I were both very busy and did not have much time to socialize, but we thoroughly enjoy our jobs. I will be going back to work there on my return,' informed Helen.

Jack raised a quizzical eyebrow. 'How long do you expect to stay with your parents? This ship will make its return passage before your stay is over.'

'I'm not too sure Jack. I will have to see how I feel when I arrive. I do miss my parents and will take the opportunity to spend as much time as I can with them.'

Jack nodded sympathetically. 'That's very wise. It is important to enjoy every moment of their company, after all you may not see them again for some time.'

They paused briefly, leaning over the ship's rails to gaze thoughtfully at the unobstructed horizon on the starboard side. 'I don't think I will ever get tired of seeing the curvature of the earth,' Jack declared, then in the same instant wondered if it would be prudent to ask questions about

Jimmy and Lucinda's relationship, without appearing to pry. He hesitated briefly before deciding to approach the subject from a different perspective. 'So, Helen, do you have a man friend now?' Jack asked casually.

Understandably, Helen jumped to the wrong conclusion, immediately deciding the question was being asked from a romantic perspective. She was unaware of his actual motive. 'No, no I don't, why do you ask?' she replied coyly.

Her answer put Jack on the back-foot, as he was expecting a reply in the affirmative, so continued headlong down a slippery slope. 'Oh, I don't know really, but an attractive woman like yourself, can't be short of admirers!' As soon as the words escaped his mouth, the expectant look on Helen's face, gave him cause to regret. It was a foolish thing to say and he quickly tried to backtrack. 'Not that I mean anything by that of course. As you know, I am in a relationship with Rosie, so I hope I didn't give you the wrong impression.'

Helen's heart sank, but she had no intention of letting Jack know of her disappointment. *There is plenty of time to change his mind*. 'Of course not Jack, don't be silly. I know you were only making conversation, but the fact is, we have so little time off, that we nurses don't get much chance to meet anyone.'

'No, I suppose it is a bit like my job, away for months at sea with little time for socializing,' said Jack, relieved Helen hadn't read anything meaningful in response to his ambiguous question.

'Yes, that's very true, so you can understand why I'm not presently with anyone,' Helen concluded.

Jack nodded sagely, whilst noting that their conversation could now include Lucinda's relationship with Jimmy. 'I am glad Jimmy met with Lucinda again,' he observed, then paused to wait for corroboration from Helen. She remained non-committal, so he decided to risk a statement, which wasn't entirely true, but one he felt sure would draw a reaction. 'He was keen on her when we first met in Australia.'

Helen took the bait. 'Really, that explains the instant attraction. It wasn't long before they became close friends after they'd met again. I did feel that Lucinda was more keen than Jimmy, initially, but after Christmas, their relationship changed. In my opinion, they became equally taken with each other. Just before Jimmy left to join this ship, he made the grand gesture. He gave Lucinda his mother's ring, to wear on her engagement finger, with the promise he would make it a more permanent arrangement on his return.'

Jack felt a sense of relief, knowing Jimmy had more or less committed to Lucinda. 'Well that was certainly a bold move and I am genuinely pleased for them. I always thought Jimmy probably committed to Rosie before he'd had the chance to meet any other women. It would appear that my intuition was correct,' he concluded.

It was the opportunity for Helen to be equally bold. 'You are probably right about first loves. How do you see your relationship with Rosie?'

'Ah well.' Jack grinned, taken aback at Helen's audacious remark, but finding it strangely evocative. 'That's an emotive question, Helen, but to answer honestly and between ourselves, Rosie and I are very close, but I have to admit, I have not had many encounters. Most of them were platonic and they didn't last very long. We will have to see how things progress and Rosie is still very young. Does that answer your question?'

Helen smiled agreeably. 'Mmm that depends. Are you saying Jimmy was right to take your advice, but, conversely, you might not necessarily follow the rules to which you subscribe?'

Jack realized Helen was enjoying playing 'Devils Advocate', which he found slightly unnerving. *She is feisty and a clever manipulator, but I doubt she is a match for me.* 'I'm not saying that at all, I am realistic when it comes to relationships and no one can foresee the future. Rosie is, in actual fact, a very similar personality to you, in as much as she can hold her own in a discussion. She is younger than you and maybe not so worldly wise, but she is a master at getting her own way and a very determined young woman. I hope we will become as close as you suggest Jimmy and Lucinda are, but time will tell and whatever the future holds, I believe things will work out as they are meant to. I am a great believer in fate.'

Helen felt somewhat deflated with Jack's reasoning, but was not discouraged in her resolve to enjoy an intimate relationship with him. Time was on her side, but for now, she thought it prudent to discontinue her probing. 'That's very interesting, Jack, a fatalist eh? I am not such a believer in that respect, as I think we fashion our own destinies, but as you say, time will tell and we will see which one of us is proven right. I hope you get what you want in life, Jack, if, of course, you know what that is!' she laughed. All was not lost she thought, as they strolled back to her cabin.

※

Meanwhile, Lucinda and Jimmy finished lunch and sat on the small settee in the main cabin. Up until that point, Jimmy hadn't had much time to think about the situation he found himself in, following his reunion with Rosie. However, this first real close contact with Lucinda brought that dilemma very much to the surface. He was in turmoil as their eyes met. He knew she wanted him to kiss her, now they were alone. One part of him wanted to rush out of the cabin, but seeing her looking longingly at him, made him feel sad and guilty. His thoughts wandered back to Christmas, when they had made love and he felt he was free to give himself wholly to her. Would she be able to arouse those feelings in him now...he owed it to her to at least find out.

Lucinda moved closer and snuggled into his shoulder. 'Oh Jimmy, I have been waiting to have you all to myself since we boarded the ship,' she whispered.

Jimmy responded by kissing her softly on the lips. He was immediately concerned at his lack of arousal and had to admit Lucinda did not evoke the same excitement he had felt when they had first made love...he wondered if she could tell his heart wasn't in it. What the hell was he going to do? The voyage would take almost six months overall. How, he asked himself, would he manage to keep up this charade? Should he even attempt to? All these thoughts swam around in his head, while he continued to caress her.

Without warning, Lucinda suddenly pulled away, hand over her mouth she rushed to the bathroom. The sickness had inexplicably returned. A surprised Jimmy, followed her and stood outside the door. 'Are you all right, Lucinda? Is there anything I can do?' asked Jimmy, who stood silently waiting for an answer.

After a few minutes, Lucinda took out her hanky and wiped her mouth, as the sickness abated. She leaned against the door still feeling slightly faint. 'I am okay Jimmy. Give me a moment and I will be right out.'

Jimmy helped Lucinda to the bed and poured her a glass of water. 'This should help you feel better. Apparently, sea-sickness can come on unexpectedly, but we are in calm waters at the moment, so I wonder if it could be something you ate?' suggested a concerned Jimmy.

Lucinda took small sips from the glass. 'I'm not sure, Jimmy. I began to feel dizzy and then sick, but now I feel perfectly fine. You have eaten the same food as me, how do you feel?' she asked perplexed.

'I feel okay, but I only ate one chicken sandwich. You ate two crayfish salad sandwiches, perhaps we should ask the others when they return?'

'I'm so sorry to spoil the moment Jimmy, but I think I should just rest a while. Perhaps all the excitement over the last few days has been too much. I did rush around a lot before we embarked and perhaps I overdid things,' explained Lucinda.

⁂

Helen and Jack returned a short while later and tapped lightly on the cabin door. 'Lucinda, can we come in?' she asked.

Jimmy opened the door and explained Lucinda's predicament.

'Oh dear, I was hoping she would have fully recovered, as she was feeling so much better earlier,' declared Helen.

Lucinda sat up. She was dismayed, but anxious to get to the bottom of her inexplicable sickness bouts. 'You're right, Helen, I did and then it suddenly returned,' she explained, pausing to take another sip of water. 'We were discussing whether it could have been the crayfish. Did either of you eat that?'

'I did, but I didn't have any ill effects,' confirmed Helen, turning to Jack and raising her eyebrows. 'What about you Jack?' she asked.

'I had one of each and feel fine, but if you overdid things and coupled with the sea-sickness, you might still be feeling vulnerable. I think it would be best if Jimmy and I left you to sleep and we will try to see you tomorrow,' suggested Jack.

Jimmy nodded his agreement, secretly pleased to vacate the cabin early.

After they left, Lucinda slept for a couple of hours, while Helen took the opportunity to catch up with the notes she was making in her journal. Jack had suggested they write an account of their travels, but neither had had much opportunity to keep abreast of their entries. Helen's summary of their daily exploits up to now, were wholly concerned with her success in developing a relationship with Jack, rather than a detailed commentary of their journey. The last words she wrote were *'Making headway!'* Satisfied with her progress and noticing Lucinda beginning to stir, she abandoned her writing, deciding to make a hot drink.

'How are you feeling now?' asked a concerned Helen, as Lucinda shuffled up the bed. 'I'm making a cup of tea, would you like one?'

'Oh yes, thank you Helen, although I don't think I will risk any food just yet. Strangely, I feel really well again, perhaps it has nothing to do with sea-sickness; as Jack suggested I might just be run down. I've not been sleeping too well, due to all the excitement of the last week,' Lucinda reaffirmed. Secretly, she knew there could be another unspoken reason for her recurring sickness...in a couple of days, her menses would be several months overdue and there was the very real prospect she might be pregnant.

Unaware of Lucinda's concerns, Helen concurred with her friend's reasoning. 'You're probably right. I expect you will feel much better tomorrow. Neither of us got off to a good start, but unlike you, I have been sleeping very well. Everything has probably caught up with you. Don't worry, apparently we expect good weather for a few days, so you will be able to relax more and recover accordingly.'

'Mmm, yes I hope so,' ventured Lucinda, who grimaced after taking a sip of the tea. 'Actually, do you mind if I have a fruit juice instead of the tea? I seem to have taken a strange dislike to my favoured beverage. Maybe I could manage a biscuit though. However, I don't trust myself to venture to the dining room,' confessed Lucinda.

'Of course; you should take the opportunity of retiring early, so that you are bright and breezy tomorrow,' suggested Helen.

The next morning Lucinda rose early and although initially she felt tired and a little queasy, she washed and dressed and sauntered down to the restaurant with Helen. A couple of slices of toast and a coffee later, she was anxious to throw off her earlier lethargy and take a brisk walk.

After two circuits of the ship, the girls relaxed on deck, taking in the view of the Atlantic. They ate cake, drank coffee and wrote in their journals, until Helen turned the conversation around to Jack. 'I had a lovely afternoon yesterday with Jack. He is such a gentleman and very thoughtful. I really feel we have a connection,' chirped Helen, who actually couldn't wait to spend more time alone with him.

Lucinda was cautious in her reply. 'Mmm, as I said before, Jack is very friendly with everyone, but we'll see. Just don't get too enthusiastic. If you really want to renew your friendship, you should take things one step at a time. Men generally don't cope well with women who are too keen. You should also find out just what his relationship is with Rosie,' advised Lucinda.

'Well, maybe you have a point. I'll try holding back, but Jack makes it so easy to flirt with. As to his relationship, he told me he hoped he would become as close with Rosie as you are with Jimmy, but then followed that up with 'time will tell', which, in my mind, means 'Que sera!'[46]

'Mmm be careful you are not reading too much into that. As I said, Jack flirts with everyone, but it doesn't mean he wants to start up a relationship. You may just find yourself in too deep with someone who may not be thinking along the same lines,' explained a concerned Lucinda.

'I know, I know, you are right and will try not to let my feelings run away with me. I am just repeating what he said, 'time will tell' and 'no-one can foresee the future',' quoted Helen, who had managed to take Jack's words out of context, to suit her own misguided interpretation of their actual meaning. She sighed contentedly and the faraway expression she held, betrayed her thoughts. She turned her attention to Lucinda. 'Anyway, how are you and Jimmy doing? He seemed very attentive yesterday.'

'We are good thank you. Although this silly sickness bout meant we didn't get the chance to enjoy our time alone together. It's a good job Jimmy is so understanding. He was really kind and looked after me.'

Once again, the prospect of being alone with Jack raised its head. 'Perhaps I can arrange for you to have another opportunity later on today. I could suggest Jack and I take a walk and leave you both to enjoy the afternoon. Hopefully,

---

46 'Que Sera' - *'Whatever will be, will be'* - *The origins of the saying and the identity of its language - the Spanish-like spelling used by Livingston and Evans (which appears on a brass plaque in the Church of St Nicholas, Thames Ditton, Surrey dated 1559) and the Italian-like form ('che sara` sara`) was first adopted as a family motto by either John Russell, 1st Earl of Bedford, or his son, Francis Russell, 2nd Earl of Bedford. First documented in the 16th century as an English heraldic motto.*

this time, there won't be any interruptions and that way, both of us will benefit,' Helen suggested, looking expectantly at her friend.

Lucinda's mood brightened. 'Okay, that sounds good, but just remember what I said and keep the conversation light,' insisted Lucinda.

Helen grinned and nodded in agreement. 'It is just about lunchtime, shall we eat in the restaurant? But you should stay clear of the fish dishes, just in case,' chortled Helen.

The women enjoyed their lunch, but on the way to their cabin, Lucinda once again began to feel nauseous. 'Oh dear, the sickness is starting again. I need to lie down.'

Helen, concerned, made a suggestion. 'I think you should see the ship's doctor and hopefully he will be able to diagnose the problem. In fact you should go now, it is down the alleyway to the right. I will wait for you in the cabin.'

'You are right, he will probably be able to give me something to help. I will see you later,' agreed Lucinda, whose underlying concern was growing by the minute.

༺༻

Half an hour later, Jimmy, who had finished his watch, saw Lucinda disappearing down the companionway. He followed her to her cabin, but she had already entered, leaving the door slightly ajar. As he approached, he heard her sobbing and speaking in whispered tones to Helen. Jimmy refrained from entering and stood tentatively outside the door.

'Whatever is the matter? Was the doctor able to give you something for your sickness?' asked a concerned Helen.

Between sobs, Lucinda explained. 'There is nothing he *can* give me for my condition Helen. You see'—she paused, not wanting to admit what was probably the truth—'the doctor is practically sure I am pregnant[47].'

On hearing the shocking revelation, a horrified Jimmy clamped his hand to his mouth to stifle a gasp, then turned and walked quietly away. His face was ashen and his eyes wide in total astonishment.

In the cabin, Lucinda continued to sob uncontrollably; Helen put her arms around her friend. 'How can he tell that?' asked a bewildered Helen. 'You and Jimmy only made love just over two weeks ago.'

Lucinda remained silent. Should she admit to her friend about her encounter with Harry and the fact that she had now missed three menses? The doctor had estimated the gestational age was three months and the timeline coincided with her unfortunate liaison with Harry. Did she have a choice? Helen would soon realise it wasn't Jimmy's, if the pregnancy was confirmed. She made her decision. 'I need to talk to you about something I am now living to regret. It was before I met Jimmy,' she blurted, looking sheepishly at Helen. 'There was this man, Harry Benfield, who I had known in my college days. I stupidly slept with him at my apartment,' she fibbed, unable to share the fact she had been unceremoniously raped. She continued—'It was before we joined the *Dreadnought* and it might be his!' admitted Lucinda.

'Oh dear, what on earth'—Helen began to ask, then seeing the distraught look on Lucinda's face, decided to

---

47 *Nineteenth Century - Various theories abounded, such as the possibility that pregnancy urine contained certain identifiable crystals or bacteria. Scientists did not know enough about pregnancy to develop a reliable test. However, for sexually active women, the best method for diagnosing pregnancy remained careful observation of their own physical signs and symptoms (such as morning or even daily sickness).*

continue in a more conciliatory tone—'I am so sorry Lucinda, what will you do?' asked a non-judgemental Helen, shocked that her friend had found herself in such a dire situation.

'I don't know what I will do, but I can't lose Jimmy over this—I just can't,' sobbed an hysterical Lucinda, her eyes pleading to Helen in the hope she would find a solution.

Helen remained thoughtful. How could she help her friend? At first she seemed bereft of answers, as thoughts danced wildly around in her head…Eventually she concluded there *was* only one way out of this mess. Lucinda, although terrified, encouraged her to suggest her plan. 'You will have to pass the baby off as Jimmy's,' Helen stated matter of factly.

Lucinda sat in stunned silence but knew Helen was right—there *was* no other solution!

CHAPTER TWELVE

A Dark Day
January 1856

Friday, 18th became a day Lizzie and Marcus would not forget. They hoped to breakfast with Rosie, only for her to grab a slice of toast and skip the rest of the meal. She had other plans it seemed at her father's house close by.

※

Elspeth's usual practice was to place the morning mail on a silver plate on the dining table. Included in the delivery were two letters addressed to Marcus and postmarked Philadelphia. Marcus was expecting a letter from his father, to confirm his attendance at their wedding in March, although his father would be unaware that they postponed the wedding until June. Marcus's second letter, informing him of this change, would probably have crossed somewhere mid-Atlantic.

The first letter, bearing an official embossed seal, was clearly not from his father. Placing it to one side, Marcus examined the second letter, written in an unfamiliar script. It appeared to be from his father's business associate, Edward Bernstein, introduced to him by his father when they last met. His name and address was clearly annotated on the back of the envelope.

Marcus frowned, unable to fathom why Mr Bernstein would write to *him* personally. He carefully slit open the cream parchment envelope and extracted the two sheets of paper. It began: *'I was so sorry to hear of the death of your father...'* Marcus's reaction was immediate. He was visibly shocked and paled noticeably, as he tried to comprehend the dreadful news.

Trembling and barely able to communicate, he attempted, almost incoherently, to inform Lizzie. 'He's dead...my father is dead,' he managed.

Lizzie's hand went involuntary to her mouth to stifle a gasp. She was equally stunned. 'Oh Marcus, how dreadful. What on earth happened?'

Marcus, disbelieving, scanned the first page again. 'It appears he had a heart attack, Elizabeth. He was drinking at his club and suddenly clutched his chest. He was taken to hospital, but did not survive. Oh Elizabeth, this is such a shock. I was expecting a reply to my letter which informed him of the good news about Jack and our wedding, but it is evident he didn't receive it, as he died on the 6th January. He wouldn't have known that Jack and I were reunited, or that we were to be married.'

Lizzie poured Marcus a brandy and put her arms around him in a gesture of comfort. Marcus continued reading: *'Bernstein says the authorities advised him that I had been informed by urgent telegram on the day he died*...but it must have gone astray. Had I received it, I would have secured an immediate passage across the Atlantic. It goes on...*Edward, of course, was very upset, as he too was out of the country and unable to make the funeral. However, he understands it was well attended by all father's friends from his club, his business associates and his employees from the mill[48]. It closed for three days as a mark of respect. Edward assures me that he will assist with everything when I finally arrive.*

'My God Elizabeth, someone should be held to blame for this error, although, of course, that won't bring my father back.' He shook his head again in disbelief before mechanically opening the second letter, from a well-known firm of solicitors, used on occasion by his father. It contained a formal request for him to attend the reading of the will, delayed to facilitate the time needed to cross the Atlantic. 'Oh Elizabeth, I have to go right away. I am sorry to leave you alone, but will you be all right my love? Rosie will be here to keep you company while I am away, but it still concerns me somewhat.'

'Don't fret Marcus; you have enough to worry about. I am so sorry not to have had the opportunity to meet your father, but I feel I've known him through you. There aren't any words of comfort I can offer, only to say my heart goes out to you. The hurt you are feeling will take time to heal. When my father died, I thought I would never smile again. I felt totally empty inside, as if part of me died with him, but it is true that you will smile again and it will no longer hurt when you recall the wonderful memories you have of him. Why don't you take a day off from the factory while you

---

48 *Textile mills of the Waltham-Lowell system sprang up across the northern New England countryside between 1814 and 1850 and grew steadily across the second half of the century. Mills of the Rhode Island variety expanded as well, and the earlier regional differences faded over time. At mid-century, New England's textile workforce had grown to number 85,000, producing cloth goods valued at $68 million annually, adding to a substantial textile industry in the Philadelphia area. Cotton and woollen textile mills were the nation's leading industrial employers at this time.*

organise your passage? We will go for a walk by the river later. It is so peaceful and quiet and it will give you time to reflect.'

'Thank you Elizabeth, that is exactly what I need to do. I love you so much, you are always so kind and thoughtful, I don't know how I would manage without you,' Marcus proclaimed.

※

Later as they walked hand in hand by the riverside, Marcus felt calmed and thanked God he had such a wonderful woman by his side. He would suggest she take a trip to Nottingham to see Clara during his absence. After all, he reflected, one never knows how long one has on this earth and Clara and Arthur *were* in their twilight years.

Just before Christmas he'd thought about retiring, or at least taking a back seat in the factory's management, now he wished he'd considered it sooner. He could have taken Elizabeth to Philadelphia, instead of spending the winter in England. Of course, that would have meant the reunion with his son, would have been delayed. Maybe some things were not meant to be and he was actually a big believer in fate, particularly as it apparently lent a hand in him first meeting Elizabeth.

His father's death actually crystalized reasons for taking stock of his own life. Maybe they should move. He loved *The Beeches*, but his son would need an apartment of his own, when he wasn't at sea and Rosie could certainly do with more space. Then there was the matter of Clara and Arthur. He knew Elizabeth had often thought of welcoming them to their home, although Clara wouldn't want to leave Nottingham.

An hour and a half ticked by, during which, many random ideas peppered his brain, forming a tangle of mostly unachievable goals. He dismissed them one by one, until suddenly, out of the blue, one idea catapulted itself clear of the others. What if he *was* to retire and sell the factory, there wouldn't be anything keeping them in Littleborough. They could actually move to Nottingham. Granted Rosie would have to choose between remaining with her father, or moving with her mother. The more he thought about the possibilities, the more he warmed to the idea.

He had spoken to a business associate, Howard Faraday, only a few months ago. He presently lived in Southwell, a town on the outskirts of Nottingham. He'd extolled its virtues and mentioned it had a Minster, which incongruously elevated the town to a place of importance in relation to its actual size. Indeed, Howard had chosen Nottingham's textile industry, with its use of innovative machinery and an emphasis on lace, cotton and hosiery, providing the impetus. He'd also mentioned the fact that James Hargreaves left Lancashire for Nottingham, a century earlier, which highlighted its potential and provided another reason for moving there. Perhaps he would also invest in a small business after he sold his factory. He would investigate the property market and with Elizabeth's approval, find a suitable house. It would need to be bigger than *The Beeches*, to accommodate Rosie and possibly Jack, along with Clara and Arthur. Two or three more staff would be required, of course…so maybe something with a couple of wings. He grinned to himself and despite his early melancholy, his enthusiasm was gaining momentum. Elizabeth would at first probably be cautious, but the benefits outweighed the problems. He was sure she would agree, so intended broaching the subject at an appropriate moment.

Marcus was sad that Elizabeth and his father would never meet, but was nevertheless, uplifted in that his passing had brought his own future sharply into focus, for which he was grateful. He would miss his father, always a great source of wisdom and strength. Even in death, he had somehow managed to focus his son's mind on what was important in life. He'd once said to him...*'never leave that 'til tomorrow, which you can do today'*:[49] A reference to Benjamin Franklin, a man much admired by his father. One of Franklin's legacies was the facilitation of Philadelphia's Fire Department, which apparently extinguished a potentially devastating fire ravaging his father's mill and saved two of his employees from certain death.

Before he retired that evening, he offered a silent prayer of love and gratitude for his father's guidance and the sadness he felt in his passing.

---

[49] *Benjamin Franklin was born in Boston (17 January 1706 – 17 April 1790). He was the tenth son of soap maker, Josiah Franklin. Benjamin's mother was Abiah Folger, the second wife of Josiah. In all, Josiah would father 17 children. Benjamin Franklin was one of the Founding Fathers of the United States. A renowned polymath, Franklin was a leading author, printer, political theorist, politician, postmaster, scientist, inventor, civic activist, statesman, and diplomat. As a scientist, he was a major figure in the American Enlightenment and the history of physics for his discoveries and theories regarding electricity. As an inventor, he is known for the lightning rod, bifocals, and the Franklin stove, among other inventions. He facilitated many civic organizations, including Philadelphia's fire department and a university.*

CHAPTER THIRTEEN

'SS Pacific'
January 1856

Marcus booked a passage on the SS Pacific[50] and embarked on the 23rd January. Once again, Lizzie found herself waving goodbye to him from the dockside. Sad that she would not see him again until early March, she kept smiling as he'd requested. She mouthed the words 'I love you' and Marcus reciprocated her simple, meaningful words as the ship left the berth and slowly moved out into the open sea.

His visit would hopefully be brief, only gone for a relatively short six weeks, including the time spent in Philadelphia. She reflected that when Marcus searched for Belle and Jack, his absence rolled into months. That had been unbearable.

༺༻

Closeted in the first class carriage of the train back to Manchester, Lizzie observed the grey stone built cotton mills

---

50 *On 23 January 1856, Pacific departed Liverpool for her usual destination of New York, carrying 45 passengers (a typically small number for a winter voyage) and 141 crew. Her commander was Captain Asa Eldridge, a Yarmouth, Cape Cod skipper and navigator of worldwide reputation; in 1854 he had set a trans-Atlantic speed record on the clipper Red Jacket from New York to Liverpool, which remains unbroken.*

and chimneys, billowing smoke into a sky, laden heavy with dark clouds. She hoped Marcus's journey would be comfortable.

Prior to the *Pacific* sailing they were in a café, holding hands across a table, adorned with just a simple blue chequered print cloth. He'd noticed her worried, furrowed brow and had sought to reassure her by extolling the virtues of the *Pacific's* credentials.

She recalled his enthusiasm for this luxurious ship and its remarkable speed, making a record passage in 1850 from Liverpool to New York. It had won the coveted *Blue Riband*, he'd said, adding that the ship's high freeboards and straight stems provided added protection from sea spray and a steadier motion through the waves. *'So,' he'd said, 'I will be home very soon.'* Laughingly he'd told her how cosseted he would feel, as there were only forty-five passengers amidst the one hundred and forty one crew. He expected only top class cuisine from the nine cooks aboard, which included a French maitre de! Of course he would miss her terribly, but the ship's home comforts would help compensate. He'd noted that the cabins and saloons were very generous, extremely spacious and elaborately decorated. Its revolutionary steam heating was almost unheard of in other passenger ships. The quarters seemed magnificent and he intended to take full advantage of the barbershop service on the return journey! A light-hearted comment, which he'd hoped would calm her fears.

⁂

The Beeches seemed very empty without Marcus, but Lizzie consoled herself with the fact that there would be so much to do during his absence. She determined that her first priority was to arrange a visit to Nottingham to persuade Clara and Arthur to move in with them. That might prove difficult, but ultimately, she was confident they would accept her offer with all its benefits.

CHAPTER FOURTEEN

Deliberation
January 1856

Just over a week after Marcus's departure, Lizzie and Rosie strolled along the familiar streets of Narrow Marsh. Little had changed since their last visit, but as they approached number fourteen Knotted Alley, Lizzie couldn't fail to notice the flaking paint and the first signs of footboard rot. It was obvious the maintenance of the property was being neglected by the landlord and, in all probability, Arthur, who could not possibly undertake such tasks himself. *Another reason to persuade them to move in with us,* she thought.

She knocked, her mood lightening when she heard Clara chastising Arthur. 'Arthur, Arthur, that'ull be our Lizzie, 'urry up and let her in, she don't want to be standing aht in the coad.'

An obedient Arthur opened the door with a grin. 'C'mon in Lizzie, Rosie,' he greeted, adding…'yer can see her voice 'an't lost its ability to holler, even if the rest of 'er body in't what it used ter be!'

Lizzie entered the parlour and rushed to embrace a frail looking Clara, firmly ensconced in her rocking chair. She'd already noticed Clara's red mottled legs, a combination of bad circulation and a bad habit of sitting too close to the coals. 'How lovely to see you Clara. Do you realise it has been three months since I last saw you? I was hoping you'd come for Christmas, but I know you prefer to stay at home these days. However, I do hope you had a lovely time together with all the family.'

'Aye Lizzie, wi did, although I din't da much in the way of cooking, our Tillie managed all a that. Did us proud as well. Anyrode, 'ow yer managing wi'out Marcus? A got yer letter yestady. It wah terrible news of 'is father's death and 'im 'aving ter rush off ter *Phillidelfa*. I expect 'e'll not be gone long, the speed some of them ships travel these days. Mind, yer wun't get me on one…me feet's better on good old English soil…well, not ser much at the minit, as me rheumatism is playing up, but yer catch me drift.' Clara laughed in amusement, before the second tirade of the morning was once again directed at Arthur. 'Can a 'ear that keckle boiling Arthur? Lizzie 'ull think 'er throat's bin cut!'

Arthur defended himself before scampering off. 'A wah just go-an to fill it Clara. Shall a get aht the best crockery and some of that Madeira cake?'

Clara grunted. 'Of course, yer shud, yer daft oaf,' she teased, before addressing Lizzie. 'A sometimes wonder what he'd do wi'out me to lead him by the nose?'

Lizzie smiled, she missed Clara's forthright manner. She acknowledged that they loved each other to bits and their chiding was actually endearing. Clara, they knew, would insist on being told everything that had happened since she last saw them. Arthur's steaming cup of tea, faithfully delivered, instigated her inquisition. 'Nah then our Rosie, what've yer bin up ta? If I know you, they'll be a lad involved?'

Rosie grinned. She loved visiting her grandma, despite her determined efforts to elicit all her secrets, usually when they were alone. 'You remember a while ago when you were ill grandma and you asked me about boys, well my answer is still the same, there's only one for me and that's Jimmy!'

'Aye well,' grunted Clara, unsure whether it was a good thing or not. 'Both yer mam and Ida wrote me abaht Jimmy turning up and we was all relieved abhat that. Ida said he wah courting a nurse off a ship. She seemed ta think it wah serious. 'As summat 'appened ter change 'is mind?' Clara questioned, directing a quizzical eye at Rosie.

'Well grandma, you could say that. It's true he *is* seeing a nurse, Lucinda, but when I turned up to wave Jack off on his voyage to Australia, Jimmy and I knew we still harboured feelings for each other'—Rosie paused, glancing at Lizzie then back to Clara—'You must keep that to yourself grandma as it's not completely sorted yet. I need to talk to Jimmy on his return.'

Clara nodded understandingly, taking another sip of tea and slowly eating a second slice of Madeira before replying. 'So long as yer sure, Rosie, there's noat worse than being wi someone who doesn't love yer more than life itssen! Teck a word of advice from yer mam and me, we've both been lucky there, an't we Lizzie?'

Lizzie agreed wholeheartedly. 'I've explained to Rosie that she has plenty of time to decide Clara, but she seems adamant Jimmy is the one, so we shall see!'

'Yer mam's right Rosie, a lot can 'appen in a short space of time. Yer think everything is mapped out, only for a big foot to 'ovva above and trample yer dahn. Yer can't count on oat 'til it 'appens, mark my words.' Clara nodded as she raised a finger then attended to the fire, prodding the coals around with the poker. This caused several fiery sparks to fly out and land on the pegged rug. Furiously she stamped her feet on the embers, to prevent the fabric catching alight.

A hush descended on the room, while Lizzie and Rosie, mesmerised at Clara's antics, stared fixatedly at the small burn marks left on the rug.

'Can I get yer another cuppa Lizzie?' asked an unperturbed Arthur, who had remained fairly quiet throughout, with an occasional nod of agreement, when he thought it was right to do so.

'That will be lovely Arthur and then I must book into an inn if we are to stay for a few days,' asserted Lizzie.

Clara, sad at the thought of Lizzie staying elsewhere in Nottingham, was astute enough to realise that home comforts were in short supply in her own home. Realistically, Clara knew she could not hope to provide them, but persisted. 'Yer know yer welcome to stay wi us Lizzie,' she said smiling and winking at Rosie—'but a know it's not really practical. Yer'l pop in every day fer a visit though?'

'Of course, Clara, every day! I was thinking I'd stay at the *King's Head,* until Marcus suggested the *Blackamore's Head* as a rather splendid alternative. However, the King's Head is just a short walk away and it's where I stayed when I first arrived in Nottingham.'

※

Lizzie left them none the wiser and without mentioning the subject of moving. She needed more time to explain the advantages to Clara, exactly as Marcus had done on the day he received the terrible news of his father's death.

After they'd returned from the walk by the river, he had mooted the idea about the possibility of relocating to Nottingham. They'd come to the conclusion, after extensive discussion, that it was the best thing to do. Secretly Lizzie was delighted that Marcus had shared all his thoughts. He'd explained how the death of his father convinced him to take stock of his life and he was adamant he would sell the factory. He'd also informed Lizzie they would be exceedingly well off after he inherited, so, could afford a substantial property to accommodate, not only Rosie, Jack and themselves, but also Clara and Arthur, if, of course, Lizzie could persuade them to move.

⁂

After booking in at the *King's Head*, Rosie and Lizzie took a walk along the cliff tops, overlooking Narrow Marsh in its entirety. Lizzie needed to gauge Rosie's reaction to a possible move, so consequently broached the subject with a good deal of trepidation. 'There's something I need to discuss with you Rosie. It is a difficult subject and one that will require a lot of thought and consideration on your part.'

Rosie's ears pricked up. She imagined it might be connected with her decision to break up with Jack. 'That sounds serious Mam, has something happened?'

'Not exactly Rosie, but you remember when you visited your father on the day Marcus received the news of his own father's death? Well, we returned from our walk by the river and Marcus suggested something important, which I want to share with you.'

Rosie breathed a sigh of relief, the break up was clearly not the subject being raised. 'Oh, I see Mam, so what is it all about?'

Lizzie hesitated for a moment before proceeding cautiously. 'Marcus has been thinking for some time to release the reins with regard to his business; in fact, he has considered selling the factory,' she stated, pausing for the expected response from Rosie.

'Gosh Mam, that's a big step, as he has always been so committed to his business,' she declared, arching her eyebrows.

'Yes, that's true, but his father's death affected him greatly. It inspired him to reflect on his own life and whether the future, as it stood, was in fact what he wanted. He came to the conclusion that it wasn't. His reunion with Jack and our forthcoming marriage put his life into perspective. He wants to spend quality time with his family, which is most important to him,' explained Lizzie.

Rosie considered her reasoning before replying. 'I can see how he would feel that way'—she paused, half expecting her mam to continue with perhaps something more startling—'Is that all?—'I thought there was some big plan on the horizon!' she concluded, rather disappointed.

Lizzie continued her carefully considered explanation. 'There is actually a little more to it'—she paused, taking a deep breath—'Marcus suggested we move house,' declared Lizzie, bracing herself for loud objections from Rosie.

'Where? Do you mean to the country, away from the hustle and bustle of the Mills?' asked Rosie, actually warming to the idea of a great country pile with acres of land for horses and stables. *At least it would be a stab in the eye for Beatrice...as she never misses an opportunity to brag about her own home with its grass paddocks and stables* she thought.

'Well!' Lizzie grinned, 'it could be, though not in Lancashire. Marcus has suggested we move to Nottinghamshire. What do you think?'

Rosie was astounded. 'Nottinghamshire? What close to Grandma?'

'Well that is the other consideration, we were hoping Grandma and Granddad would come and live with us.'

Rosie speculated on where in Nottingham this grand house might be located, but nowhere came to mind, within the town centre. 'But there's nothing suitable, even St James

Street doesn't have houses big enough for everyone,' reasoned a disappointed Rosie.

Her dreams of a large house with paddocks were fading fast, until Lizzie restored her hopes. 'Marcus was thinking somewhere a little further out, where there are sizeable properties with land. In fact, a business associate of his lives in a town called Southwell. It's surrounded by a rural landscape, near Nottingham, but less inhabited. He suggested we consider properties possibly with two wings. Jack needs a private apartment, for when he returns from sea and you will undoubtedly need more accommodation before you eventually marry, prior to buying a house of your own. How does that sound?' asked Lizzie positively.

'Mmm…it sounds interesting. Would I have my own suite of rooms Mam?' Rosie beamed, as dreams of a large house with a paddock were suddenly resurrected.

'That's the idea Rosie, but the most important thing is to persuade Grandma and Granddad to join us; we envisaged them occupying the ground floor of one wing of the property. Marcus and myself would live in the main house and you and Jack could share the other wing, with separate accommodation. Of course we don't know yet what size property we would be able to afford, but Marcus expects it would be large enough to accommodate us all comfortably on the proceeds of the business, our present home and his father's inheritance. We would also retain a substantial sum in the bank for every day expenses, should Marcus decide to retire from business altogether.' By now, Lizzie was confident that Rosie was not opposed to the idea, surprisingly, she appeared to be embracing the concept.

Rosie walked on ahead, speculating whether it was prudent to ask her mam if, when she was older, Jimmy could live there too, but *perhaps, now wasn't the best time*.

However, she was definitely warming to the idea, until the thought of leaving her dad suddenly appeared like a dark cloud circling above. She waited for Lizzie to catch up before posing a very important question. 'What about my dad? Will he have to remain in Littleborough?' ventured a slightly downhearted Rosie.

It was the question Lizzie was dreading. It could make all the difference to Rosie's decision. 'I'm afraid so Rosie, but it is only a short train journey away and you're bound to spend a lot of the time down at Kate's. The point is, does it change your mind about moving?'

Rosie hesitated, weighing up the pros and cons. It was true she spent a good deal of time in Oxford and it would mean that she would have three bases to choose from, no less: A room with a bathroom at Kate's; a room at her dad's and an apartment in Nottinghamshire. *That would definitely make Beatrice envious! Maybe it wasn't so bad.* 'You're right Mam and I'd have three houses to live in...how lucky!'

At this point, Rosie recalled the time when they lived in the Marsh with her Grandma. She'd shared a room with her mam, the toilet was in the yard and the bath hung on a nail outside the back door. Now here they were, about to purchase a large house with inside bathrooms, a paddock and stables and she was dithering whether it was a good idea. Of course, it was a good idea and she would embrace it wholeheartedly.

CHAPTER FIFTEEN

Taking Stock
January 1856

Following a hearty breakfast at the King's Head, Lizzie and Rosie walked the short distance to Knotted Alley; their conversation focussed on the potential move. Marcus had previously contacted Howard Faraday to assist with finding a suitable house for the family. Howard, delighted to have been asked, was soon in contact to advise of a wonderful property that had recently come on the market. This particular residence was one he had viewed, whilst his family were considering their own move. Unfortunately, his wife considered it too large, as their recently married daughter had moved to Dorset and his son, Duncan, intended commencing a new career, sheep farming in Australia. Howard had reluctantly given him his blessing to embrace this significant position in a land of opportunity.

On Howard's advice, Marcus suggested Lizzie visit Southwell, to view the property, when she saw Clara. With his approval, Howard contacted the present owners, who were anxious to sell, to inform them that he had a possible buyer for their substantial, late-eighteenth century, brick built house. Lizzie was impressed with its specifications. It faced east and boasted a central three-storey canted bay, flanked by single Venetian windows and three smaller sashes, flanked by single Diocletian[51] windows. The house on Back Lane also offered a large walled garden and adjacent paddocks, which was ideal for Lizzie and Marcus. She was very excited, of course, but Clara and Arthur needed to agree on the move, before she revealed what they were considering. Having Rosie on board was advantageous, but persuading Clara and Arthur to leave Narrow Marsh would be more of a challenge.

Rosie, who had thought of nothing else all morning, was busy devising a plan of her own. 'I've been thinking Mam and I agree, it would be good to move to Nottingham. There isn't anything to keep us in Littleborough, after Marcus sells his business. As we are in Nottingham, can we visit Southwell and look for a property? I'm informed it actually has a train station,' said Rosie quite knowledgeably—'but the line only runs between two villages. We would need to take a cab from Nottingham to the first,' explained Rosie.

Lizzie acknowledged Rosie's comments, but now had a dilemma. She needed to convince Clara and Arthur, before she could agree to Rosie's suggestion; then actually take her to view the property that she had in mind already, so prevaricated. 'Maybe, Rosie, but there's little point unless Grandma and Granddad agree, so perhaps you could help me persuade them what a good idea it would be,' suggested Lizzie, anticipating Rosie's co-operation.

'Mmm...well, as you know Mam, I can be pretty persuasive.' Rosie grinned, already deciding that the move would definitely go ahead if she had anything to do with it.

---

51 *Diocletian windows are large segmental arched windows, which are usually divided into three lights (window compartments) by two vertical mullions.*

TANGLED WEB

As they neared Knotted Alley, Clara's 'dulcet' tones emanated from the open window. 'Arthur, 'ave yer got that keckle on? they'll be here any minute and there's an icy wind terday. When a went aht ta the lavvy, a thought ter messen 'ow good it 'ud be ta 'ave one inside, but that in't gonna 'appen is it? It blew right up me skirts and a felt chilled ter the bone, it's a wonder me wee din't turn inta an icicle! Evry time we oppen the door, it's like a blast from the North Pole. Pull that curtain across the door Arthur, afore, we freeze ter death and get another scuckle of coal on the fire,' ordered Clara without taking breath.

Arthur wasn't sure which task to carry out first and decided the kettle might be the most urgent, followed by filling up the coal-scuttle and lastly drawing the curtain.

Lizzie and Rosie grinned at each other, both thinking Clara might be easier to persuade than they thought. Lizzie knocked on the door, not expecting Arthur to answer immediately, considering the tasks he had to perform, but it was opened snappily with a cheery 'good morning'.

'Come through, I've got the keckle on,' Arthur assured, before turning to address Clara. 'It's Lizzie and Rosie, Clara.'

Clara tutted and rose from her chair before replying. 'Oh am glad yer let me know that, a wah thinking it might be Queen Victoria hersenn, she said she might pop ovver,' Clara declared, in a voice showing more than the merest hint of sarcasm. Shaking her head in despair, she addressed her visitors. 'Sit yersenn dahn you two,' she said smiling, whilst patting her hand on the small settee then settling herself back in her chair.

Arthur glanced over at the kettle coming to the boil on the hob. 'Shall a—'

Clara interrupted him mid sentence—'A very good idea Arthur and yes, use the best crockery. The butter fer the

Madeira's on the table, a took it from the stone slab in the cool pantreh[52] earlier as it wah as hard as a brick bat,' she exclaimed, pausing for a moment, until another thought emerged—'and, Arthur, a noticed the mesh at the winda 'ad a little 'ole in it, me duck, it'ull need replacing before the weather warms up and a 'erd of flies get in or woss. A caught young Alfie Waplington, poking a piece of wire through it the other day, trying hook a piece of me cold pie. 'is movver 'ud 'ave a fit if she knew what 'e wah up ta. She's as toffy nosed[53] as they come and 'ad 'ave a job proving oat,' Clara explained, as a cup of tea magically appeared in her hand. 'Thanks me duck, a don't know what ad do wi'out yer!' Clara smiled, secretly grateful Arthur was a very attentive husband, who never raised his voice...or his hand. She made a note to tell him how appreciative she was...but immediately decided he already knew.

'Well then Lizzie, 'ave yer settled in at King's 'ead?' asked Clara.

'Yes Clara, we have adjacent rooms and I am occupying the room I took when I first arrived in Nottingham. It has been re-decorated of course and is most comfortable.'

---

52 *The 'cool pantry' was often located on the coldest (North) facing wall of the house/cottage and had a tiny window high up. This window was often protected by a metal sieved screen to keep the flies out. On the inside, the walls were shelved and on the shelves were kept perhaps a jug of milk or cream cheese in a specially shaped china wedge; perhaps a ham or other cold meat, rashers of bacon, a pot of butter or a few slices of cold pie or brawn. The cooler temperatures in there would have been enough to keep the food cool for two to three days, especially if a 'cold slab' was installed.*

53 *The origin of 'toffee-nosed' has nothing to do with the sugary, brown sweet, but derives from 'toff', (toffy-nosed), which was the slang term given by the lower-classes in Victorian England to the stylishly-dressed upper-class.*

Clara noticed Rosie eyeing up the Madeira cake. 'Arthur, cut our Rosie a nice chunk of that cake and don't stint wi the butta,' she ordered, taking another bite of her own piece.

After everyone was settled and several cups of tea later, Lizzie subtlety broached the subject of mutual interest. 'I see the landlord hasn't done much with regard to the upkeep of your home Clara. Would you like me to contact him to remind him of his obligations?' asked Lizzie, in the hope Clara would make some complaints about the run-down state of number fourteen.

A look of discontent crossed Clara's brow as she fiddled with her apron, before delivering her verdict. 'It wun't da na good Lizzie, he int a bit intrested in pouring good money after bad. There's talk round 'ere that 'ell let em ga ter rack and ruin, rather than do oat abaht crumbling paint and rotting wood,' replied a disheartened Clara. 'We're better off than most, as we allus 'ave enuff coal fer the fire and food in us bellies, thanks ter yo Lizzie. Some poor souls 'ave to scrat abaht dahn the embankment picking up fallen tree branches and oat that 'ud create some sorta flame. Then others risk gaol, nicking coal at night from the slag heaps, although them with a long memry, remember what 'appened ter Sam Armstrong, when George Rowan 'ad finished wi 'im; 'e could 'ave got deported to Australa! No Lizzie, we can't complain…wun't der no good if wi did.' Clara laughed, turning to Arthur. 'Anyrode, when Arthur's fully recovered from 'is bad coad, 'e reckons 'e cun fix most on it, sa long as 'e dun't 'ave ter climb a ladder, eh Arthur?'

Arthur nodded sagely. 'Aye me duck, I'll da me best, but neither on us is getting any younger,' concluded Arthur, before adding—'The only thing that worries me Lizzie, is Clara struggling up them stairs wi me pushing 'er from behind. I keep saying one a these days, we'll both land in a 'eap at bottom.'

Clara chuckled, making light of the situation. 'Well Arthur, we'd probbly be there fer days, as neither on us could get back up.'

Lizzie decided now was the time to inform Clara of her plans. She placed her hand over Clara's and began tentatively. 'I have something to tell you Clara. I think you will be pleased, but I want you to listen until I have finished, before you comment,' declared a determined Lizzie.

Clara nodded, curious what Lizzie had in mind. 'Right oh, am all ears,' she clucked.

'Well, when Marcus's father died, he took stock of his own life and came to the conclusion that he should sell the business before relocating to Nottingham. He wants to spend more time with his family,' explained Lizzie.

Clara's eyebrows arched in surprise and she could not keep quiet. 'Yer can't come dahn 'ere Lizzie, yer'l not find oat suitable, sept up St James Street, or that posh place they call *The Park*[54].' She digressed. 'That land used ta be the deer park fer the castle. It wah public land, but the rich din't care and still built on it.'

Lizzie smiled at Clara's early interruption, which she studiously ignored. 'We intend to find somewhere on the outskirts of the city Clara, big enough to house Marcus and myself, staff quarters and hopefully separate accommodation for Rosie and Jack. We will also need a paddock, as Rosie

---

54 *The first domestic building in the park was built in 1809, opposite the castle gatehouse, the building served as the vicarage to St. Mary's Church. Despite much opposition from locals, who regarded the area as public land, major development began in the 1820s under the 4th Duke of Newcastle-under-Lyme. Development continued under the 5th Duke, who appointed architect Thomas Chambers Hine to design many of the houses.*

would like a horse,' she explained, then waited for Clara's reaction.

A smile began to form on Clara's lips. 'Well now that's exciting innit Arthur?' she stated and without waiting for a reply, continued—'Will yer be able ter come and see us more often,' queried Clara.

Lizzie drew in a deep breath, realising the time had come for her to acknowledge the rest of her plan. 'Indeed we will Clara. In fact, if I have my way, I will see you every day,' promised Lizzie.

Clara could barely contain herself. 'Der yer 'ear that Arthur? A think we need another cuppa ter celebrate.' An ecstatic Clara chortled, despite the fact she would have to brave the cold wind in the yard to the lavatory, if she did have another 'cuppa'.

Lizzie was anxious not to lose the momentum. 'There is one other thing Clara and that is a proposition I would like you to consider,' indicated a still nervous Lizzie. 'We would like you to come and live with us.'

Clara's eyebrows shot up and her mouth gaped in total surprise. She gulped down her tea, as Arthur followed suit, both staring incomprehensibly at Lizzie. The clock ticked loudly in the background until, surprisingly, Arthur broke the silence. 'Well Lizzie, if yer serious abaht it'—he began, turning his attention to Clara—'I think we need ta give yer offer some thought. If it wah just fer messen, I'd probbly stay here, but fer our Clara's sake, the answer ud be an easy one, what der yer say Clara me duck? No more traipsing aht ter the lavvy, no cold wind blowing up yer skirt and seeing our Lizzie every day! Sahnds like 'eaven!'

Clara was shell shocked, it was a lot to take in. On the surface she agreed with Arthur, but then they would be leaving their friends behind and she felt she would be a 'fish out of water' living somewhere she considered too posh and way above their station.

Lizzie had already determined that Clara would have some misgivings so quickly reassured her. 'There's no need to worry about missing your friends or visiting the shops, as Jacob, our gardener will take you in the gig to Nottingham any time you want.'

Clara nodded vacantly, as if she hadn't heard Lizzie, *would it be such a bad thing?* she wondered. *There were distinct advantages and Arthur seemed keen. If she could get back to see her friends, then perhaps it was the answer to their prayers.* She observed Arthur, whose face suddenly appeared younger than his fifty-four years, as if a great weight had suddenly been lifted from his shoulders. She immediately realised the strain he had been under, struggling to keep up the maintenance of the house. She would be fifty-three this year and was already suffering greatly with rheumatism, which seemed worse in the damp, cold weather. Even in the summer, the house never seemed to dry out, sometimes flooding when the swamps of the River Leen overflowed. The horrible miasma[55], which rose from the swamps, brought on ague, rheumatism and other unpleasant diseases. Up until now, they had both managed to keep most serious illnesses at bay, apart from the relatively mild dose of cholera last March, which Clara miraculously survived, but perhaps now they needed to face up to reality. If Arthur was right in his summation of their nightly

---

55 *In 19th-century England the miasma theory made sense to the sanitary reformers. Rapid industrialisation and urbanisation had created many poor, filthy and foul-smelling city neighbourhoods that tended to be the focal points of disease and epidemics.*

struggle up the stairs, they might stumble and fall. If they survived, who would find them?

Lizzie, Rosie and Arthur waited patiently as Clara continued to ruminate on the pros and cons of a move. Several minutes passed, before she noticed three pairs of expectant eyes focussing on her. She reached a decision. 'Well Lizzie, tekking everythin inta consideration, a think wi could possibly move in wi yer,' Clara confirmed.

Lizzie breathed a huge sigh of relief and Arthur responded by pouring everyone yet another cup of tea to celebrate. 'e're me duck, 'ave put an extra spoon of sugar in it,' informed Arthur, handing Clara a cup. Then he bent down and whispered in her ear, 'Wi doing the right thing Clara me duck, you'll see and there's a drop of Indian brandee in that, by the way…for medical purposes of course.'

A delighted Rosie put her arms around her grandma. 'I am so glad you want to come Grandma. Now you can both be looked after properly, with no more suffering from the damp conditions and Mam and me will know you are safe.'

There were a hundred and one questions Clara wanted to ask, but for now she would enjoy the moment. Arthur felt ten years younger, in the knowledge he wouldn't have the worry of Clara falling or succumbing to an illness she couldn't survive. Lizzie, for her part, was reassured that her family would all be housed in the same place, where she could keep an eye on them. Rosie was ecstatic in that she'd have her own apartment and a place to keep a horse. If her future included Jimmy, they could remain there, until they found somewhere of their own. The only fly in the ointment would be Jack, but if he no longer figured in her plans, he might want a property of his own, as he enjoyed his independence. It could be a perfect solution all round.

CHAPTER SIXTEEN

Unexpected News
January 1856

The following morning, as Lizzie and Rosie exited Leenside then turned in to Knotted Alley, they were surprised to see an official looking gentleman hovering outside Clara's front door. Quickening their step, they reached number 14, before the man had chance to knock. 'Can I help you,' asked Lizzie, concerned that Clara might be receiving bad news.

'I have an important message for a Mrs Clara Milligan, but who might you be?' he asked witheringly.

Thinking quickly, Lizzie claimed ownership. 'I am she,' she said assertively.

The man accepting her identity and forthrightness confided abruptly. 'I don't think the news is particularly good.' He then slapped the envelope in Lizzie's outstretched hand, just as Arthur threw open the door, while an agitated Clara hollered, 'What's up Arthur? Don't leave 'em on the doorstep.'

'Right yer are,' he obliged, allowing Rosie to walk past him into the living room, leaving Arthur staring perplexedly at Lizzie.

She pushed the envelope into her pocket, intending to read it before Clara set eyes on what she considered might be unwanted news, then hurriedly made an excuse of forgetting to pick up an item from the local shop. She cast

Arthur a pleading look before she disappeared down the alley.

Clara was surprised that Arthur closed the door behind him. 'Where's Lizzie Arthur? I thought she wah wi Rosie at the door,' asked a concerned Clara.

Arthur was quick to respond. 'Aye she wah, but she mumbled something abaht forgetting summat at the shop. She said she wah go-an to get a pie for lunch. She'll only be two shakes of a lamb's tail[56] and she'll be back me duck.'

'Okay Arthur, well hurry up and pull the curtain across, else Rosie u'll 'ave ter sit in her coat for the duration.'

༺༻

Lizzie quickly retraced her steps to the River Leen then sat down on a bench. She took out the crumpled envelope, opened it and began reading:

'Dear Mrs Milligan,

Please be advised that Mr Tommy Bradley, inmate at the Asylum, is very ill and not expected to last the night. Your name is on file as the person to contact in the event, if Mrs Elizabeth Van der Duim is unavailable. We request that you visit him urgently. Mr Bradley has something he wishes to give to you.'

Lizzie's hand shook as she processed the alarming information. She must go at once to see Tommy before he passed,

---

56 *First recorded by Richard Barham in 'Ingoldsby Legends' in 1840, but probably much older. Means with no loss of time, for a lamb can shake its tail twice 'before one can say Jack Robinson'.*

but first she needed to inform Clara. She would be very upset, but Lizzie was thankful it wasn't an actual 'family' emergency.

Lizzie spoke to Clara and Arthur, then took a cab to the Asylum. She stood outside the gates and observed the window to Tommy's room, remembering the day she'd taken him there. He had settled quickly and been happy, but now her attendance was vital and very different. Tommy's life was coming to an end, although he was still relatively young. He was never expected to live to an old age, but nonetheless, it came as a shock. Lizzie had already planned a visit to Tommy the next day to impart the good news that she was moving to Nottingham and consequently, would be able to visit him regularly. Sadly, this visit would be her very last.

Her shoulders slumped in resignation as she made her way to the main door. Once inside, she reported to reception then ascended the stairs to Tommy's room on the first floor, but was surprised to find matron and two other staff hurrying towards her. The matron beckoned urgently to Lizzie. 'Mrs Van der Duim, come quick, Tommy is fading fast and I fear the end is near for him,' she hurriedly explained.

As Lizzie entered the room, Tommy turned his head toward her. He smiled, despite his anguish. She sat at his bedside, as the unmistakable notes of Robert Schumann's 'Dreaming', filled the room. Lizzie placed his hand in hers. 'It's all right Tommy, you are safe now, don't be scared, I am here with you,' she whispered.

Peaceful recognition invaded his consciousness. He was overjoyed that Lizzie was here to help. He felt serene and ready to pass. She kissed him on his cheek and, as always, Tommy pressed his hand to the spot. As the last notes of the melody faded away, Tommy Bradley closed his eyes. The little box, with its fine engraving of an angel floating on a cloud, slipped out of his hand on to the coverlet. With tear filled eyes, Lizzie retrieved it and held it to her breast.

The staff in attendance were witness to this most tender of moments. So often, residents died in total isolation, without family and friends, but Tommy was special. He never demanded anything and was respected by all. He'd spent most of his last few months sitting on a bench in the grounds or in his chair by the window, looking out across the valley. The enamelled music box was always by his side and he would constantly tell the staff that Lizzie had given it to him and how precious it was. He never tired of listening to its haunting melody, saying it made him feel happy and secure.

Lizzie, sad and subdued, eventually left the room and walked slowly to the main entrance. Once outside, she paused by the bench Tommy frequented and admired the view across the valley, that he had enjoyed during the twelve years he had been resident. She stopped again at the large ornate gates, turned determinedly, then gazed at Tommy's window just one last time.

CHAPTER SEVENTEEN

A Stormy Passage
February 1856

On the 18[57] February, the Champion of the Seas rounded the Cape of Good Hope[57], catching the Agulhas[58] current before running into a ferocious storm. Lucinda and Helen, along with other passengers, were ordered to stay in their cabins for at least forty-eight hours, while the storm did its worst. Huge swells and tremendous seas caused the ship to pitch and roll dangerously, which made all deck areas treacherous and inhabitable to the unwary.

Both girls became violently sea-sick again. Lucinda considered she shouldn't have made the journey at all. If she had stayed in England, she could have made plans and hidden her pregnancy from everyone.

---

57 *The Cape of Good Hope is at the southern tip of the Cape Peninsula, about 2.3 kilometres (1.4 miles) west and a little south of Cape Point on the south-east corner. In the fifteenth century it was referred to as the Cape of Storms, being renamed by King John II of Portugal - 1455–1495.*

58 *The southernmost point of the Cape of Good Hope, is Cape Agulhas, about 150 kilometres (90 miles) to the east-southeast. The currents of the two oceans meet at the point where the warm-water Agulhas current meets the cold water Benguela current and turns back on itself—a point that fluctuates between Cape Agulhas and Cape Point (about 1.2 kilometers east of the Cape of Good Hope).*

Jack and Jimmy were unable to spend any time with the women, as all crew were involved in essential deck duties; reefing sails, battening down hatches and stowing gear. Only sufficient canvas remained on the masts to maintain steerage. Jimmy was probably the only sailor on board who welcomed this distraction, as the overheard conversation still preyed heavily on his mind.

Off duty time became non-existent, as the storm surged, but prior to this, Jimmy had managed to pen a letter to Rosie, laying bare his feelings for her. He anticipated that the ship would have to dock at Port Elizabeth for repairs to a mast footing; which presented the ideal opportunity for him to ensure his letter reached home via the ship chandler. He did consider writing to his mam, but his situation was so complicated, he decided it was better to explain everything to her on his next visit.

※

A day after the storm abated, the *Champion of the Seas* limped into Port Elizabeth. It was the first time in almost three days that the friends managed to spend time together; although for Lucinda and Jimmy, these brief periods were fraught and awkward silences prevailed.

Helen and Jack could sense the atmosphere. Helen, now fully aware of the circumstances, was, however, puzzled about Jimmy's reticence. Jack, for his part, was also curious, but made it his mission to get to the bottom of it. Eventually, he encountered Jimmy alone, whilst making his way to his own cabin. 'Hey there Jimmy, have you got a moment?' Jack called out.

'Yes Jack, come over to my quarters, I could do with a chat. Some of the crew have been bandying tales of ghost ships passing by without anyone aboard! Quite spooked me to be honest.'

On reaching the accommodation, Jimmy tumbled into his hammock, propping himself up on his elbow, while Jack perched himself on a stool. 'Thank God she weathered the storm, Jimmy. The only real damage was to the mast footing, so we were lucky,' commented Jack turning his eyes to the heavens, then crossing himself to praise the Lord for keeping them safe.

'Well, it was pretty bad I have to admit, but no worse for me than when I dived overboard to save the bosun.' Jimmy grinned as he reminded himself how lucky he was to survive such an ordeal.

'Mmm, at least there weren't any incidents to rival that!' said Jack thankfully, gauging that the time seemed right to approach Jimmy on the other matter. 'So, how are you and Lucinda? Not getting much time alone with her must be disappointing,' probed Jack.

Jimmy stared at the floor and fiddled with the edge of his hammock, wondering whether it would be prudent to tell Jack about the conversation he'd overheard between Lucinda and Helen. He noticed Jack frowning, he was obviously expecting at least a semblance of a reply, but as Jimmy was silent, Jack pursued the subject. 'Nothing wrong is there Jimmy? You haven't had a row have you?'

Jimmy hesitated before deciding to come clean to his friend. 'No, no nothing like that, it is just...well...I overheard a conversation between Lucinda and Helen, which, to be honest, really shocked me. In fact, I haven't been able to think of anything else since.' Jimmy fell silent once again.

Jack's brows knitted in a frown, he was at a loss to understand what Jimmy was struggling to tell him. 'Well it's clearly nothing good Jimmy. What on earth has been going on? We haven't seen them for almost three days. I thought you two were getting on well. Has Lucinda voiced doubts about your future together?'

'No, just the opposite. There is something, however, on which I must make a difficult decision. One minute I am sure what I should do, the next, I am at sixes and sevens, agonizing on whether I am about to make a big mistake.' Jimmy grimaced, still unable to come clean to Jack.

'Sounds serious! Why don't you just tell me what it is? You know what they say, *two heads are better than one* in solving a problem, Jimmy.'

'All right, but you have to swear you won't mention it to either of them, as Lucinda is unaware that I know,' stated Jimmy.

'Of course I won't. We've shared secrets before and I've never let you down Jimmy,' argued Jack.

Jimmy took a deep breath, then began his tale. 'It was the last day we spent with them. Lucinda had been feeling really sick and I think Helen must have suggested they retire to their cabin. I had just come off duty and wanted to spend some time alone with Lucinda. I reached their cabin and found the door slightly ajar. I was just about to knock, when I heard voices inside. Helen was asking if the doctor had been able to give Lucinda something for her sickness. Lucinda said no and began sobbing. She then told Helen the doctor was certain'—he paused, looking vacantly into space, still unsure whether he should be sharing this information with Jack. He decided there was no going back, so continued—'certain she was pregnant—' Jimmy blurted, but was immediately interrupted by an intake of breath from Jack.

'My God, Jimmy! Are you sure?' Jack gasped, a deep frown conveying his total astonishment.

'Of course I'm sure Jack. It was at that point I walked away; they don't know I was eavesdropping,' confirmed Jimmy, as his eyes darkened, giving him a slightly haunted look.

Jack remained silent, unsure what to say to make his friend feel better, as they both sat quietly, each with his own thoughts on the matter.

Jimmy eventually broke the silence, coughing surreptitiously to gain Jack's attention. 'So you can understand my dilemma Jack. What I can't fathom, of course, is the fact that we only made love at Christmas, so how could the doctor be so sure, less than a month later?' queried Jimmy.

Jack raised his head after staring at the floor, a deep frown creased his brow. 'That doesn't sound right Jimmy. He must be mistaken. Not that I am particularly knowledgeable on the subject, but by my calculation, she wouldn't even be due her next menses yet.'

Jimmy gave him a quizzical look, so Jack expanded on his theory. 'Oh it's the bleeding thing. I think I heard my mother referring to it as that. She always went to her bedroom for a lie down once a month. She would draw the curtains, place a hot water bottle in the bed and apply a cold compress to her head. I had to keep refilling the bottle and Oliver took over the household tasks. Sometimes she didn't surface for days. When I asked what was wrong, she would reply, *'It's the menses John, another thing we women have to contend with.'* I asked Oliver what it meant and he explained about the monthly bleeding. Apparently, if they miss one, they could be pregnant. However, it's impossible to tell before then, which makes me believe the doctor making this passage would merely have suggested she could be, when in actual fact, she probably isn't. It is most likely panic on Lucinda's part. If I were you, I'd forget it. Why don't you arrange to meet with her and see if she mentions anything?

I do think you are worrying over nothing Jimmy. Now what say we have a tot of rum and make the most of our off duty period by playing a game of cards. It should take your mind off the matter,' suggested Jack.

Jimmy, somewhat relieved, slid down to the floor and sat opposite his friend. 'You're right Jack, it does sound improbable. Now where's that rum you suggested?'

Jack drew out a hip flask containing the rum, obtained from the ship's chandler, for helping him out when a burly able seaman accosted him for no good reason, whilst storing was in progress. He swigged a good mouthful from the flask, wiped his hand over the top and handed it to Jimmy. 'Now then Jimmy, what's this nonsense about ghost ships...' he taunted laughingly.

Helen decided to have another heart to heart with Lucinda, who had been down in the dumps since the doctor declared she could be pregnant. An ideal opportunity arose before they left Port Elizabeth. The ferocious storm still preoccupied all the passengers' minds and most were relieved to have survived. Fortunately, it was now behind them and the ship had only suffered relatively minor damage; consequently, the captain decided to hold a special dinner that evening, to celebrate their good fortune and minimal delay. Lucinda and Helen were to be the special guests of the captain, complements of Jack, who'd arranged their presence.

The women were looking forward to eating in the dining room, having been confined to their cabin with only a brown paper bag for company during the storm. Lucinda vigorously brushed her hair at the dressing table, in preparation. Now that her 'sea-sickness' had passed, she felt quite well and began to think the doctor must be mistaken. She had only made love twice in her life, so surely that couldn't result in a pregnancy. It must only have been seasickness, she surmised, due to the rolling and pitching of the ship. Admittedly, Helen was less affected. Anyway, as soon as she was able, she would meet with Jimmy on his next off duty period and rekindle their relationship. However, her optimism was tempered with one disturbing thought: her menses were overdue again by almost two weeks; her last showing was in November and it was now February. She had also put on a small amount of weight, but she put that down to the delicious meals they had eaten and a distinct lack of exercise. The non-appearance of menses was, she convinced herself, due to the emotional upset she had suffered.

They'd both finished dressing and were relaxing, before they made their way to the dining room for dinner. 'You seem much better Lucinda,' Helen remarked. 'In fact you look positively blooming! Is that what mothers' are supposed to look like,' she added undiplomatically.

The remark surprised Lucinda, whose determination wavered for an instant, refusing to embrace the possibility. 'That reason never crossed my mind and I really don't think I could be pregnant, everything considered. I do feel much better now the sea-sickness has abated. I am not going to dwell on the alternative, unless I have definite proof. I intend to see Jimmy and get our relationship back on track. In fact, I feel so well that a pre-dinner walk on deck would be welcome. Are you coming?' Lucinda asked, rising from the sofa determinedly.

Helen, embarrassed by her thoughtless comment, followed her. They might also run into their respective beaus. As it happened, neither was disappointed as both men emerged from the forecastle accommodation, heading in their direction, bearing broad smiles.

Jack spoke first. 'How are you girls? Most of the other passengers have remained in their cabins, so we are surprised to see you on deck. It's been a busy forty-eight hours for us, getting the ship ready for departure, so what say we retire to my cabin for a drink? We have a couple of hours off duty before things get hectic again and you get to dine with the Captain.'

※

There was definitely a more relaxed atmosphere, partly due to Jack's talk with Jimmy and Lucinda's renewed optimism, which improved as more tots of rum were consumed, although the women opted for tea, with just a dash of the spirit.

Eventually, a slightly intoxicated Jimmy, on impulse, contrived to manipulate time alone with Lucinda. Despite Jack's assurances, he still felt the need to discover whether or not a pregnancy was a possibility, which would determine the path of their relationship. He fervently hoped that she was not pregnant, which would ease the burden of guilt he was feeling. He also knew she would be devastated if he ended their relationship. However, that seemed inevitable, because he'd convinced himself that the woman he wanted to spend the rest of his life with was Rosie. Indeed, his love for Rosie had been reignited at the café, although up until that point, he had been certain she was indeed part of his past. His future, he had genuinely believed was with Lucinda. Now all that had changed; some how or other he needed to extricate himself from his present relationship and the sooner the better.

He mulled that over in his mind as he sat next to Lucinda on the day bed, with Jack on his bunk and Helen in a chair. Jimmy put his arm around Lucinda and whispered that they could spend the last hour in her cabin before his return to duty. A delighted Lucinda agreed and they left, taking the inboard stair to Lucinda's stateroom.

Jimmy was apprehensive as he settled himself on the sofa with Lucinda beside him. Now they were alone, Jimmy's confidence suddenly diminished. He coughed nervously as he summoned up courage. 'I was thinking'—he began—'was the doctor able to give you anything for your sea-sickness, as you seem much better now?'

Lucinda flushed alarmingly at Jimmy's direct question, becoming momentarily silent. How did Jimmy know she had been to see the doctor? Had she mentioned it? She couldn't remember, but thought it unlikely. 'How did you know I had seen the doctor Jimmy?' Lucinda asked innocently.

This time it was Jimmy's turn to think on his feet. He was kicking himself, realising the only way he could have known was if he had been privy to the conversation. He needed to brazen it out. 'Er, well, I think Helen mentioned it, I'm not sure, but someone did, otherwise I wouldn't have known,' he said confidently.

Lucinda relaxed, maybe it had been mentioned following the storm. 'Well the doctor said sea-sickness was the problem, but that would subside when the ship reached calmer waters. Now we are alongside, I feel really well. I am also glad you wanted time alone with me. I have missed you Jimmy,' she said, quickly disrobing and kissing him sensuously on the lips.

Jimmy pretended he was excited by her actions, but now he knew that Lucinda had lied about the doctor. Inexplicably, he felt unable to tell her that their future was in doubt. He decided to wait a while longer. Either Lucinda came clean, or, some other information would surface. He thought he owed her that much. It wasn't Lucinda's fault that his chance meeting with Rosie had changed everything. It wouldn't be fair to upset her unnecessarily and the time would come soon enough when he had to tell her the truth.

A confused and disheartened Jimmy continued with the pretence, despite his misgivings and he reluctantly removed his clothes. He tried his best to focus on making love to her because Lucinda wanted him urgently. Her undisguised need for him to enter her was overwhelming, but for Jimmy, it wasn't going to be easy to feign such an act.

As his hands lingered over her tummy, a deep sense of fear enveloped him; Lucinda had put noticeable weight on her stomach since the last time they were intimate. At that moment, he wanted to call a halt and confront her once again about the possible pregnancy, but as he entered her, his excitement waned. He felt sick; the likelihood she could be pregnant suddenly became very real. For the first time he feigned orgasm, which luckily went unnoticed by Lucinda who was elated that Jimmy still wanted to make love. Unbeknown to her, it would be for the very last time.

᎒

Later at dinner, a happy Lucinda told Helen that her and Jimmy were definitely back on course.

A slightly tipsy Helen also shared a piece of news. She and Jack had enjoyed the last hour drinking rum and she had fallen asleep on his day bed. He had covered her with a blanket and when she awoke, he had made her coffee. She said he had flirted with her and when she stood up to go, he had held her by the shoulders. For a brief moment, she felt a spark of excitement between them as their eyes met. Was this down to the fact that Jack was missing Rosie, or was it something more intriguing? She wasn't sure, but intended to pursue the possibility and spend more time in his company.

During an off duty period, the men again discussed Lucinda's perceived pregnancy, while playing a game of cribbage[59]. Jack had won all the previous games and Jimmy's pride was at stake.

The cards were dealt, before Jack raised the subject. 'Have you spoken to Lucinda Jimmy?' he asked, curious as to whether there had been any developments.

Jimmy, studying his hand, was making a decision on which card to discard, but still managed to answer Jack's question. 'Yes I did ask her what the doctor advised before I realised I wouldn't have known that she had actually seen the doctor. I made the excuse that Helen might have mentioned it, which seemed to satisfy her. Anyway, she said the doctor had not given her anything and that her 'sea-sickness' would clear up on its own.'

Jack inclined his head to one side and pursed his lips in a gesture of scepticism. 'Oh, I see, so in effect, she lied,' suggested Jack.

---

59 *Dealing in the game of Cribbage - Cribbage uses a standard 52-card deck. The jokers are removed; the suits are equal in status. The players cut for first deal, with the player cutting the lowest card dealing first (ace counts as one, lowest card). The dealer shuffles, the cards are cut and he deals cards singly to each player, starting with the player on the dealer's left. Cards must be dealt so that each player ends up with four cards, after the crib is formed, and the crib should also have four cards. Once dealt, each player chooses four cards to retain, discarding the two face-down to form the 'crib' that will be used later by the dealer. The player on the dealer's left cuts the un-dealt portion of the deck and the dealer reveals the top card, called the 'starter' or the 'cut', placing it on top of the deck face up.*

'Yes, I suppose she did,' Jimmy agreed, whilst placing his cards face down on the table.

'What will you do?' Jack asked, staring intently at his friend.

'I'm not sure,' Jimmy replied. 'I've decided to hang fire and see what happens. I hope Lucinda may slip up and say something without thinking, which may confirm a pregnancy. Helen may even confide in you'—he paused, desperate to employ whatever means it took to arrive at the truth—'I don't suppose you could speak to Helen to try and glean something,' begged Jimmy, his brow contorted into an anxious frown.

Jack, with lots of sympathy for Jimmy, said he would help him if he could. However, a suspicion had been preying on his own mind since the day they sailed and it was eating away at him. Perhaps now was the time to take the 'bull by the horns' and confront Jimmy about his feelings for Rosie. He began tentatively. 'Helen seems to want to spend a lot of time with me and, between ourselves, I think she wants to take our friendship to the next level, which affects my relationship with Rosie; albeit that's progressing very slowly,' he confided, looking directly into Jimmy's eyes. 'On that particular subject, there is something I want to discuss with you. I have been reflecting on the situation between you and Rosie. I thought everything was through between you, but looking back to the day we sailed, I am now not so certain. You probably thought I hadn't noticed the meaningful looks, which passed between you. At the time, I put it down to the fact that an exuberant Rosie was pleased you had survived, but perhaps I have been fooling myself and it was something more than that. Be honest with me Jimmy, do you still have feelings for Rosie?'

Jimmy blushed; he was beginning to regret asking for Jack's help. He had been backed into a corner, so felt obliged to confess. 'Maybe, Jack, but she is with you and I don't want to move in on someone else's girl. We both know she is still very young and may not wish to embark on a serious relationship just yet. Do you remember advising me to 'play the field' before settling down?

'In hindsight, it could be said that we are taking this love business too seriously and should not feel pressed into making such life-changing decisions…I think I may have been a bit hasty placing a ring on Lucinda's left hand, not long before we sailed. I should have just left it as a gift of gratitude given to her by me mam, but I felt pressured into making a commitment. I didn't believe she had made love with anyone before, so foolishly made a snap decision to assure her I wasn't just using her.

'The day I discovered Rosie was seeing you affected me more than I wanted to admit, but when I made love to Lucinda, I thought I had managed to put my feelings for Rosie behind me. However, when we met again, they came flooding back,' concluded Jimmy, his eyes darting nervously from the cards lain face down on the table to Jack. Would this be the end of their friendship he wondered?

Jack grinned wryly; he now had the confirmation he sought. He knew at that moment he had lost Rosie. Did he ever really have her love? Probably not. What Jimmy said made a lot of sense. Even he had been having doubts about his own feelings, since spending time with Helen and admitted to himself that he enjoyed her company. That wasn't the way it should be, if he was committed to Rosie. The fact that he had been tempted to kiss Helen after Lucinda and Jimmy left was all a bit of a mess. The only saving grace was, that he knew Jimmy and himself would always be friends, even if the other relationships failed.

He leant over the table and placed his hand on Jimmy's shoulder. 'Don't worry Jimmy, we won't come to blows and neither will it be an end to our friendship, which I value too much. Whatever happens, I can see us having many more trips together around this great planet of ours. You might have a point about Rosie's age, she's young and she might change *her* mind too. We should remember that being a sailor isn't really a platform for settling down Jimmy as you will be away from home for months at a time,' he concluded.

Jimmy breathed a sigh of relief. Jack's reaction was what he had hoped for; although he wasn't sure he agreed with 'playing the field'. It was how he felt in his heart. However, it was certain that he needed to find out the truth about Lucinda's perceived pregnancy. Either way, he needed to end his relationship with her. 'I think you are right Jack. It's easy to start a relationship, but when you don't see 'em for months, things can change...on both sides. Anyway, how confident are you that you can elicit any information from Helen?' he asked, hoping Jack already had a plan.

Jack tapped the side of his nose. 'Leave it with me Jimmy. I'll do my best to get to the bottom of it. Now let's see if you can beat me this time around my friend.' Jack laughed, as he confidently placed two discarded cards on the 'crib'.

༄

Despite his bravado, Jack spent a long time, alone in his cabin, ruminating over Jimmy's confession. The truth hit him hard, but he needed to come to terms with it. He'd realised for a while now that Rosie wasn't fully committed to their relationship. He suspected she still yearned after Jimmy, although she hadn't known whether he was alive or dead. Her tender age was also a consideration, as Jimmy had pointed out and obviously not ready for a sexual relationship. He could have waited until the time was right, but there would always have been the ghost of Jimmy, hovering. Of course, had Jimmy not survived, Rosie may have eventually moved on. However, his friend was very much alive and it had changed everything. He could not deny he was genuinely delighted, despite the fact it had destroyed any chance of a future with Rosie.

It was then he remembered a piece of advice given to him by his step-father, Oliver Jamieson, that gave him the strength to move forward. He intended to give Helen a chance and see where it took them. It would not be a knee-jerk reaction, as over the period of time they had spent alone together, his feelings towards her had strengthened, despite Jimmy's revelation.

He hoped she was as keen as him to take their relationship further and he was ready to embrace that. The only fly in the ointment, as far as he was concerned, was his promise to Jimmy. He needed an answer to Lucinda's possible pregnancy. If there was any truth in the fact that Lucinda was pregnant, he needed Helen to persuade her to tell Jimmy, that way his loyalty to both would remain intact.

※

The first opportunity Jack had of being alone with Helen came early the following morning, before the ship sailed that afternoon. She was seated on a deck perusing the '*The Champion of the Seas Times*'. An article, which highlighted a dinner hosted by the Captain, caught her attention. Lucinda and herself were listed as being guests at the Captain's table. John McKirdy was overheard to have said that he was honoured to be in the company of such glamorous guests.

Jack could not fail to notice the article as he looked over her shoulder. 'I see our Captain has impeccable taste,' he teased, grinning as Helen blushed at Jack's sudden unexpected appearance.

'Oh, hello Jack,' she said, not raising her eyes from the paper, lest Jack should notice her embarrassment. 'I was just taking some air and picked up the paper left behind by another passenger.' A demure Helen smiled, pleased that Jack had stopped for a chat.

When Jack looked directly into her eyes, both felt a strong attraction for each other. He felt liberated now that his relationship with Rosie was no longer relevant.

Helen's heart began to beat faster at Jack's obvious intense affection, which gave her confidence. She responded flirtatiously, 'Your Captain is very attentive and complimentary. I am sure he considered all of the ladies at his table to be glamorous. Everyone made an extra special effort to look as attractive as possible. We've not had much opportunity recently, as we've been languishing in our cabins, some of us with our heads in brown paper bags,' she jested, flashing her most disarming smile.

Jack didn't waste any time implementing his plan to win Helen over completely, offering little subtlety in his reply. 'Oh I am sure they did Helen, but I bet you and Lucinda were the most attractive, so before someone else spots that fact, perhaps you would accompany me on a walk? I am not on duty until later this afternoon when the ship sails.' Jack winked, grinning at Helen's attempts to disguise her discomfiture.

Despite her astonishment at Jack's behaviour, Helen was overjoyed that he was so attentive, offering such lovely compliments. It was obvious that something in Jack's demeanour had changed so she decided to embrace it wholeheartedly. As she rose from her chair, Jack boldly placed his arm around her waist. The promenade deck was pretty much deserted; most of the passengers were engaged elsewhere and the crew were readying the ship for departure. Helen did wonder about Jack's sudden show of affection, but was happy to enjoy it while it lasted.

Jack broke the silence with a speculative question. 'Do you wonder just what the future might hold for all of us Helen'—not waiting for an answer he continued—'I really do believe it is all mapped out. You remember, when we last discussed the topic, you called me a fatalist? You said *you* thought people made their own destinies. Well perhaps that's true, but often events don't quite work out how they imagine.

'For instance, do you think Jimmy went to great lengths to secure a berth on the same ship as me, or was it fate? And what about ourselves? Neither of us could have envisaged any life changing occurrence happening, because of something we orchestrated. For me, it was just another journey to a foreign land, without any prescience as to whether my future would be determined by some precipitated act.

'Your objective, of course, was to see your parents in Australia, but it wasn't going to affect your future life. How could it when you intended to return to your nursing duties again on the *Dreadnought?* What I am really saying is sometimes a series of unplanned events…let's call them fate, might totally change our future to one that we didn't anticipate.'

Helen didn't speak at first, but looked adoringly into Jack's eyes. She would at that moment have agreed with anything he said. However, she *had* followed his logic, so commented. 'Jack that's very profound and you could have a point, when did you become so worldly wise?'

Jack grinned. 'I think it was all the time I spent with Oliver Jamieson, the man who brought me up from a young boy. He once told me that my mother was always plotting and scheming, but very often, to her surprise, her plans went awry. It was Oliver who informed me that he was not my biological parent. My mother convinced me that Oliver *was* indeed my father. He *was* a good man, but knowing I had a parent who had no idea where I was and whom I might never meet, was hard. It was then he said, *'If only your mother wouldn't try to go down a path that she wasn't meant to travel, she would be much happier with life. Unfortunately, she was never satisfied with her lot'.*

'Sadly, I only remember my mother complaining how life hadn't been what she had planned and hoped for. She used to say, '*Life has treated me very badly, John. No matter how hard I try and achieve something, I am always let down!*'.

'Oliver tried hard to offer me guidance and once quoted me a few lines from a poem by Robert Burns. He said I would do well to remember it—

> *'The best laid schemes, o' Mice an' Men,*
> *Gang aft agley,*
> *An' lea'e us nought but grief an' pain,*
> *For promis'd joy!'*[60]

'Can you see what I mean Helen? It's no good trying to continue along a path that is littered with obstacles. Fate is telling you to choose a different route, that you might not want to take, but in the end, it might make sense of everything,' explained Jack, confident of his own convictions.

---

60 *Meaning: The best laid schemes of Mice and Men (mankind), often go awry, and leave us nothing but grief and pain, for promised joy!*

'I think I am convinced Jack, but where is this all leading?' asked Helen hopefully.

Jack responded in his usual cryptic manner. 'I think you know the answer to that Helen. Let's go back to my cabin to continue our conversation with a little more privacy.'

Helen agreed, hardly able to believe her luck. Whatever Jack had in mind she wouldn't raise an objection. Significantly, he placed his hand once more around her waist, as they walked the short distance to his cabin.

Once inside, Jack poured Helen a brandy, part of his secret stash of spirits he kept for special occasions, given to him by his father as a gift before he left.

A nervous Helen availed herself of the day bed, which, when the four of them were together, was usually occupied by Lucinda and Jimmy. The whole situation felt surreal and she could not believe what was happening.

Helen placed her glass on the side table and encouraged Jack to sit next to her. He didn't need asking twice and sat, putting his arm around her shoulders, before cupping her face and gently turning it towards his own. He kissed her softly on the lips. Helen trembled, as their kiss became more urgent. Her breathing deepened, as Jack planted kisses along her shoulders, simultaneously slipping off her blouse. He pulled her gently to her feet, then loosened her silk skirt, which glided effortlessly to the floor. Helen assisted by removing her underwear as Jack took off his uniform. They delighted in the other's nakedness, stroking and caressing as their excitement mounted. Finally, Jack carried Helen to the bed and lay beside her. He moved his hand slowly and sensuously over her breasts and down to her stomach, where he lingered, caressing the velvet softness of her inner thighs. Helen gently directed his head towards the heart of her femininity and Jack's tongue caressed her inner lips, bringing her to the brink of ultimate arousal. Holding back himself, he continued to give her pleasure until she begged him to enter her. He straddled her body then covered her lips with his own; his eyes bored into her soul, as he guided his erection into her. Both reached orgasm simultaneously in an all-consuming intense culmination of their love-making.

Neither spoke as they lay in each other's arms. Helen wondered if it had been a good experience for Jack and hoped this would be the beginning of a more permanent relationship. Jack was surprised by the intensity of his feelings for her and had to admit, he didn't feel any sense of guilt with respect to Rosie. Helen, he thought, was a good lover, as well as someone who could match him intellectually and share his sense of humour. He had no doubt that this relationship would strengthen and continue when Helen returned to England.

There was, however, still the matter of Lucinda's predicament, but now wasn't the time to raise the subject. Jack poured them both another brandy, before they made love a second time. When Helen eventually left, Jack sat at his writing desk. He took out a single sheet of paper and, unknowingly, commenced writing the second letter to be posted in Port Elizabeth, destined for the same recipient. He would just have enough time to give the letter to the ship chandler to post, before he commenced his shift.

※

In just under four weeks the ship would dock in Melbourne. Lucinda's menses had been absent since she had slept with Harry Benfield. Despite continued bouts of sickness, she reasoned her cycle had been disrupted due to emotional upheaval, firstly her encounter with Harry, followed by a new job and lastly the excitement of meeting Jimmy. However, realistically, she knew that was stretching parallelism too far.

The first menses missed was on the 23rd November, with another due on the 20th December. Her third should have been 16th January, a week before they sailed, but now alarmingly she was overdue a fourth time. She was concerned that her relationship with Jimmy was doomed. Lucinda realised that Jimmy's ardour had waned. He was still kind and attentive, but they hadn't made love; something had fundamentally changed. He was reluctant to talk about their future and in their most intimate moments, Jimmy no longer professed his love for her. Now she was once again overwhelmed with feelings of nausea, despite the ship having a relatively calm passage. She hadn't had much chance to confide in Helen, who'd spent every last moment with Jack. She realised that their relationship was going from strength to strength.

Jack and Jimmy were on duty for the whole of the day, so Helen relaxed on deck, having left Lucinda in bed. She had tried to cajole her friend into accompanying her, citing fresh air as a probable help in relieving her symptoms, but Lucinda had declined.

Helen closed her eyes and after day dreaming about Jack for what seemed hours, made an entry in her journal, open on her lap, noting the third of March as a 'special' occasion. It was the date Jack had made love to her for the first time. She added her feelings in consequential detail, so it became close to lunchtime before she sauntered back to their cabin. She wanted to confide in Lucinda to what had occurred, but as Lucinda wasn't feeling well again, she decided to shelve her news for another occasion.

On hearing the door open, Lucinda sat up in bed and called out, 'Is that you Jimmy?'

Helen, sighed, noting the desperation in her friend's voice. 'No Lucinda, it's me. How are you feeling?'

Lucinda groaned, swinging her legs over the side of the bed and pulling her dressing gown over her pyjamas. 'Not so good. I was about to order lunch to eat in the cabin, as I cannot face going to the dining room. Would you sit with me a while? There's something I want to discuss with you.'

'Of course, Lucinda, I will order lunch for the two of us.'

Twenty minutes later, their food arrived. 'Shall I play mother and pour the tea?' Helen remarked light heartedly, but Lucinda made a dash for the bathroom, without managing a reply.

Helen followed her and knocked tentatively on the door. 'Are you all right Lucinda? Is there anything I can do?'

A tearful reply came back. 'No, there's nothing anyone can do. I will be out in a minute.'

Lucinda emerged a few moments later and, making no attempt to dress, sat forlornly at the small table Helen had set for lunch.

'Perhaps if you ate something, you might feel better,' suggested Helen.

'I might,' agreed Lucinda. 'In fact, eating small meals seems to alleviate the problem, but we both know that it is looking less like sea-sickness and more like I might be pregnant,' bemoaned Lucinda, whose anxious frown and the dark circles around her eyes gave away the fact that she had not been sleeping well.

Helen fell silent, unable to offer anything positive in response. She felt sad for her friend, as a pregnancy was the last thing she needed.

'I am not sure what to do Helen.' Lucinda frowned, dabbing her eyes with a handkerchief.

At this point, Helen felt she could not go along with the seasickness excuse any longer, as she had noticed Lucinda's growing belly. It was time to advise a best course of action. 'Dear Lucinda, I agree a pregnancy is the likely cause of your sickness and gain in weight,' she said kindly, placing her arms around her friend's shoulders.

Lucinda acknowledged Helen's appraisal with tear filled eyes. She spoke quietly between sobs. 'It's true Helen and I need to face up to it...I thought Jimmy and I had become close again, but there are signs that his ardour is cooling. He never says he loves me anymore, even during our most intimate moments...and they are rare. If I try to pass the baby off as his, he's bound to be suspicious. I have the feeling sometimes that he has something to tell me, but the moment passes and we just carry on; neither of us brave enough to face the inevitable...that we break up.' Lucinda dissolved in a flood of tears, throwing herself on to the bed. 'I once said, I cannot lose Jimmy, but I think I have already lost him Helen. What would you do?'

Helen comforted her friend, but realised she needed to be honest. 'I believe you have a choice Lucinda, admit to Jimmy that Harry is the likely father, or pass the baby off as his, as we discussed; although, like you, I am not sure the latter is now a viable option. Apparently, he knew you saw the doctor around seven weeks ago, so he has probably calculated that the baby could not be his. Your encounter with Harry was on the 9th November and your menses was due on the 23rd. If my calculations are correct, you are around four months pregnant. You could, of course, carry on with the pregnancy and when it is born, pretend the birth is premature,' proposed Helen, unconvinced by her own suggestion.

Lucinda sighed resignedly. 'No, this charade has gone on long enough; I cannot do that to Jimmy. I love him Helen and for that reason I cannot deceive him. I am going to tell him the truth and he can decide whether he is able to accept another man's child, or we finish…I'—Lucinda's voice tailed off and it was a few minutes before she regained her composure—'I think I know the answer Helen. I have known for a while things aren't right between us, but I don't know what I will do when I hear him tell me it is over. It was a stupid mistake and now I am paying the price.' Shaking uncontrollably, heartbroken and with tears tumbling down her face, she stared ashen faced at Helen.

Helen wrapped her arms around her friend, guilty that her own life had suddenly taken an upturn. 'Whatever the outcome Lucinda, I would like it very much if you stayed with me and my parents for a while. We can contact matron and tell her that you have decided to take a break and stay in Melbourne for a few weeks. This will give you time to see a doctor and decide what you will do with respect to your ongoing pregnancy and birth.'

Lucinda dabbed her eyes, trying desperately to get her emotions under control. 'Oh Helen that is so kind. I think you are right, Jimmy and I need time apart. Maybe he might change his mind,' she muttered unconvincingly.

Helen was also not confident that would happen, but her friend needed time to come to terms with and realise that her relationship with Jimmy was probably over for good. 'Right, that's settled then. We are still weeks away from Melbourne, so if you want me to, I'll ask Jack to have a word with Jimmy, to calm the waters before you tell him.'

'No, I need to do this, but you could ask Jack to give us some time alone together when they are next off duty.'

'Of course, I will make sure you have a few hours undisturbed, but if you need me, I won't be far away,' Helen assured her.

Two days later Lucinda had composed herself, but still sat tense and apprehensive in her state-room, awaiting Jimmy's arrival. She had invited him for lunch and after what seemed an age, he finally appeared, after giving the door a perfunctory knock. He was unaware that Helen and Jack had orchestrated their few hours of privacy together.

Lucinda poured Jimmy a brandy from Helen's exclusive reserve. The large glass *she* had consumed before Jimmy arrived, hadn't done anything to calm her nerves. She smiled uneasily, as she passed the glass of golden liquid to Jimmy, who, equally uncertain, took a large gulp before sitting down next to her on the sofa. Jimmy would rather have been anywhere but there, if it saved him having to participate in the inevitable discussion.

Jimmy felt obliged to put his arms around Lucinda's shoulders. He turned to kiss her but was surprised when Lucinda pulled away. 'Is there something wrong?' he asked, caught slightly off-guard at Lucinda's reaction.

Lucinda fell silent and looked down at the floor. She knew the time had come for her to explain to Jimmy the predicament she found herself in. She also knew that following her confession, their relationship would probably end. She took a sip of brandy and placed the glass back on the table, then turned to face the man she loved. 'Jimmy'—she said quietly—'there is something I have to tell you.' Her stomach flipped and she took a deep breath, before tentatively beginning her explanation. 'You know how much I love you Jimmy. I hoped we would eventually be together forever, but I fear it is not to be'—she paused, searching Jimmy's countenance for some sign that he still wanted her, but his face was taut and his eyes lacked emotion. She continued—'I haven't been well for some time and I thought my malaise might be down to sea sickness, but it turns out that's not the case.

The truth is, I have not had my menses since November, which means I am probably around four months pregnant.' Lucinda fell silent waiting for Jimmy's reaction, but staggered by her forthright revelation, he became transfixed, unable to utter a word.

His head was whirring. He was perplexed; he had seen her lips forming the words, but they didn't fit with what he expected. Shocked and surprised by her admission, he gulped down what remained of his brandy, as the ramifications of her words slowly sank in. She had missed a menses *before* he made love to her, so the baby could not possibly be his. What did she want him to say? Had she had sex with someone just prior to their relationship? if so, when? She had given him to believe he was the first; why would she do that? he conjectured.

He wasn't angry, but was disappointed she had now lied for a second time. 'When…who?' he blurted, as he continued silently ruminating on the likely time the baby was conceived. *November* he repeated inside his head, *before she joined the Dreadnought, or was it*? He had forgotten when she did join, as he met her on the 1st December, but perhaps she was there before that date? His mind went blank, as he tried to assimilate the information.

He observed Lucinda's eyes filling with tears and for a moment he felt sorry for her, but that sentiment quickly disappeared when, in a voice trembling with emotion, she delivered a forthright statement. 'It was before I took the job on board the *Dreadnought*, I bumped into someone I knew years earlier. He was living in the block of apartments in Shoreditch, where I resided, just prior to me joining the hospital ship. His name is Harry Benfield,' she murmured quietly, repulsed at the sound of his name. She continued— 'He used to be a boyfriend of my best friend, Anne, when we were students in'—Lucinda broke off as she suddenly saw the hurt look in Jimmy's eyes, realising he thought she had continued an affair during their time together. She was quick to allay his fears—'It ended Jimmy the day after it began—'

Jimmy interrupted abruptly—'So, just a passing fancy then?' he spouted, unable to hide the sarcasm that had unceremoniously crept into his voice.

'No...no Jimmy, it wasn't like that—'

Jimmy interrupted for a second time, as his voice took on an irascible tone. 'So what was it *like* exactly?' His direct manner, so unlike Jimmy, brought a fresh flood of tears from a broken hearted Lucinda. Jimmy would not be silenced, as his unaccountable urge to belittle her continued unabated. 'I didn't realise you were that sort of girl. I wouldn't have entered into a relationship with you if I had known.'

Despite Jimmy's unbridled tirade, Lucinda managed to calm herself. She knew he would be hurt and angered, but he deserved the truth and needed to hear the whole story. Determined to reveal all, she continued—'Jimmy, please let me explain. You are making it sound sordid, but for my part, I didn't see it like that.

'Harry was someone I had admired from afar for a long time, but he never knew I existed when he courted Anne. He was someone who's always used women and discarded them when he got his way.

'When I met him years later, he seemed a changed man. He helped me with my shopping, which spilled out of my bag, after he literally bumped into me on the stairwell of my apartment. I foolishly invited him in for a coffee and he behaved like the perfect gentleman. He asked to see me again and in my naivety I agreed; little did I know the only thing he wanted me for was sex. He told me his girlfriend had just finished with him and I felt flattered that he wanted to get to know me. I must admit, he made me feel good about myself, at a time when I lacked confidence.

'The following day, however, after he had wined and dined me, we went back to my apartment and...and Jimmy'—she broke off and stared shamefaced at the floor, before continuing in a voice full of emotion—'he seduced me. In fact, some would say he raped me, then he walked out of my life. I never saw him again...That's the truth Jimmy.'

A shell-shocked Jimmy stood up and pulled his hands through his hair in a gesture of anger and distress. *What on earth should I do now? What a shocking thing to have happened.* He gathered himself together and pulled Lucinda into his arms, holding her close. *She hadn't deserved that,* he thought. They stood for several minutes before Jimmy released her. He spoke soothingly. 'I am so sorry Lucinda. Why didn't you tell me sooner? The man is a monster. Did you report it?' he asked.

'No, Jimmy, I couldn't prove anything. He would have said I was a willing participant and up to a point I was. I wanted him to like me and allowed him to kiss me, which I admit to enjoying, but that was all. However, he wouldn't stop and continued, despite my protestations.

'After he'd finished, he treated me with disdain, called me a tease then walked out, slamming the door. I felt ashamed and stupid. I stayed in my flat for days until I started my job on the *Dreadnought*. I thought I could make a fresh start and put it all behind me, especially when you and I got together. I was so happy Jimmy. I never meant to deceive you and maybe I would have told you eventually, but I was scared you wouldn't want me and I didn't want to lose you,' Lucinda explained, hoping there was still a chance for them, but as she looked into Jimmy's eyes she knew she had lost him; all she could see was pity. It was all over for them.

※

After a long interlude where neither spoke, she decided she would be the one to settle their future, to save them both from embarrassment. 'I understand that we cannot possibly continue with our relationship Jimmy. You don't have to worry, I won't make a fuss. I just ask that we remain friends. I have decided to leave the ship when she docks. Helen has invited me to stay with her parents for a few weeks. I will return to England for the birth and later take up my nursing post again on the *Dreadnought,* unless an opportunity presents itself closer to my parents home, where I hope to live for a while.'

Jimmy breathed a sigh of relief. He couldn't help but feel very sorry for Lucinda; after all, they did have something special for a short time and the circumstances were almost beyond her control. He would try to help her all he could in the time they had left together. 'I am so sorry things have turned out the way they have Lucinda. Please believe me when I say, I thought my future was with you, but I find I cannot bring up another man's child. I hope you understand. It is a good idea to stay with Helen's parents; it will give you time to come to terms with your pregnancy. I am sure your parents will help you through this when you return to England. Would you like me to stay with you for a while, as I am off duty for the rest of today?'

Lucinda wanted more than anything to spend time with Jimmy, but found herself declining his offer. 'It's okay Jimmy, if you don't mind I would like some time on my own. Perhaps you could find Helen and ask her to come and see me?'

'Of course, is there anything else I can do? Otherwise, perhaps the four of us could meet again soon?' said Jimmy benevolently.

'No there is nothing you can do Jimmy, but I would like for us to meet up when you and Jack are next off duty,' Lucinda confirmed.

Jimmy placed his hand on Lucinda's arm and kissed her lightly on the cheek, before leaving her alone in the room.

Several days later, they all met for lunch in the women's stateroom. The atmosphere, although initially tense, became less so as time moved on. Helen and Jack behaved sensitively by keeping the conversation light and Jimmy included Lucinda in his conversations. After lunch Lucinda intimated she needed to talk to Jimmy. 'Would you come for a walk with me on deck Jimmy, there is something I have to say?'

Jimmy was unsure but whispered, 'Okay, but I cannot be too long, as I am on duty again in half an hour.'

'I understand Jimmy. Please don't be concerned, it isn't connected to us getting back together, rather the opposite.'

Jimmy was intrigued. What could Lucinda have to say to him?

There was a cool breeze blowing on deck and Jimmy took off his coat, placing it around Lucinda's shoulders. 'Thank you Jimmy, I hadn't realised the temperature had dropped so dramatically since yesterday.' As she looked out over the ship's rails at the miles of ocean spread out before her, it reminded her of the emptiness she would feel when Jimmy was gone. The act of placing his coat over her was just one of many things she would miss of his kind and thoughtful ways.

Jimmy turned to face her. 'What is it you wanted to talk to me about Lucinda?'

Lucinda bit her lip as she conjured up the courage to speak. 'I wanted to say thank you for everything you have done for me since we met. You have made me understand that not all men are the same. Some like you are caring and unselfish, loving and loyal. I will miss you so much Jimmy and will always regret that my foolish mistake, deprived me of happiness,' she admitted.

Jimmy was embarrassed by her forthrightness and felt guilty that her pregnancy wasn't the only determining factor in their break up. He lay his hand on her arm to comfort her, but could not think of anything to say to lessen her sadness.

Lucinda continued, 'It is because you are such a wonderful person, that I want you to take back the ring your mother gave to me,' she announced, twisting it off her finger and holding it out to Jimmy.

Jimmy hesitated before folding her hand to cover the ring. 'Keep it Lucinda, my mam gave it to you for saving her life. I know she would want you to have it and I told you that whatever happens between us, the ring should remain with you.'

Tears formed in Lucinda's eyes as she held the ring out to Jimmy once more. 'That's very kind of you Jimmy, but I have my reasons for returning it to you—'

Jimmy interjected, 'What reasons?'

'The first reason is, every time I look at the ring, it will remind me, not of the happiness we shared, but the sadness I will feel every day after we part and secondly, the ring has been in your family for a very long time and meant so much to your mam. I feel that when she generously gave the ring to me, she believed we would be together forever. It's only right that the ring should pass down to you Jimmy and you should give it to the girl you intend to marry. It should be kept in the family, do you understand?' asked a determined Lucinda.

Jimmy solemnly took the ring and placed it in his pocket. 'Perhaps you are right and perhaps not, but I will do as you suggest. I won't forget you Lucinda and I am still very fond of you. I hope everything works out well and believe me when I say, you will find someone else, someone who will return your love. You are a wonderful person and deserve to find happiness.' Jimmy spoke with honesty and a certain sadness, even though he knew it was right for them to part.

Lucinda turned and hurried towards the companionway back to her state-room to be alone with her sorrow. Jimmy watched her go and then looked out over the horizon. What, he wondered, did his future hold? Would his love for Rosie be reciprocated? Whatever the outcome, he knew for certain, being 'fond' of someone wasn't enough. He had known true love with Rosie and nothing less would do.

CHAPTER EIGHTEEN

Mixed Emotions
January 1856

Lizzie and Rosie, full of anticipation and excitement, approached a pair of gates, supported by brick pillars, beyond which lay the imposing late eighteenth century property on Back Lane. Lizzie engaged the rope pull, which sounded an ornate bell, beside the heavily panelled door on the east side of the house. Almost immediately, the door opened. A smartly dressed butler greeted them cordially and introduced himself as Joseph, but regretted that the owners were not presently at home. However, he was to give the women a tour of the house instead.

Once inside, they became spellbound, in awe of the grandeur of the spacious hall, the large open panelled staircase with its scrolled handrail and stick balusters. Rosie already had visions of wearing an expensive 'Charles Worth' gown and making a grand entrance, with Jimmy waiting patiently in the hall to accompany her to dinner.

Her thoughts were interrupted by Joseph, who suggested they follow him to the dining room with its splendid wall panels and cornice. They noticed that the central classical wooden fireplace, had a hob grate and the whole room was light and airy. The front living room to the left had panelling and door-cases with dentillated cornices, similar to the hall; most rooms presented exceedingly well. In fact, the whole house they judged to be spectacular, on all three floors and both wings. Joseph, their inspirational guide was both informative and solicitous during their hour and a half tour, which continued outside. The grounds extended on all sides, with two paddocks and a stable block. Lizzie felt that, if anything, the house might be too large, but Rosie instantly fell in love and set to convincing her mam of its advantages. 'Remember Mam, Marcus did suggest you take a tour so he must have considered its size after he'd viewed the plans. You did mention we required a couple of wings, along with the main house; one for Grandma and Granddad and the other for myself and Jack. There's staff quarters too, so can we buy it Mam…please?' Rosie was at her most persuasive.

Her excited demeanour and extremely determined face, it seemed, persuaded Lizzie. She had to admit that the large house had a welcoming feel and, as Rosie correctly pointed out, Marcus had apparently already made up *his* mind.

'Very well Rosie, but there is nothing we can do before Marcus returns, which will not be before the 6th March; that's another five weeks, so you will have to be patient until then. It will be May before we are able to move,' Lizzie explained.

'Oh Mam, I don't care, May will be here sooner than you think. Will Grandma and Granddad move in then or will they come later?'

'Oh, a couple of months after I would imagine Rosie. All our furniture has to be sent down and we'll need extra staff. I hope Elspeth, Polly, Annie and Jacob will relocate with us and we will need dedicated staff to take care of Grandma and Granddad. Apparently, a workhouse was built thirty years ago on the outskirts of Southwell, so we might be able to recruit our staff from there. I believe everyone deserves a second chance in life and there are good people who end up there because they cannot find work.'

'Of course Mam, some from Narrow Marsh may have gone there as a last resort, when they could not make ends meet.'

'Indeed Rosie, but for now, let's explore the rest of the town. I know Granddad will be pleased there is an inn on this very lane, the *Black Horse*, so he won't have far to go for a quiet pint of ale. Grandma will love the small market in the centre where she can buy any small items she needs. It seems every convenience is within walking distance in Southwell and interestingly, there is talk of a new train branch line linking Southwell to the main line to Nottingham. That would be splendid and so convenient,' enthused Lizzie.

The following morning, Lizzie stumbled out of bed, pulling on her dressing gown to sit by the window. Nothing had changed since yesterday. The publican was rolling empty barrels across the yard of the inn before stacking them against a wall. Several pigeons were scratching around seeking crumbs. The drayman, whose cart contained replacement barrels of beer, was guiding his large Shire horses through the back gates into the yard and beyond them, several people were hurrying to and fro. She observed a baker's boy returning to the bakery, after his delivery, ringing the bell on his bike to alert everyone walking along the cobbles, which was just as well, as without brakes, he was unable to stop. The daily hustle and bustle of life was continuing, but Lizzie, felt empty and alone, she missed Marcus and couldn't wait for his return.

His ship was due to arrive in New York about now. He would then finalise the will with the solicitor and agree all other matters with Edward Bernstein, before his return journey. For her, that could not come a moment too soon. For a while, she continued to observe the now deserted yard. All the hustle and bustle had abated, but alone with her thoughts she chastised herself. She needed to be strong, while Marcus was away; consequently, she would start planning their move, which would mean less for him to do on his return. She acknowledged that he would still be grieving, so would need her support.

※

A minute later there was a tap on the door, then Rosie breezed in before exuberantly plonking herself down on Lizzie's bed. She was puzzled to find her mam sitting at the window in her dressing robe, oblivious to her presence. 'Good morning, Mam,' she said cheerily, but received no reply. She approached slowly, then placed her hand on her mother's shoulder. 'Mam, are you all right?' she asked, noting the thoughtful look on her face.

Lizzie reluctantly acknowledged Rosie's presence. 'I…I'm fine Rosie. It's just that there is so much to do and I miss Marcus. I can't wait for his return.'

'Oh Mam, I do understand. By my reckoning, he should arrive in Liverpool in around three weeks time. Don't worry though, we will be that busy, it will fly by. Let's cheer ourselves up by joining Grandma and Granddad for breakfast. If I know Granddad, he will have the kettle on and Grandma will be cooking her famous bacon and eggs. If we are lucky, there will be fried bread as well. I will wait for you downstairs, while you get dressed then we can go straight over.'

Lizzie attempted a brave smile, as it was impossible to remain downhearted in Rosie's company for long. 'All right Rosie, I will be fifteen minutes. I am sorry I am not in fine fettle this morning, but you are right, I need to keep myself busy.'

Rosie turned to go, but remembered a message received from Kate. 'Before I forget Mam, you know mamma Kate delayed her birthday celebrations, well, I received another letter today inviting us down to Oxford for an alternative celebration on Marcus's return. She wants to discuss a suitable date with you,' explained Rosie.

༺༻

In no time at all, they were tucking in to a hearty breakfast at number fourteen. Clara bustled around from kitchen to living room and back, adding to the pile of bacon, until there was enough to feed the entire street. Lizzie's melancholia disappeared as she was caught up in the familiar jovial atmosphere of Clara and Arthur's home, which reminded her how lucky she was to have such a supportive family.

CHAPTER NINETEEN

End of the Road March 1856

A clear blue sky greeted the *Champion of the Seas* as she sailed into Port Phillip harbour and then Melbourne docks. It was the last day of March.

Lucinda, Jimmy, Helen and Jack descended the gangway and stepped foot on Australian soil with mixed emotions. All were looking forward to a bright future, except Lucinda, who seemed apprehensive. She'd blossomed during the voyage and now, at almost five months pregnant, could not deny she was with child.

Jimmy was supportive, but she knew their relationship was at an end. Lucinda realised that today would probably be the last time she would ever see him and her sadness was multiplied by the uncertainness of her future. She tried to put on a brave face, suggesting they find a café for a final meal together, before she and Helen left for Helen's parents home. Jimmy agreed, eventually finding a table in a popular café favoured by visitors from the ships. He ordered everyone sandwiches and coffee, but even this failed to erase Lucinda's melancholia.

The somewhat surreal atmosphere, gave rise to a speculative question from Jack, designed to break the ice. 'How long do you envisage staying with your parents Helen?' he asked, hoping the answer would be 'not too long'.

Helen smiled, making eye contact with Jack. 'Well Jack, I initially planned to stay for two months; however, that now depends on Lucinda. If she decides to return home, it may be less, but I will support her whatever she decides.'

Helen's statement gave Lucinda the opportunity to share her thoughts without the embarrassment of speaking directly to Jimmy, which would have been awkward; consequently, she was grateful.

She took a deep breath and controlling her voice, she laid bare her plans. 'I intend to stay for around two weeks with Helen's parents, subject to them agreeing to accommodate me.' She thankfully noted that Helen was eagerly nodding in the affirmative and gaining confidence, she continued—'I will then return to my parents home for the birth. I don't know if I will keep the baby, but I know I need to think long and hard before I make such a big decision,' she said trying to gauge their reaction.

Helen smiled encouragingly, but Jack raised his eyebrows in surprise at the notion that Lucinda might have the baby adopted. However, Jimmy remained non-committal, shielded by his coffee cup, as he took a slow sip. Unfortunately, his attempt to hide his embarrassment failed, as he felt a rush of blood creep up his neck. He was aware that all three were expecting a comment from him, but words seemed to stick in his throat as he stared fixedly past Lucinda at the exit to the café. He would have given anything at that moment to be able to walk straight out of the open door and into the fresh air.

Luckily, Jack came to his rescue, making light of the situation. 'It sounds as if you have thought this out Lucinda. No doubt you'll receive help and support in Australia and back in England, but I admire your fortitude and courage. Your nursing skills will be a big help when your baby finally arrives and who knows, it may even be a very exciting time for you'—he paused—'If, of course, you decide to keep it?' encouraged Jack meaningfully.

At this point, Helen offered her advice. 'Jack is right Lucinda, you have so much support already and I expect your parents will want you to move in with them if you keep the baby. They could employ a nanny, if you wish to continue your career. You never know, you might meet a handsome young doctor to sweep you off your feet at the General Hospital.' Helen laughed conspiratorially.

Lucinda took the bait and smiled confidently before answering. 'Of course Helen. I am still young and I know my parents would love a grandchild. Maybe I will meet my knight in shining armour...we'll see. There are plenty of opportunities in Cambridge,' she asserted, focussing on Jimmy, who could no longer dodge making a contribution to the conversation.

He had to step up to the mark, so intended to make a bold suggestion. When staying with Lucinda's parents he'd grown significantly in confidence and stature and more recently aboard ship. Could he carry it off? He judged by their expectant faces, that there wasn't a choice.

'Well,' he began emphatically, holding Lucinda's expectant gaze, 'I think you could do really well Lucinda. I for one do not doubt your ability, both in securing a nursing post and bringing up a baby. You are really organised, so with your parents help, you could make it work. I also have no doubt that a worthier person than myself will come along...I'm sure there will be many because you are a beautiful woman Lucinda, inside and out. I am just sorry that it did not work out for us. Of course, you must let us know as soon as the baby is born...we are still your friends and you must count on us for support in the future.' Jimmy, surprised at his assured delivery, finished abruptly. He looked around the table and realised all three were staring at him in awe of his magnificent oration. Indeed, from their expressions, he half expected a rousing cheer and a round of applause. He had never before spoken at such length and with such deliberation, which surprised even himself. With the ice truly broken, their animated conversation flowed like old times, all being relieved and, therefore, uninhibited by unforeseen circumstance.

Later, as Helen and Lucinda hailed a cab to take them to Helen's parents, an air of optimism reigned. Helen and Jack's kiss goodbye was slow and sensual, which promised a future together after several months apart. Jimmy hugged Lucinda and kissed her on the cheek, before whispering 'good luck' in her ear. Although she'd quickly turned away, she'd taken courage from Jimmy's assessment of her future. A life without him was inconceivable in that instant and despite her bravado, a tear slid down her face. She knew she would miss him terribly.

Helen eventually tore herself away from Jack. He, concerned at the length of time they would be apart, asked her to write to him, pressing a note with the address of *The Beeches*, into her palm, before she embarked on the coach. Delighted with his commitment, she held his gaze until it rounded a corner and he was lost from view. Jack and Jimmy exchanged a brief acknowledgement of understanding then turned together to return to the ship. Their lives had changed dramatically and significantly since the *Champion of the Seas* departed Liverpool just twelve weeks previously.

CHAPTER TWENTY

Reflections
February 1856

Twelve days into February and back at home for almost a week, Lizzie and Rosie had successfully organised *The Beeches* sale; having already agreed the Southwell property purchase. Of course, it was a big decision, but one, which Lizzie believed Marcus would want her to make in his absence. However, embarking on such a venture was not so exhilarating as she'd imagined. Two more weeks remained before Marcus would return and the time was dragging interminably.

Fortunately, this morning her feeling of loneliness did not last long. Rosie, true to form, began talking animatedly about their forthcoming move, as she swept in for breakfast. Lizzie counted her blessings; Rosie had a knack of lifting her spirits.

'This is so exciting Mam,' enthused her daughter and Lizzie couldn't help but agree.

Rosie offered her a cup of breakfast tea, whilst wondering whether, despite the decision to move and their initial exuberance, that Marcus's absence might be affecting her mother more than she envisaged.

'Thank you Rosie, you've cheered me up already. I was just thinking how Marcus's negotiations with the solicitor were faring and how long it will take to tie up all the loose ends, before returning. His ship was due in Philadelphia on the sixth, so he will have been there for almost a week already.'

'Well Mam, if I know Marcus, he will conclude everything as soon as is humanly possible. There isn't any reason for him to delay as he will be keen to return. Don't worry Mam, Marcus could be back by the 1st of March and that's only just over two weeks away.'

Lizzie cupped Rosie's face in her hand and smiled lovingly at her daughter. 'Do you know Rosie, your optimism always reminds me to look on the bright side of life. Why, at this very moment he may be purchasing a ticket for the return journey to England.'

'Absolutely and by the end of June, Jack and Jimmy will be in England too. We have so much to look forward to Mam. Marcus would be cross if he knew you were mouching[61] about, feeling sad. What we should be doing is deciding what furniture we need to take and clearing out some of our clutter[62]. If you like, we could take some boxes of items we no longer need to the church, so they can be distributed to the poorer people of the parish.

'Do you remember the rag and bone man[63] coming before dawn in the Marsh and the sound of his gruff voice

---

61 *Mouching - 1425-75; late Middle English, apparently variant of Middle English michen < Old French muchier to skulk, hide.*

62 *Origin of clutter - 1550-60; variant of clotter (now obsolete). Disorganised items*

63 *In the UK, 19th-century rag-and-bone men scavenged unwanted rags, bones, metal and other waste, from the towns and cities where they lived. Henry Mayhew's 1851 report, 'London Labour and the London Poor', estimates that in London, between 800 and 1,000 'bone-grubbers and 'rag-gatherers' lived in lodging houses, garrets and 'ill-furnished' rooms in the lowest neighbourhoods. White rag could fetch 2–3 pence per pound, depending on condition. Coloured rag was worth about two pence per pound. Bones, worth about the same, could be used as knife handles, toys and ornaments, and when treated, for chemistry. The grease extracted from them was also useful for soap-making. Metal was more valuable and*

crying out 'Rag, bone, rag, bone'? Grandma would be out the door in an instant, struggling with her bag of rags, ensuring Granddad had a few pence to afford his half pint of ale.' Rosie laughed, which elicited a smile from Lizzie.

'Indeed I do, but that seems a very long time ago.' She sighed as she reflected on how life had changed dramatically since those early days. Neither dreamt of purchasing such a magnificent property just a few miles from the centre of the beautiful Borough of Nottingham[64]. However, they would never forget the harsh times when Clara helped Lizzie to bring up Rosie. If Arthur and David had not found Lizzie on the tow path, she probably would have died, or at best been condemned to the workhouse, which reminded Lizzie that she needed to visit the Southwell Workhouse sooner rather than later.

'Rosie, I suggest that tomorrow we take a train to Nottingham; I have something I need to do. We can stay at the King's Arms and, of course, visit Grandma and Granddad again. Unless, of course, you've made other plans to visit mamma Kate?'

'street-grubbers' could be seen scraping away the dirt between the paving stones of non-macadamised roads searching for horseshoe nails. Brass, copper and pewter was valued at about 4–5 pence per pound. In a typical day, a rag-and-bone man might expect to earn about six pence.

64 *Nottingham was one of the Boroughs reformed by the Municipal Corporations Act 1835 and at that time consisted of the parishes of St Mary, St Nicholas and St Peter. The population in 1851 totalled 58,000. Nottingham has a very small official city boundary, hence the small population of just 306,000 (2017). In the early 18th century, an amateur botanist and historian, Dr Deering, chose Nottingham to live in, since, with its orchards, river meadows and large gardens 'were a naturalist in quest of an exquisite spot to build a town or city upon'. Nottingham became known as 'The Garden City'*

Rosie pulled a face then inclined her head, instantly reviewing her options. She had not seen Kate since Christmas and in February, her mamma's birthday plans had been put on hold until the end of the March. Consequently, she really needed to see her. 'Mmm, Mamma did suggest I visit, so I should probably do that this weekend, but that still gives me a couple of days to see Grandma. Would that be all right?'

'Yes of course, Rosie, but first things first, let's pack the boxes and take them over to the church this afternoon, before we depart for Nottingham in the morning.'

CHAPTER TWENTY-ONE

The Workhouse
February 1856

Lizzie set out for Southwell[65] Workhouse[66] very early on a bright February morning. She noted it was located a short distance from the small settlement of Upton on Greet Lane. When her coach drew up on the forecourt, outside the main entrance, Lizzie thanked the driver, requesting he return in two hours time.

She did not enter the building immediately, but walked the length of a long path, which cut through the gardens, to get a feel for the institution. She needed to decide how best to approach the matter of hiring an 'inmate' to look after Clara and Arthur.

Several thin wiry men, in workhouse uniform, were working the large vegetable plots on each side of the path.

---

65 *The population of Southwell (South of the Well) remained fairly static during the 19th century, around 3,000. Today it is has doubled to about 6,000.*

66 *The Workhouse, Southwell - The Workhouse is a huge building, or, rather, a set of connected buildings, constructed in 1824 by Rev John Becher of Southwell, as a residence for the poor. Men, women, and children had separate quarters, which meant that families were split up and not allowed to meet. Becher aimed at moral improvement; by dint of tedious, hard work idle folk were supposed to be converted to a more upright lifestyle. Rules were strict and transgressions were harshly punished. Life was regimented and strictly controlled, under the watchful eye of a paid Master and Matron.*

They were engaged in hoeing, digging and weeding, overseen by a warden. None dared to look up as she passed, but when she reached the bottom of the gardens, she turned to survey the imposing three storey high building. She counted fifteen bays, noticing a central, full height canted bay with a hipped roof, which constituted the entrance. Shallow stone arches and sills encased the windows, divided into thirty small panes by iron strips. It seemed a forbidding place and presented a daunting prospect for Lizzie.

After a few minutes lost in thought, she walked back to the main forecourt. Taking a deep breath, she pulled the cord, which activated a brass bell. The door was immediately opened by a large military looking woman with a sallow face, whose pinched lips showed a row of large teeth. She vociferously gave the order to *'step inside!'* and Lizzie nervously obeyed, finding herself in a large area, known as the 'Committee' room. Only then did 'severe woman' enquire as to her identity.

The Master's room stood to the right and a kitchen to the left. At the end of the Committee room was a door to the schoolroom and in between, strictly for the Master's use, a wide staircase to the first floor.

Lizzie was announced to the Master in the same cutting voice and ushered in. 'Sit here,' ordered the woman, before turning to leave. Her 'designated' upright chair faced a large oak desk, behind which sat a rather austere gentleman, who appeared much older than his forty-five years. His lank greying hair poked out from beneath a black top hat, continuing into straggly side burns, before culminating in a sparse beard. His neatly tended moustache seemed totally incongruous to the rest of his appearance. It was indeed unfortunate that his black frock coat, high collared white shirt and black cravat, accentuated his pallid skin, which gave him a haunted look. However, this didn't prevent him staring salaciously at this good-looking visitor, whom it would appear required his assistance. Peering over his pince-nez, he produced a weak pencil-lipped smile, which failed to disguise his innermost thoughts.

Lizzie gained the measure of Mr Edward Fullerton within the first few minutes of being in his presence. He was, she believed, a man of few words, but capable of getting his own way by fair means or foul. She took an instant dislike to him but, as she required his assistance in recruiting a nursemaid for Clara, she returned his 'What can I do for you madam?' with a warm smile.

He was curious. She had piqued his interest. It was highly unusual for ladies of wealth and breeding to require an audience in an establishment such as this. It put him on the back foot. Maybe, he thought, that despite her obvious good looks and friendly manner, she could be just another frigid 'spinster' from the church, who would offer to 'heal' some of the scum under his control, by paying them a monthly visit; thereby changing filthy habits and lazy personas. She would fail miserably, of course, as the majority of inmates were, without doubt, a lost cause. Nevertheless, he would still grant such a request, as the prospect of conversing with this woman on occasion was certainly preferable to the daily, unavoidable ritual, of negotiating with his sour faced Matron.

Since being widowed ten years previously, Edward Fullerton had had little contact with women. He had secured the respectable post of *'Master of the Workhouse'*, shortly after his wife's death. He no longer had designs on becoming the *'Lord of the Manor'*, where he'd be expected to attend church and maintain a high profile around town. Neither did he have any desire to take another frigid wife. He was more than happy to have meals served to him with staff kowtowing to his every need. The constant daily nagging and 'holier than thou' attitude of another wife, who would undoubtedly spend his money and deprive him of his conjugal rights, was not something he wished to embrace.

He'd closed up the large house he owned on the Burgage in Southwell, much to the annoyance of neighbours. Most were appalled at the prospect of such a wonderful property going to rack and ruin. Fortunately for him, there were no children in the marriage to inherit, a fact to which he was eternally grateful. He'd had no desire to be surrounded by loud, offensive, demanding brats, who as they grew older, would no doubt bleed him dry, demanding money because they believed they should not work.

However, he could now please himself as to how he conducted his life. His leisure time consisted of visiting a gentlemen's club in the centre of a wealthy part of Nottingham, which his now deceased wife considered an unacceptable past time. As an atheist, he did not attend church; however, his wife had devoted most of her time to flower arranging, visiting the sick and other 'god-fearing' matters.

She also suffered from 'women's issues' early on in their marriage, so all his sexual needs were curtailed. Fortunately, a 'maid of all works', an orphan, whom his wife had taken in after she found her praying in the church, was the poor unfortunate, to suffer his demands.

He was secretly disgusted at lowering himself to seek gratification with such a woman and it left him with a deep contempt for any woman without breeding. The maid, who felt genuinely indebted to his wife, left immediately after she died. The fact that the position of 'Master' at the Southwell Workhouse became vacant, determined him to abandon his property, until he decided what to do with it.

At the Workhouse, Edward had a large private office and a bedroom on the first floor, accessed by his own private staircase. He enjoyed fortnightly visits from a mystery woman of ill repute; unbeknownst to all staff, bar the Matron, who chose to turn a blind eye. However, this particular woman, he reconciled, was the antithesis of her kind, previously a person of breeding whom had fallen on hard times. This, in his mind, lent respectability to the liaison.

She was the wife of one of his close friends at the club, but after his death, she drank away the money left in his will, after discovering he had re-mortgaged their home, in order to buy his mistress a property on the other side of town. She managed to survive for a short while, by inviting men from her husband's club to sleep with her for money. This included Edward Fullerton; but eventually the Bank foreclosed on the mortgage. She later came to an agreement with Fullerton. If he bought her a modest property on the outskirts of town, she would repay him in kind with her 'favours'. However, Fullerton remained oblivious to the fact that she continued to prostitute herself, which enabled her to afford the expensive clothes and lavish lifestyle to which she had become accustomed.

She always arrived by coach, dressed as a respectable upper class lady, but refrained from speaking to anyone at the Workhouse, entering the building with her own key, like clockwork, once a fortnight. She would silently make her way to Fullerton's bedroom up the broad staircase, adjacent to his office. There she would wait for him to arrive. Usually, their sexual liaison took less than half an hour, before she left by the same route.

She presumed that this arrangement, distasteful as it was, would eventually result in him asking her to become his wife. She could then take up her rightful place as the new mistress of his substantial property and would once again become a woman that commanded respect. No longer would she suffer the humiliation of being abused by men from all walks of life. She reflected that she loathed them all, including Edward Fullerton. If she were mistress of his house, her first priority would be to hire a willing maid to provide her husband with sexual favours. Perhaps then he would leave *her* alone. However, her patience was wearing thin. This was the second year of her visits and yet no mention had been forthcoming from Fullerton of a permanent relationship. She could not have known, but Edward Fullerton had no desire to remarry and was happy for the 'arrangement' to continue ad infinitum without commitment.

༄

Fullerton, who had initially been appraising Mrs Van der Duim as a possible replacement for his present mistress, with whom he had become bored, suddenly realised she was waiting for an answer. He had half-heartedly followed the gist of her conversation, when he belatedly realised, much to his disappointment, that she was not to become a regular visitor.

It dawned on him that he would probably never see her again. This fact significantly diminished his interest in her as a woman and prospective lover. How anyone could want anything to do with the scroungers and *ne'er do wells* that inhabited his Workhouse was beyond him.

Consequently, he decided Matron would be the best person to sort out his dilemma and advised Lizzie as such. He didn't care whether Mrs Van der Duim secured a nursemaid, or not, only that she took leave of his office. Her use to him had dwindled to only that of nuisance value in the last few minutes.

Hardly concealing a yawn, he glanced at the large clock on the wall behind Lizzie. To his horror, he realised his mistress would be arriving at any moment. Despite the repetitive nature of his trysts, he still needed his gratification, until a replacement could be found, so needed to keep her sweet. To this end, Fullerton, rang the bell, to summon Matron to take over. Unfortunately, a prior incident with an inmate required her immediate attention and an unforeseen delay occurred, resulting in an embarrassingly uncomfortable silence.

A few minutes passed. Lizzie's attention was drawn to Fullerton's impatient drumming of his fingers on his blotter, while he seemed fixated on the view out of his window. She followed his line of sight and saw inmates being steered into the tiny exercise yards. She shuddered, realising they were observed by this obsequious man, even at 'rest'. All inmates were watched over like criminals it seemed, so much so that Lizzie became more determined to employ at least one of the inmates, saving them from humiliation and other abuse.

Her attention returned to Fullerton, who remained impassive waiting for Matron to arrive. His inadequacy to hold a conversation with Lizzie, whose eyes were now boring into his own, was causing him considerable embarrassment, which added to his annoyance. The absence of the Matron meant he was compelled to spend more time than was necessary with Mrs Van der Duim and less with his mistress.

He fidgeted in his chair, as he watched the seconds slowly tick by on the mantel clock. He was becoming anxious and pushed his pince-nez to the highest point on the bridge of his nose, until they slid again, settling on the large bulbous part containing his nostrils. This action resulted in Lizzie's sudden urge to laugh, as she remembered Myrtle Barnes, Rachael Phillips private tutor to her children, Olivia and

Isobel, before Lizzie took over. Their disrespectful but humorous name of 'Speccy', personified the continual adjustment of her pince-nez worn for myopia. Fullerton's unintentional mimicry meant Lizzie's powers of self-control were pushed to the limit.

⁂

More minutes passed agonisingly slowly; neither Fullerton nor Lizzie uttered a sound until finally, the door opened and Matron entered, her lips already contorted into a formal cold smile. She raised an eyebrow, following an explanation by Fullerton of Lizzie's unusual request.

An extremely brief 'good-day' signalled Fullerton's departure, leaving Lizzie to follow Miss Barnfather out into the Committee room. However, not before she noticed Fullerton's 'visitor', flaunting her skirts as she ascended the stairs. Another 'unusual' guest today, she thought wryly.

Miss Barnfather, ushered Lizzie into her office and indicated a chair. 'Now Mrs Van der Duim...oh, have I pronounced that correctly?' she added dryly. 'Am I to understand you actually wish to offer a job to one of the women presently under our jurisdiction?'

Lizzie sitting upright, was not intimidated by this formidable woman, so answered forcefully, 'I believe,' she began, 'that everyone deserves a second chance in life and to that end, I propose to offer a position in my household to someone deserving of such a post,' explained Lizzie, confusing Miss Barnfather with an engaging smile.

Miss Barnfather, totally unconvinced, continued to interrogate Lizzie. 'I see Mrs Van der Duim and do you expect to find such a creature within these walls?' she asked, an expression of incredulity clouding her face.

'Indeed I do,' ventured Lizzie. 'I would also hope that you could recommend someone to me, as you should know the women here very well.'

'Humph,' breathed Miss Barnfather. 'You will understand that a request such as this would have to be put before the Board, as it is highly unusual,' she stated, observing Lizzie's obvious resolve.

Lizzie decided to reveal something of her own early life, before becoming a woman of means. It might appeal to Matron's better nature she thought. 'I realise that, but I didn't always have an easy life myself and if it were not for certain people helping me through a very difficult time, I might have found myself in an institution such as this one,' said Lizzie forcefully, after abruptly ending her tale, to gauge whether Barnfather would accede to her request and to convince her that not everyone was an unworthy, lazy *creature* beyond redemption.

Miss Barnfather held Lizzie's stare, but her resolve began to crumble. There was something about this determined woman, that appealed to her sensibilities, which in turn reminded her of her own sister's unfortunate position, a few years earlier when her husband became bankrupt. He'd made a bad investment and their modest house was put on the market, to cover his substantial debts. Soon after that sale, the couple parted and her sister was left penniless. She could have taken her in of course, but that would have meant her sister moving two hundred miles away from her present home and friends.

However, help came from an unlikely source. Her sister's neighbour wanted to invest in a property close by, to provide accommodation for a nursemaid to administer to her ailing husband. A live-in 'nurse' was out of the question, so she capitalised on the opportunity to buy the house.

Miss Barnfather's sister could continue on as a tenant, if she agreed to become nursemaid to her husband. In the event, the arrangement worked very well and her sister's pride was left intact.

※

Maybe, she *could* help Mrs Van der Duim and furnish her own coffers at the same time, by recommending someone who had been in the Workhouse for a few years, along with her elderly and ailing mother. The younger woman was able bodied, but by getting rid of both, she could save money, as the old lady contributed hardly anything in labour. She would ask Mrs Van der Duim for a reasonable sum of money, without recourse to any approval by the Board. In truth, she would, of course, pocket the money, which she felt should be hers. After all, an arrangement such as this needed careful planning and a great deal of subterfuge, which risked her position. This salved her conscience somewhat.

Segregation remained an important part of the harsh day-to-day regime and the woman she wanted rid of, frequently disobeyed orders and often sneaked up the back staircase to spend time with her infirm mother. This could not continue. If the Master found out, the woman would be reprimanded and placed in a punishment cell. The end result: two inmates with idle hands, so this solution was opportune indeed.

※

The Workhouse had a sophisticated system of double stairs, ensuring that none in one group ever came into contact with inmates of another group. The four dark, steep staircases were separated from each other. This meant that the woman, known as Mary, had little chance of visiting or consoling her mother, who had recently been in isolation in the infirmary, with a severe sickness and diarrhoea. Before she became sick, her mother was to be seen in the infirm dormitory and exercise yard, or engaged in light manual work in the kitchens most days. On one occasion, Matron caught Mary sneaking into the infirm dormitories via a separate staircase, adjacent to the able bodied women's staircase. Locked doors at the top of the landing meant she also had to return to her quarters via the same staircase.

Matron was not amused at Mary's latest disregard of the workhouse rules, which resulted in her being placed on extra duties and severely chastised, although she hadn't reported the incident to the Master.

❦

Eventually, Matron looked up and smiled deviously, which caused Lizzie some disquiet. 'Well Mrs Van der Duim, I have considered your request and I believe I may have someone… in fact two people, who may be interested in accepting your proposal. However, we need to be discreet in this matter, as I don't wish to place your request before the Board, which could take many weeks to gain approval. I'd prefer that these inmates leave with you as soon as possible…today in fact, when everyone will be at lunch.'

Lizzie was shocked and apprehensive at Matron's suggestion. It meant she would have to take the two women back to Littleborough, after saying goodbye to Clara. She was totally unprepared, but it seemed she did not have much choice in the matter, so agreed.

Matron, however, had one final demand, which she enunciated slowly to avoid doubt. 'Of course, the Workhouse will lose two of its inmates, so compensation in the form of a money order to the value of fifty pounds is required. You understand, I am doing this as a favour to you and I will be putting my job on the line, by excluding the Board from this decision. I hope we understand each other,' she emphasised almost menacingly.

'Yes, of course, I understand,' agreed Lizzie, opening her bag to write the money order, before passing it to the Matron. It was, she considered, a small amount to pay to save two poor women from spending one more day in this hell-hole.

'Come with me please,' she ordered, whilst placing the money order in her uniform pocket. 'Both women are engaged in the inner courtyard; Mary is presently employed in the bake-house but her mother is in the infirmary.'

Lizzie followed the Matron into the Committee room, through the schoolroom and into the inner courtyard. There were very few inmates or staff around, as most had moved to the main building for lunch, except those who were tasked with cleaning up the bake-house and two in the infirmary.

The Matron entered the bake-house and was relieved to find Mary alone. Lizzie stepped inside, before Matron shut the door behind them, locking it securely. Mary was surprised and stopped scrubbing the tins, recently used to make bread. The room was hot and her lank hair had escaped from underneath her poke-bonnet, falling forlornly down her thin face. Lizzie noticed the coarse stiff uniform; a shapeless shift, made of striped calico[67], which reached to Mary's ankles. The long stockings and knee-length drawers, obviously adding to her discomfort. Mary stood to attention

---

67 *Calico (in British usage from 1505), is a plain-woven textile made from unbleached and often not fully processed cotton. It may contain unseparated husk parts, for example.*

by the deep sink and stared incomprehensibly at the two women.

Neither Matron, nor Lizzie were prepared for what happened next. A second passed before Mary threw herself at Lizzie's skirts, then pleaded uncontrollably, as she gazed into her eyes. 'Lizzie Cameron! Is it really you?' unable to believe it *was* her long-lost friend standing there as large as life.

Lizzie's eyes engaged Mary's. She felt faint in the room's heat and the shock of finding her best friend, Mairi Mackenzie here in Southwell, but Lizzie didn't hesitate. She pulled Mairi off the floor and hugged her close. Matron looked on in total disbelief.

'Do…do you know this woman Mrs Van der Duim?' she stammered, aghast that there could be any connection between the two.

'Oh yes Matron, I certainly do,' she replied, but I almost did not recognize her. It has been over twenty years since we last saw one another. We were childhood friends in Strathy; that's in the Highlands of Scotland, before I moved to Glasgow with my father.'

Matron composed herself, whilst evaluating the situation. She quickly realized she could turn this meeting into an advantage, finding a valid reason to allow both inmates to leave the institution. 'Fortuitously', a relative had come to take them away. A little white lie, of course, as they were friends, not relations. Nevertheless, that reason would be given to the Master *and* the Board.

'Well now, Mary or should I say Mairi,' Matron corrected herself. 'Your friend'—she paused, showing unconcealed contempt for both women—'Mrs Van der Duim, has requested that you be employed by her to look after her parents and has agreed to take your own mother as well.'

Mairi's eyes filled with tears, which she wiped away with dirt ingrained hands.

'Is it true Lizzie? Can we both come with you?'

'Yes Mairi, it's true, although I cannot believe it myself. The Matron even insists we leave immediately.'

Matron obviously wished to hasten the women's departure and her voice betrayed guilty panic. 'Go immediately and pack a bag, while we collect your mother from the infirmary. Do not speak to anyone, but meet us outside the entrance,' ordered Matron.

Mairi did not need a second invitation and within ten minutes all were standing under the front entrance porch. Bridget Mackenzie, totally speechless after being manhandled by Matron out of the infirmary, thought she recognized the good-looking woman, standing next to her daughter, who was about the same age. There wasn't the chance to study the woman more closely, before a coach and horses pulled up abruptly and she was bundled aboard.

As the horses cantered off down the long driveway, Matron returned to her office with a big smile on her face. She carefully stowed the money order in a locked drawer and made a mental note to visit the bank the following morning.

Shortly afterward, the carriage pulled out of the Workhouse grounds and made its way along the narrow lanes towards Southwell. Bridget peered intently at the woman before she gasped in recognition. She leaned over and took Lizzie by the hand. 'Lizzie Cameron as I live and breathe. It is you isn't it? My I canna believe it. How did you know where to find us?'

'Oh Bridget, it is a very long story, one which I will have the pleasure in telling, but for now you should relax and enjoy the journey.'

A while later, the coachman halted the horses in the courtyard of the Saracen's Head Hotel. Lizzie had already decided that the journey to Littleborough would be too taxing for Bridget and a night at the Saracen's would be prudent and beneficial.

The coachman helped the ladies down. Mairi and Bridget, with much trepidation, followed Lizzie inside the entrance to a small lobby. 'Do sit here, while I book rooms for us.' Lizzie smiled encouragingly, overjoyed at seeing her old friends again.

Mairi and Bridget felt very uncomfortable sitting on beautifully upholstered armchairs attired only in their workhouse uniforms, but did as they were bade, which made Lizzie suddenly remember her first visit to a hotel in Glasgow. Kate had taken her there so that Lizzie could change her clothes before they went shopping. She remembered feeling awkward, until she walked out wearing the glorious cloak given to her by Kate. Consequently, she understood their unease but assured them there was nothing to be embarrassed about. Lizzie walked boldly up to the reception desk and pressed the small brass bell on the counter. Almost immediately, a staff member appeared. 'How can I help you madam,' asked the impeccably dressed, but friendly receptionist.

'I would like to book rooms for one night for three people and wondered if you had a suite available,' enquired an assured Lizzie.

The young woman opened the booking register and smiling informed Lizzie there was a choice of two. 'We have a lovely suite on the first floor with a double and two single beds, a large seating area and its own bathroom, or a suite of slightly smaller proportions to the rear of the hotel, madam.'

Lizzie returning her smile, suggested they would take the former suite on the first floor.

'Does madam have any bags,' enquired the receptionist, noticing Lizzie appeared not to have any luggage.

Lizzie grinned. 'No, as a matter of fact, it was a last minutes decision we made, so no luggage, but I would like to place an order for room service. A pot of coffee, a plate of sandwiches and some fancies would be lovely, if that could be arranged? Would you also arrange for the local doctor to attend to one of my party? She has become very dehydrated and I would appreciate his advice.'

'That's not a problem Madam. The porter will show you to your room.' Up until that point, the receptionist had not seen Lizzie's two travelling companions and was indeed surprised to see two women dressed rather inappropriately for such an establishment as *The Saracens Head*. However, unflinching, she instructed the porter to escort the three guests to the first floor before alerting the kitchen of their needs.

Lizzie followed the porter up the stairs with Mairi and Bridget trailing behind; totally out of their depth. Rather wearily they ascended the stairs with their heads bent. After the porter closed the door behind him, Lizzie hugged her friends in an outpouring of love. All were delighted that they had, at long last, been reunited. Their stories could wait until the food arrived.

Lizzie inspected the bathroom before inviting her friends to make use of the dressing gowns provided. They needed to wash their hair and have a bath[68], before relaxing in the comfortable armchairs.

---

68 *Wealthy households did have splendid bathrooms with some very elaborate and somewhat Heath Robinson-like shower attachments.*

Mairi and Bridget luxuriated in the hot bath, taking time to soak their weary bodies. They had never seen such beautiful soft fluffy towels, placed in the room for their personal use. Lizzie had to remind them to use separate water for each. They had only ever bathed in a tin bath in the scullery in Strathy and then in a shared sink in the Workhouse, so this was indeed a luxury.

A tap on the door announced that the doctor had arrived. He gave Bridget a thorough and efficient examination before declaring that she had a sickness virus. Dr Johnson did not believe it contagious and thought it was probably gastroenteritis. He considered she was over the worse. He left medicine, along with a bill for his services and advised Bridget drink plenty of water and get rest accordingly.

Mairi and Bridget were enjoying the luxury of coffee, sandwiches and fancies when Lizzie enquired how they came to be in Nottingham and finished in the Workhouse.

⁂

Free standing roll top baths were in use in finer homes and hotels during the eighteenth century, but it was during the Victorian era that these became more easily available to the middle classes. These baths may have had a system of hot water running to them thus enabling the bather to enjoy the luxury of turning on the taps. Thomas Crapper, whose name has become synonymous with all things 'toilet' (plumbing) was born in 1836 at Thorne near Doncaster. The name Crapper has been explained as being old Yorkshire, from cropper (possibly some agricultural occupation) and is not, as is popularly believed, the origin of the vernacular term widely in use today. At the age of eleven he left home and walked 165 miles to London and got himself apprenticed to a plumber in Chelsea. By 1861 he had his own business, which became Thos Crapper & Co, Marlborough Works, Chelsea. Thomas Crapper did not invent the flushing lavatory - this was invented by John Harrington in 1596 and Joseph Bramah of Yorkshire patented the first practical water closet in 1778. Plumbing also extended to providing running water for the bath.

Bridget glanced at Mairi and began their story. 'Oh Lizzie, we'd been searching for you for over five years. We decided to leave Strathy and seek work in Glasgow…following in your footsteps. We had no choice but to leave the croft, after the landlord put up the rent. We were practically penniless when we arrived in Glasgow. Fortunately, an old priest took pity on us and invited us to the rectory. He gave us food and a hot drink and even allowed us to use his bath. We mentioned we were looking for a Lizzie Cameron; Josiah Monks was his name and said he knew you very well. He told us you had been employed at Low Wood Hall, but understood that you left some years previously. He did not know where you had gone and told us the Hall now had new owners.

'We almost gave up hope of ever finding you, but Mairi said we should visit the Hall and ask if anyone there knew where you had gone. I wasn't too keen, as them sort o' folk look down on crofters, seeing them as unworthy of breathing the same air'—Bridget paused to finish her sandwich. Then after one more sip from her second cup of coffee, without warning, fell fast asleep, her head lolling on the back of the chair. Lizzie frowned as she covered her with a blanket. 'Poor love, she's totally spent,' said Lizzie.

As Mairi finished most of the fancies, Lizzie remembered her own time with Josiah and the kindness he'd shown. So many years had passed but her recollections were as vivid as the day her father and herself huddled in the shop doorway, when Josiah Monks whisked them back to the rectory.

However, Mairi was keen to continue their story. 'We eventually found the Hall and, as luck would have it, there was a woman there by the name of Dottie. We first saw her coming through the gates on her way to the town. I plucked up courage and asked her if she could help. She was only too pleased to assist and grinning broadly, told us you went down to Nottingham originally, but now thought you may be in Lancashire. Unfortunately, Lancashire covered a very big area, so we decided to try Nottingham first, in the hope of finding someone who might know your whereabouts in Lancashire.

'It took us a long while to save enough money to afford the fare. Mither and me worked really hard. I managed to get a job as a maid in Glasgow, but they said Mither was too old'—she paused, then laughed—'They were probably right but, as you know, Mither has always been used to hard work. We secured lodgings in the Gorbals[69] by the river Clyde and Mither used to 'pull lace' to help pay the rent. It was a terrible area Lizzie. It always smelt awful and we really missed the good clean air of Strathy.

'A year later, having saved enough money, with a little over, to get us to Nottingham, we left, hoping to find you of course and possibly some work. We could not afford lodgings, so made a home in one of the caves just out from the centre of the town. We lived there with a widow and her two children, helping each other out with food and clothing. The only work we could find was 'pulling lace', which affected Mither's fingers. She suffers from arthritis so could only do small amounts.

When she fell sick, I had to look after her, so could not do much in the way of work. Unfortunately, I also fell ill. The

---

[69] *The Gorbals is an area in the city of Glasgow, Scotland, on the south bank of the River Clyde. By the late nineteenth century, it had become densely populated and adversely affected by local industrialisation. Many people lived there because their jobs provided worker housing and they could not afford their own. Poor sanitation and poverty contributed to problems. As industrial jobs declined during restructuring, this area became widely known as a dangerous slum associated with drunkenness and crime.*

widow told us she could not look after us both, so we would have to leave. She could not afford to catch the sickness you see. Anyway, after that we wandered the streets, begging for food.

'Our situation eventually became dire and Mither could hardly walk. I tried to find sanctuary under railway arches and doorways and even scavenged food from bins. We drank water from the standpipes, but in the end Mither could not carry on, she became so ill and weak,' explained Mairi, pausing to wipe the tears that rolled down her face.

'Inevitably, we made the decision to seek refuge at the Workhouse as a last resort. We spent one night under a bridge and the following morning, walked for half the day to Southwell. We'd been told it was better than the Workhouse in Nottingham. It might have been in the countryside, but there was very little 'fresh air'.

'The Master and Matron are very strict, as you know and soon we were parted. Mither slept in the infirm dormitory and I in the able bodied dormitory. I tried my best to keep in contact with her and disobeyed the rules by sneaking over to see her whenever I could. She was concerned I would be punished and placed in the punishment cell'—Mairi paused, before smiling at Lizzie—'A few years passed and we began to rue the day we left Strathy, then a miracle happened when you walked into the bake-house and our prayers were answered. I couldn't believe it was you, Lizzie,' she said tearfully.

'Well, thank goodness I did,' commented Lizzie. 'I am so happy to have found you, but now we should get some sleep; we can continue our stories tomorrow at breakfast,' suggested Lizzie. 'Then we need to do some shopping. You both require new clothes and shoes. There is a lovely women's dress shop on the High Street, where we should find something suitable. Later you must come to Clara's, who is the one I refer to as my mother. She took me in when I was most vulnerable. Finally, after a stay at the *King's Arms*, we will catch the train back to my home in Littleborough, Lancashire.'

☙❧

The following morning, they enjoyed a substantial breakfast, which Bridget requested they ate in their suite. She still felt embarrassed in her workhouse uniform and preferred the privacy of the suite to the dining room. They tucked in to eggs, bacon, sausages, tomatoes, mushrooms and fried bread, followed by toast, preserves and several cups of tea. Bridget reflected that they hadn't eaten such wonderful food since Strathy.

During breakfast, Lizzie briefly recounted her own amazing story, before they left to purchase more befitting outfits.

They left the outfitters' store happy and uplifted, which prompted Bridget to comment, 'Oh Lizzie, you really didn't need to do this for us. The chance of employment in your household was enough, but it is very generous of you. We will pay you back as soon as we are able,' promised Bridget.

Lizzie frowned. 'You will do no such thing Bridget Mackenzie. I remember how you helped my mother whilst giving birth to Robert, it is I who should be indebted to you. After you have changed clothes at the hotel, I will arrange a carriage to take us to Nottingham, so we can visit Townsend & Daft department store. They sell everything you will need under one roof, so you can choose clothes for your winter and spring wardrobe.

☙❧

A while later, as they entered the main doors of the store, both Bridget and Mairi were wide eyed in wonder. Bridget acknowledged that they had never been inside a department store before.

'Gosh Lizzie, it's like a wonderland,' exclaimed Mairi.

'Are you sure you will be able to afford the clothes?' asked Bridget.

'Of course Bridget. Some would consider me a very rich woman, but to me real riches exist in the people you love and cherish. So don't worry, I can afford everything you will need.'

Two hours passed before the women exited the store laden with bags; their coach ready and waiting to take them to the *King's Arms*.

❦

The coach ride gave Lizzie chance to explain her relationship with the Milligans. 'You will love Clara and Arthur, they are good people and very welcoming. If it wasn't for them and their son, David, I would not have survived. They'll fuss around you and not stint with the tea and cake. Clara maintains a roaring fire, even when it's not cold'—she laughed, remembering the many happy times she had spent in Clara's home—'but I must warn you that the Marsh is a world away from affluent Nottingham with its shops and grand houses.

'The streets in the Marsh are dirty and the houses cramped, but there is a good community spirit, for the most part anyway. Neighbours support one another through good times and bad. They live in a small terraced house, not much bigger than your croft in Strathy, but they get by…at least they have until recently. Clara's rheumatism gets her down and Arthur does the repairs himself, because the landlord refuses to do any maintenance on the property. For a long time I have wanted them to come and live with me in Littleborough, but they say Narrow Marsh is their home and the only one they know. They moved in when they first married and all their friends live in adjacent houses and nearby streets. However, I've now convinced them to move with me to Southwell, which is only a few miles from Nottingham. There is plenty of room for us all and you'll also have your own suite of rooms. I will be most grateful if you keep an eye on them both. You won't need to cook for them, but I need to know that they are safe, especially if we are away. Occasionally, we visit Kate, Rosie's birth mother and also my friend in Oxford, so we could be away for a week. Would you be able to manage that Bridget?'

'Why Lizzie, of course; we are both used to hard work, so it will be a pleasure,' assured Bridget.

'Mither's right Lizzie, we will do all we can to make them comfortable, so you've no need to worry. We can't believe this miracle has happened to us; to have found my best friend again after all these years is wonderful and we can never repay you, but we will do our best to help you all we can,' enthused Mairi.

'I know you will and I am so happy to have found you both. We have a lot to look forward to—Oh, we are almost here. Don't forget your new handbags,' reminded Lizzie. The coachman will assist with the rest of our shopping, after helping you down from the coach.'

They deposited their purchases at the King's Arms, then walked to Knotted Alley to surprise Clara with their news.

※

Clara and Arthur were finishing their morning chores and were ready for a break. 'Put the kekkle on Arthur, I'm dying for a cuppa char[70],' said Clara slumping down in her chair, before flipping off her slippers and resting her feet on the fender.

'Yo and me both me duck,' he responded before adding as an afterthought, 'By the way Clara 'ave fixed the mesh in the pantreh, so Alfie Waplington's days of free pies are ovver.'

'Aye, well, a wun't mind, but 'is mam cun afford to buy 'er own from the butchers. It in't as if they 'ant the means. Cut us a chunk of Madeira Arthur and don't stint the butta. We'll 'ave five minutes, then, if yo sweep the yard, I'll do a bit of dusting. Me washing's blowing nicely, so there'll be a load of ironing tamorra. My, it's like being on a treadmill, Arthur,' commented Clara. 'Yer nevva get ta the end on it. Eee, I can't wait til we move in wi our Lizzie. Best decision wiv ever made me duck. Course, al miss me friends, but our Lizzie sez we cun come back ta see 'em whenever we want and, Arthur, she toad me thiz a boozer[71] on the same road as we go-an to live. A tell ya what Arthur, we go-an ta need new bedding. That straw eiderdown's seen better days. Thiz more straw scattered in our yard than stuffed in that,' Clara added.

---

70 *Tea has been around for a long time, and so has the British slang term for it - 'char'. In fact, it was known in the west by that version of the Mandarin ch'a before it was called 'tea'. The Dutch adventurer Jan Huygen van Linschoten was one of the first to recount its use as a drink, in Discours of voyages into ye Easte & West Indies, 1598: The aforesaid warme water is made with the powder of a certaine hearbe called Chaa.*

71 *The origin of the word 'booze' is often mistakenly credited to E. C. Booz, who was a distiller in the United States in the 19th century. But the first references to the word 'booze', meaning 'alcoholic drink', appear in the English language around the 14th century as 'bouse'. The spelling we use today didn't appear until the 17th century.*

TANGLED WEB

'Aye yer not wrong me duck, but Lizzie said we not ta buy oat new just yet. Shiz tecking us ta Market Square[72], to buy stuff from some of them posh shops, so wi better wait.'

'Yer probably right Arthur. Lizzie knows what shiz doing. Talking of our Lizzie, she said she'd be ovver later taday, praps around tea-time, so we'd better be ready fer 'er visit. Oooh, a can't believe the new 'ouse dun't 'ave an outside lavvy. Yer'll not miss disposing of the ash pit Arthur—'

※

Their conversation was suddenly interrupted by loud a knocking. Clara, totally panicked, eyed the door. 'Who cun that be Arthur? 'ave not done me dusting yet.' Clara groaned at the thought of anyone turning up unexpected.

'Ave no idea Clara, a cun turn me 'and ta most things, but a can't see through wooden doors me duck,' said Arthur sarcastically, as he got up to open the door.

He was surprised, but delighted, to see Lizzie and two other women on the step. 'It's our Lizzie,' shouted Arthur.

Clara quickly relinquished herself of her apron. 'Well let her in then. I don't know Arthur...really she shun't 'ave ter knock. Door's allus oppen.'

Clara was surprised Lizzie had company. 'Oh goodness Lizzie, I must apologise for me state, we weren't expectin yo

---

[72] *The Market Square has long been at the centre of Nottingham life. In the early days before the City of Nottingham was formed, the area was the centre-point between the Norman town of Nottingham, situated around the Castle Rock and the old Anglo-Saxon town, which was based around the current Lace Market at St Mary's Church, also called Snothryngham, Snottingaham or Snottingham. The central point between the two towns became a major market point, and hence the square has been at the centre of Nottingham's growth around it for hundreds of years since.*

til this afternoon. Wiv just sat dahn fer a cuppa and a 'aven't 'ad chance ter dust,' explained Clara.

'Don't worry Clara, no one's going to worry about a bit of dust. Let me introduce you to my friends. This is Bridget and her daughter Mairi. I told you all about them when you first took me in.'

'Well Bridget and Mairi am very 'appy ter meet yer. Sit yersenn's dahn on the sofa'—she paused and looked expectantly at her husband—'Arthur, can yer get everyone a cuppa? A think thiz enough cake left and yer'll need another slab of butta.'

Arthur exited to the kitchen to perform the task allotted to him, as everyone made themselves comfortable.

Clara pushed her swollen feet back into her slippers, tucked some stray hairs under her mob cap and smoothed down her skirt, in an effort to regain some respectability. 'Well now, let's 'ear how yer found one another,' she smiled whilst giving the coals a poke, which immediately sent flames rushing up the chimney. Inevitably some sparks and cinders flew out on to the pegged rug, but quick as a flash Clara stamped them out in her usual fashion. 'Ah, there's more burn marks on this rug than enough. I'll definitely need ta peg another fer the new place. Mind me rheumatism's playing up, so it'ull 'ave ter wait til summer comes,' stated Clara, moving her slipper across the burnt area in an effort to distribute the charred loops.

Lizzie grinned but allowed Clara to believe she would be doing something useful in the furnishing of their new home. She realized Clara may want to take a few items to make her feel less like a 'fish out of water', so if she wanted to peg a rug, then that was fine by her.

Arthur duly arrived with the tea and a plate of Madeira. He'd succeeded in cutting enough pieces to feed the street.

Whilst they enjoyed the cake, Lizzie revealed her plan for their living arrangements, as she had had time to determine the layout and possible combinations. 'I think you should live in the south wing Clara, it's nearer the lane. The rooms are all on one level, so no stairs to climb,' she emphasized. 'You and Arthur will have a sitting room, a bedroom and bathroom, but you won't need a kitchen, as everything you need will be provided by the cook. Just think, tea and cake throughout the day! You only have to ring the bell.'

Clara was astounded. She turned excitedly to Arthur. 'Da'ya 'ear that Arthur. Yer'll 'ave that much time on yer 'ands, yer'll not know what ter do wi yersenn me duck.'

Lizzie grinned, remembering the first time she 'rang a bell' for Elspeth to serve afternoon tea. She continued, 'Bridget and Mairi will have rooms on the first floor of the same wing, so they'll also be on hand should you require anything at all.

'Well we're 'appy wi that, aren't we Arthur? Da ya have any idea when the move 'ull teck place Lizzie?'

Lizzie hesitated, as she didn't want to raise their hopes. A lot would depend on Marcus's return. 'I can't say for sure Clara, but Marcus should be home by 1st March, that might give you an inkling. Any time from the end of March, I expect. Oh and don't pack anything Clara. I will arrange for a company to pack for you, but let me know if you have any special items of furniture you wish to take, I will ensure they are collected and delivered. If you prefer, we can choose some new furniture, especially for the bedroom. You could even choose some pictures to hang on the walls. There are good quality shops in the Market Square so we should be able to find everything we need, including some new towels for the bathroom; you too,' she said indicating Bridget and Mairi.

The three women stared incomprehensively, as Lizzie continued. Bridget, listening intently, posed a question. 'Will we have to wear a uniform Lizzie,' she asked.

Lizzie smiled in understanding. 'No Bridget, I wouldn't wish it. You will be able to wear your own clothes. My other staff do wear comfortable uniforms, the maid and my housekeeper for instance, but they are happy to do so. You are part of my family, so no curtseying or bowing down to anyone.'

Relief spread across Bridget's face. 'Oh thank you, Mairi and me have had enough of uniforms to last us a lifetime.'

Lizzie noticed that Clara seemed contented, as did Arthur as he stood protectively behind her chair. It was clear that a big weight had been lifted from their shoulders and that their new life in Southwell promised their twilight years would be happy and comfortable. Lizzie felt lucky that all her loved ones would be accommodated under one roof. She couldn't wait for Marcus's return to complete the picture of happiness, as she counted down the days. All would have a bright future. Marcus and she were also about to begin a new chapter in their lives with many happy years ahead of them.

CHAPTER TWENTY-TWO

The Secret
February 1856

Rosie, slightly breathless after a last minute detour to meet with her father, boarded the train to Oxford as the guard was about to blow his whistle. Nearly all the seats had been taken, but she managed to secure a vacant window seat. As the countryside rushed by, her excitement grew. Jimmy was foremost in her mind and she was looking forward to meeting him again, but for now a short break with her mamma was just what she needed.

༺༻

Just after a quarter to five the train pulled into the station. Rosie retrieved her valise and disembarked, to see her mamma hurrying along the platform towards her, closely followed by Edward, their coachman, already out of breath.

Kate had missed her daughter, so much so that she gave Rosie a huge hug in anticipation of a splendid time during the forthcoming week. She had not had any further contact with Robert, since New Year's Eve, as her birthday celebrations had been cancelled, so was feeling depressed; however, she knew she could rely on Rosie to cheer her up.

'It's lovely to see you again Rosie.' She smiled ecstatically, before turning to Edward, requesting he take her daughter's valise.

They were together again at last and Rosie was eager to share her news about Jimmy. As they neared *The Chestnuts*, she smiled to herself. She wondered what her mamma would think of Lizzie's plan to move to Southwell.

James and Beatrice were waiting on the porch to greet her. Surprisingly, her sister appeared to be in an unusually good mood, kissing Rosie on each cheek. Somewhat taken aback, Rosie responded with equal heartiness.

'Come in Rosie,' James encouraged standing aside. 'Edward will carry your valise to your room and we can take tea in the drawing room, before you unpack. I expect you've lots to discuss with Kate and Beatrice before dinner.'

Later, Beatrice watched Rosie unpack her clothes. She complimented her on her choice of outfits, keeping up the pretence of liking her half-sister for a whole three minutes, before making an insidious remark. 'I expect you have been looking forward to coming here, as we do have much larger rooms than you have,' she asserted condescendingly, before folding her arms in anticipation of a retort from Rosie.

Rosie, however, refused to rise to the bait. 'Yes, it is especially lovely to be here and spend some time with Mamma and James…oh and you of course,' she said smiling warmly. Rosie was saddened by Beatrice's continued dislike of her; it seemed there was nothing she could do to change her attitude or opinion. She sighed, realising her sister might never change. Their relationship would inevitably be one of tolerance and not friendship. Nevertheless, she would not give up trying. Maybe, when Beatrice matured, she would realise that having a sister was a joy and not something to be endured.

'Shall we go down and join Mamma for pre-dinner drinks?' suggested Rosie.

'If you like. I think Mamma will allow me an aperitif before dinner, as I am twelve in March, so nearly an adolescent,' said Beatrice confidently, paraphrasing her mother's use of the word, during discussions with her friends. Some of their children were about to embark on a life at University; although it would be several years before Beatrice would be eligible.

Rosie kept quiet, knowing her mamma would not allow Beatrice an alcoholic drink. She had only just been allowed the odd glass of wine on special occasions herself.

'Are you coming then?' asked Beatrice offhandedly, before Rosie reluctantly agreed to follow her down to the sitting room.

Olives, pork rillettes and a pickle of dried apricots accompanied the Blanc-cassis[73], which Beatrice was determined to try. 'May I try the aperitif Mother?' asked Beatrice.

Kate did not want to embarrass her youngest daughter, but, neither did she have any intention of allowing her to drink the aperitif. Her plan was to let her daughter have a very small glass.

Beatrice gloatingly took the glass, whilst looking at Rosie, who smiled politely. She swallowed a large mouthful of the liquid but her distaste of the spirit could not be disguised, as she grimaced.

Kate, however, quickly came to her rescue and poured her daughter a glass of fresh pink lemonade. Rosie, somewhat amused, couldn't resist an 'I told you so' expression, which succeeded in embarrassing Beatrice, but soon the drama was over, as everyone moved to the dining room for dinner.

---

73 *Blanc-cassis is a common and very popular apéritif-cocktail made with a measure of crème de cassis (black currant liqueur) topped up with white wine.*

'Well Rosie,' began Kate, instigating conversation. 'What news have you from Littleborough?'

Rosie surveyed the others around the table. Her mam had not said anything about keeping the move a secret, so she delighted in telling them what plans were afoot. 'I have big news Mamma,' asserted Rosie, which gained everyone's full attention. 'We are moving house,' she announced coolly, sitting back in her chair to gauge the reaction.

Beatrice spluttered food on to her plate in surprise, which drew a raised eyebrow from James, although he noticed that Kate was equally astonished. 'Where are you moving to Rosie?' Kate asked, secretly hoping they would move closer to Oxford along with Robert.

'We are moving to Southwell in Nottinghamshire. Grandma and Granddad are going to live with us. Of course, I will miss my father, but intend to still see him regularly. Oh, by the way, he sends his love, he's really looking forward to seeing you all again. Anyway, the property, Oak Tree Lodge, has two wings. Mam and Marcus will occupy the main house and Jack and me are having our own apartments in one wing. Grandma and Granddad will live in the other wing. Mam intends to employ an extra three staff, in addition to Elspeth, Polly, Annie and Jacob, who will probably relocate with us. She will also require a nurse to take care of Grandma and Granddad, so around eight staff altogether.'

'I see'—Kate smiled, hiding her disappointment that Robert would not be joining them; although she was secretly elated by her perceived 'hidden' message she believed was intended for her. She continued—'I've always thought Lizzie did not have enough staff to run their present home, so I am glad she is thinking along those lines. Incidentally, what decided Marcus to consider moving?' she added guardedly.

'Mam told me that Marcus wanted to spend more time with the family, now that his father had died. He's decided to sell his business, his father's house and business and *The Beeches*. He realized that Mam wanted Clara and Arthur to live with us, so immediately set to with the help of a friend and found a house to the north east of Nottingham. Mam and me went to see it last week. It's really lovely and there's a paddock, so I will be able to have a horse!' she exclaimed.

Beatrice askance, believed Rosie was making the whole story up. 'I don't believe you,' she said pouting. 'Your mam cannot afford such a big house and—'

Beatrice was immediately interrupted by an angry Kate— 'Go to your room Beatrice, I will not tolerate such an outburst, which is untrue and totally uncalled for. You can return when you have considered your behaviour and apologized to your sister,' admonished Kate, pulling Beatrice from her seat.

Rosie, very surprised at her mamma's reaction, dare not make a comment. The room fell silent, as Beatrice stomped out of the dining room and up the stairs.

An embarrassed Kate tried to regain the convivial atmosphere that preceded her daughter's outburst. 'I am so sorry Rosie, Beatrice's behaviour was totally unacceptable. Now then, where were we?' she asked directing her attention to Rosie.

Although Rosie was upset at Beatrice's remarks, she didn't want to spoil the occasion so continued with her news. 'Mam intends to visit the Workhouse and recruit staff from there. She says everyone deserves a second chance'— she paused, detecting looks of disdain, although she knew her mam would not be discouraged—'She is very determined,' explained Rosie, almost apologetically, as she glanced from one to the other. Oh dear, she hoped the second course would arrive and relieve the tension that had built up. Fortunately, she didn't have to wait, the second course duly arrived, before either James or Kate could raise an eyebrow.

Nothing more was said on the subject throughout the meal. Beatrice did not return from her room and James excused himself immediately after dessert, muttering something about a cigar and glass of brandy.

Kate was mortified that Rosie's first day had ended in disaster and strove to retrieve the situation by ringing for two mugs of hot chocolate and Rosie's favourite shortbread biscuits that evening. Once they were alone, they relaxed once more and began to enjoy each other's company. 'So tell me how you and Jack are faring,' asked Kate.

Rosie pulled a face, testament to the fact that her love life was very unsettled. 'Mmm, well Mamma, it's not going well. I went to see Jack off on his ship in early January, just after Marcus's father had died. On the dockside he told me that he wanted me to meet someone. You will never guess who that someone was Mamma…Jimmy, it was Jimmy, he is alive and well! He was accompanied by two women, Lucinda and Helen. Apparently, Jack and Jimmy met them in Melbourne on their last trip and both were nurses on the *Dreadnought* hospital ship where Jimmy convalesced after an accident at sea. It's a long story Mamma, but it appears Jimmy jumped into the sea to try and save the bosun, who had fallen overboard during a storm. They thought both were lost, but it transpired Jimmy had only broken his leg before fetching up exhausted on an island. He eventually returned to England to convalesce aboard the *Dreadnought*.

'It was obvious Lucinda and Jimmy were in a relationship. She was wearing his ring on her engagement finger, so it appeared serious. I was heartbroken, until we all went for a goodbye drink and I realized Jimmy still had feelings for me and I for him. I knew instantly that Jack wasn't the man for me. On my return, Mam had a long talk with me about being too young to settle down, but I know my own mind Mamma.

I love Jimmy and intend to wait for his return,' said Rosie emphatically.

Kate nodded her head slowly and deliberately, she understood Rosie's enthusiasm, but was she too young to know what she wanted? 'He was your first love wasn't he Rosie?'

'Yes, I have known Jimmy since I was very young. He always looked after me and our feelings grew as we grew. Am I wrong to believe our love is forever? Mam told me I should not make such monumental decisions just yet, that there is plenty of time for me to find the right one. What do you think Mamma?'

Kate sighed as she wondered what she should tell her daughter. She needed a sensible answer, but Kate was not sure she could provide one. 'It is difficult to say Rosie. I do know how you feel. You believe you are in love when you are young and hope it will last forever, but that does not always work out how you think it will.'

Rosie took a sip of her hot chocolate, while she took in her mamma's words, deciding to ask a very pertinent question. 'Did you think your love for my dad would last forever Mamma?'

Kate struggled with her reply. 'Of course Rosie,' she hedged, pausing to think before offering more advice. Her eyes darted to the Christmas group photograph, which stood on the small but elaborate oak sideboard. One face stood out…Robert, her one and only true love. She feared for her daughter as she realized she was even younger than herself, aged seventeen, when *she* fell for Robert. There could be so much heartache ahead, but whatever advice she gave, Rosie would probably pay little heed. She hoped her daughter would not suffer the same fate as herself…to be married to a man she did not love.

Rosie waited patiently for her mamma to continue, noticing with some concern, the sudden sadness, which clouded Kate's countenance. 'Are you all right Mamma?' she asked.

Kate brought her attention back to her daughter. 'Yes Rosie...yes I am fine. I just remembered something that occurred long ago. Now what was I saying...oh yes, the truth is that at your age, it is difficult to know whether you *are* in love, or just in love with the idea of being in love,' Kate explained. She did feel in her heart that Rosie probably did love Jimmy and if her own experience was anything to go by, love would continue to thrive.

Rosie frowned. 'I see...well I think I see. When did you stop loving my dad Mamma?'

Kate felt compromised, unsure what she should say, but her daughter was waiting for a reply. She sidestepped the truth. 'The thing is, we didn't ever stop liking each other, but over the years, we both came to terms with the fact that we had moved on and our lives were very different, we both married other people and now have our own families. Some say you can never recreate the past, so you have to look to the future,' explained Kate, who, not thinking straight, tagged on a thought provoking statement that in reality, should have been left unsaid. 'Rosie, if you can't be with the person you love, you should learn to love the person you are with'—she paused, before adding—'Do you understand Rosie?'

Rosie was even more confused. 'I think so. Life is very complicated isn't it and I suppose we don't always follow the path of our destiny?'

Kate smiled understandingly and took her daughter's hand. 'That's very true Rosie. The best advice I can give is, you must be true to yourself.'

'Mmm, I suppose so Mamma.'

Kate rose from her chair and bade her daughter goodnight. Their conversation had been difficult but she intended to be more positive on the subject when, inevitably, Rosie raised it again.

※

Kate spent a restless night, tossing and turning, her jumbled thoughts continuously whirring around and around in her head. Eventually she got out of bed, put on her dressing robe and tiptoed across the landing, before descending the stairs to the dining room.

Her attention was drawn to a beam of light generated by the full moon, which shone through the window on to the photograph she had focussed on earlier. She picked it up and held it close to her breast, as tears flowed freely down her cheeks.

She stared out through the French doors and spoke out loud, her eyes following the curve of the driveway to the large entrance gates. She imagined Robert Cameron standing there. 'Robert, oh Robert, why can't you see we are meant to be together. One day you will realise it's no good fighting your feelings and come to me.' She sobbed, lifting the photograph up to her lips and softly kissing Robert's image.

Rosie transfixed to the spot, concealed by the half open door, was a shocked spectator to the short drama being played out in front of her. She had also been awake for some time now and heard muffled sobs as someone passed swiftly by her room. Curiosity took hold and so she opened her door to see her mamma descending the stairs. She followed, making sure she remained in the shadows, unseen by Kate. Her mamma's spoken admission filled her with alarm, as she raised her hand to her mouth to prevent herself crying out.

While Kate returned the photo to the sideboard, Rosie quickly retreated to her room, but she was unable to sleep and began evaluating the consequences of her parents indulging in an illicit affair. She concluded that her mamma's secret should remain just that 'a secret'. She would never admit to overhearing Kate's anguish, but hoped her mamma would abide by her own philosophy *'if you cannot be with the one you love, learn to love the one you are with'.* It seemed to be the only solution, any other scenario would result in at least two families being torn apart. She was heartbroken that her mother seemed to be living a lie and, possibly too that her father was also struggling with his feelings. She began to question the meaning of the message he sent, but ultimately, there was nothing she could do. It would be out of the question for her to intervene. She would have to live with the secret and hope her mother could find happiness with James in the future. If only she could learn to love him; but, as she had recently discovered herself, that was seemingly impossible.

CHAPTER TWENTY-THREE

Rendezvous
February 1856

Robert remembered his first meeting with Kate with some clarity, on the pretext of a spurious business meeting in Oxford. After taking a cab to *The Chestnuts* from the station he'd stood apprehensively at James's large oak door. He'd nervously rung the bell and was more than relieved when Kate herself opened it. She was, of course, surprised to see him, but enthusiastically ushered him inside, as James apparently, was not at home and she was alone in the house. Her euphoria was, however, short lived, as he stayed only long enough to suggest another meeting at the *Star Inn* in Stone, Staffordshire.

❦

Now for the second time in just over a week, Robert, with some trepidation entered the inn, snuggled alongside the canal in the quaint village of Stone. Mercifully, the train journey had been long, which afforded him valuable thinking time. He was unsure what he would say when he eventually saw Kate, but their future, or lack of it, depended on this meeting.

He'd arrived early at a quarter past eleven, so ordered a brandy, choosing a booth by the window, which overlooked the towpath. *The Star,* situated only a small distance from the train station gave him a distinct vantage point. He would see Kate immediately she arrived by coach. She, of course, would be punctual, so it was no surprise when fifteen minutes later, her coach drew up for their eleven thirty assignation.

His heart beat faster as he watched her alight from the coach. She always took his breath away, this time in a dark blue coat, over a pale blue wool day dress, complemented by a hat with a small feather, which was perched jauntily on her head. Her dark blonde curly hair framed her face and tumbled on to the collar of her coat. In a few seconds, she would enter the inn and they would be reunited once more. He shuffled nervously in his seat and his mouth became dry. He hurriedly took another swallow of brandy to give him courage, then moistened his lips in anticipation. When he looked up, she was standing immediately in front of him. Her smile invaded his consciousness as she moved to kiss him on the cheek. Why, he considered, did she make him feel so hopelessly in love with her after all this time? He could never admit his deepest feelings for her, but despairingly his was a true longing. Could he, therefore, convince her that they had no future together and that he intended to stay true to Amy?

His intentions melted away in confusion as once more her soft, sensual voice penetrated his innermost being.

'Hello Robert, it's good to see you. Thank you for agreeing to meet with me,' she said softly, whilst stroking his arm with her hand.

He knew full well this meeting would be difficult, but he needed to control his emotions if he was to succeed in his bid to put a halt to their, as yet, unfulfilled affair.

He heard himself offering her a seat and asking what she would like to drink, as if he was witnessing the scene from afar. He shuddered uncontrollably when she smiled seductively and removed her hat, before he took her coat, hanging it on the stand next to his own. 'How are you Kate?' he muttered unnecessarily. It was clearly obvious how she *was*, her actions were already indicating a subtle determination to seduce him before he had any chance of escaping.

'I am well Robert thank you. I have been looking forward to seeing you again,' Kate added brightly, her focussed eyes burning into his soul as only hers could.

'Good, good, would you like a gin and tonic or something else?' he asked with a nervousness he had never felt before in her presence.

'That would be lovely Robert, with a slice of lemon, please.' Hers was a confidence Robert wished he could share.

He returned to the table and watched her as she sipped the gin. She lowered her eyelashes seductively and moved her tongue over her lips in a suggestive manner. For a moment he was transported back to their intimate meetings near Low Wood Hall. He visualised them tethering their horses in the top field before walking down to the disused cottage, where they made love and talked about their future…a future that never materialised.

Kate suddenly interrupted his train of thought as she covered his hand with hers. 'Robert, I understand the inn has rooms. Would you would feel more comfortable discussing our situation in private, out of the public gaze?'

Robert, taken aback, flushed, due to the undeniable sensations that flooded his body at the touch of her hand and her forthright suggestion. 'Is that such a good idea Kate? We never seem to be able to resolve anything when we are in such close proximity to one another. I thought we could be reasonably objective if we keep our distance, albeit at the same table.'

Kate inclined her head to one side and raised her eyebrows, before once again teasing Robert. 'Why Robert? are you concerned you might lay bare your true feelings if we are totally alone and uninterrupted?' countered Kate, suggestively squeezing his hand.

Robert sighed. He felt his resistance waning, as he stared unblinking into Kate's eyes. 'Listen Kate, whatever feelings we have for each other cannot be acted upon. We are both married and it would be wrong for us to behave irresponsibly. If we embarked on an affair, there would be no going back and there would be serious consequences, not only for us, but our families.'

Kate responded, 'I don't want an affair Robert! I thought you understood that. I want to be with you for the future. I have no desire to be the *other woman.* I love you deeply, but I won't sneak around or become deceitful, having to lie to James and wait for you to contact me so we can take some snatched hours together,' she confided. Kate held his gaze, before adding, 'If you want to be with me Robert, we have to walk out on our respective marriages and, eventually divorce our present partners.'

Robert fell silent for several seconds before responding. The enormity of her proposal sinking in. 'I can't leave Amy,' he stammered, pausing to take another glug of brandy, before lowering his voice. 'At least not yet and not in the foreseeable future Kate,' he finished.

Kate seized the moment, acknowledging in that instant that Robert had all but declared his love for her. Her desire to tell him *'she had told him so'* on many occasions, tempered her response. 'So, you do not discount a future with me, only not yet?' she hedged.

Robert admitted defeat. 'I suppose that's true...I realised I still loved you when we met again a few years ago, but, at the time I believed there was too much water under the bridge for us to rekindle our love. We were both married with children, but'—he paused to look out of the window, still unsure whether to be honest about how he felt.

Kate interrupted his thoughts again—'but...but now...you find you can't live without me, isn't that the truth Robert?'

Robert stood up unexpectedly without replying and walked over to the bar, with his back to Kate. 'Do you have a room available for my wife and I?' he asked of the landlord. 'It would be for one night.'

The landlord raised an eyebrow, as if he too knew that Robert was unsure he was making the right decision, before he responded. 'As a matter of fact we do sir, we have a room above the lounge which overlooks the river. Do you wish to see it?' he asked, glancing suspiciously at the very attractive woman sitting at the window seat.

'No, I am sure it will be suitable,' confirmed Robert sheepishly. 'We will take it. We don't have any luggage, as it is a spur of the moment decision.'

The landlord nodded and inappropriately tapped the side of his nose, as he reached over to a wooden board containing several hooks. He removed one of the keys and handed it to Robert. 'You will find the room very quiet, sir, it's away from the bar area and the only one on the right off the small landing. Go down the corridor'—he indicated—'and the stairs are on your left. Can I trouble you to sign the visitor's book?' he asked, with a conspiratorial wink, handing Robert a pen, which he had already dipped into the small inkpot to the side of the bar, before adding, 'Would you like lunch in the lounge bar or your room, sir?'

'In the lounge bar, after we freshen up, we will be down shortly.'

'And dinner, sir? Would you prefer to eat dinner in the restaurant too?' he queried.

Robert hesitated before making a decision. 'We will eat in the restaurant, thank you,' confirmed Robert, determined to stamp out any idea in the landlord's mind that they were not a respectable married couple. He signed the guest book, *'Mr & Mrs Carmichael, Cambridge'*

Robert returned to the table and spoke softly, just audible enough for the landlord to hear, in an effort to prove their legitimacy. 'Kate, the landlord does have a room for one night. We should take breakfast early tomorrow so that we can return home mid-morning to coincide with the children returning from their grandmamma's.'

Without hesitation, Kate, hardly able to disguise her joy, continued the charade. 'That would be wonderful Robert. A week away at their grandmamma's has seemed much longer. I have really missed them and am looking forward to seeing them again.'

'Come my dear, we are lucky, the room overlooks the canal.' He exaggerated his observation with a sweep of his hand, glancing confidently at the landlord, who nodded his approval.

Kate, secretly elated at the thought of spending the night with Robert, followed him meekly to the room.

Once inside, Robert put his arms around Kate and pulled her close, then kissed her passionately before stepping back. 'I love you Kate, but like you, I do not want to embark on an affair. I feel guilty just meeting with you and will not make the ultimate betrayal of Amy. Do you understand?'

Momentarily, Kate's heart sank and she turned her head away. Robert immediately placed his hand gently under her chin, tilted her face upwards and looked directly into her eyes. 'It has to be this way Kate, but I promise you, one day we will be together.'

Kate was encouraged, but also disappointed. 'When... how long do you envisage it will be?'

Robert sighed. 'I can't promise, but when our girls reach an age where they are not totally dependent on us...probably between eighteen months and two years.'

'Two years?' Kate gasped, a tear sliding down her face.

Robert experienced a sudden rush of sadness and emotion, as he too realised the implication of maintaining the pretence for such a long period. 'We can meet Kate. I do want to see you, but we must be careful. Amy and James must not find out.'

Kate was appeased, although she wanted Robert to make love to her more than anything, she knew he had made the right decision. She would not be able to change his mind...at least for the present, so she agreed, accepting his proposal; their future seemingly resolved.

Robert once again gathered her into his arms and kissed her tenderly. He held her tight, but needed all his emotional restraint not to give in to his desires. He also knew that, the more he saw her, the more his resistance would be tested. He realized, that despite Kate's verbal acceptance of his decision, she would not give up easily, but his need to continue their meetings was now overwhelming.

They lunched in the bar and spent an idyllic afternoon walking by the canal. They discussed their future and how to manage the break up of their marriages. In the evening after dinner, they retired to their room, but did not share the bed that night, with Robert opting to sleep on the couch. The night was long and tortuous for them, but their love for each other made them blind to the devastation they would cause their families. Now the decision was made, there *was* no going back. They could not imagine life without the other and both realised that despite their pact not to make love, inevitably, at some point, they would.

CHAPTER TWENTY-FOUR

Headlines
February 1856

Bridget and Mairi settled in to their new home at *The Beeches*, sharing a large bedroom and sitting room. They joined Lizzie in the main dining room for their meals, where they astonished one another with personal tales, which helped curb Lizzie's anxiety concerning Marcus's safety.

When Rosie arrived home from her stay in Oxford, Lizzie detected an air of dejection in her daughter. It was apparent that she returned with troubling mixed emotions. So far, Lizzie had not had the opportunity to speak at length with her, as her days had been filled organising the packing of boxes and indulging Bridget and Mairi. However, later that day she encountered Rosie in the sitting room with a mug of chocolate and a plate of shortbread, a sign that she was eating to forget whatever was bothering her. To cheer her up, Lizzie proposed she take her shopping in Liverpool and so on Thursday morning they caught the train from Manchester central. They would include lunch and return later that afternoon.

By mid morning, they were already firmly ensconced in the Kardomah on Bold Street, planning a new spring wardrobe for Rosie, who was excited about recounting her special bond with Jimmy. 'This is the very table at which we sat on the day Jimmy and Jack left for Australia,' she stated as her mind recalled that auspicious day.

Lizzie smiled, because of the noticeable difference in her daughter's demeanour then made a suggestion. 'I think we'd better order coffee and cake because if we continue to sit here at an empty table the waiter's agitation will increase.' Lizzie grinned. 'What would you like Rosie?'

'A slice of Madeira cake and a pot of freshly ground coffee, thanks, Mam.'

The relieved waiter, took their order while Rosie remembered how she and Jimmy couldn't take their eyes off each other, as if they were the only people in existence, but Lizzie's thoughts were elsewhere. These docks were the last place she'd seen Marcus. She could picture him in her minds eye, leaning casually against the ship's rails, waving optimistically from the deck. He'd blown her a kiss and his love surrounded her. She'd returned his wave, but could not prevent a tear forming, consoling herself that time would pass swiftly and that he would come home safely. In relentless fashion and oblivious to their thoughts, the *Pacific* had sailed into open water and out of sight. Right now, she wished she was standing on the dockside, waiting for him to disembark, but sadly that was still another week away.

Uncomprehendingly, a sense of foreboding enveloped her. She glanced anxiously around, watching people hurrying to and fro, outside the cafe window. They were going about their daily business—then, in one terrible moment, seemingly frozen in time, she caught sight of a billboard outside a newsagent's. Her body trembled, as she focussed on the heart stopping headlines:

'PROBABLE FATE OF THE PACIFIC'

Her heart pounding in anguish and desperation, she staggered out of the Kardomah and across the road, until she stopped transfixed on the pavement's edge, opposite the billboard. Her tearstained eyes blurred as she tried to decipher the small print, which contained the story beneath the headlines. Several shoppers walked briskly past, obscuring her view, but eventually she focussed; the words confirmed her worst fears. She became hot and swayed to and fro, stumbling closer to the board. Disbelief and a torrent of emotional turmoil enveloped her as her whole world collapsed and she was no longer capable of conscious thought. She became aware of several unfamiliar concerned faces staring down at her, speaking incoherently, as if in a vacuum. Still unable to utter a word, she stared blankly at the sea of faces, as she was carried to a chair inside the newsagents. *This can't be happening* she thought, *it can't be true*, but then, through tear filled eyes she sighted the headlines in a newspaper held by a gentleman who was comforting her. It read:

The following was posted in the Underwriters' Rooms to day: -

"GLASGOW, FEB. 27. The Edinburgh (s.s.), which arrived here on the 14th inst, from New York, passed on the 7th inst. a large quantity of broken ice, and in it saw a quantity of broken cabin furniture, fine ornamental doors, with white or glass handles, such as might have belonged to a first class steamer or ship."

THE PACIFIC SAILED FROM THIS PORT ON THE 25TH ULT.
LONDON, FRIDAY

Lizzie once again lost consciousness but after a few seconds, felt Rosie's presence as she regained a semblance of composure.

'Mam, Mam, is it true,' asked Rosie fearfully. 'Has Marcus's ship foundered? This gentleman'—she paused to indicate an elderly man holding up a newspaper emblazoned with the horrific headlines across the whole of the front page—'This gentleman showed me his paper Mam...it is Marcus's ship, isn't it?' she sobbed.

Hollow voices resonated around the shop, as Lizzie half listened to the man holding the paper. 'Do you know someone who was on the ship ma'am?' he asked with concern, but Lizzie remained silent. Hot tears welled up in her eyes, which fell uncontrollably down her cheeks and on to her coat. Her anguish was plain for everyone to see in her vacant look and sad eyes. The man spoke to her again and tried to comfort her. 'There...there might be survivors,' he offered, but he really didn't believe there could be, as he had scrutinised the whole story, which included a paragraph by the Times, establishing the fate of the crew and passengers:

'The Times', London, Friday.
Insurance for small amounts were effected to-day at Lloyd's
upon the Pacific steamer, overdue at
New York, from Liverpool,
at 50 per cent free of average—

'Someone fetch a doctor,' the man with the newspaper commanded. 'This woman isn't well. It appears she has received some very shocking news and she needs attention.'

His words had the required effect, in that several of the customers immediately rushed out of the shop in an effort to find a doctor.

An immeasurably long time afterwards, although it could only have been half an hour at the most, still in a state of shock, Rosie and Lizzie found themselves in a local doctor's surgery. They had no recollection of how they'd arrived there.

Rosie explained their circumstances to a kindly doctor in his early sixties, who held Lizzie's hand across his desk. 'Mrs Van der Duim, I am so sorry for the situation in which you find yourself. It will take some time to come to terms with your husband's apparent demise in this disaster. Unfortunately, there is very little anyone can do to help you feel any better. There aren't any magic cures to take away the pain, but I can give you something to aid your sleep over the next week. Try and get plenty of rest and if possible call upon a relative to arrange to matters. Unfortunately—' he continued—'it appears everyone went down with the ship and it is almost inconceivable that anyone survived and nigh on impossible to recover any one for a Christian burial,' explained Dr Richards, expressing his sorrow for the poor woman in front of him, who hadn't even raised her head. The best thing you can do is to make sure you are surrounded by family and friends. They can be a great source of comfort to you during this dreadful time,' he advised, as he passed Rosie a dark brown bottle containing a sleeping draught.

In a daze, Lizzie belatedly thanked the doctor for his attention and for arranging a carriage for their journey home. A return by train was out of the question. Rosie acknowledged her mam needed a period of solitude, without having curious passengers staring at her obvious distress.

Neither spoke during their two hour journey home, but once there, Rosie immediately put her mam to bed, asking Mairi to keep an eye on her while she went to the post office to send a telegram to her mamma. On her way home, she called in on her father to inform him of the devastating news.

⁕

Rosie's insistent knocking on the door surprised Robert, who opened it to find a composed but obviously distressed Rosie standing there. 'Come in Rosie, what on earth's happened?' he asked, ushering his daughter into the living room before sitting her down in an armchair.

'Oh, father it's Marcus…he…it seems his ship has foundered…and…and there aren't any survivors. We heard of the news in Liverpool. Mam saw the headlines on a billboard,' spluttered Rosie, breaking down at last, her eyes filling with tears.

A shocked Robert immediately pulled his daughter into his arms and held her close. 'Oh my goodness Rosie, this is awful. Are you sure there are no survivors?' he asked hopefully.

'Yes—*The Times* newspaper confirmed it along with something about insurance and Lloyds. What will we do father? Mam will never get over this.' Rosie sobbed, her eyes darting from side to side, in fear and panic.

'I'm not sure Rosie'—hedged Robert with concern—'but I will do everything possible to help Lizzie, both practically and emotionally. You will have to step up Rosie, despite your own grief. Can you do that?'

'Yes, yes of course. I loved Marcus, he was like a second father to me, but to my mam, he was her world. I am scared that she will not be strong enough to survive. What if she becomes ill—how will we cope?' Rosie asked, trying desperately to keep her fear and emotions under control.

Robert acted quickly, by first getting his daughter a strong brandy. 'Drink this darling, it will help you to calm yourself. I am so sorry Rosie, we will have some tough times ahead and your mam will need our support. I will make sure she is never alone and Amy and I will visit every day. She should see a physician, as there is medicine she could take to help her sleep,' suggested Robert.

'She already has some. A doctor in Liverpool prescribed a sleeping draught for her to take over the next few days.'

'That's good Rosie. As soon as possible, I will contact Lloyds to claim on the insurance, which should be straight forward, but the underlying problem lies with Marcus's father's will and the sale of his businesses and houses. However, don't worry, I will employ a good solicitor. Hopefully, Marcus will also have put his affairs in order, so you can still move to Southwell. I believe that to be Lizzie's best option at present, but it is early days. She needs to be strong and recover.'

Rosie agreed with her father then suddenly remembered something. 'Jack! Oh no, Jack's ship won't dock in Melbourne until the 31st March. That's another month and he won't be back before the end of June. There is no way of letting him know,' she sighed.

Robert fell silent. He tried to think of a way of informing Jack, but eventually shook his head in defeat. 'You are right Rosie, we are unable to message him, but as soon as he returns we must be there. I suspect he will want to leave for Philadelphia himself and conclude his father's affairs. Jack is the next of kin, unless Lizzie was Marcus's beneficiary and named in his will, but I am not aware of that.'

'Oh dear, I don't know father. Neither of them ever mentioned a will. I'll have to ask Mam, but not yet, it will have to wait. We must delay a Memorial Service for Marcus, until July, after Jack returns, although It will be very difficult for Mam not to say her goodbyes until then,' said Rosie feelingly.

'Mmm...it is indeed a dilemma. We cannot arrange anything before Jack returns. I need to talk to Lizzie, possibly next week about the practicalities of such an arrangement, but for now, all we can do is support her. You should contact Kate. She will probably want to come and see Lizzie,' suggested Robert.

'I have already sent a telegram father, so she will receive it quite soon, but now I need to go home. I don't want to leave Mam for too long,' Rosie advised, her eyes filling with tears once more at the thought that Marcus would no longer be by her mam's side.

'I'll come with you,' stated Robert.

CHAPTER TWENTY-FIVE

Acceptance
March/April 1856

Every night since learning of Marcus's death, Lizzie slept on his side of the bed. Tears frequently tumbled unabated down her face, accompanied by anguished cries of his name, followed by the question…*'Why…why?'* She must find answers, but just how, she knew not.

During the last month, Lizzie acquired several newspapers containing articles, which alluded to poor management of the ship and negligence by a succession of Captains in their quest to obtain the *Blue Riband*, without regard to the safety of passengers. She knew it would not bring Marcus back, but she needed to confirm the reasons for the ship's loss and ultimately, who had been responsible.

She often sat in a chair by the window sipping a mug of hot milk and honey, which she believed, assisted in helping her sleep. One night as she sorted through papers piled high on an occasional table, she selected the *Cork Examiner, dated the 5th March 1856*, and began reading. It was allegedly an account provided by a gentleman whose voyage on the *Pacific* the previous April had almost resulted in catastrophe, when the ship was battered by a hurricane.

'We (Dublin Evening Post) have now before us a letter, written by a gentleman, late of this city, who left Liverpool on the 'Pacific' on the 14th of April last, giving an account of the almost miraculous escape from a hurricane, which caught that vessel with all sail set, and threw the ship on her beam-ends, whilst amongst banks of field-ice, off Newfoundland, on the 20th April last. This occurred, notwithstanding repeated warnings given by the sudden fall of the mercury, which made the ship's captains', of whom there were seven on board, as passengers, declare, several hours before, 'that they were in for a gale'. The account says:

'On the Friday afternoon (the 20th), the weather became very cold; the temperature of the sea having fallen twelve degrees in four hours, and an iceberg appeared to the northwest, which obliged us to change our course a little; after this came a storm of hail and snow, which ended with lightning from the coast, which gradually spread round, and ended at the N.W., according to the opinion of the nautical men, the very worst possible sign. They all said we were in for a hard blow. At this time the wind was blowing pretty fresh from the eastward and we had all sail going at 13½ knots an hour. At midnight the wind veered suddenly round to the N.W., which blew so hard that the sails could not be taken in, and consequently flew to shivers, the jib, foresail, and foretopsail, all went over, and were torn into ribbons.'

After describing the storm, which lasted for two days, the writer thus speaks of the management of the vessel:

'It is most astonishing that the Captain, an officer of great experience - especially with so many unmistakable signs of a gale - should have been caught with all sail set. He had plenty of time to have all down, and topmasts and yards lowered. The only way I can account for it is, that having so far made a most rapid passage, he wanted to do something wonderful; even when the gale was blowing its worst, he

kept the steam on, and drove on at five knots, in the very teeth of the hurricane - for hurricane it must be called. They all agreed, that in all their trips across the Atlantic, they never experienced so heavy a gale. One old sea captain said, that he once knew it to blow as hard when off Cape Horn.'

Lizzie had discovered that on Marcus's voyage, the *Pacific* had both a new captain and first mate, neither of whom had much transatlantic experience. Also aboard was a new chief engineer, totally unfamiliar with the *Pacific's* engines. The gentleman's account of his voyage seemed almost beyond belief. She concluded that the inexperienced Master, intent on securing the coveted *Blue Riband*, put his passengers in danger. Therefore, it seemed hardly surprising that the inexperience of the officers commanding the ship on the 23rd January, also fell foul of another hurricane, with catastrophic results. When the ship failed to arrive in New York, several other ships conducted a search. Sadly, not a trace of the vessel was found and not one body was recovered. Consequently, the loss of the ship would always remain a mystery[74].

Lizzie had to accept that all the 'what ifs' and 'blame', scenarios, could not hide the cold, hard fact that Marcus was never coming home and so reluctantly agreed to a Memorial Service, to take place after Jack returned.

---

[74] *Fast forward 135 years, where in 1991, divers in the Irish Sea discovered the bow section of the ship a few miles northwest of Anglesey. The ship had only travelled about sixty miles from her Liverpool departure point before sinking. The cause of Pacific's demise is still unknown.*

For an interminably long period, Lizzie would be unable to say goodbye to the man she loved. She became morose and reclusive, eating her meals in her room and only venturing out to walk alone in the gardens during the evening. She spent most nights sat by the window. The fact that she could not bring Marcus's body home for burial made acceptance doubly hard, so much so that the sparkle left her eyes and her soul filled with sorrow. When she slept at all, it was fitful, despite the doctor's sleeping draughts, which caused her to believe her frequent nightmarish dreams were exacerbated by the medicine's hallucinatory effects.

Her nights became intolerable, as she sat for hours staring out over the garden. Often her mind played tricks. She believed she could see Marcus walking through the gates and for a few seconds, she would feel incredibly happy, until the harsh reality of his death surfaced. Although he was no longer with her, he remained her last thought at night and became the first when she awoke, if she managed to sleep at all. It was not surprising that nothing and no one could relieve the loneliness and desolation she now felt, even when surrounded by friends and family.

She always tried her best to carry on when guests arrived who would talk animatedly, as they tried to raise her spirits. Ultimately, she knew she would have to move on with her life, but it was so difficult to smile anymore because now her future looked bleak. There didn't seem to be any light at the end of the tunnel.

She acknowledged she would not have coped at all without support from the family. Kate travelled up and remained at *The Beeches* the day after she received Rosie's telegram and Robert, Amy and Rosie made sure she was not short of company. Bridget and Mairi assisted Elspeth, Polly and Annie with household tasks, as friends and family visited most weekends. Jacob the gardener ensured fresh cut flowers were always available for Elspeth to replace when their colours faded, although Lizzie hardly noticed in her ongoing grief. However, the house ran smoothly and guest bedrooms were always ready for occupation, no matter what time of the day or night.

※

Two months later, on the eve of what would have been Marcus's birthday, on 26th April, Lizzie sat alone in her room, on the window seat. The full moon shone and giant shadowy fingers reached out across the lawn whilst stars twinkled in an ink black cloudless sky.

Despite the coolness of the evening, Lizzie flung open the window and breathed in the scented honeysuckle, which covered part of the wall under her room above the main entrance. She felt particularly sad, in that she had planned a combined welcome home and birthday party for Marcus. The unwritten card she'd bought several months ago lay on the dressing table. Her sleeping draught stood untouched on the bedside cabinet, alongside the book of poems by Byron. She'd given the book to Marcus shortly after they'd first met and recently rediscovered it in his bedside cabinet, with a bookmark on the page of her favourite poem.

Four lines of 'A Red, Red Rose' had been copied by Lizzie on to a piece of vellum[75], but three lines had been struck

---

75 *The term vellum is actually used describe a variety of different types of paper. Some vellum papers are heavy, while others are thin and transparent. What these papers have in common is the smooth, even quality of their surface.*

through. She'd changed the words in a sad and pitiful attempt to accept Marcus's death:

'And fare thee weel, my only love,

~~And fare thee weel awhile!~~ And fare thee weel *forever*

~~And I will come again, my love...~~ For you won't come again, my love...

~~Tho' it were ten thousand mile...~~ Nor yet we'll be together...'

She read the words out loud, then placed the paper on the front page of the open book. As she stared dejectedly at the poem once again, a sudden gentle breeze invaded the room causing the book's pages to flicker. The sheet of vellum floated up and out of the open window, as if guided by an unseen hand. Lizzie watched it hover and then gain height, disappearing over the tree-line.

Astonished by the occurrence, she turned to find the page of the book was open, revealing the poem in its original form. Comforted beyond measure, her fingers traced the lines of the poem. For the first time in many weeks she decided against taking the sleeping draught. She again approached the window and her eyes were drawn to a group of stars, which appeared to be shining extra brightly. Suddenly, she remembered Marcus's retelling of the romantic legend surrounding *Perseus and Andromeda*[76] and his eternal promise.

'See there below that 'W' shape which is Cassiopeia, the group of stars dangling from the left edge of the

---

[76] *Legend says that Perseus and Andromeda were married and led a long, happy life together. He keeps watch over her.*

'W' is Perseus. It is high up in the sky all winter, so it is not too hard to find. Every evening at 6 p.m. wherever we are, we can both look up and seek out Perseus. Legend says that Perseus and Andromeda were married and led a long, happy life together. He keeps watch over her. I will watch over you Elizabeth when we are together, but for now, I must leave you...'

It was at that moment she realised Marcus had never really left her. He would remain with her always, holding her close and watching over her. A cool breeze wafted the curtains to her room, but she felt strangely cocooned by a sensation of warmth and love. For the first time since Marcus's death, she found herself smiling...the knowing smile shared only by lovers. She felt at peace as she slipped into bed and drifted into a deep sleep. The nightmares did not return. In their place were vivid dreams of loved ones past, her mither[77] and father standing together with Marcus. She could see him quite clearly as he drifted towards her, encircling his arms around her one last time. He spoke softly to her of the day they would be together again, but for now she must embrace the life God had given her and live it to the full without him. She felt his lips pressed tenderly to hers. She tried to hold on to him, but he pulled gently away and the vision began to fade...

Lizzie awoke suddenly to the sound of a cock crowing and the sun rising in the sky. She did not shed tears that morning.

---

[77] *Mither – Scottish form of Mother*

Although her life had changed forever the moment she discovered Marcus had died, she knew now she had to look to the future. There would be bad days and better days and the journey would be long and difficult, but eventually she would comply with Marcus's wish. She felt comforted by the knowledge that he would be with her in spirit. In the fullness of time, they would be together again.

CHAPTER TWENTY-SIX

Letters
April 1856

It was bright that particular morning when Rosie sauntered down for breakfast. Much earlier, she'd heard Lizzie pottering around downstairs, so assumed she'd probably not slept well. Elspeth had anticipated Lizzie's need for an early breakfast. On entering the dining room, Rosie immediately noticed something different about her mam's demeanour. Most days she was to be seen with a cup of coffee, staring but not seeing what lay beyond the bay window, sorrowfully contemplating a future without Marcus, but strangely today she was tucking into croissants and jam.

'Good morning Rosie!' she smiled. 'It is going to be a lovely day. The sun is shining and there's a vibrant a chill in the air, the birds have been singing since 4 o'clock. What would you like for breakfast?'

A little perplexed and detecting a distinct change in her mother, Rosie replied cautiously, 'I...well, if they are Elspeth's delicious croissants, I will join you.'

Lizzie noticed the concern in Rosie's voice and her expression, so decided an explanation was required. She recounted her unusual experience during the previous evening. Rosie listened intently, her eyes widened as the tale unfolded. 'It had a profound effect on me Rosie, so much so that I put aside my sleeping draught. I still slept soundly but woke early and, more importantly, my nightmares disappeared'—she paused as Rosie frowned uncertainly—'I've at last come to terms with my life. I know that my path will be difficult and all the crying in the world will not bring Marcus back. I will have bad days and better days but today will be a better day. I owe it to Marcus to be strong and brave…it is what he would have wanted'—she paused again as she drew Rosie's attention to two letters on a silver tray—'I think you will have a good day too Rosie. The letters are for you.' She smiled, handing them to her daughter.

Rosie swallowed a mouthful of croissant, before scrutinising the writing on the envelopes. She recognised Jack's 'neat' and Jimmy's 'not so neat' hand immediately. She was, never the less, excited and decidedly curious. She ripped open Jimmy's letter and read the valediction first…'My love forever, Jimmy'. 'Oh Mam, it's from Jimmy! Do you mind if I take them to my room and finish breakfast later?'

Lizzie laughed. 'Of course not Rosie. I hope there's good news?'

'Oh yes Mam, I believe it will be very good news. I'll be down shortly. Will you still be here?'

'Yes Rosie, I intend to sit a while and enjoy a leisurely breakfast. I feel stronger today, so will begin sorting through Marcus's clothes and correspondence. On another day, I may not feel able to accomplish such a task.'

'Right Mam, I will help as I know it will be difficult,' she asserted, before rushing headlong down the corridor.

In the privacy of her room, Rosie read Jimmy's letter.

'My darlin Rosie, you will be suprised to receive a letter from me. Please forgive me spelling it's not improved much, but I had to write and tell you how I feel. I am hoping I read your own feelings right when

we last met befour me ship sailed. I have bin doing a lot of thinking since then and altho I thort I had gotten over you and moved on with Lucinda, I new that day, I hadnt. As soon as I saw you agen the love I had fer you came rushing back. I dint want ta sail that day. I wanted ta run down the gangway and gather you up in me arms. I hope Im not mecking a fool of meself and that you feel the same. I intend to finish with Lucinda and I will explain everything when a see you agen. I cant wait ta come home. Hopefully you will be there waiting fer me. Thats all fer now as 'ave got ta get this letter ta the ship chandla who will pass it on fer me. My love forever Jimmy xxxxxxxxx'

A big smile formed on Rosie's face as happiness surged through her entire body. She re-read the letter again before slipping it back into the envelope and holding it to her breast. She knew now that she and Jimmy would share a life together. She couldn't wait for his ship's arrival, expected to be in just over eleven weeks' time.

Nervously and with a certain anxiety, Rosie opened Jack's letter. She hoped more than anything that he would not want to resume their relationship on his return. She was, however, surprised by its formality and content.

My Dear Rosie,

I hope you are well. We have had rather a rough passage and have docked in Port Elizabeth for repairs to a mast. Consequently, I've decided to take this opportunity to write to you. You will undoubtedly receive it before we arrive home, courtesy of a fast mail steamer.

I have given a great deal of thought to the last time I saw you in Liverpool. I admit I was saddened and disheartened that you and Jimmy still appeared to have feelings for one another. Of course, I tried to dismiss these thoughts earlier on in our voyage, but as time went by, my conversations with Jimmy changed my understanding of Lucinda's relationship with him and his actual feelings for you, which are still strong. I hope I am not speaking out of turn, but I would be very surprised if Jimmy did not write to you to explain his innermost feelings.

I believed I was in love with you, but I also knew you did not feel the same...and probably never would. You now know Jimmy is alive and well and cannot be blamed for the vagaries of life and fortune. Consequently, I wish you both well for the future. Please do not feel sorry for me. I am a strong person and I will survive. I will always love you in my own way, so I know we will always be friends.

I am going to be honest with you, to prevent you feeling guilty. I became close to Helen on this trip. I don't love her, in the true sense at the moment, but feel we might have a chance in the future. I hope there won't be any difficult or embarrassing moments between us when we return. I will be a good friend and we will always have a connection through my father. I expect I will see a lot of you when I return, but, until then, take great care of yourself and give my love to Lizzie and father. With love, your good friend Jack xxx

Tears formed in Rosie's eyes, because Jack would be devastated to hear of his father's death. They'd agreed he should not hear before he returned home from Liverpool, but inevitably, their task would be extremely difficult. He would need all the support and love they could offer.

She secured Jimmy's letter in her keeper box, but put Jack's letter in her dressing gown pocket, returning downstairs.

Lizzie was surprised at Rosie's studious and thoughtful demeanour when she reappeared at the breakfast table, which prompted her to comment. 'Oh dear, Rosie, isn't the letter from Jimmy what you hoped for?'

'It's not the letter from Jimmy that has upset me,' replied Rosie warily. 'I am reminded that Jack does not know about Marcus. You can read his letter,' she offered, passing Lizzie the single sheet.

Lizzie read the contents thoughtfully, but could not prevent the tears that followed, making little effort to wipe them away. 'Oh Rosie, our task will be very difficult, especially so because we too are grieving for Marcus. I fear this will be a massive blow for Jack. I hope he *has* genuinely moved on and that Helen can provide some comfort to him, although he hasn't mentioned that she will be returning any time soon.'

Rosie shook her head. 'No Mam, I understood that when I waved them goodbye. Lucinda planned to return but Helen would stay with her parents for a while.'

'Would you like me to accompany you when their ship arrives?' Lizzie offered with compassion.

Rosie fell temporarily silent, unsure of what best to say. 'It might be an idea Mam and Jimmy will most likely refrain from showing his affections if you are there. Of course, I am looking forward to his homecoming, but the time to enjoy our reunion will come later. It is more important that we support Jack.'

'Yes Rosie, we must all pull together and support one another.'

Lizzie's optimism had waned slightly, following her reading of Jack's letter, but she was determined to regain it. She decided not to tackle the job of sorting out Marcus's private papers and possessions immediately, but she did take a look in his wardrobe. She removed the sweater he wore on their last walk together down by the river and pressed it to her face. She inhaled the manly scent then held it close for a few moments before placing it in her own chest of drawers. This particular item of his clothing, she would keep forever. Whenever she felt low, she would cuddle the magnificent woollen garment and remember the happy times they shared.

CHAPTER TWENTY-SEVEN

A Discovery
May 1856

It was over a month later, when Lizzie and Rosie finally began the task of sorting out Marcus's personal effects and packing boxes in anticipation of the move to Southwell. *The Beeches,* as expected, sold relatively quickly, but their moving date was still to be decided, as Marcus's business had not yet sold. Co-ordinating the sales of both assets was proving difficult and would take at least another month it seemed. Robert toyed with the idea of buying the business, but decided his own substantial cotton mill, which was booming, must take priority. He was also undertaking the onerous tasks of purchasing Lizzie's new property and overseeing the sale of her assets.

Rosie conscientiously helped Lizzie with the sad and distressing task of parcelling up Marcus's belongings for distribution amongst the poor at the church. It proved harrowing in the extreme, but it had to be dealt with. Rosie sorted Marcus's clothes, which Lizzie had been unable to undertake herself, while she tackled the paperwork.

'I'll start on the contents of his study desk,' stated Lizzie. There's heaps of correspondence. Although Marcus was extremely organised and efficient, it might not take as long as one might imagine. I hope so anyway.'

'Of course Mam, when I have finished my tasks, I will ask Elspeth for a pot of tea. It's very thirsty work, so we should take a break, say around half past ten in the sitting room,' suggested Rosie, as she efficiently packed yet another box with shirts, cravats and handkerchiefs. Some items were left in the wardrobe, still requiring a decision by Lizzie on their intended destination.

They had both been up since five thirty and Lizzie was quite exhausted already, so appreciated Rosie's suggestion. She hoped they'd finish by the end of the afternoon.

⁂

As she determinedly entered Marcus's study she couldn't help noticing its hollow, dark and soulless aura. In consequence, she flung open the curtains and allowed the morning sun to filter into the room. Its targeted rays illuminated the desk and floor and highlighted tiny particles of dust disturbed by her entrance.

No one had entered the study since Marcus's departure for Philadelphia, when the curtains were drawn and the door locked. Dust sheets had not been placed on the various pieces of furniture, as was usual when a room was not in use, so each item displayed a thin layer of dust on its surface. Lizzie sat tentatively on the blue leather Captain's chair. She intended emptying the desk drawers first, before starting on the oak filing cabinet. His numerous books would remain on the shelves, but she deemed it important to sift through all his papers for any important documents.

The top drawer contained pens, pencils, rulers and other small stationery items. It was here that Lizzie found an ornate key to a smart large oak writing slope, which took pride of place on the beautifully polished desk. She unlocked the slope gingerly. It contained a neat pile of papers; these she placed on top of the blotter. The title deeds to the house were among these documents, as were important papers relating to Marcus's business. All were read then placed in a pile. The remaining, less important documents, were returned to the slope. Her next task was to unlock the centre compartment of the main desk, which appeared shallower than its exterior suggested. Puzzled, but anxious to continue, Lizzie removed all the papers and sorted them into three piles: 'important papers to be discussed with Robert', 'papers requiring her attention' and lastly 'bills' which required Robert to instigate payment. Her latest task completed, she tried to close the drawer, but it resisted her attempt...something appeared to be stuck under the lip of the desk, interfering with its smooth closure. As she pulled the offending article, an envelope, from the underside, her fingers brushed against a small brass lever, which moved easily to one side. A false bottom had unexpectedly sprung open. Curious and with mixed emotions, because she was reminded of the Keeper Box made by her father, she examined the secret compartment containing old birthday and occasion cards neatly piled to one side. Several official looking envelopes occupied the remaining space, some with broken seals. She removed them before closing the drawer. There were several letters from a local solicitor and letters from Marcus's father. A third sealed envelope, shocked and surprised Lizzie, in that it was marked 'Last Will and Testament – Marcus Van der Duim, 31st December 1855.'

She carefully slit open the vellum envelope with an ivory and silver letter opener and extracted a letter plus the parchment Will, bound with blue ribbon. Her hands shook as she read the letter, obviously written by Marcus himself:

My Darling Elizabeth,

If you are reading this letter, it suggests I have unexpectedly had to leave you. If this is the case, I am so sorry my love...I realise this will mean I have met my maker earlier than I thought, but none of us have any control over how long we have to live on this earth. Rest assured, even though I have passed, if it is in my power, I will still watch over you.

My father always maintained, that making a Will does not hasten one's death! With that in mind, I made this Will on the afternoon of New Year's Eve 1855, after returning from my visit to Thomas Taylor, Solicitor. He advised that, as a beneficiary, you should be referred to as 'Elizabeth Cameron'. Even though you have taken my name, in the eyes of the law you are still a 'Cameron'.

In the unlikely event that I have met with my demise! I shall not have the opportunity to change the wordage of my Will again, which I hoped to do after our much-awaited marriage on the 1st March 1856, to reflect your new name. Incidentally, if the former is true, you will find the rings I bought when I was over in Philadelphia last, in the safe behind the picture...My father and I visited New York for a couple of days. He advised me then to buy matching rings from Tiffany, Young & Ellis on Broadway, I hope you like them.

In respect of my inheritance...I leave the business and our home, The Beeches, to you, also my father's house in Philadelphia, if he and I should die before we marry...(as mentioned, that is very unlikely, as he is still a very fit and healthy man, as am I my love).

Of course, if my father should die, before I get the chance to alter the Will, Jack will inherit his business to do with it as he wishes. We, of course, would have sufficient funds and property to live very comfortably from the sale of my father's house. Rosie should be given a substantial sum of money to guarantee her future and, of course, if all goes to plan, after we are married, she should eventually (post our deaths) inherit half of everything we own...the other half will go to Jack, together with my father's business. I hope he might continue the family tradition, but it will be entirely up to him.

I find myself smiling as I write these requests, as I truly believe you will never have to carry them through, but I am reliably informed that it is always prudent to make a Will! I am, with all my heart, looking forward to a long and happy life together...Just like Perseus and Andromeda...I still remember our romantic night when we stood at the hotel window looking out at the stars. Of course, if you are reading this, you will know wherever I am, I will watch over you. If this be the case, I want you to lead a full and happy life, albeit without me in the physical sense. I know that will be difficult. Don't be afraid to remarry in the future. You have my blessing, as all I wish for is your continued happiness.

Well my love, that's about it! It feels very strange writing this to you, as you are at this moment, busy preparing for our New Year's Eve party. I can hear you humming 'My Love is Like a Red, Red Rose', which you always do when you are happy. Let's hope our happiness continues until we are both well in to old age. We will be able to look back on a life together, filled with love, hopes and dreams, all of which we can achieve. I have been thinking as I write this letter to you, that I just might keep it and show it to you one New Year's Eve, when we are old and grey and sitting in rocking chairs in front of a blazing fire, just to celebrate the fact that we both made it to that moment.

My love to you always, Marcus xxx

Tears flowed unashamedly down Lizzie's cheeks as she folded the paper and inserted it back in its envelope. Several minutes elapsed before she rose to leave the room, but unexpectedly she experienced an overwhelming sense of love and peace. Strangely the hollow, dark soulless energy, she'd identified on entering the room had disappeared. The sun's rays were now filling the room with warmth and light, which lifted her spirits. The letter enhanced her belief that Marcus was indeed watching over her, just as she'd dreamt on the eve of his birthday. Thoughts of him would see her through her darkest moments as she trod the path of life alone.

CHAPTER TWENTY-EIGHT

The Decision
May 1856

Midway through May, Robert and Kate were due to meet for the second time at The Star Inn. Robert arrived first and secured the same room, then waited in the window booth for Kate's arrival.

The clock above the bar showed the time to be a quarter to twelve. Kate was already fifteen minutes late. He frowned in consternation because it wasn't like her. He ordered a brandy whilst absently noticing the lock gates were opening, to allow access for a cargo-laden narrow boat.

Just as he was resigned to the idea that she may not turn up, a clatter of hooves attracted his attention. A coach pulled up outside, much to his relief and the familiar figure of Kate disembarked. He was shocked to realise just how important Kate was to his life and now knew he would be bereft without her.

Kate was all smiles and apologies as she entered the inn. 'Oh Robert, do forgive me, I am so sorry I am late; one of the horses threw a shoe and we had a lengthy wait while the driver, who used to be a blacksmith, re-shoed her,' she advised, before kissing him briefly in compensation for the delay.

Robert returning her kiss, smiled. 'It's okay Kate, I haven't been here long myself,' he lied, glancing over her shoulder to ascertain if the landlord was listening, but fortunately, some other customers required his undivided attention. When the landlord was free, Robert ordered a gin and tonic for Kate, thinking it might be the right moment to broach a delicate subject. Uncharacteristically, however, he blurted out his earlier decision. 'I have taken the liberty of booking a room for the night, Kate. I hope that meets with your approval?' he stated bashfully, which seemed at odds with his earlier confidence.

'That is fine with me Robert, although I am not sure one is required,' she replied teasingly. 'Last time our room wasn't used to best advantage.'

Robert flushed, fingering his collar. 'Yes, but this time, I'll put that right,' he affirmed quietly, as he moved to hold her hand across the table. He realised that his need to make love to her was overwhelming. Despite the moral dilemma, it seemed ludicrous that they should not sleep together, when they were so much in love. He hoped their affair would remain a secret, but felt capable of accepting the consequences, should the unthinkable happen. His resolve to stay true to Amy no longer seemed possible. As he gazed into the eyes of Kate, his first love, his heart melted. It would take all his willpower to resist the temptation of making love to her. He doubted he was capable of lasting five minutes, let alone his self-imposed target of eighteen months.

A short while after, they found themselves outside the bedroom on the first floor. Robert opened the door hurriedly, before removing his coat. He pulled Kate towards him, kissing her passionately. 'Oh Kate, you must know how much you mean to me and how much I love you,' he whispered.

'I have never stopped loving you Robert and long for the day we can be together,' she responded, but his love could no longer be denied, as his urgent kisses left her in no doubt of his intentions.

Deftly he unbuttoned the bodice on her dress and undergarments, which slid to the floor. The years melted away as they rediscovered their passion for one another. It was as if they had never been apart. Robert carried Kate to the bed, then disrobed quickly himself. He pulled her close and planted kisses across her shoulders, determined this moment would be special, as he slowly caressed her naked body. Initially, Kate responded fervently, before it dawned on her that they had the whole afternoon and night to be together, so allowed Robert to dictate the pace. They were uninhibited in their eagerness to pleasure one another. As long lost lovers they remembered the many times they had made love in the deserted cottage. Their desire to fulfil needs was all consuming.

Despite their determination to savour this long awaited reawakening, they were carried away on a sea of emotions. Robert's need to enter her overwhelmed him and they became one. Later as they lay in each other's arms, they knew they were destined to be together always, despite Robert's intentioned promise to be faithful to Amy. From that moment, he wanted more than anything, to stay with Kate and not return home, but knew they would have a cruel wait before they became free to spend the rest of their lives together.

At this point, Kate remembered something she'd brought with her. 'I felt so sad that I couldn't celebrate your birthday with you, but I do have a gift.' She smiled as she reached over to her bag and extricated a small box, which she opened to reveal a pair of exquisite *Faberge,* egg shaped, Nephrite Jade, diamond and gold cuff links. 'I do hope you like them Robert, although I realise you won't be able to wear them for some time,' she said ruefully.

Robert was overwhelmed by such an expensive gift, but did not want to embarrass Kate. 'My goodness Kate, they are absolutely splendid, but I am not sure I am worthy of such a gift. However, I will treasure them forever and, as you advise, I will have to keep them somewhere safe, until such time as we are together. Thank you,' he said, slipping the box into the inner pocket of his frock coat, which he had hung on the back of the chair.

Later that afternoon, they spent an idyllic time walking by the river, before returning to make love for a second time. When the sun rose the following morning, they knew their time was limited.

They promised to meet again on the 25th July, after the family 'get together' on the 12th. They took separate coaches to the station ready to immerse themselves in their every day lives' once again. Neither could have envisaged that their next meeting would be sooner than they imagined.

CHAPTER TWENTY-NINE

Turning Point
June/July 1856

The Champion of the Seas docked in the port of Liverpool on the 28th June. The passenger quay bustled with excited people, welcoming home relatives, friends and loved ones. Merchants hoping to sell their wares mingled with flower girls selling their posies to passers by before the blooms faded. The sweet smell of lavender seemed at odds with the smell of recently caught fish in baskets brought by the Fisherman to sell to the highest bidders at market.

Alone and in complete contrast, Lizzie and Rosie waited patiently on a bench at the far end of the quayside. Only when the last of the passengers dispersed would Jack and Jimmy finally disembark, after completing all their essential duties. They were surprised that Lucinda was not among the passengers, but Lizzie concluded that she was probably waiting until the men were ready to accompany her.

They realised they could not wait any longer so approached the magnificent ship as the crowds thinned. Almost immediately, Rosie caught sight of the familiar figure of Jack leaning over the ship's rails, desperately trying to attract their attention. 'There's Jack Mam, but he is alone. Maybe Jimmy and Lucinda have already disembarked. Oh, I do hope we haven't missed them.'

Rosie waved back as Jack reappeared at the top of the gangway. He smiled as he began his descent. Only then did

Rosie realise the implication of their reunion. She knew his reaction to the news of Marcus's death would not be pleasant and his smile would be gone in an instant, to be replaced by extreme sadness. Inevitably, the process of coming to terms with his loss could take some considerable time. She walked towards him, then noticed Jimmy following close behind, but no Lucinda, which she found slightly perplexing. Nevertheless she was excited to see Jimmy and welcome their safe return. For now, she must keep up the pretence that all was well, until Jimmy and Jack exhausted the retelling of their adventures. Just how long would she be able to delay imparting the news of Marcus's death?

Jack grinned broadly as he put his arms around Rosie and whispered in her ear, 'Don't worry Rosie, everything will turn out all right. There's no need to pretend everything is as it was. Jimmy and me had a long talk last night and we are good.'

Rosie kissed Jack on both cheeks and conveyed her gratitude with a smile. Their conversation was cut short, as Lizzie stepped forward to greet Jack, manoeuvring him to one side to ask how the voyage had been, especially with respect to the rough weather and the unexpected detour to Port Elizabeth.

Jack responded enthusiastically, but finished by asking about Marcus. 'So was father not able to get away from his business?' he asked Lizzie speculatively.

'Something like that Jack, you know how it is. Men have different priorities to women. Anyway, we should make our way to the coach,' she added, delaying the inevitable. 'We must be at the station, in time to catch the train to Manchester. I expect you can't wait to unwind and have a glass or two of brandy,' Lizzie commented.

'Well I can't say the thought of being home, a comfortable chair and brandy, doesn't have a certain appeal,' said Jack, disappointed that his father was not there to welcome him home.

Jimmy's excitement changed to one of confusion on seeing Rosie again. Although she was smiling, she did not look overjoyed to see him and for a moment his heart sank. It was not what he was expecting. Had he read the signs wrongly when he last saw her several months ago? He thought not, but kept his emotions in check just in case. Despite Jack's assurance that his involvement with Rosie was over, he realised he should restrain himself from sweeping her up in his arms.

Whilst speculating on his next course of action, he noticed that Lizzie was dressed all in black, which seemed odd. However, he did not have time to dwell on this, distracted by an after thought that Rosie's reticence might be related to her break-up with Jack.

I'll remain calm, he thought to himself, but inwardly his heart was beating out of his chest. Rosie had greeted him with a friendly, 'Hello Jimmy', but that was all. Did she long for him to hold her in his arms and kiss her?

Rosie also hadn't imagined that their reunion would be like this either, but the reality was, that she also needed to show restraint.

However, she did wish to reassure him, so reached over and squeezed his hand, before whispering, 'I love you Jimmy, but we must respect Jack's feelings at least until we arrive home,' explained Rosie.

Relieved and elated, Jimmy tentatively placed his arm around Rosie's waist as they made their way to the waiting coach.

The journey seemed interminable. Lizzie and Rosie were keeping up the pretence that everything was well with the world, both on the coach and the train, until eventually they arrived at *The Beeches*.

On entering the living room, Elspeth efficiently and diplomatically placed the promised bottle of brandy and four glasses on the table, before bustling away to prepare a lunch, which most probably no one would feel remotely like eating.

Jack poured everyone a good measure then contentedly sank back into a comfortable settee. Lizzie sat next to Jack while Rosie and Jimmy occupied the two armchairs. A lull in conversation gave Lizzie the opportunity she required. She moved closer to Jack and took hold of his hand. It would be the worse news she had ever had to convey. She took a deep breath. 'Jack, I am afraid I have some news that will shock and upset you greatly. Your granddad, died while you were away and your father needed to visit Philadelphia to finalise his will and attend to other matters. He sailed on the 23rd January on the *Pacific*, for New York. It departed Liverpool less than two weeks after you set sail for Australia. Unfortunately, *The Pacific* never made its destination and foundered somewhere on route. I am so sorry Jack, but there were no survivors,' advised Lizzie, her voice full of emotion.

Jimmy looked on incredulously, not quite grasping the enormity of Lizzie's statement.

Jack paled. He struggled to understand Lizzie's words. 'Oh my God, no...no it can't be true, we have only just been reunited. Why? How can that be? Surely there must have been survivors. My father was a strong swimmer, I know he would have fought for his life—' He stopped abruptly; tears welled in his eyes then unashamedly spilt down his cheeks.

'It is true Jack. We know your father would have done his best to survive, but it was an exceptionally violent storm.

He didn't stand a chance. Wreckage was found, but no bodies were recovered. According to a report posted in the Underwriters' Rooms in Glasgow on 27th February, the wreckage was spotted by the S.S. Edinburg *[sic]*, which arrived in Liverpool on the 14th from New York. Apparently, it passed a large quantity of broken ice, interspersed with broken cabin furniture, fine ornamental doors with white or glass handles, such as might have belonged to a first class steamer or ship.' Lizzie confirmed, as she held back her own tears.

Jack stroked his chin, in one last vain attempt to maintain hope. 'So, there isn't really any confirmation that the wreckage belonged to *The Pacific*,' he argued.

Lizzie knew he was in denial and clutching at straws, but her heart went out to him nonetheless. The tragedy had hit him particularly hard. 'You are right Jack, there isn't any absolute proof, but what is undeniable is that the ship did not reach its destination. We have to believe it foundered and there weren't any survivors. If Marcus had survived, he would have done his utmost to make contact with us, but that hasn't happened. We have to accept, he is not coming home,' stated Lizzie, her own intense sadness almost overwhelming her.

Jack took a large slug of brandy and shook his head, before abruptly exiting the sitting room, his rapid footsteps clattering along the hallway before ascending the stairs.

'Should I go after him,' suggested a stunned Jimmy.

'No Jimmy, he will probably wish to be alone to assimilate his thoughts and work through this terrible event,' advised Lizzie. 'I'm sure he will return when he feels able. I reacted in much the same way myself and I just wanted to be alone, despite everyone's attempts to comfort me. I will ask Elspeth to take a light lunch to his room and hopefully we will see him this evening. Whatever Jack wants to do, we will respect his wishes, but Jimmy, that was really thoughtful. I realize how difficult this is for you, to arrive back home and walk into such an horrendous situation. We must not forget that this is also your homecoming, which I imagine you would have been looking forward to. Rosie and yourself will have a lot to discuss. Why don't you walk by the river, to enjoy some privacy? Elspeth will pack a picnic basket for you. You can have lunch and return this evening. Take the chequered tartan rug with you. You'll find it in the cupboard by the stairs. I will look after Jack. I am sure he will speak to us in due course,' confirmed Lizzie.

'Thanks Mam, we'll do as you suggest, if Jimmy is agreeable,' posed Rosie.

'I think that is a good idea,' he agreed, it will give us time to think.

❧

When they reached a peaceful stretch of the river, Jimmy turned and faced Rosie. He knew there was a lot to get off his chest and now they were alone, he intended to discuss the future with her. 'I thought the moment would never come when we would be together again'—he began—'but here we are, though not under the best of circumstances.' He smiled ruefully as he intimately put his arms around her waist. However, he was extremely conscious everything had changed dramatically in the time they'd been away.

Although still grieving herself and sad for Jack, it didn't seem fair that Jimmy's homecoming should be wholly centred around Marcus's death. To remove the shadow that had been cast and in an effort to dispel his concerns, she determined to lift their mood in her own inimitable way. 'Jimmy Mitchell, are you just going to carry on talking or are you going to kiss me. I too have waited for this moment. We have been apart quite a while now...too long to waste any more time on the spoken word,' she announced truculently, before looking up expectantly.

Jimmy did not need a second invitation and pulled her close to him, kissing her passionately. It was the first kiss they had shared since he boarded *'The Lightning'* in the May of 1855. He'd almost lost his life on that ship, he recalled fleetingly. He remembered that kiss had been soft and sensual, but not like this one. As they struggled to keep their emotions at bay they became almost breathless with desire. Jimmy now experienced in the art of making love, was especially affected, but still managed, rather reluctantly, to release Rosie from his embrace, deciding to lead her instead to a spot beneath a large oak tree, where he laid the tartan rug on the grass. 'Let's sit here and enjoy the afternoon sun,' he suggested, unwilling at this point to start something that he would be unable to stop.

Rosie, somewhat piqued at Jimmy's reticence, unpacked the picnic box. For what seemed an age, they ate their lunch in silence, as they each reflected on what just transpired, but soon Rosie capitulated and snuggled into Jimmy's shoulder. Without looking up at him, she asked the question she had been wanting an answer to as she waved goodbye on the dockside, prior to the *Champion of the Seas*, sailing. 'Jimmy, I want you to tell me about Lucinda. What you had planned and what she meant to you?'

Unsure as to how much he should reveal, Jimmy only gave a brief account of their relationship. He neglected to mention the fact that they had made love on several occasions. Rosie listened avidly, but felt sure Jimmy had purposefully missed out on how far their intimacy had progressed. He did, however, underline the fact that, at that time, he believed Rosie was also in a relationship with Jack. His mother had confirmed it when he and Lucinda visited her on Christmas Day. Undoubtedly, his intimacy with Lucinda only started after he discovered that her and Jack were seeing each other. 'So you see Rosie,' he ended, 'I didn't feel I was being disloyal to you when I embarked on a relationship with Lucinda. I had no reason to doubt that you had also moved on,' he concluded.

Studiously avoiding Jimmy's gaze, she asked him the ultimate question, 'Did you make love to her?'

Stunned, but wanting to make amends, Jimmy felt he had no choice but to come clean. 'I will not lie to you Rosie. We did make love, but I was never sure that I was actually *in love* with her,' he finished lamely, in the fervent hope that more difficult questions would not follow.

His hopes were dashed however, as Rosie persisted. 'I can understand that Jimmy and why you became lovers, but what I am not sure about is how, in such a very short space of time, you decided you still had feelings for me and was happy to end your relationship with Lucinda?'

He fell silent; he would have to tell Rosie everything, that Lucinda was pregnant. Before he revealed all, he tilted her chin toward him and pulled her close to kiss her. In consequence, Rosie almost forgot her question, allowing herself to enjoy Jimmy's kiss, but the fact that he'd made love to someone else, made her jealous beyond comprehension. She believed their first sexual encounter would be with one another. She wanted him to make love to her more than ever, as she was several years above the age of consent.[78] Would Jimmy even now think her mature enough?

---

[78] *The age of consent was changed for the first time in the nineteenth century in 1875, when the felony clause was raised from 10 to 12 and the misdemeanour clause from 12 to 13.*

They separated abruptly, surprised by the strong sexual feelings that were surging through their bodies. Jimmy broke the silence. 'Rosie, I do love you and I always have. The day we sailed, I regretted committing to Lucinda, but by then I didn't have the opportunity to tell you how I felt. I knew we still had strong feelings for one another, when our eyes met just as the ship pulled off the berth. I even told you as much in the letter I wrote to you.'

'I know Jimmy. I felt the same as soon as I saw you again, but when I noticed the ring on Lucinda's finger after we were introduced I felt confused. Only later when you squeezed my hand as we left the café did I realise and my heart soared; I knew you felt the same, but tell me about the ring Jimmy?'

'Okay. I renewed my acquaintance with Lucinda aboard the *Dreadnought*. We bumped into one another almost daily, her being a nurse on the ship. I did write to you and also me mam and gave the letters to an older nurse to post. Time passed and as I did not receive a reply, I assumed you didn't want a relationship with me. It turned out neither you nor me mam received my letters. I felt low but decided I had to change my life. I admit to liking Lucinda so asked her if she would like to spend Christmas with me and she seemed keen. We spent the first part of the holiday at her parents and then travelled to Derbyshire to be with me mam on Christmas Day. That's when I discovered you were in a relationship with Jack, so I decided then I must forget about you and move on. Lucinda actually saved me mam's life'—he stated matter of factly—'as when we arrived, Mam had slipped into unconsciousness due to the cold. Lucinda's nursing skills brought her back from the brink. Mam was so thankful that she gave her the ring. She wore it on sailing day. I'd foolishly asked her to wear it on the third finger of her left hand as a sign of commitment because I felt I owed it to her to put our relationship on an official footing. At first everything seemed good between us but later that changed. It was at me mam's house that we first made love incidentally. Had I known you were still interested in me, I would not have made such a commitment. Do you understand Rosie?'

Rosie fell silent and struggled to prevent tears forming in her eyes. She realised how close she had been to losing Jimmy for good, but understood his dilemma. Jimmy went on to explain how Lucinda *eventually* informed him she was pregnant and that the child wasn't his. This shocked her, but as Jimmy revealed the whole story, she was relieved at his decision to end the relationship with Lucinda.

'Oh Jimmy, it must have been very difficult for you, but where is Lucinda now and what does she intend to do about the baby?'

Jimmy enlightened her, 'She is staying with Helen's parents in Melbourne for a while, before returning home and I believe she will go through with the pregnancy. Her parents are very supportive and I expect she'll live with them and continue her nursing career.'

'Oh I see, well I do feel sorry for her, but it may be the best alternative. Did you know Jack wrote to me when the ship was in Port Elizabeth by the way? He told me then that he knew you and I still had feelings for one another and that he had become close to Helen over the course of the voyage. He is hoping they might have a future together.'

Jimmy grinned. 'I thought he might, following a conversation we had. Jack is a good man Rosie and accepted our situation. I will always consider him to be a good friend and a good shipmate. We must support him as best we can during this sad time, even if it means any plans for our future are kept on hold. Do you agree Rosie?'

'Yes...yes of course Jimmy. It will take some time before he will come to terms with his father's death. I expect him to stay at our home for some while; although we will, of course, be moving to Southwell soon.'

It was Jimmy's turn to be surprised. 'Southwell? Where is that Rosie and why will you be moving there?'

'Well, It is on the outskirts of Nottingham Jimmy. Clara and Arthur will move in with us, but as it is a long story, I will tell you about it later. For now, let's just enjoy the rest of the afternoon together,' she suggested, laying her head on his shoulder.

Jimmy gently turned towards her then placed his lips on hers. As he did so, he moved his hands down over her breasts. Rosie responded eagerly, as she whispered in Jimmy's ear—'Make love to me Jimmy.'

Jimmy however, moved away, held her gently by her shoulders and as the moment was lost, apologised. 'We can't...not here Rosie, it is too risky. I do want to, but not now. Somehow it doesn't seem right with Jack's grief casting a shadow over us,' he explained.

Rosie fell silent studying Jimmy's face. 'I know you are right, but I want us to become more than friends. Please tell me we won't have to wait too long?' She sighed, disappointed their relationship remained platonic.

'Of course not,' he promised, smiling, before reaching into his pocket to take out the posy ring that Lucinda had returned to him. 'What would you say if I asked you to wear me mam's ring?'—he paused then continued—'I will understand if you do not want to wear a ring I once gave to Lucinda. I can buy you a new one if you like, but I want to show you that I am serious about our future together,' Jimmy explained, as he held the ring in the palm of his hand.

'Oh Jimmy, yes, I would like to accept your mam's ring. I really don't need a new one and it would mean more than any other.'

Jimmy grinned. 'Give me your hand Rosie.' Not thinking, Rosie proffered her right hand.

'No, silly, the left hand. What I am trying to say is, will you marry me Rosie Cameron?' he asked anxiously.

Rosie flung her arms around him immediately he placed the ring on her finger. 'Of course I'll marry you. I love you Jimmy Mitchell and can't wait for us to be together. In fact, that might be sooner than you think. I know Mam will give you a room at our new home until we get married,' she stated, as she admired the small gold posy ring that fitted perfectly on her third finger. 'Oh Jimmy, I am so happy.'

'So am I Rosie. This time I know I am doing the right thing, I feel it here,' he said placing his hand on his heart. 'I do need to ask you one thing, however; just for a while, can we keep this to ourselves? You can tell your mam and dad and your mamma, but for Jack's sake, would you wear the ring on a chain around your neck until the time is right to tell him of our plans?'

'Of course Jimmy. It is the right thing to do. Now kiss me again before we pack up our picnic.'

Jimmy willingly obliged. Soon they were walking hand in hand along the river and back to *The Beeches*, overjoyed at the thought of spending the rest of their lives together. The following morning Jimmy would take Rosie to visit his mother.

Lizzie's family moved into their new home in Southwell, although the sad thought that they would be saying their goodbyes to Marcus was uppermost in their minds.

His Memorial Service took place at St Denis village church, in the Parish of Southwell on a fine summer morning. It was well attended by his family, friends and many of his employees who'd travelled from Lancashire to pay their respects. The vast amount of flowers, placed reverently near his memorial plaque, close to the centuries old Church, were testament to the high regard in which he was held.

Jack read the eulogy, but was hardly able to contain his emotions as he extolled the many virtues of his late father, whilst Lizzie looked on, a sad and lonely figure, although surrounded by friends and family.

It would be a long time before, Lizzie, Jack and Rosie, came to terms with the loss of Marcus. The impact he'd made on their lives would never be forgotten and their love for him would last forever... Marcus could now rest in peace.

༺ৡ༻

The service was held the day before Jack left for Philadelphia, when he received a letter postmarked 'Melbourne', forwarded from *The Beeches*. He knew immediately it was from Helen. He'd torn the envelope open, hoping the letter contained news of her arrival, desperate that it should not coincide with his visit to America. His ship, the *Lucy Thompson* was due to sail to New York on the 5th July, but not return to Liverpool until the 19th September. Fortunately, Helen was due on the 26th, exactly a week after his return. This gave him the focus he needed for the future, which sadly would not include his father. Finding a bench in a secluded part of the garden he read Helen's letter again:

'My Dearest Jack,

I hope you are well and your return journey was uneventful. I am missing you terribly and hope you miss me too. Lucinda's baby is due in early July (around the time you will receive this letter) and despite being heavily pregnant, she intends returning to her parents' home in Cambridge. She boarded a ship for home last week, after deciding to keep the baby. Perhaps you could let Jimmy know. She appears to have come to terms with losing him but is determined to pursue her nursing career after the birth.

I spent a lovely couple of months with my parents Jack, but I am looking forward to coming home and seeing you. I hope you feel the same as I and will be waiting for me when the ship docks. It's scheduled to arrive on the 26th July all being well. It would be lovely if you could come alone then we could book into an hotel for a couple of days before seeing everyone. I assume you are staying at The Beeches with Lizzie and your father. I can imagine how delighted he would have been to see you again.

I hope Rosie and Jimmy have renewed their friendship. I'm sure they will have a wonderful future together. Rosie is such a lovely person. I know she's young, but if they genuinely love one another, age shouldn't matter.

I was standing on the afterdeck leaning on the ship's rail and looking at the stars last night, thinking of the time you asked me back to your cabin. I couldn't believe that you wanted to make love to me, but I was really delighted, (as you may have noticed!). I am praying you feel the same way about me. My feelings haven't changed and I cannot wait for us to be together again. I miss your kisses and our lovemaking.

I want more than anything for you to be waiting for me Jack and dream of that moment.

My love to you, Helen xxx

Jack shed a tear as he read the line concerning his father, but was delighted Helen had laid bare her feelings for him. He needed comfort at this awful time and realised she could and would provide it. Placing the letter in his jacket pocket, he returned to the empty house. Lizzie was absent, visiting Clara and Arthur in Nottingham and Rosie and Jimmy were in Derbyshire to surprise Ida. They'd already promised to see Jack off on the 5th, but he was glad to be alone right now; despite the family's anxiety, he'd insisted he would be able to cope for a couple of days in their absence.

Alone in the study, he poured a brandy then sat in his father's captain's chair, which gave him comfort. He relaxed as his thoughts turned to the future. Helen would surely play a large part of course, probably as his wife. His father's death mostly occupied his waking moments, but he also recalled his time with Helen on the *'Champion'*. He realised he missed her more than he'd ever imagined.

He took out the letter again and re-read the pages, which made him stronger and able to face the future, whatever that held. He knew that her love would give him the strength and wit in Philadelphia, to settle the legal aspects of his grandfather's will, which his father was sadly unable to accomplish. At that moment, he felt confident of the challenges that lay ahead. Lizzie had already briefed him about Marcus's will, which provided for him. In addition, he would also inherit a large sum of money after the sale of his grandfather's business. He had already decided he would not take on the mantle of the family business, as his father may have wished, but his heart lay in sailing the great oceans of the world. *How would Helen fair as the wife of a sailor* he wondered absently.

They would have to move to an English port town, as Nottingham was landlocked, but they could live anywhere they chose. That particular question did not require an immediate answer, but first he must make the passage to New York and then, on his return, after the memorial service for his father, he would take stock of his life.

CHAPTER THIRTY

Approval
July 1856

Rosie and Jimmy boarded the train to Darley Abbey. Jimmy was desperate to see his mam again, although he needed to explain the circumstances surrounding his parting from Lucinda and his engagement to Rosie.

A nervous and preoccupied Rosie twisted the ring around her finger, whilst staring blankly out of the window.

'Is something wrong Rosie?' asked Jimmy with ill concealed concern.

Rosie laughed nervously, trying to make light of her preoccupation. 'Not really Jimmy, but I do wonder what Ida will think when we turn up on her doorstep, because the last time you met, you were practically engaged to Lucinda.'

'Aw, don't worry about me mam, she'll understand right enough. Leave it to me Rosie. The fact that Lucinda's baby isn't mine, will be reason enough. I bet she'll be pleased we are back together again, you'll see. Mam's rather old fashioned in that respect and believes couples should wait until they are married before they do it...if you catch my meaning?' Jimmy coughed, somewhat embarrassed, before continuing tentatively. 'Which reminds me, I was thinking we could perhaps book somewhere this coming month; go away for a few days. What do you think?'

'Oh, yes, Jimmy, I would like that,' she willingly agreed, realising *he* wanted a meaningful relationship and pleased that he had become so manly and masterful. 'Maybe the time is right because I did want you to make love to me when we walked by the river,' she reminded him with a grin. 'I realised then that we had all the time in the world to be together so didn't need to rush anything,' she added, allowing Jimmy 'the upper hand'.

'Are you telling me, I've actually made a good suggestion Rosie Cameron? I have waited many years for that ta happen,' he said laughing with her.

'I only said, *maybe*, Jimmy,' she teased, looking out the window again to conceal a grin.

Soon the train drew in to Derby station. In good spirits they signalled for a coach to take them on to Ida's. It was Rosie's first time in Derbyshire and the beautiful countryside surrounding Darley Abbey impressed her. 'Perhaps we could stay somewhere in Derbyshire,' suggested Rosie enthusiastically. 'We've already passed a river on our way and I'd love to spend some time picnicking and walking along the river bank.'

'That's a great idea Rosie,' Jimmy agreed. Despite her earlier approval of his judgement, he realised it would be some time before she truly believed that all his suggestions earned merit. However, it was an excellent start.

The coach dropped them off near Ida's cottage. Jimmy raced to her door and knocked loudly, wherein Ida duly appeared, totally astonished but delighted to find Jimmy on her doorstep. He swept her up in his arms. 'We thought we'd surprise you Mam and here we are,' exclaimed Jimmy.

Ida, laughing at his antics, felt more secure when her feet touched terra firma again. It was then she noticed Rosie standing behind Jimmy a little uncertain of her reception. Rosie stepped forward. 'Hello Ida, you look well. I've been looking forward to seeing you again.'

Ida, perplexed, hid her consternation beneath a welcoming smile. 'Come in, come in. I was just abaht ta mash,' she said, as she disappeared inside.

Jimmy and Rosie followed. Ida indicated Rosie seat herself on one of the two old, but comfortable armchairs. 'While Rosie is mecking herssen comfortable, praps you could help me in the scullery Jimmy,' she suggested, hoping that a quick explanation for Rosie's presence would be forthcoming.

'Okay Mam,' Jimmy agreed, as he winked conspiratorially at Rosie.

Ida spoke in whispered tones. 'What's up son? Where's Lucinda and why 'ave yer brought Rosie?' she queried, her eyes wide in expectation.

'It's a long story Mam'—he began, slipping easily back into the local dialect—'But briefly, me and Lucinda broke up on our voyage ta Australia. Turned out she was having someone else's baby and I didn't want ta bring it up as me own. I knew Rosie and I still had deep feelings for each other when she came ta see Jack and me off. I decided ta write ta her on the voyage and now we are tagether agen,' he concluded.

Ida's eyes widened. Jimmy never ceased to surprise her. 'Well blow me down wi a feather.[79] What on earth wah Lucinda thinking on Jimmy? A thought she wah a good gel,' Ida said, although her expression of disdain was not lost on Jimmy. He only just managed to smother a grin at his mam's turn of phrase.

---

79 *Originated in the 19th century or earlier Likely derived from an African/American song sung by sailors, 'Blow the Man Down'.*

'Actually she is Mam, but it's more complicated than that. I'll tell you the ins and outs[80] later, but now let's have that cuppa,' Jimmy suggested, rejoining Rosie in the parlour.

The pair had treats: a bottle of wine, chocolate truffles, shortbread biscuits, cooked ham and a newly available tin of condensed milk, which Rosie presented to Ida, along with a large bunch of sweet peas from the garden of Oak Tree Lodge. Delighted, Ida studied the items on the table. 'Why Rosie, yer shunt 'ave spent yer money on me, but thanks me'duck. Jimmy, fetch us a vase from the scullery. Thiz a nice cut glass un in the cupboard that 'ud suit. I've some fresh bread and butter in the larder, we'll have some of that ham for lunch,' she said smiling, whilst handing Rosie a cup of tea.

'Let's have a shortbread biscuit with the tea Mam,' Jimmy suggested noticing Rosie was already eyeing up the elaborately decorated tin.

'That's a good idea son, you cun put some on a plate,' she directed, before launching into question mode. 'I'm aching with curiosity,' she admitted, waving goodbye to subtlety. 'Now then Jimmy, tell me again how you and Rosie got tagether?'

Jimmy grinned at his mam's undisguised inquisitiveness, then began the long story, ending with Marcus's death. Ida shook her head in sadness then Jimmy changed tact. 'There's another thing yer should know Mam, Lucinda insisted on giving me back your ring, despite yer wish for her ta keep it, so I've given it ta Rosie,' he said gingerly, hoping Ida would understand.

---

80 *'Ins and outs' - The first meaning turned up in 1670 in a memorial by Bishop John Hackett on John Williams, Archbishop of York: 'Follow their Whimsies and their In and outs at the Consulto, when the Prince was among them.'*

'Ah well, Jimmy, when I gev it ta her, I imagined yer would get married and yer would pass it down the line. A couldn't imagine the situation yer found yersenn in messen Jimmy, so of course a don't mind. 'ave known yerv loved Rosie a very long time and a knew yer weren't 'appy abaht her and Jack, but thought yer'd got ovver it. Seems yer cun nevva tell what the future holds, but if yer both 'appy, then I'm 'appy. Am very sorry ta 'ear abaht Marcus's death Rosie. A 'ope yer mam's coping all right. It can't be easy fer yer all,' Ida commiserated.

'It was a great shock. Jack and I had just broken up when he was informed of his father's death. It meant Jimmy and I needed to keep our engagement a secret. I've worn your ring for the first time today. The only saving grace in all of this is that Jack renewed his friendship with Lucinda's friend Helen. I believe he will see her when she returns from Australia. She will be of great comfort to him,' explained Rosie, turning the ring on her finger and appreciating how important it was to have the right person to share life's fortunes.

ॐ

After lunch, of ham and fresh bread, they decided to visit Matlock Bath where they gazed in wonder at the scale of the limestone crags of *High Tor* and *Wild Cat Tor*. They walked by the *River Derwent* then later treated Ida to dinner at the *New Bath Hotel*. It occurred to Jimmy that this would be the perfect romantic place for him and Rosie to stay, so, halfway through dinner, he made an excuse to leave the table. It would cost him more than a week's wages, but he considered it worthwhile so made a booking for the following month.

Back at Ida's home, they exhausted all topics under the sun. Ida could barely keep her eyes open, with all the conversation and her consumption of a very large glass of wine, something she wasn't used to. Eventually, Jimmy suggested Rosie should use the room Ida made up on his last visit, while he slept on the couch, to which Ida gave her sleepy approval, before he helped her to her bedroom.

As was their want, they knelt to say a prayer, before sitting on the bed for another intimate chat. 'Well Jimmy, it looks as if you two will finally marry. Seeing you tagether terday made me heart soar. This is one marriage a know will last. Hopefully you will be blest with grandchildren…there will *be* grandchildren?' she enquired expectantly.

Jimmy blushed before replying positively, 'I am sure you will have grandchildren Mam. Rosie is keen to start a family straight away'—he paused as Ida raised her eyebrows—'but after we are married of course,' he laughed.

Ida nodded, 'Oh well then, I must pray that I will live long enough to become a good grandmother…Amen! Jimmy, you're a good lad and I know yer'll treat her right, but now I'm fair bushed,' she said, her eyes closing as she slipped contentedly into bed. 'Goodnight Jimmy, sleep tight,' she murmured. She was asleep before Jimmy gently pulled the bed covers up to her chin. He stared down at her with a compassion that only a son knows, before leaving the room. He too prayed she would live many more years. He descended the stairs, determined to secure Rosie's agreement that Ida move in with them after their marriage, provided he could afford a house big enough for them all.

Unbeknown to him, Rosie was already wrestling with her own property conundrum. Would Jimmy agree to a substantial contribution from herself to purchase a large property with at least two servants. Despite acknowledging Jimmy's desire to provide for her as his wife, she determined that she would share the financial burden of their marriage—A point on which she would be unable to compromise.

CHAPTER THIRTY-ONE

Disclosure
July 1856

Kate's Birthday celebrations, planned for the first week in February had eventually been abandoned. Initially, postponed to accommodate Marcus's return from Philadelphia in March, but his untimely death dictated events from then on. Lizzie's birthday on the 12th June, as per her wish, was not celebrated, but now, five months later, the family were attempting to heal the heartache of bereavement. Kate persuaded Lizzie that she should embrace life with her family and begin picking up the pieces by attending Kate's latest attempt at holding a party.

The second week in July was gloriously hot, which boded well for a family 'get together'. The guests were mostly congregated in the garden of *The Chestnuts* enjoying the late sunshine. Some occupied the comfortable chairs on the rear veranda, while the younger guests amused themselves playing hide and seek in the extensive grounds. This gave the adults the opportunity to enjoy a glass of wine and generally relax in the peace and tranquillity of the secluded gardens, until the sun disappeared beyond the treeline.

At Amy's suggestion, Robert accompanied her on a romantic stroll along the pergola, adorned with sweet smelling honeysuckle. Her intention was to rest on the rustic bench under the wooden arbour, alive with pale pink roses and a favoured secluded spot of many visitors. Once there and for almost an hour they talked without interruption, until Amy requested Robert left to check on Harriett. Now alone, she reflected on her happy state of mind and the fact that Robert had apparently distanced himself from Kate. She felt certain he had succeeded in persuading her to see the error of her ways. Sadly, she still remained oblivious to Robert and Kate's plans.

Several minutes passed before Amy reached for her bag, which lay open beside her. She felt inside for a hanky, as she was suffering from a mild hay fever. As she did so, her hand encountered the envelope, which contained the note to James, hastily written at the Christmas celebrations. She studied the unsteady scrawl and a feint smile crossed her lips as she read the name and address of the intended recipient. *How quickly one's perceptions of a situation can change* she thought, as she recalled the game of 'sardines'. She'd witnessed Kate and Robert's whispered conversation about meeting secretly. Her mind had been in turmoil but still she was angrily motivated to write the ill-conceived accusatory letter. Now, several months later, she decided to tear it up and burn it, because she no longer perceived Kate to be a threat.

Happier than she'd been in months, she saw Robert returning, waving cheerily atop a steep bank, before his descent to the manicured grass of the formal gardens. A feeling of love and wellbeing overwhelmed her, until a totally uninvited anxiety crept malevolently into her soul. She observed an, as yet, unidentifiable figure running across the lawn, obviously intent on intercepting Robert's passage. The scene unfolded rapidly and she watched with incredulous fascination, as the person's identity became known— It was Kate! who smiling, linked her arm through his.

Galvanised, Amy, grabbed her bag and hurried toward them, but in her haste, failed to notice the envelope slip from her grasp as it fell between the slats of the oak bench, becoming hidden from view.

Amy drew close. Robert, fearing the worst, immediately disentangled Kate's arm and brushed her to one side, before striding purposefully toward Amy, leaving an anguished Kate in his wake. Taking Amy gently by the arm he led her back to the gardens, where other guests were chatting and drinking wine.

Neither spoke when Daniel greeted them. 'There you are,' he observed, indicating vacant seats beside them at their trestle table. 'We wondered where you had disappeared to. I was just going to refill our glasses, despite Lizzie's protestations. Anyway, I'll get you a Claret-cup each and we can relax while the children play.'

Relieved, Robert threw himself wholeheartedly into the conversation, making sure he paid close attention to Amy, who by now had disregarded the incident as just familiarity on Kate's part. She would not let it spoil her otherwise enjoyable afternoon. Regrettably, her decision to destroy the letter had completely slipped her mind.

Kate, however, was disappointed not to have had the opportunity to be alone with Robert for even a short while.

⁘

When Kate married James and moved to *The Chestnuts*, they required a gardener. Providentially, Jimmy, previously a gardener at *Low Wood*, after George's death, decided to take the vacant post at *The Chestnuts*. Over the ensuing years, he worked tirelessly on the gardens and which became his pride and joy.

On the afternoon following the garden party, James instructed Jimmy to tidy the garden and collect any stray glasses, left inadvertently by guests. Jimmy's search included the pergola and the oak arbour, where Robert and Amy talked. He noticed the bench's two front legs were in desperate need of a coat of varnish. He'd recently treated the rear legs with a coat but had not yet had the time to finish the job.

It was definitely on his list requiring attention, but as he'd run out of varnish that day, he'd not got around to it, with such a lot to organise before the big day. Now, anxious to finish the job, he determined to start that afternoon before the forecasted showers arrived.

He thought the honeysuckle entwined around the arbour might impede him in his task, but on inspection, only the weeds beneath the seat presented a problem. It was then that he noticed an envelope apparently addressed to James Renwick, near the rear legs, which puzzled him. How had the letter found its way under the bench, was anyone's guess, but it went into his pocket for safekeeping anyway. It wasn't until the following morning, that he remembered the letter and hurriedly placed it on the silver plate on the hall table. James would undoubtedly pick it up, together with the rest of the morning's mail.

James retrieved the mail from the hall and placed it on the blotter on his study desk. One small, square envelope immediately caught his attention. The lack of his official title, which usually preceded his name, perplexed him somewhat, but he jovially slit it open anyway and unfolded the single sheet of vellum. The missive was devoid of a signature. He read the one line of text written in the centre of the page:

'Your wife, Kate is having an affair with Robert Cameron'.

No longer jovial, but shocked and angered beyond belief, he grabbed a bottle of brandy and hurriedly left his study to seek the privacy of their bedroom to fully evaluate the meaning of such an unbelievable statement. Apart from the servants, James was alone in the house as Kate was shopping and Beatrice riding. He took the stairs two at a time, anxious to shut himself away from the world. He closed the bedroom door firmly behind him, picked up a glass from the bedside table and poured himself a stiff drink before slumping on to the window seat, facing the front garden. Ashen and shocked, he tried to calm himself. *Why,* he thought, *would anyone write such a damning letter, unless an element of truth existed?*

Despite his initial all-consuming anger and disbelief at the insidious words, penned by an unknown author, he knew he must try and regain a sense of objectivity. Another slug of the amber liquid calmed him somewhat, allowing him to reflect and be transported back to the long distant past.

***

He remembered the holiday in South America when he informed his parents of his intention to ask for Kate's hand in marriage. He'd already decided to secure her father's approval on his return. Consequently, he was not, therefore, officially betrothed to Kate at the time of her infidelity with Robert, but he believed that they had an understanding and that they would indeed become husband and wife.

Eventually, after Kate's mother's death and Howard's decision to leave Low Wood, he married Kate, forgiving her earlier indiscretion. His marriage, although not the most passionate, was stable. He believed Kate was happy, especially since the birth of Beatrice. It was true his wife enjoyed the company of men but he turned a blind eye to what he perceived to be innocent flirting. However, he did begin to wonder whether his wife shared his perception of a happy marriage.

James turned his attention back to the letter. His hands shook visibly as he re-read the bold statement. Agitatedly he folded the single sheet and replaced it in the envelope, then almost distractedly, pushed it into a chest of drawers. He could not, however, shake the niggling doubt that was dominating his thoughts. *Perhaps Kate's harmless flirting wasn't harmless at all. Could it be his love for her blinded him to the truth.*

There had been occasions over the years, when he suspected she might still have feelings for Robert, but these were fleeting and he dismissed them instantaneously. What was the good of suspecting her of being unfaithful, without solid proof, of which he had none? He would not live his life constantly doubting Kate. It would destroy him. The letter, he decided, was probably written by someone out to cause trouble, but whom could that be and for what reason?

Several more minutes passed by as he stared aimlessly out of the window across the grounds. He poured himself another glass of brandy, but once again began ruminating on his own version of the known facts, which might substantiate or discredit this anonymous bold accusation. Kate was a good wife he thought. She looked after Beatrice and they got on well together...but was that enough for someone like her? Her passion for life and the constant need for excitement were the exact qualities that had drawn him to her all those years ago. Did he provide that? he asked himself. He certainly did his best to ensure she had every conceivable comfort in their home. However, in truth, he had to admit that home comforts were probably not at the top of her list of desires. From her perspective, he as a husband, would probably be best described as dependable and trustworthy, but lacking in passion. He knew that in the bedroom, he could be described as predictable, as opposed to adventurous. He didn't have a high sex drive and it was mostly Kate who instigated their love-making. Perhaps, he concluded, she had become bored with him over the years. He was not a risk taker, like Kate. She took risks in all areas of her life, unlike himself, but he believed one of them should bring stability to the union.

As he took another slug of brandy, his attention was drawn to movement on the drive outside. Kate had returned from her shopping and their driver, Edward, was following her into the main entrance, carrying numerous bags. He needed to pull himself together because a confrontation right now was inappropriate. It was essential to prepare a course of action commensurate with the situation. The accusations might just be true and he needed time to think before deciding on their future. Then Kate suddenly appeared at the bedroom door.

'Hello James, what are you doing up here? I thought you would be in your study, which is usually where you retreat when I'm shopping.' She grinned, pleased that James never questioned the amount of money haemorrhaging from their bank account.

'I decided to buy you a silk neckerchief and couple of new shirts, because I noticed the one you wore yesterday was looking a bit tired. Would you like to try them on?' she offered, whilst placing the items on the bed.

James's mind was still on the letter and trying on clothes was the last thing he wished to do. 'I...er...well, do you mind if I leave that until later? I have been quite busy this morning, organising the clearing up in the aftermath of the party,' he lied. 'It is almost eleven and I was going to have an early lunch, as I have been up since six,' he continued, his voice taking on an anxious tone.

Kate scrutinised his ashen pallor, noticing the empty glass in his hand. 'I'm not driving you to drink am I?' She laughed guiltily, wondering if perhaps her spending *had* got out of hand. It's not like you to drink before lunch. Are you all right James, you don't look too well?' she commented, touching his arm in concern.

James nodded. 'Yes, well, I do feel a little out of sorts. It was silly of me to have a drink. I could probably do with a black coffee. I think I overdid the drinking yesterday.'

'Oh well James, I shouldn't worry. There isn't anything wrong with letting your hair down occasionally; although, I agree it's probably not the best idea to carry on with the *hair of the dog*[81]. I'll arrange for a pot of coffee to be served in the dining room and perhaps something light to eat would be prudent.'

James indicated his acquiescence by nodding, then watched her disappear to arrange an early lunch. Later Kate, excited with her purchases, tried to revive James's melancholy as they tucked in to a smoked mackerel salad, but was disappointed to find him distant and pensive. Eventually she left him to sober up with a third cup of coffee, having given up the cause.

༺༻

---

81 *'Hair of the dog', short for 'Hair of the dog that bit you', is a colloquial expression in the English language predominantly used to refer to alcohol that is consumed with the aim of lessening the effects of a hangover. The expression originally referred to a method of treatment of a rabid dog bite by placing hair from the dog in the bite wound*

She hung the shirts she had purchased in the bedroom wardrobe. James' lack of interest in trying them on dismayed her, but as she handled the exquisite silk neckerchief she wondered for a moment whether Robert would appreciate it more. Unfortunately, she could not possibly give it to him as a gift, so she reluctantly placed the item in the chest of drawers. At that moment her hand brushed against the envelope, placed haphazardly in the drawer an hour earlier by James.

Slightly bewildered to find a letter in amongst socks and other small items of clothing, she nevertheless retrieved, then examined the envelope with its lack of a formal title to accompany her husband's name. It appeared to be written in an unsteady hand and this aroused her curiosity. Intrigued and hesitating only briefly, she took out the single sheet of folded paper. Before she could read the contents, James, who had left the dining room shortly after his wife, strode across the room and quickly relieved her of the letter.

Kate was totally surprised by the determination of her husband to conceal the letter from her, so she at once confronted him. 'What on earth are you doing James? Why was this letter secreted in the chest of drawers?'

James, visibly shaken himself, was annoyed at his own inability to give a viable answer to her question, immediately pushed the paper into his pocket. An awkward silence prevailed as a bewildered Kate stepped forward to face her husband with an exasperated frown. 'What are you hiding James? Why don't you want me to see the letter? I didn't realise we had secrets from one another and it obviously is a secret if you felt the need to squirrel it away in a drawer and not file it in your study desk,' accused Kate.

James, unsure of his next move, shrugged his shoulders and remained silent, but Kate could not leave the question unanswered and continued with her interrogation. 'Is there something wrong James? Are we in some kind of trouble you feel unable to discuss with me?'

James, unwilling and unable to enlighten her, stared vacantly, so Kate, unceasing in her bid to discover the contents of the letter persisted. 'Answer me James, you are frightening me now. Is it something very bad?' she asked fearfully.

James focussed on his wife, but displayed clear signs of distress. He would have to concede sooner or later as Kate seemed determined not let the matter drop. He made her sit on the bed then sat beside her. Drawing a deep breath, he made his opening gambit. 'I also didn't think we kept secrets from one another Kate, but this letter subjugates that hypothesis. Here, why don't you read it yourself,' he suggested, stony-faced, handing the offending note to Kate.

Kate unfolded the letter and quickly read the contents. She let out an audible gasp; it wasn't what she was expecting and she was shaken. She realised the truth was there in black and white, so stood up to face him. Although it could not be certain who had made the accusation, she could make a calculated guess. Amy! She had every opportunity to leave the letter for James. In addition, she was the only person who could have overheard their conversation at Christmas. Yesterday was the only time since then, that everyone had met.

Amy had been descending the stairs during the game of *Sardines*. She must have overheard Robert and herself arranging to meet, as they suspected. No one else was present; it must be her.

They had met secretly only on three occasions since that decision, so it was nigh on impossible for any friends or family to be aware of their meeting place in Stone, but there was no point in a denial. The truth was out and any denunciation would only prolong the inevitable. She crumpled the letter tightly in her hand, then hung her head. There was no going back. In a voice filled with emotion she dealt James a killer blow. 'We aren't having an affair in the physical sense,' she lied, 'but I cannot deny Robert and I have fallen in love again and plan to be together'—she paused, waiting for a reaction, but none came—'Not now,' she muttered, 'later… much later, when Harriett and Beatrice leave home; and that could be several years from now. I am so sorry James. I did not plan this, but I will admit, I never stopped loving him…I know it wasn't fair but I married you in good faith and hoped, over time, I would come to love you and in my own way, I do,' Kate stated, hoping it would soften the impact. James was horrified. The bones on his cheeks stood out and his lips pursed angrily. At last he spoke, quietly but with intent. 'Please go…just go. I have no words to describe how I feel at this moment, but I do know that I never want to see you again.'

Shocked at the venom in James's voice, Kate turned and ran from the room. She hurriedly descended the stairs, grabbed her cloak from the peg in the hall and called out to Edward, their coach driver, who happened to be passing on his way back from the stables. 'Take me to the station Edward…now,' she ordered. Surprised, Edward, who had only just unshackled the horse an hour previously, galvanised himself to the task in hand, preparing the horse and buggy, whilst he considered the implications of the raised voices heard earlier from the master bedroom. It signalled something very serious was taking place and his was not to reason why his mistress was intent on leaving in such a hurry. Within minutes, Kate was on her way to the train station, her intention to warn Robert of the magnitude of the event, uppermost in her mind.

Meanwhile, James, sad but resolute, remained in their bedroom. In one momentous minute, Kate had confirmed the unthinkable!

CHAPTER THIRTY-TWO

The Plan
July 1856

Alighting from the train, Kate frantically hailed a coach to take her to Littleborough. A short while later, she reached Amy and Robert's substantial residence. The driver reined in the horses a short distance from the majestic ornamental wrought iron gates. Kate stepped down and requested that he wait the short while she intended to be there. With fear and trepidation she approached their substantial front door. She'd already decided how she would broach the subject of their affair on the long train journey to Manchester, but had not anticipated the possibility of Amy being at home.

Fortunately, luck was on her side as Robert answered. He glanced fearfully left and right before ushering Kate swiftly in to the hall. He confirmed that Amy, Harriett and Lizzie were engaged on a shopping expedition to Manchester, then steered Kate along the hall and into the sitting room. 'What on earth are you doing here Kate? Has something happened at home?' he asked agitatedly, as by now he'd become extremely concerned

'Oh Robert, it is the worse news possible,' she declared hysterically. Robert, shocked and alarmed, still had the presence of mind to pour her a brandy, insisting she sat down.

She continued, 'It's James'—she sobbed—'He knows about us…someone sent him a letter informing him that we are having an affair.'

Aghast and dismayed, Robert attacked the brandy decanter himself before sitting disconsolately beside her. He took her hand before asking the inevitable question. 'Who… and how would anyone know?'

'I'm not sure Robert, that's just it. It was only one line and not signed,' she explained.

'What *exactly* did it say,' Robert asked incisively, trying desperately to remain calm.

Kate dissolved into a deluge of tears, as she handed him the crumpled letter. 'I think I already know who it could be, Robert. There is only one person who could possibly have arrived at that conclusion.'

Robert placed his arm around her shoulder. 'Listen Kate, we have been very careful on the few occasions we have met'—but stopped abruptly in mid-sentence as he read the note. The handwriting raised alarm bells. 'Do you think it was Amy? She most probably heard our conversation that night at *The Beeches*, when we arranged to meet.'

Kate, severely overwhelmed by all the implications, looked to Robert for support. 'Who else could it have been? As we've have been very careful to hide our meetings. What will we do Robert? We didn't plan for this to happen. James is furious, he ordered me out of the house and said he never wanted to see me again,' whispered Kate fearfully, concerned now that Robert would be annoyed because she'd not denied their affair.

Robert shook his head in disbelief. 'What's done is done Kate and there is little point in us denying it. We did not plan it this way and that is unfortunate in the extreme, but now we have to make this as painless as possible for all concerned,' he stated. His determination to protect Amy, by providing a stable home and financial security was possible for him to achieve, but how could he take away the total devastation and betrayal she would feel. He needed time to think, away from everyone, including Kate; however difficult that might be. Would he appear cowardly, by walking out instead of facing up to the enormity of the situation? He knew not, but there was no other way. The best way was to admit everything to Amy, then leave the marital home. He would rent a property. Kate must do the same. She should not return to *The Chestnuts*.

***

Robert was unsure what to say next, as he observed Kate staring into the distance, but taking a deep breath he outlined his plan. 'This is what we must do Kate. You cannot return to your home, so why not spend the night at Aunt Jayne's, then with her help, you must rent a property. It would probably be best if it were a few miles outside Oxford…somewhere close enough to see Beatrice, who will undoubtedly be distraught. After all, she is just twelve years old. You will need regular contact with her, but I cannot see James objecting to that. Some how or other, you'll both need to maintain a civil relationship for Beatrice's sake.

'I will tell Amy and together we will tell Harriett, before I leave here. I'll move into rented accommodation, probably on the outskirts of Manchester, so that I'll be able to commute to Littleborough. I don't know how long it will be before we can be together Kate, but it will be as long as it takes for all concerned,' he stated matter of factly, as if in that instant he removed himself from the terrible and overwhelming situation.

Kate, her tears still flowing, declared falteringly, 'Oh Robert, I am so sorry things have turned out this way. You do understand why I couldn't deny the allegation. If I had James and Amy, already suspicious would be watching us like hawks. We would not have been able to meet as we had done previously. I couldn't bear not to see you and share precious moments for possibly years to come, when Harriett and Beatrice are old enough to be less dependant on us.'

Robert, on hearing this, was touched, so sympathetically kissed Kate in mutual understanding, before pulling away. 'I couldn't bear that either Kate. Since rekindling our love, I've realised I can't live without you. What we did was wrong, but I couldn't help myself. However, we won't have to tell lies any more. I have hated all the deceit, having to make excuses to Amy, knowing full well that ultimately, I would break her heart.'

One more lingering kiss was all that he could offer Kate at that instant. They could not see each other for the foreseeable future, which would be unbearable, but they must do the right thing. 'You must leave now Kate, before Amy returns. She is taking tea at Lizzie's after their trip, but intends to return home early this evening. Perhaps you should write to James explaining your intentions. I am sure he will be magnanimous enough to send your personal possessions on to you. You must realise that, initially, we will be in a relatively poor position financially, as I intend to leave this house to Amy, but I will keep the business. It is also my intention to allocate a large allowance which will pay all her outgoings,' he stated.

'I realise that Robert and it is the right thing to do,' she replied. 'I have no idea whether James will cut me off without a penny. Either way, I do not care, so long as we can eventually be together. I love you Robert and always have.' Kate smiled wryly as he accompanied her to the front door.

'I love you too Kate. I will endeavour to meet you at our usual place at the *Star Inn* on Sunday 24th August at 11.30. If, for any reason, I am prevented from meeting you, don't worry, I will send word to you and rearrange. Take care my love.' Robert smiled encouragingly, as he let go of her outstretched hand and watched as she disappeared through the gates. He closed the door, then turned to stride down the hall to the sitting room to dispose of the two glasses before Amy returned. Taking a seat at the window he contemplated the future, which now seemed as elusive as the shadows in the garden. Soon he would bear witness to the unbearable sadness and anger of his wife when she learnt of his infidelity. She had done nothing wrong and did not deserve such an indefensible betrayal from the man she loved unconditionally. However, despite acknowledging the terrible consequences of his affair, he felt powerless in that he could not alleviate her misfortune and his undeniable guilt.

CHAPTER THIRTY-THREE

Bittersweet
August 1856

Rosie was dismayed to learn that her father, Robert and mother Kate were to leave their marriage partners, after it became common knowledge within the family, following Amy's bombshell. Rosie feelings were mixed: On the one hand, she knew they were both unhappy and their chance of happiness lay with each other, but from another perspective, she realised that her sisters' Harriett and Beatrice would suffer enormously from their parents' divorce. She would, of course, help them both despite the circumstances and maybe...just maybe, Beatrice and herself might even become closer.

※

Rosie visited her father shortly after the breakup. It was hard for him to explain that he had ignored his feelings for Kate for many years, but could no longer live without her. It was, he explained, the right thing to do. Rosie actually understood perfectly, as her own short life paralleled theirs in some small way; Jimmy, after all, was her first love. At least a clean break meant they would not have to meet one another in secret, anymore and live a life of lies and deceit for the sake of a few snatched hours together.

Although she did not condone their actions, she knew a marriage bereft of love would always be second best. Jimmy and herself were destined to be together and it would have been folly indeed to continue her friendship with Jack any longer. Their relationship would always be as friends.

Jimmy, her one and only love, would see her through this difficult time, while both her parents divorced.

∽∾

Jimmy booked the *New Bath Hotel*[82] in Matlock for a romantic break and a month later, he and Rosie entered the foyer of the grand building. They were extremely nervous, acutely aware that shortly they would be sharing a bed for their special moment.

Jimmy wanted everything to be perfect, as soon he would be joining a ship bound for Brazil, with a general cargo. His pay would supplement his savings for their wedding.

Jimmy approached the reception desk with new-found confidence and announced their arrival, which obviously impressed the receptionist as well as Rosie, who smiled somewhat guiltily at what they were doing. He signed the visitors book with a flourish in the names of *'Mr and Mrs James Mitchell*. They were shown to their room, overlooking splendid grounds and a beautiful miniature lake.

---

[82] *The New Bath Hotel (so called because the date of its discovery was later than that of the Old Bath, which flows through the bath room of the Hotel). In 1852 it was described by William White as: "pleasantly situated at the South end of the Tufa Terrace, owed its existence to the second hot spring, that was discovered some years after the Old Bath. It has been enlarged at various periods, and now forms three sides of a quadrangle, and is a large and commodious establishment, with beautiful grounds". Francis White thought it "a spacious building, replete with every comfort*

The porter shut the door behind him after receiving a tip from Jimmy, who then turned to Rosie. 'I am so lucky to be betrothed to you Rosie. When I first saw you in the Marsh, I knew there was something special between us. I know we were very young, but I felt an immediate affinity with you and that has never gone away,' he said, sincerely, surprising himself in the use of the word *'affinity'*. He determined to expand and improve his vocabulary and in this respect, Rosie had thoughtfully taken out a book from the Campfield Library[83] in Manchester, on the English Language, in an effort to help his progress.

Rosie smiled too, conscious of his close presence in the confines of the bedroom. 'Oh Jimmy, you know I've always felt something special, even when everyone thought you had perished at sea, I never gave up hope that you were alive and would one day return. We were always meant to be together. Now kiss me Jimmy, before I totally throw myself at your mercy,' she said laughing seductively.

Jimmy held her in his arms then kissed her tenderly, acutely aware that later she would give herself to him. When he accepted the room Lizzie offered him at Oak Tree Lodge, the opportunity existed for them to sleep together. However, he had not felt the time was right and he was too embarrassed. It was also Jack's home. Additionally, Jack was coming to terms with the death of his father, so he didn't want to

---

83 *Among the many important political and social reforms of the mid 19th century concerning working conditions, public health and education was the Public Libraries Act of 1850. This allowed municipal boroughs in England and Wales to establish public libraries. The first free public library was opened in Campfield, Manchester in 1852. The rate that boroughs could charge for libraries was increased to one penny in 1855.*

upset him either. Now that Rosie and he were removed from that awkward situation he felt liberated.

Rosie brought him back to the present rather abruptly. 'Shall we unpack Jimmy and walk by the river. It's still only 2 o'clock and dinner isn't until 7.30. Let's explore outside. Matlock[84] is such a romantic place and there is plenty to see,' she enthused, as she unlocked her valise to hang her clothes in the spacious wardrobe.

'That's a wonderful idea Rosie. We should change into something more appropriate for walking. I for one feel rather uncomfortable trussed up in this formal jacket and cravat. Did we really need to arrive looking like the lord and lady of the manor?' he asked, grinning as he loosened his necktie.

In that instant, a fleeting memory resurfaced, as he remembered Christmas at Lucinda's home and his embarrassment endured in the gents outfitters. The owner, Mr Pollykoff, had insisted *he* tie the silk cravat. Ties, he decided, were the most uncomfortable items of clothing ever invented.

For once, Rosie, laughing at Jimmy's viewpoint agreed. 'Yes, we should change, I did notice that some of the male guests were wearing expensive but more casual sack coats[85] and Tweed[86] suits, but we will still have to dress for dinner,' she said pointedly.

---

[84] *Princess Victoria of Kent's royal visit in 1832 confirmed Matlock as a society venue of the time. Victoria's party visited a pair of museums and a petrifying well. John Ruskin and Lord Byron were visitors, Byron comparing it with alpine Switzerland, leading to a nickname of Little Switzerland.*

[85] *In the 1850s, the sack suit, walking suit or business suit (or, in Britain, the "lounge suit") was leisure wear for men who might wear a frock coat.*

[86] *Tweed suits, normally consisting of a jacket, waistcoat and trousers (or skirt) have been an icon of the English country gentleman and lady since the 1840s*

'Okay, but for now, I'll wear the Tweed jacket and trousers that Lizzie insisted I accept from Marcus's wardrobe. Apparently, she originally earmarked them for the church, along with several other items, which I've also inherited. Actually, I'm grateful that Marcus and me were about the same stature, his clothes fit perfectly.' He laughed somewhat guardedly, hoping Rosie did not think he was being disrespectful, although it reminded him of an amusing occurrence before he joined *The Lightning.* 'Do you remember when you stayed with your Aunt Amy a couple of years ago in spring? Your mam and dad were in Glasgow and Marcus was in Philadelphia.

'Well, I turned up unexpectedly and saw you before I boarded *The Lightning*'—he paused, waiting for Rosie's confirmation; instead she began to laugh, which absolved Jimmy of any disrespectful feelings with respect to Marcus—'I needed a bath and a change of clothes remember? You found a key in Aunt Amy's hall table drawer and we let ourselves into *The Beeches*. You'd already sneaked some clothes from your dad's wardrobe and a pie from Aunt Amy's kitchen, then you found a pair of boots and an old hunting jacket of Marcus's in the potting shed—I bet they wondered where they'd disappeared to—Mind, I had to wear two pairs of socks to stop the boots slipping, but I was very grateful nonetheless,' he said.

They both laughed heartily as they recalled the incident, sharing the moment. 'Oh Jimmy, we do have wonderful memories, some sad, some happy, but especially those when we played together in the Marsh. Those moments bind us together. When we are old and grey, we will sit and reminisce.' Rosie smiled as Jimmy once more put his arms around her to give her a deep, meaningful kiss.

'Rosie Cameron, I love you so much,' he said releasing her before his emotions overcame him.

Rosie shared his passion, but showed restraint herself. He'd planned a romantic evening, so she wasn't going to spoil it. Instead, she busied herself putting on her coat and some sensible shoes. 'Right Jimmy, grab your coat and let's take that walk before we spend all of our time in this room'—she paused for a moment before adding—'not that I would complain,' she said suggestively, half hoping after all that he would abandon their plans to explore.

On this occasion, Jimmy, using all the strength he could muster, declined. His seduction, he decided, would begin with dinner this evening, hopefully setting the scene for romance. He wanted it to be special for them both.

***

They spent a wonderful afternoon in Matlock. They discovered a petrifying well, some magnificent caves and even visited a museum, until eventually it was time to return to the hotel and change for dinner.

***

Jimmy couldn't take his eyes off Rosie. She was wearing a midnight blue silk *Charles Worth* dress. The childhood friend he'd first met in the Marsh had disappeared. In her place was a mature, independent and beautiful young woman.

Rosie imagined wearing such a dress in their grand house at Southwell, but was speechless when Lizzie bought the dress as an early birthday present. Jimmy would cherish this image of her on his voyage to Brazil. It gave him an added incentive to provide for the wedding of Rosie's dreams.

Rosie admired Jimmy in his dinner suit and cravat, also courtesy of Marcus and Lizzie. 'Are you ready Madame?' Jimmy asked, putting the emphasis on the two 'A's to impress Rosie.

'Why thank you kind sir,' she mocked, as they left the room to descend the stairs and on to the dining room, which featured splendid high ceilings and beautiful half-panelled walls. The separate tables, with their crisp white cloths and exquisite flower vases were spaced for privacy. They were shown to a table for two in a corner, adjacent the French doors, which looked out across a terrace to the Derwent gorge. The impressive fireplace, at the end of the room, featured a grand display of flowers in the hearth.

Although Rosie enjoyed the experience, Jimmy felt uncomfortable and awkward in the intimidating and imposing surroundings. However, he would be eternally grateful to Lucinda and her parents, in that their dining etiquette rubbed off on him. Rosie, justifiably proud of Jimmy, congratulated him on his composure in ordering their meal. Jimmy, for his part, made sure he only had one glass of wine and made light choices for each course, so that he was alert and not over full.

When later they returned to their room, both were apprehensive but excited. Their bed linen had been 'turned down' by the maid, which unnerved Jimmy, but Rosie took everything in her stride and changed in the bathroom into a beautiful long silk robe, which accentuated her naked form. She brushed her hair and applied a light spray of perfume before sensually gliding into the bedroom.

Jimmy changed into a new bathrobe, then thoughtfully turned down the ornate gas lamps. He gasped in admiration as Rosie stood before him.

This was their moment! Jimmy moved closer, hardly able to control his desire, then held her in his arms as he kissed her passionately. His hands felt the silky touch of her gown and the promise of her nakedness within, as he planted kisses along her neck. He gently slipped the exquisite gown off her shoulders and watched mesmerised as it cascaded to the floor; then Rosie stood naked before him.

Jimmy removed his own robe and their bodies entwined for the very first time. He carried her to the bed and laid her gently on the coverlet, where they caressed each other. Their kisses became more urgent, as Jimmy moved his hand over her breasts and then down to her stomach, where he lingered before caressing the soft wetness of her vagina.

This was her first time, so he held back his own overwhelming needs and desires ensuring she was in a heightened state of arousal, before he entered her. He kissed her breasts and moved his mouth over her body and between her thighs. Her breathing quickened as she felt the intensity of his tongue as he expertly explored her most sensitive place. She cried out for him to make love to her and with a passion born out of love, he entered her. Both climaxed simultaneously. Only then did Jimmy realise that making love to the woman he adored made the experience overwhelming and beyond anything he'd experienced before.

Rosie's initiation was more fulfilling than she could ever imagine. She knew beyond doubt that the only woman Jimmy would ever make love to again would be her. Their passion seemed never ending as they talked until dawn, but all too soon it would be over, Jimmy would leave her to join his ship the *Cherokee*. He would not be able to hold her in his arms again for three whole months. It would seem a lifetime.

CHAPTER THIRTY-FOUR

Friendships
August 1856

Since Robert confessed to Amy and Harriett, three whole weeks had gone by. Amy would not admit sending the letter to James, despite being totally distraught. Harriett, of course, was inconsolable, especially as Robert left home the very next day, moving into rented accommodation; a cottage in Knutsford with three bedrooms. He'd taken leave from his business, in consideration of his present circumstances. His loyal manager would be in sole charge for the duration of his absence, whatever that might be. He also needed to spend time with Harriett, but Amy's demands, that he should not return to their home, presented difficulties.

Although distressed herself, Lizzie endeavoured to pick up the pieces of her brother's broken marriage. However, her new home in Southwell precluded regular visits to Amy and Harriett, to offer support. She was disappointed that Robert had left the marital home, but realised he was adamant that his future lay with Kate and that Amy did not wish a reconciliation. It was a difficult situation all round, but Lizzie, despite her concerns, would support her brother by accepting his marriage had broken down.

Lizzie determined that Kate would also need her support, so a week after their separation, she visited her friend in Staffordshire. Kate chose to rent in Stone, as she was familiar with the area where she met Robert on several occasions. The modest Georgian countryside property was close to the river, with stables and a small field to the rear to exercise her horse. Kate hoped Beatrice would be able to join her, but James quashed her request by insisting she stay at *The Chestnuts*, until she was sixteen. Only then would he allow Beatrice to make a choice, on whether to live with Kate.

Lizzie arrived mid-morning, to find Kate in the kitchen, busying herself, sorting out the many boxes of personal items James had sent to her new home. The furnished house was not up to Kate's standards, but was passably comfortable and clean.

Kate sheepishly embraced her friend. 'Lizzie, I am so happy you came. I know you must be upset, but please believe me, we did not plan for this to happen this way…at least not for several years,' explained a contrite Kate.

Lizzie observed Kate, noticing the spark had gone from her eyes. She was still the woman she had grown to love over the years since she first stepped foot into the hall at Low Wood. They were very young women then, but had soon become inseparable, despite the class difference and the fact that Lizzie was a servant, in the household.

Lizzie didn't pretend to condone the misdemeanours of her friend, but realised she couldn't change the outcome, so kissed Kate on both cheeks before allowing herself to be led through to the cosy sitting room, with its view of the river.

'I have just made some fresh lemonade, can I get you a glass Lizzie?'

'That would be most welcome Kate,' she replied. 'It is rather hot today and it was quite stuffy on the train, despite the open windows.'

Kate set a jug of lemonade on the functional coffee table, then sat opposite Lizzie in the armchair next to the window.

Lizzie took a sip of the cool lemonade, before opening the conversation. 'How are you Kate? You look a bit drawn and tired,' began Lizzie with concern.

'I am okay Lizzie, but I *am* very tired, cooking, ironing and washing. As you've observed, living here is a big adjustment for me. I have to do everything myself, but I am enjoying my freedom, even if I am exhausted. I want to have everything neat and tidy before Beatrice arrives. Surprisingly, James has agreed to her staying overnight next week. I am so excited Lizzie, it will be the first time I have seen her since I left *The Chestnuts*, so I am very grateful to James'—she paused to collect her thoughts, before continuing—'I never meant to hurt him Lizzie. James has been the perfect husband, but the sad truth is, I never loved him. My parents pressured me to get married and even Aunt Jayne advised I marry and settle down. I used to wish I had not been born into a life of nannies, servants and luxuries. It sounds idyllic, but you have to obey the rules Lizzie, whereas I imagine you had so much more freedom. If you had had the choice, what sort of life would *you* have chosen for yourself?' asked Kate.

Lizzie smiled, amused at Kate's perception of such an uncomplicated choice, in her opinion. 'That's not so difficult Kate. It was very tough growing up in Strathy, but I did, in some respects, have a lot more freedom. Even so, my own life path was littered with many emotions—sadness, excitement, disappointment and happiness; my pleasures were simple but my opportunities few.

'You know I lost my mother when I was young and had to grow up very quickly. Times were hard and sometimes I felt lonely without siblings. My father left the croft to work the fields very early in the morning and didn't return until late in the evening. I couldn't just run freely in the meadows and sit by the brook or even visit Mairi, my friend, that often, as I had so much work to do at home. Even though Robert lived a short distance away, I missed his company and would rise at dawn every day. The days were sometimes interminably long so invariably I couldn't wait to take to my bed. So you see Kate, my childhood wasn't all a carefree bed of roses. You can't change the life you were born into. You just have to accept and embrace whatever that may be,' Lizzie concluded.

Kate frowned. 'Mmm, I hadn't thought of it that way. I admit I could do pretty much what I wanted when I was a young girl. I am not sure how I would have coped in your shoes Lizzie,' Kate declared, as she poured them both another glass of lemonade. 'Do you remember when we first met? I knew very soon after that we would become good friends and friends are very important, especially when things in life don't go to plan. I will be eternally grateful to you for supporting me and Rosie. I was desperate and wanted your backing, when I asked you to go along with my plan, at the expense of your own future. I don't think I appreciated just what you would be giving up for me.' Kate smiled wryly, before taking hold of Lizzie's hand. 'I hope we will always be friends and pray you will forgive me for what I have done.'

Lizzie's face clouded in sadness as she nodded acceptance. 'You must know I can't condone your affair, but there's no going back now Kate. You will have to live with the hurt that has been caused to both families. However, we have known each other a long time and you helped me in so many ways. You befriended me, even though I wasn't in your social class and we've shared good times and bad together so our bond will never be broken,' Lizzie declared.

Kate brightened determined to share her recollections of her past and their time spent together at Low Wood. 'Do you remember Lizzie when I gave you my cloak and we went into town? That was the first time I saw Robert and I believe I fell in love with him right then. I know we cannot turn back the clock, but I was wrong not to explain to him the reason I entrusted his baby to you and asked you to take her away. I compounded everything by marrying James. It really wasn't fair on him. The fact is, some days, I wanted to wake up and find my love for Robert had died, but it never did and when I saw him again, it was just as if we'd never been apart. Of course, he told me he was married, but I knew he still loved me. Was it really so wrong to hope that we would one day be together again?' pleaded Kate, hoping her friend would understand her reasoning.

Lizzie fell silent. Who was she to judge what was right, she questioned. Should Kate and Robert live the rest of their lives in unhappy marriages? Was that fair on their partners? Probably not. They had apparently already discussed waiting until their respective daughters were old enough to be less affected by their decision, but it hadn't worked out that way and that was the tragedy. Two young girls would have to live with the disturbing consequences of their parents' actions.

Lizzie turned her attention back to Kate, who was waiting anxiously for her response. The fact was that it had happened and the whole family needed to pull together. She reached out and took hold of Kate's hand. 'I'm not sure whether anything could have been avoided, but I will help you all as much as I can Kate. You and James have to reconcile your relationship for the sake of Beatrice. Can you do that?'

'Yes, yes Lizzie, I believe we can. James is still hurting at the moment, but he has already shown a willingness for us to bring up Beatrice with as little disruption as possible.

For now, she should live with James at *The Chestnuts*. She needs that stability and consistency. I cannot provide her with the home comforts she has been used to, but James maintains she can stay with me whenever she wishes,' she explained, relieved that Lizzie promised unconditional support. 'How is Amy? What has she decided to do for the future?' asked a genuinely concerned Kate.

'Amy is not so forgiving as James. She wants a divorce as soon as possible and presently, she is not allowing Robert to see Harriett. I am going to visit her next week and hope to change her mind, but I foresee difficulties ahead,' admitted Lizzie.

'Oh dear, Robert will be devastated. I do hope you can bring about a solution, whereby Harriett is encouraged to see her father. Robert is devoted to her and it will be she who will probably suffer most,' Kate speculated, her face clouding over, as she struggled with the guilt she was still feeling.

'We shall see. I will do my best and hopefully, after a period of time, the bitterness she feels will subside and she will realise for Harriett's sake, the need to keep their relationship civil.'

Lizzie fell silent, deciding to change the subject in an effort to relieve her friend's desperation. 'Listen Kate, after lunch, I will help you empty some of the boxes I saw piled up in the kitchen, then we can go for a walk by the river. If you like, I can stay over and we can continue bringing your house into some semblance of order,' she offered. 'I've noticed some of the windows need cleaning and furniture polishing. This house has obviously been empty for some while.'

'I would really like that Lizzie. It will be like old times. I am so lucky to have you as a friend. Come through to the kitchen and while I prepare lunch, you can tell me about your life for a change. How are you settling in to your new home?'

As Kate bustled around the kitchen, Lizzie confided in Kate. 'The house is lovely, but I don't have the same feelings I had when Marcus and I lived at *The Beeches.* I am blessed with good friends and family, of course, but I still feel lonely. I thought I had turned a corner after I found a letter written by Marcus on New Year's Eve, in his desk in May, but just when I am determined to move my life forward, I find myself reflecting on our future hopes and dreams, which will never be fulfilled. It is so hard Kate and I miss him terribly.' Lizzie sighed, deep sadness showing in her eyes, as she struggled to keep her emotions under control.

Now it was Kate's turn to express sympathy and try to lift her spirits. 'I cannot imagine how you feel Lizzie or understand your loneliness. The loss of someone you imagine will be there forever has to be the most devastating thing imaginable. It will obviously take many months, even years, before you can contemplate moving on with your life. Good friends and family can only support you and make your journey less painful, but in the end, it will be you who finds the inner strength to carry on'—she paused, noticing that Lizzie was still wearing black[87], since Marcus's death and wondered if it contributed to her sadness. She made a mental note to engage Lizzie in wearing dresses of a lighter colour in the coming months to encourage her recovery, however controversial that might be; as it was still only six months since Marcus's passing, but she could not bear her friend to be consumed with so much melancholy.

---

[87] *The length of mourning depended on your relationship to the deceased. The different periods of mourning dictated by society were expected to reflect your natural period of grief. Widows were expected to wear full mourning for two years.*

Their initial conversation about life's 'ups and downs', did not deter them spending two glorious days together, walking by the river and reliving old times. They worked cheerily on spring-cleaning the house in preparation for Beatrice's visit and so put aside their troubles, which lifted their spirits. However, Kate was unaware that it would take another seventeen months before Lizzie agreed to cast off her mourning attire.

CHAPTER THIRTY-FIVE

The Outing
August 1856

Mid morning on the 22nd August, Daniel started his journey to Nottingham with the intention of meeting Howard Faraday, an old business associate of Marcus', to discuss the possible purchase of a small lace factory. If he succeeded in his mission, a relocation to Nottingham was inevitable. Lizzie, instrumental in introducing the two men, following her own move to Southwell, was acutely aware of the implication.

※

In Daniel's absence, Georgina and Victoria took the opportunity of a short break in Bilston near Wolverhampton to visit her best friend Miriam, who taught at Sunday school there. Her husband, Albert Granger, a lock maker by trade, believed their move from Ardwick near Manchester two years earlier, would enhance their fortunes.

A special event in the Sunday school calendar, which coincided with Georgina's visit seemed opportune. Miriam helped organise a day excursion for the children from several Sunday schools, including the church of St Leonard, where she taught.

The special excursion train arrived at twelve minutes past nine precisely at Wolverhampton station. Miriam, her ward, along with Georgina and Victoria happily boarded the carriage. Victoria was especially excited to be making the short journey to Worcester with a promise of a picnic by the river, with her new found friend, Mary O'Reilly, aged ten, just over two years younger than her. Victoria loved mothering younger children so took to Mary immediately.

The train, initially designated solely for children and their teachers, was blatantly disregarded by greedy ticket sellers, who seized the opportunity of making more money, by allowing extra passengers aboard. Fares were exceptionally low and therefore, appealing, with a return ticket costing just one shilling for adults and sixpence for children. Inevitably, all coaches were full to capacity. Around fifteen hundred passengers boarded the forty-two four-wheeled coaches, supplemented by four brake vans and two locomotives. In addition, the train was scheduled to call at intermediate stations on route, to pick up local Sunday school children and other 'extra' passengers. Despite the heavy load, the train arrived safely at Worcester on schedule, two hours later.

꧁꧂

Miriam planned to visit Worcester Cathedral, with its Norman crypt, The Lady Chapel, The Nave and the Chapter House. On arrival at the Cathedral, Miriam's party were amazed at the scale of the building and Mary, completely in awe of its magnificence, clung to Victoria's skirts.

When their tour finished, they continued on to a grassy bank, which fronted the River Severn. It was a beautiful sunny day so Victoria and Mary wandered off to pick wild flowers, while Miriam and Georgina laid out their picnic on a large rug.

So far they'd not had the opportunity to exchange stories, but now, with the two girls out of earshot, Miriam launched into her questions. 'Well, Georgina, how is Daniel these days? Is he still intent on a move to Nottingham?'

'Yes, more than ever. At this very moment he is negotiating the purchase of a small lace factory in the centre. If he's successful, he intends pursuing a house purchase at Fiskerton, a small hamlet near Southwell, on the banks of the River Trent. There is one particular cottage that interests him, with its own mooring. I actually think he is more excited at the prospect of purchasing a riverboat, than investing in a lace factory. I'm sure he's been influenced by Lizzie's move to Southwell, but, I must admit that Nottinghamshire does have some wonderful countryside. We have been impressed with Southwell when we've visited. The Minster has wonderful grounds, set within parkland; several local hostelries and a bustling market place. There is also talk of extending the train line into Nottingham, which will make Daniel's decision easier,' informed Georgina.

'I see, so have you changed your mind, since we met last August?' asked Miriam with a frown.

'Well, possibly yes, I am beginning to embrace the idea. Since *you* left Ardwick, I haven't had anyone to confide in, or, for that matter, accompany me shopping in Manchester. If we moved to Nottinghamshire, I would at least be able to visit Lizzie and Rosie regularly. Victoria would love to see Rosie more often. I'm frequently lonely now that Victoria is at school, especially so as Daniel's usually away on business.'

'Yes, I can understand how you feel. I miss you very much too, although I keep busy working at the Sunday school. Perhaps if you were to involve yourself in the community, you might meet new friends?' ventured Miriam.

Georgina shook her head. 'You know I am quite shy, so making new friends is difficult. I'm not able to reach out as easily as you. However, on a parallel subject, you remember I told you Lizzie employed two women from the Workhouse? Well, it appears she's already involved in the community. Since Marcus's death, she's needed a focus. Apparently, she collects unwanted clothes from local residents for the unfortunates of this world.'

'Oh, I see, so taking everything into consideration, a move to Fiskerton may be a good idea,' stated Miriam, still unsure whether it would turn out well for her friend.

'Yes, it could be a new start for our family. It would give Daniel a new purpose in life, as his heart hasn't been in his work. I feel he needs a new challenge,' Georgina speculated.

Miriam mulled over *the* question she wanted to ask Georgina, but, unfortunately, her friend's personal relationship with Daniel was fast becoming a taboo subject.

Just after Victoria was born, Georgina confided in Miriam about the sexual problems she was experiencing. In consequence, Miriam advised Georgina how to be more adventurous in the bedroom. Georgina, strait laced and self-conscious at best, tried to heed Miriam's advice, but with limited success. She loved Daniel, but her strict upbringing by her mother did nothing to enhance her conjugal obligations. Despite a lot of patience shown by Daniel, she still floundered. She wondered if he would eventually lose interest and seek an affair; despite his assurance that he was true to her.

Unbeknown to Georgina, if Daniel's strong feelings for Lizzie were reciprocated, he knew he would leave her. However, despite Marcus's recent death, Lizzie remained fiercely loyal to Georgina and, therefore, would not instigate any impropriety between herself and Daniel.

༺❦༻

Inevitably, Miriam courageously broached the subject she'd been contemplating. 'I worry about you Georgina, you've not mentioned your problems, but I have the feeling, they have not gone away. Once upon a time, we could have talked about anything...and did,' she reminded, regretting the distance that now existed between them.

Georgina blushed before lowering her eyelids. It was true, she had confided in Miriam many times in the past, but somehow she had become too embarrassed to mention that her inhibitions prevailed. Sometimes she wanted nothing more than her friend's advice, but as she rarely acted on that advice, there seemed little point.

She looked up to see Miriam raising her eyebrows questioningly; having reluctantly decided an explanation was in order. 'Maybe, I can be less inhibited if we start a new life in Nottinghamshire. I must admit I am much less tired since Victoria has reduced her demands on my time. She often rides with her friend and at weekends, stays over, which means Daniel and I have more time alone. Unfortunately, he has faced my rebuffs too many times and seldom makes any suggestion to make love any more. I've never had the confidence to make sexual advances myself, so the moments pass us by,' explained Georgina, saddened by her own perception of an impossible situation.

Miriam placed her hand on her friend's arm and gave it a gentle squeeze. 'Oh Georgina, I am so sorry. Perhaps a new start could be all you need to reignite the feelings you have for each other. I imagine Victoria will make many new friends, so you'll have even more time to get to know each other intimately again,' she assured.

'Well, I feel Daniel will be happier with a new challenge, but do you really believe I'll have the opportunity to make things right between us?' questioned Georgina, grateful for her friend's supportive comments.

'Yes, I think you will have every chance. You want your marriage to succeed and that is a real incentive'—she encouraged, then paused as the girls were returning along the river bank carrying large bunches of flowers—'We'd better leave it there,' stated Miriam. 'We'll continue our conversation this evening over a glass of wine,' she said remembering that Georgina once confided that she enjoyed a glass of wine prior to retiring to the bedroom, in an effort to enhance their lovemaking. 'Everything will work out, you'll see, but right now, we should take advantage of this beautiful weather and enjoy our picnic.'

The afternoon sped by and soon it was time to return to the station for the journey home, much later than anticipated. They reached the platform and were surprised to see the carriages filling up very quickly. The original train had been divided in two, because it was deemed safer when negotiating the downhill gradients on the line.

They noted the first eleven coaches were already full, except for the second coach, which had just two seats left. Consequently, Georgina and Miriam had little choice but to hurry along the length of the platform with the girls in tow, in search of a carriage, where they could all sit together. It soon became clear that only a few seats remained, but not for all of them together. Consequently, they retraced their steps and were relieved to find the two seats in the second coach still vacant. The girls, holding hands defiantly, made it plain that they wanted to sit together, which gave Georgina and Miriam a dilemma. Should they allow the girls to take the two seats in the second coach? It required them to locate seats for themselves at the rear of the train.

Victoria, excited at the idea of travelling in a carriage without her mamma, voiced her opinion. 'We will be all right Mamma. There are two adults in this carriage.' She grinned, pointing to two middle aged ladies, who smiled benevolently at Georgina.

Miriam advised Georgina that a second train was scheduled to leave later, but as Georgina wanted to arrive in Bilston before Victoria's bedtime, they dismissed the idea. Neither trains had carriage lights and it would already be quite late before their train arrived in Wolverhampton.

Sensing Georgina's anxiety, one of the ladies sought to reassure her. 'Don't worry my dear, we will take great care of your children. You should hurry along if you want to secure seats for yourselves.'

Her mind made up, Georgina left Victoria and Mary in the care of the ladies, but gave strict instructions to the pair. 'You must not poke your heads out of the carriage windows and when the train reaches Wolverhampton, you should both remain on the platform until we are reunited. Is that understood,' she ordered.

Victoria, nodded vigorously, so Georgina, a trifle hesitantly, kissed her daughter, then hurried along the platform with Miriam to secure the last two seats in a basic carriage at the rear of the train. The locomotive with its twenty-eight carriages and two brake vans eventually pulled away from Worcester at 6.25 p.m.

The other occupants in their carriage smiled, acknowledging their lateness as they settled in their seats. Georgina was still apprehensive about leaving Victoria to her own devices, but was reassured by Miriam, who reminded her that the two ladies seemed perfectly capable of ensuring the safety of the two girls.

Their return journey was uneventful and Georgina felt more confident about her decision as the locomotive sped through the countryside. It was becoming quite dark when they arrived at Round Oak Station just after 8 o'clock, but with a bit of luck, Victoria would still be in bed soon after 8.30 p.m.

Suddenly and without warning, everything changed, as a coupling broke with a loud snap. Horrified onlookers on the platform witnessed the last seventeen coaches detaching from the train then begin moving back in the opposite direction. They were soon hurtling out of control down the steep gradient from Round Oak station.

Moments earlier, the second train,[88] given clearance to proceed, was moving slowly out of Brettall Lane station in darkness, as it prepared to negotiate a series of curves on its ascent up the hill to Round Oak station.

---

[88] *The second train had reached Brettell Lane about eleven or twelve minutes behind the first, and therefore was clear to proceed to Round Oak. The line ran in a series of curves, limiting forward visibility, the night was dark and there were no lights in the coaches. Excursion trains did not have to have a red light on the rearmost vehicle. Smoke was blowing across the line from neighbouring factories; consequently the crew of the second train did not see the runaway coaches until they were about 300 yards away.*

With ever increasing velocity the seventeen coaches and rear brake van of the first train, rolled inexorably down the incline towards Brettell Lane, whereupon it careered catastrophically into the second train. The guard's van and the last carriage immediately splintered into matchwood. The sickening sound of the impact could be heard for miles around. A short eerie silence followed, then moments later, loud screams pierced the smoke ladened air, blowing across the track from adjacent factories. Bodies were flung unmercifully through the air, before landing with bone crunching thuds on the hard ground. Miriam and Georgina lay among the carnage littering the track. Fighting terrible pain and serious injury, Miriam called out to Georgina, but there was no reply. Rescuers, some from the factories and some locals, arrived within minutes, but there was nothing that could be done for Georgina who died at the scene from extensive injuries. Miriam was eventually pulled clear of the wreckage, but she too died before receiving medical help. Her final thoughts were for loved ones and probably echoed many of the victims. In her case, *what will Daniel, Victoria, her own husband Albert and their families do now?*

※

Albert Granger waited up until the early hours of Monday for Miriam, Georgina and Victoria's return. He put the kettle on the hob, for a refreshing cup of tea on their arrival, but as the hours went by, decided they must have missed the train. If so, they would, he convinced himself, have to spend the night at a hotel and return the following morning. Consequently, pleased with his summation, he doused the fire and washed the dishes, before going to bed. Despite his logic, he spent a restless night, constantly moving from bed to window, opening the curtains and then closing them again, concerned not to see them walking up the lane. Eventually, sleep overcame him and the next thing he knew, the sun was rising in the sky. By mid afternoon, his anxiety escalated. By late afternoon he began to panic and feared the unthinkable; what if there had been an accident? He desperately needed answers. What on earth could have happened to them? Finally, he determined to go to the village for news, but as he approached his local newsagent's shop he stopped dead in his tracks. The newspaper billboard, prominently displayed a disturbing headline.

'Frightful railway collision near Dudley - Twelve lives lost'

In a panic, he purchased a copy of the Birmingham Daily Post and scanned the headline again before returning the short distance to his cottage. He fumbled for his key to unlock the door, then stumbled through to the parlour. He sat awkwardly and began to read. The shocking, but detailed report pierced his heart and his troubled mind:

> *"The most serious catastrophe that has ever occurred on a railway in the Midland district took place last night (Monday) on the Oxford, Worcester, and Wolverhampton line, between Round Oak and Brettell Lane Stations, a few miles beyond Dudley. By it, eleven persons were instantaneously killed; another died a few hours afterwards, several more were so severely injured that their recovery is despaired of. Others are maimed for life, and a great number were more or less injured….."*

> ..."Fragments of the crushed and broken carriages, mutilated human forms, some still in death, some writhing in their last agonies, others seriously but not fatally hurt, shrieking with pain and terror, were commingled in a general melee, hardly distinguishable amid the darkness and the dust occasioned by the collision.
>
> The terrified passengers who escaped without serious injury, ran hither and thither in bewilderment, and for a time none knew what to do. A few of the more self-possessed, however, speedily bestirred themselves to render all possible assistance to the unfortunate sufferers, and remove them from the wreck that bestrewed the line, and messengers were despatched for medical and other aid.
>
> It was soon apparent that the loss of life was lamentably great. Eleven lifeless forms were discovered amongst the rubbish, in addition to many frightfully mangled and disfigured[89]."

This last sentence caused his heart to beat faster as a sense of foreboding overwhelmed him. What if Miriam or one of the other two had been badly injured? That could explain why she had not returned. He then noted a short paragraph concerning those passengers who sustained more serious injuries:

> "There is a feature in this case which is not presented by railway accidents generally. The train to which the accident happened, being a special one from a particular district; all the persons injured, and it is feared all

---

[89] *Direct (unchanged) report/quotations from the Birmingham Daily Post*

those killed also, (but up to two o'clock this morning none of them had been identified), resided within a limited area, within which all the distressing consequences of the calamity are concentrated, instead of being distributed over the whole country as in the case of an ordinary train conveying passengers to and from various parts. The bodies of some of the dead are fearfully mangled, and their identification, except by the dress, will in some cases be difficult.

From the list appended it will be perceived that all the serious casualties were sustained by persons resident at Princes End, Coseley, Tipton, Dudley, and the immediate vicinity of those places; and with one exception all are adult persons."

The written words danced alarmingly across Albert's vision as he tried to comprehend the enormity of the situation. Mechanically he filled up the kettle and placed it on the hob for a mug of tea, then stared at the resultant brew before adding a dash of brandy to calm his nerves. Unsure what to do next and in a state of shock, he sat down again and began drinking the steaming liquid. He had drunk but a few mouthfuls, when there was a loud knock at the front door. He steadied himself on the arm of the chair before transiting the hallway and opening the door, to be greeted by a young man. 'Telegram for Mr Albert Granger,' said the man. 'Would that be you sir?' he asked politely.

'Yes, yes that is my name,' confirmed Albert. 'Thank you.'

Without uttering another word, he closed the door and returned to the parlour. His hands shook as he tore open the envelope. Before he read the two short sentences, he knew his wife had not survived.

The telegram fell to the floor. Albert, distraught and immobile stared incomprehensibly into the ashes of the now extinguished fire, which had burned so brightly that morning, together with the promise of an imminent reunion with his wife.

Why? He asked himself. *How could this have happened?* Right now, despite the lateness of the hour, his choices were limited. He gathered himself together, *I will take a train to Brettell Lane Station to ascertain the condition of Georgina and Victoria and begin arrangements to bring Miriam's body back home*.

⁂

On reaching Brettell Lane, Albert mingled with many anxious relatives and friends of those involved in the crash. A list of names of those that had died and were identifiable, were posted on the station notice board, some confirmed by survivors of the crash. Very quickly Albert was able to establish that Georgina had perished along with his dear wife. However, there wasn't any mention of Victoria, either on that list or among the list of those injured, which perplexed him.

After further enquiries, the station officer informed him that a young girl answering the description of Victoria and another, younger girl, had been taken to the home of two elderly sisters; Phyllis and Ann Proudlock, who lived in Wolverhampton. They had been in the same carriage as the girls.

After ascertaining their address, he made his way there by coach. Much to his relief, the information turned out to be correct. He introduced himself and Phyllis informed him that Victoria was in bed but had not yet been told of her mother's death. She explained—'We knew both ladies had perished in the crash as we were able to identify the bodies, which helped the authorities. They'd taken seats to the rear of the train, so left the girls in our care. Victoria's friend, Mary, has already been reunited with her mother, who gave us your details. We understood she was Miriam's friend.

'We are so very sorry for your loss Mr Granger. We hope your wife did not suffer. It is a terrible business, terrible'— Phyllis commiserated, before continuing—'Mary's mother sent you the telegram, but, unfortunately, she was unable to contact Victoria's father.'

'Oh, I see,' replied Albert. I do have Mr Lorimer's address, but I needed to be certain of the facts before contacting him. I think it best if Victoria comes home with me until her father arrives. If I send the telegram now, I am certain he will be on the next train to Wolverhampton; he can then board a coach to Bilston and should arrive sometime tomorrow morning,' he concluded.

Albert thanked Phyllis and Ann for their kindness then arranged a coach to collect him and Victoria, now awake and dressed ready for the journey. Albert, by no means recovered from his own shock, rather despairingly placed his arm around Victoria and guided her to the coach. When they stopped in Wolverhampton, he sent a telegram to Daniel.

Victoria was silent during the whole journey. Albert perpetuated the story given to Victoria by Phyllis and Ann, that Miriam and her mother were injured in the accident. He agreed with them that her father should be the one to tell Victoria that her mamma had died, along with her friend Miriam.

༺༻

Daniel returned from his business meeting around midday on Wednesday, 27th August to be met by a smart but impatient telegram boy. He had already rung the brass bell located on the wall of Daniel's home several times.

'Can I help you young man?' Daniel asked; somewhat perturbed as to whom could be sending him a telegram.

'I have a telegram for a Mr Daniel Lorimer'—the boy proclaimed, adding—'I did try to deliver it earlier this morning, but found no one at home.'

'I see, well I am he,' Daniel confirmed, a hint of anxiety showing in his voice, as he handed the young man a tip.

'Thank you, sir,' said the boy, placing the thru'penny bit in his pocket, before turning and walking back down the drive.

Daniel hurried inside, removed his coat and sat down on the chaise longue in the hall, before turning his attention to the telegram. He opened it, disbelief clearly etched on his face as he stared at the words, which leapt out from the page.

He was visibly shaken and walked trance-like to his study, before pouring himself a stiff drink. He sat dejectedly in the leather armchair positioned in front of the French doors. Tears streamed down his cheeks and the tautness of his jaw showed his anguish. His eyes, dull and unseeing, stared unblinking out to the garden. He remained statue like for an hour or more, before regaining his composure. He poured himself another brandy, bracing himself as he retrieved his hat and coat to make the short journey to town. There he hailed a coach, then gave the driver instructions not to 'spare the horses', as they proceeded posthaste to Southwell. There was only one person he knew could help him through this nightmare, Lizzie! His fervent hope was that she would accompany him to Bilston and help him break the sad news to Victoria.

※

Lizzie was putting the finishing touches to a sampler she had been working on, when she heard the frantic ringing of her house bell. Elspeth, concerned by the apparent urgency of the unknown caller, hastened down the hallway to open the door.

Sensing Daniel's urgency, she quickly ushered him through to the sitting room. Lizzie immediately discerned the panic in his voice. 'Oh God Lizzie, something terrible has happened. It...it's Georgina, she has been in an horrific accident...and...she'—he faltered—'she didn't survive! Lizzie, she's dead, Georgina is dead'—he blurted, tears welling up in his eyes, before adding—'I have to go to Wolverhampton immediately and pick up Victoria. Please say you'll accompany me.'

'Oh, Good Lord Daniel, that's awful...how...why? What on earth happened?' asked an equally shocked and distraught Lizzie, as she placed her arm around Daniel's shoulder to lead him to a comfortable chair.

Elspeth waited hesitantly outside the sitting room, with two glasses and a bottle of brandy, anticipating her call, having overheard everything. She didn't have to wait long, as Lizzie's emotional voice bade her enter. Lizzie, although distressed, acknowledged Elspeth's intuition by smiling briefly, then turned once more to Daniel, who looked pleadingly into Lizzie's eyes. '*Will* you come with me Lizzie? Victoria has not yet been told of her mamma's death. How on earth will I find the courage to tell her?' he questioned. 'Just over a week ago, we celebrated Georgina's thirty-eighth birthday. We had a family picnic and she was so happy,' he said, a deep sadness creeping into his voice.

Lizzie held his hand in hers to comfort him. 'It's horrible Daniel, she was much too young to die and had everything to live for. Of course I will accompany you. Jacob will drive us to the station and there we'll catch a train to Wolverhampton. We can return here with Victoria. I will ask Elspeth to air the large double room, which also has a single bed. I insist Victoria and you stay, until you feel able to return home.

※

It was gone midnight when Lizzie, Daniel and Victoria eventually returned. Lizzie suggested they try and sleep, although she knew that might be impossible as she remembered her own experience. They would need her support tomorrow when Daniel told Victoria.

The following morning, Lizzie became aware that Elspeth, quite diplomatically, had not pre-empted the news, so she advised the staff, Clara and Arthur of the terrible events, which shocked everyone. They all agreed to keep their distance, whilst Victoria was told. Although the buffet table in the dining room had been prepared for breakfast, Lizzie was not hopeful that Daniel would have anything to eat.

In the event, Daniel managed a slice of toast and coffee before preparing himself for the ordeal ahead. Lizzie joined Daniel in the sitting room to discuss how best to proceed, when Victoria wandered through in her dressing gown and snuggled up to her father.

Daniel, uneasy and fearful, sought confirmation from Lizzie that he should begin his explanation. He kept his voice under control as he began, 'Victoria, how much do you remember of the train crash that Mamma and Aunty Miriam were involved in?'

Victoria thought for a moment before responding. 'It was awful and a little confusing Daddy. Mary and me weren't hurt, but we were told Mamma and Aunty Miriam were injured. They went to hospital...are they still there and can we go and see Mamma?' she asked anxiously.

Daniel took a deep breath and held his daughter close. He began—'Well, both Mamma and Aunty Miriam were injured. Unfortunately, they were so poorly, they didn't get better and now they are with the Angels in Heaven,' he faltered, trying desperately to prevent tears forming as he needed to be strong for his daughter. 'You see Victoria, some times people get hurt so badly, that the Lord sees fit to take them under his wing and keep them safe with him in Heaven. He realized your mamma and Miriam would not get better and lifted them up so they could be with him'—he paused, waiting for a reaction. It came in the form of a flood of tears, as she looked to him for comfort—'Do you mean I won't ever see Mamma again?' she asked emotionally.

'Yes, I am afraid so, for quite a while. We can't actually see Mamma any more, but she is safe now and will always watch over us to make sure we stay safe too,' he ended, willing Lizzie to support the notion that in some way her mamma would still be with them.

Lizzie moved next to Victoria, to try and help her understand what happens when loved ones die. 'Do you remember when Uncle Marcus was lost to us and Daddy explained how he went to be with the Angels in heaven?'—she paused as Victoria nodded sombrely—'Well, your mamma is now in that same safe place. We cannot see them physically, but their presence is all around us and always will be. Your mamma would want you to be very brave and try to understand that she couldn't stay with you, as she was so poorly. She would have stayed with us if she could, but that was impossible, just as it wasn't possible for Marcus to stay. You will be very sad for some time and it is all right to feel like that, but you can always come to your daddy or me on those days. All the family will feel sad, so you will not be alone,' assured Lizzie.

Daniel, grateful for Lizzie's intervention, suggested they go out for the day by the river with a picnic. He would grieve alone for Georgina in the evening and at night, when Victoria was asleep. Right now, his daughter was his only priority. 'Why don't you put on that dress Mamma bought you before you went to visit Aunty Miriam? You can also wear your new shoes. Perhaps Aunty Lizzie will plait your hair around your head, so Mamma can see how pretty you look,' suggested Daniel, struggling with his emotions, but hoping that Victoria wouldn't notice his own sadness.

༺༻

The picnic was a big distraction. Although the future would never be the same, with Lizzie's support, they would all survive this terrible ordeal. They would continue to live with Lizzie in Southwell for a while, but Daniel realized, that eventually, they would need to return home.

The Round Hay Train Disaster 23rd August 1858
For the purpose of this story, the year has been changed to 1856

CHAPTER THIRTY-SIX

'Woodgate House' August 1856

Robert and Kate met at the *Star Inn for* the first time since leaving their respective marital homes. Both were inexplicably nervous as they sat at their usual table by the window.

Small talk seemed appropriate in the light of recent events, so Kate tentatively broke the ice. 'The sun's shining'—she stated unnecessarily—'so we should make the most of it and take a walk by the canal after lunch. Oh and my house is only a stone's throw away. Why don't we take tea there later?' she suggested, simultaneously engaging her most appealing smile which couldn't fail to melt Robert's heart.

He reached across and took Kate's hand in his own, squeezing it gently. 'That's a wonderful idea Kate, I would like that'—he paused, before adding a speculative question—'I did wonder now that you have lived in this location for a while and had chance to explore, what you think of Staffordshire?'

'It has already made a favourable impression on me Robert. There are so many bridleways, rivers and wooded areas where I can ride. There are shops nearby in the Borough of Stafford and two churches, St Chad's and St Mary's, which Giles Gilbert Scott restored only fourteen years ago. Did you know, he was also the architect who restored Ely Cathedral,' she commented knowledgably, having discovered that particular fact shortly after her arrival in Stone.

Robert seemed impressed; especially as he was unaware Kate knew anything about architecture. He even raised an eyebrow in amazement.

Kate, pleased with his reaction, continued—'There are also good railway links to Manchester and the south,' she emphasised, still intrigued by his original question and hardly daring to believe he might be suggesting they embark on their lives together, sooner than she expected. Now extremely excited by his newfound interest in the area, she boldly asked, 'Were you thinking we could buy a home here?'

Robert nodded to emphasize his willingness. Despite the heartache and hurt their love had caused to so many people, this *was* their destiny. 'I can't wait for us to begin our lives together Kate. I have missed you so much. If you agree, we could start looking for a property right away?'

'Oh Robert, that's wonderful. I have been so lonely without you by my side. I know we could be happy here and as it is only a short train journey to Manchester, you could visit Harriett as often as you like. Perhaps one day, our girls will choose to live with us, or at least come and stay.'

'Actually, I have good news on that front Kate. Last week I received a letter from Amy, who appears to be coming to terms with the situation. She wants to buy a home further north, possibly the Lakes, near a distant cousin and she's even asked for my help to find the right place for her and Harriett. It would be most crass and inconsiderate of me not to oblige.

'As you say, the railways are expanding rapidly, both north and south, which helps us both with our commute[90].

---

90 *Commute - Late Middle English (in the sense 'interchange (two things)): from Latin commutare, from com- 'altogether' + mutare 'to*

I have other news too; Amy is anxious that I secure a house large enough for Harriett to have her own suite of rooms and has generously agreed to give me a quarter of the money remaining after the purchase of her new home. She was surprised by my generous allowance for herself and appears to have softened towards me. There's also a possibility that her elderly parents may consider selling their own home in Glasgow to buy a joint property with Amy. I suspect this may account for Amy's willingness to part with a quarter of the remaining money, as I understand her parents would be contributing most of their money from the sale. Apparently, they've holidayed in the Lakes when Amy was small and as Glasgow is becoming rather overcrowded and industrialised, they feel that this is the right time to leave. This means we can afford a larger property than I initially thought.'

Kate, quite astounded at their apparent change in fortune commented—'Well that is very generous of Amy. For my part, James has determined he will remain at *The Chestnuts* until Beatrice is sixteen and she can then decide where she would like to live. I agree with this solution. He is giving me a very good allowance and he's already placed a substantial lump sum in to my account, possibly because my father initially made a large contribution to our property in the first instance. Father will, of course, continue to occupy a wing there with a live in nurse to attend to his needs in my absence. He and James always got on well and I cannot see that changing.'

---

change'. Commute (sense 1 of the verb). In the 1840s, originally meant to buy and use a commutation ticket, a US term for a season ticket (because the daily fare is commuted to a single payment).

'In that case Kate, it seems our respective divorces will be less acrimonious than we imagined. Right, let's order lunch and then spend the afternoon by the river.'

Later, the couple stepped out into bright sunshine and blue skies, anxious to make the most of their day together. 'Look, there's a footpath over there, winding up the hillside to a wooded area, away from the lock. Let's explore where it goes,' Kate suggested eagerly.

'That's adventurous Kate, but as your shoes aren't exactly made for hiking, wouldn't you rather walk beside the river? teased Robert.

Not one to shirk a challenge, an adamant Kate responded—'No, I'll be fine.' She grinned, lightly punching Robert's arm in a gesture of defiance—'Although I've not ventured there before, the path does seem fairly flat until it reaches the wood.'

They initially hugged the bank for a hundred yards, following the meandering river, until the path forked up an incline, towards the trees. Beyond these, they found a quiet lane, dotted with white painted cottages, where they stopped to admire the view. A panorama of several small copses and green pastures, full of sheep and wild flowers, criss-crossed with footpaths and bridleways, stunned them almost into silence.

'It's like being on top of the world,' Kate remarked, eventually turning to Robert, who seemed somewhat distracted, his eyes obviously drawn to a wooden post and board, leaning at an angle some distance away.

'Look there Kate, can you see that wooden post, almost overgrown by foliage? Well, it looks remarkably like a 'For Sale' sign.'

She strained to catch sight of the hand made board. 'Oh yes, I do see it. Why its almost fallen over. Come on Robert,' she urged, pulling him by the arm.

They hurried along the path and eventually came across two large ornamental wrought iron gates, a little worse for wear. 'Well, well,' Robert declared, excitedly. 'The sign does appear to have been here some time. This lane looks like a dead end, so I doubt many walkers bother coming this far. Do you suppose the house is still for sale?' he asked in anticipation, but Kate was already trying to push the gates open.

'I do hope so,' she managed in her haste. 'It looks inhabited, but oh what a magical place. Help me open the gate. Do you think anyone will mind if we take a look?'

Robert grinned, knowing full well that she was going to anyway. He put his foot on the bottom edge and pushed hard until one side of the gate begrudgingly opened. They passed through, then along an overgrown gravelled path which was just passable. It curved, narrowing around an area of rhododendron bushes, which over shadowed smaller herbaceous plants, eventually widening as it swept up to the front of a large Georgian property. Although the grounds were unkempt, the house itself looked impressive, highlighted by the afternoon sun.

'Goodness Kate, no one would ever know it existed. Look to the right, there is a driveway, which appears to descend to a road. This is really exciting Kate, what do you think?' asked Robert, impressed by the extent of the property and its grounds.

Kate's eyes widened enthusiastically. Her thoughts transparently communicated by a gleeful smile. 'I love it Robert. If it is for sale, we *must* buy it. Do you really think it might be?' Kate conjectured, marvelling at the house's stunning location and obvious potential.

'Well, I am sure no one lives here at present, but I wonder if we could gain entry anyway,' Robert pondered, as he approached the arched oak door. On closer inspection it appeared slightly ajar. Out of courtesy and still unsure, he rang the bell. The hollow sound seemingly confirmed the property was indeed empty, as it echoed around inside. Robert pushed and the door swung open easily, but he did wonder why it wasn't locked.

They stepped inside and gasped in wonder at the large hall with its central staircase. Heavy curtains were drawn, but even in the half-light they could ascertain that the interior seemed to be in surprisingly good condition, with no significant tell-tale damp. On the contrary, a smell of wax polish invaded their nostrils. Who ever had owned the property had not mismanaged or neglected the housekeeping. However, the thickness of the dust, which covered the mantle and the dust-sheets on the furniture, suggested no one had lived here for some while. Strangely, this looked at odds with the main footfall areas, which appeared dust free, indicative of other tell-tail signs that someone visited regularly, which included remnant charcoaled logs in the fireplace and a basket of fresh wood in the hearth.

Curious and eager to explore, Robert placed his hand on the rounded finial of the elaborate staircase to the first floor, but was stopped in his tracks, as a voice boomed out across the hall. 'Can I help you?' came the question, from a tall bespectacled gentleman who had suddenly appeared just inside the front door.

Shocked and embarrassed Robert turned in his direction. 'Do forgive me sir, we thought the house was empty and decided to take a look around,' he answered, hurriedly taking Kate by the arm. He ushered her towards the entrance. 'We will be taking our leave immediately and again my most profound apologies,' he offered, tipping his hat towards the stranger as he passed him to exit the property.

'Wait!' ordered the man as they partially exited. 'If it's not too impertinent'—he asked sarcastically—'might I ask the reason you decided to invite yourselves into my home?'

Robert, totally flummoxed, attempted an explanation. 'I...we, we saw the 'For Sale' sign at the gates and were interested to discover if the property was still for sale.'

Bemused man took a step forward and, in the same instant, dramatically changed tack, breaking into a friendly grin. 'I see, well it is still for sale as it happens. I must have inadvertently forgot to lock up when I was last here a few days ago, hence the ease in which you were able to make entry. No matter, you *are* here now, so if you don't have to rush off, I will gladly show you around. It is still very warm outside so I didn't really need this,' he said, as he placed his lightweight jacket on the hallstand before stretching out his hand to grasp Robert's. 'Dr Jonathan Crawford and you are?'

'Robert Cameron, sir and this is my wife Kate,' he fibbed, which amused her somewhat, although she refrained from speaking. She knew that an opportunity to buy the property now appeared to be a realistic option. Robert squeezed her hand in a gesture of reassurance, as her heart beat rapidly in anticipation.

Dr Crawford indicated they follow him to the drawing room. He whipped the dustsheets off a Victorian sofa with a flourish, then bid them sit. Dr Crawford offered them a brandy from a half empty dusty Tantalus, adorning an oak table just inside the door, which they declined politely, but which didn't stop Dr Crawford pouring himself a large measure.

'Right, that's the formal introductions out of the way, now I suppose you would like to know why I am selling *'Woodgate'*, the home I shared with my wife for over forty years,' he added, raising his brows.

'Well, yes we would,' Robert said as he found his voice. 'Although it's not really our business,' he said politely, followed by—'But we would be interested in the purchase of your home. My wife fell in love with it, the moment she set eyes on it,' he explained, as he gave Kate's hand another gentle squeeze.

'Regardless of whether or not it is your business'—he smiled encouragingly—'I would, however, wish you to know.'

Kate and Robert sat patiently, as Dr Crawford explained. 'Briefly, my wife also fell in love with 'Woodgate'. We came to Stone on our honeymoon, a little over forty-nine years ago. We were partaking of lunch in *The Crown*, a coaching inn in the village, when a gentleman at an adjoining table interrupted our conversation.

'Impressed with the area, we were discussing the possibility of purchasing a local property, with enough land to accommodate our horses. My wife loved animals and devoted her life to looking after workhorses, after their productive lives were over. 'Putting them out to graze, so to speak.' He laughed at his own joke. 'Well, the man made his apologies for interrupting, then proceeded to extol the virtues of a property he had for sale…this one!

'Inevitably, we showed a keen interest, so he arranged for a coach to take us to view 'Woodgate House'; which, is a surprisingly large Georgian property in several acres, as you've already observed I think. The main drive, by the way, is situated off the highway, but only two miles from the village centre, so it isn't quite as remote as you might have thought. As you appear to be on foot, I am guessing *you* accessed the property via the public footpath, then past the line of white cottages, which, incidentally, are included in the price. Of course, the future owner will also be responsible for their upkeep. Some of the present occupants have rented their homes for over forty years and some have passed the tenancy on to their offspring.

'Anyway, I digress; to cut a long story short, we subsequently purchased the property and we lived here until my wife died last year. At the time I was inconsolable and moved into a smaller property, a rather splendid Victorian town house, in Stafford, this February actually. My gardener left shortly afterward, but I didn't wish to employ another, especially as I wouldn't be there to keep an eye on him. That's why the grounds have been neglected. I suspect it will cost a decent amount to bring them back to their former glory so, naturally, this will be reflected in the price. I still visit the house once a week to ensure everything is in order and occasionally light a fire to ward off damp. Generally, the housekeeping has been neglected; hence the dustsheets, but for the most part the furniture is in good condition and will remain in situ. They are too large to fit into my modest town house'—he added as an afterthought—'Of course, you would be at liberty to dispose of any unwanted items as you wish.'

Kate was ecstatic with Dr Crawford's proposal, as neither of them had retained any furniture, but she continued to take a back seat in the proceedings, allowing Robert 'Carte Blanche'[91] in the negotiations.

'So!'—Dr Crawford eyed them expectantly, as he looked from one to the other—'If we can agree a price, the place is yours. I only want a nominal amount for the furniture, because it's of no use to me. You could move in, as soon as

---

91 *17th Century – When King Charles the Second was fleeing the Roundheads, he is reputed to have offered his helpers a 'Carte Blanche'. This was a 'White Card', a blank sheet of paper with his signature at the bottom. The recipient of this could then write anything they wanted above the royal signature and it would be legal.*

we have concluded the necessary paperwork. What do you say, Robert?'

Robert, still shell-shocked at the rapid turn of events, looked to Kate for agreement.

'I do love it Robert,' she said, breaking her silence. '*Woodgate'* could become our new home, but the final decision lies with you. I know nothing of finance and the implications of purchase,' Kate graciously admitted.

A brief discussion ensued, wherein a settlement on a price was agreed. Robert shook hands with Dr Crawford. 'I believe, sir, you have just made yourself a sale. I will contact my solicitor in the morning, to set the ball rolling. Would you mind if my wife and I take a further look around before we return home,' Robert requested.

'By all means, Robert,' he agreed trustingly, handing him the keys to the property. Please lock up when you leave and I will meet with you tomorrow at 3 o'clock in *The Crown* to collect the keys and place them with my solicitor. That's a Mr Pemberton, of *Hand, Morgan and Owen*. Their offices are on Martin Street in Stafford. Consequently, if you wish to visit the house again before completion, you may obtain the keys from there. I expect your wife will wish to take measurements for soft furnishings etc. Anyway, I'll bid you good day Robert and thank you, it's been a pleasure and you my dear, enjoy many happy years together at 'Woodgate'.'

Kate, stunned into silence for the first time in her life, managed some garbled thanks herself. Dr Crawford picked up his coat from the stand and strolled out into the late afternoon sun. He boarded his buggy, then commanded the horses to 'walk on'. With a wave, he disappeared down the drive to the main gates.

Robert, flushed with excitement, picked Kate up and swung her round, hardly able to believe what had just occurred. 'Well Mrs Cameron! May I call you that?' he joked. 'Welcome to our new home...at least it will be as soon as I organise payment. I am sure my bank manager can provide a loan, until I settle the amount later. I would need to offer my business as collateral of course, but that is a matter of formality.'

Kate, deliriously happy, couldn't wait to be the official Mrs Robert Cameron. 'It's perfect Robert and fate that we came across it on our unplanned walk. Even the name 'Woodgate House' reminds me of the times we'd meet and make love in the disused cottage, near Low Wood. It's where Rosie was conceived. I used to light a candle in the window, which could only be seen from the *gate*, to let you know I was waiting for you.'

'I do remember Kate. How could I ever forget? I will always hold those memories dear. It was the last place we met before you left. Hopefully, we will make new memories in this wonderful house. I love you Kate and I know we made the right decision.'

'I've always loved you Robert Cameron and I always will,' sighed Kate happily.

CHAPTER THIRTY-SEVEN

Reunited
September 1856

A week had passed since Jack returned to Liverpool from Philadelphia on the *Lucy Thompson*. Now an anxious Helen, making an epic journey herself, aboard the *Morning Light* from Melbourne, was preparing to disembark at Liverpool Docks.

Jack noted the date, 26th September, as he paced the quayside in anticipation of a welcome reunion. It would be just three months since he'd learnt of his father's death. Unfortunately, it would be another long month before his Memorial service could be held. Despite his continuing grief, he longed to be reunited with Helen, the one person with whom he could reveal his feelings.

Lizzie was as supportive as ever, but he realised she too was grieving and was struggling with her own emotions. Before he journeyed to New York, he had turned to Jimmy for support, but his and Rosie's notable absence meant he had had to cope alone.

※

Heaving lines were thrown and hawsers attached as the *Morning Light* came alongside. Jack spotted Helen immediately, as she waved her handkerchief and leant on the ship's rail. The gangway was lowered into position and soon she was descending the final few steps to the dockside.

'Jack, Jack,' she shouted excitedly, rushing headlong into his arms. He held her close then kissed her passionately in an emotional release, until they reluctantly pulled apart.

'I've missed you so much Jack and I'm really pleased you're here to greet me. I thought you might have had second thoughts as I couldn't spot you in the crowd, momentarily my heart sank, but then you were there as handsome as ever.'

'Of course I came to meet you.' Jack grinned, elated at Helen's obvious joy and her welcoming sensual kiss, which held a promise of a blossoming relationship. 'I've missed you Helen,' emphasized Jack. So much so that I've booked a room in an hotel in Liverpool, as you suggested,' he remarked boldly.

'That's lovely Jack.' Helen smiled, hardly able to believe they were together again at last. Although she'd allowed herself to dream about the possibility as the English coastline drew ever closer.

Jack took her by the arm then flagged down a cab, one of the many waiting on Strand Street for those disembarking from the passenger ships. Soon they were standing in the foyer of the *Adelphi Hotel*.

Jack could hardly believe it was only nine months since his father shared the story of his own stay at the Adelphi, fourteen years previously and sadly, the last place they were *all* together, Marcus, his mother Belle and himself.

Jack clearly remembered his exact words: *'It was three months after your second birthday, Jack, on Tuesday 16 March 1841, a day I will never forget. It was the last time I would see you. My heart broke as I kissed and waved you goodbye. Belle walked out holding you in her arms. Her intention was to begin a new life with you and Andries and I was left totally alone.'*

He recalled that the ill-fated *William Brown*[92] later sank at 10 p.m. on the 19th April, after hitting an iceberg off Newfoundland. Andries perished, but thankfully his mother and himself survived.

The Adelphi was also the place, which held happier memories for his father. It was where he'd met Lizzie and much later, his own long awaited reunion with his father.

༄

Jack blessed his lucky stars that the same room was available, as he wished to recapture that moment in time, where he had known happiness in the company of his father. Although he couldn't remember, he knew he had been a big part of his father's life until he was two years old. Sadly, they had shared only two short weeks after being reunited.

Jack shuddered uncontrollably as he unlocked the door. On entering, he experienced an overwhelming sense of love enveloping him. He wasn't sure he believed in the after life, but this surreal moment concentrated his attention. Regaining his composure, he placed his arms around Helen, eager for human contact, from someone he hoped, completely understood his emotions.

'Are you all right Jack?' asked Helen, aware that Jack seemed preoccupied, without making any attempt to kiss her in the privacy of the room.

'Yes...yes Helen, I am okay, although, I think I owe you an explanation,' he admitted, as he began the story of his father's death and his own need to find solace.

---

[92] William Brown was an American ship that sank in 1841, taking with her 31 passengers. A further 16 passengers were forced out of an overloaded lifeboat, before the survivors were rescued.

He had tears in his eyes when he finished. Helen responded by holding him close. She whispered, 'I'm so sorry Jack. I would do anything I can to help ease your pain.'

'There isn't anything you can do about the loss I feel, but I have a need to be loved by someone who can comfort me in a physical way. Does that sound selfish Helen?'

Helen, at that moment, felt confused. She wondered if Jack's motives were genuine. Did he see her as a lover, or just someone who could provide a physical solution to his pain? She fell silent and stepped away, awaiting his next move, but Jack reacted swiftly, pulling her towards him then kissing her softly before releasing her. 'I think you may have misunderstood me Helen. On my journey back from Australia, I really missed you and when I journeyed alone on the ship to Philadelphia, I realised just how important you were to my life. It is true, I do seek comfort from the pain of my loss, but I also need you because'—he paused—'because, I love you Helen.'

Shocked but delighted, Helen accepted Jack's unexpected declaration. During her nursing career, she had observed men who needed the assurance of a woman, particularly following the loss of someone dear, or if they were dying themselves. She always obliged by holding and comforting them. It was natural for her and perfectly logical to assume, that Jack wanted that closeness now. However, she realised that she meant more to him than to provide comfort, so responded eagerly. 'I love you too Jack and I do understand.'

'Mmm, I'm not sure you do—'Jack smiled—'but to prove I don't just want you for sexual gratification, I suggest we go down to the bar for a drink? We can talk, without you feeling pressured and you can tell me about the time you spent with your parents in Australia, then maybe return to the room later, but only if you want to,' proposed Jack.

'Thank you Jack,' said Helen understandingly. 'Perhaps we could have a bite to eat'—she added—'I missed breakfast this morning, as I was feeling anxious about meeting you again,' she admitted.

'I understand, I too felt apprehensive.' Jack grinned as he placed his arm tenderly around Helen's waist before escorting her to the dining room.

Downstairs, they were shown a discreet corner table for two, overlooking the gardens. Jack studied the menu, eventually suggesting a crayfish salad, which he knew Helen would enjoy. 'Would you like a glass of Perrier?' he asked.

'That would be lovely Jack, thank you.'

While they waited for their meal, Jack opened the conversation. 'How are your mother and father Helen? I hope they are well. I expect they were really pleased to see you.'

'Yes, they are both well and I had a lovely time. Lucinda's problem took over initially, but once we settled and she made the decision to keep her baby, everyone relaxed. I was missing you of course and wanted to tell my parents about you, but I didn't think it appropriate to mention your name whilst Lucinda was present. She was obviously devastated that Jimmy ended their relationship. I considered that it would have been cruel of me to appear so happy.'

Jack smiled, before taking hold of Helen's hand. 'Well I am here now and there isn't anywhere else I would rather be,' he said, sincerely, lifting her hand to his lips and tenderly kissing her fingertips.

Helen blushed and hastily scanned the other tables in case anyone had observed Jack's manoeuvre, before changing the subject deliberately. 'Are you still living at *The Beeches*?' asked a slightly embarrassed Helen.

'No.' Jack laughed. 'We moved to a large house in a small village on the outskirts of Nottingham. Rosie and I have a suite of rooms each. The area is lovely and quite close to a river. However, I would eventually like a place of my own, maybe nearer to Liverpool. I understand the town of Crosby has many attributes to recommend living there. It became a suburb of Liverpool eight years ago, since the new railway[93] was built. It is also close to the docks, so especially convenient if I am to remain in this profession. Apparently, my father hoped I might follow him into the business, but my heart lies in travelling the world. Will you return to the *Dreadnought*? That's if you aren't considering a move north,' Jack probed.

Helen lowered her eyes, unsure whether he was suggesting they actually move in together. 'I suppose it depends on where our relationship is heading. You know how I feel about you, it's really up to you where our future lies,' Helen concluded.

'Mmm, maybe,' he hedged, while engaging Helen with a look that expressed his desire. 'After lunch, I propose to show you how much you mean to me, which may give you an inkling about my feelings on our future,' Jack teased.

Lunch arrived almost unnoticed as they flirted with each other. Helen's coquettish replies left Jack in no doubt that she was as keen as he to resume their intimate relationship.

⁂

After an idyllic two days, Jack suggested he take Helen to Southwell. He'd already requested Lizzie's permission, in anticipation of the event. In addition, he'd decided that, when his father's will was settled, he would definitely look for a property in Crosby.

---

93 *The Liverpool, Crosby and Southport Railway opened in 1848.*

Their stay at the Adelphi was beneficial for two reasons. He'd found immeasurable peace in occupying the same room he shared with his father and he had become closer than ever to Helen. That thought came to him as he was admiring Helen's soft curves, accentuated by her small waist. She had her back to him and was packing her valise ready for the journey to Southwell. How lucky he was to have met up with her again on the passage to Melbourne. It prompted him to encircle his arms around her waist, before kissing her neck seductively.

She turned to face him, other things on her mind. 'Oh Jack, I have had such a lovely time here. I do hope Lizzie won't mind us staying at her home together,' she confided.

'She won't mind at all. My father and Lizzie lived together for several years without being married, but hopefully it won't be for very long. I intend purchasing a property in Crosby, which I mentioned to you yesterday. That's my plan, but everything depends on whether you would like to move in with me,' Jack stated, nonchalantly raising his eyebrows.

'Oh Jack, I would love to,' she cried, her eyes sparkling at the thought of such a bright future. Of course, I will have to inform the Matron on the *Dreadnought* that I won't be re-taking up my post and should do that sooner, rather than later. Perhaps I will return the weekend of the 11th, which will give you opportunity to have a look around Crosby in my absence,' suggested Helen.

'Why don't I wait until the 11th and we could take a look at a property together, staying at the Adelphi if you like.'

'That would be lovely,' confirmed Helen, ecstatic that she at last had a future with Jack.

'Excellent, that's settled then. Now we should hasten to the station to catch the next train to Nottingham,' he said, as he picked up Helen's valise. A new chapter in their lives had begun.

CHAPTER THIRTY-EIGHT

A Realisation
December 1856

The last few years had taken its toll on each and every one of the four friends gathered in the sitting room of *Woodgate House*. Daniel suffered depression, following the loss of Georgina, Lizzie, widowed almost a year and it had been five months since Kate and Robert's affair was exposed. Their profound hope was that their catharsis would begin at *'Woodgate'*, commencing with a combined house warming and very belated birthday celebrations for several guests.

⁓⁕⁓

Kate never stopped trying to lift Lizzie and Daniel's spirits, but she wasn't succeeding as well as she hoped, as their emotional struggles still seemed insurmountable. Robert's futile warning not to interfere had fallen on deaf ears; being Kate, she not only ignored his advice, but persisted in her determination to inject a modicum of happiness into the people she loved, which previously included himself. However, she wasn't going to give up and persevered with her encouragement.

She acknowledged Robert and herself were now very happy, despite the ongoing divorce proceedings. Luckily, both Amy and James now accepted the breakdown of their respective marriages, concluding that the best solution for their children's happiness was to work closely with their respective spouses and share the parental responsibilities. Amy had jointly purchased a house in the Lakes with her parents and, for the last two weeks, Harriett and Beatrice had both been allowed to stay at *'Woodgate'.*

Kate secretly hoped the family party would bring Lizzie and Daniel closer together, despite Georgina's tragic death in the train crash. She was mindful that it would soon be Christmas, which warranted extra special enthusiasm from herself. The rest of her family and friends, Rosie, Jimmy, Helen, Jack and Aunt Jayne were due on Saturday, when they planned to go horse riding.

༄༅

Congregated around the blazing fire, Daniel, was seated on the sofa, adjacent to Lizzie, who occupied a comfortable armchair. Robert relaxed on another. Kate was disappointed that her plan to sit Daniel and Lizzie on the sofa had backfired when they claimed their seats. Undaunted, she remained standing, on hand to serve drinks and eventually manoeuvre Lizzie on to the sofa next to Daniel, given the opportunity. At present, both of them seemed to be struggling with their emotional memories.

Kate noticed her fine spread of canapés and hors d'oeurvres lay untouched on the buffet sideboard, which increased her determination to act. 'Sherry Cobbler[94] and

---

[94] *Sherry Cobbler - Sherry Cobbler when you name it long; cobbler, when you name it short. Recipe: Fill tumbler with shaved ice, add 2 wine glasses of sherry one tablespoon of sugar and two to three slices of orange; shake well and ornament with berries of season.*

canapés anyone?' she asked pointedly. 'Oh Lizzie, do have a glass, it's rather delicious,' coaxed Kate, which precluded any attempt by Lizzie to decline. She took the proffered glass reluctantly, but smiled her thank you.

Daniel followed the episode with interest and, as Lizzie raised her glass to her lips, realised he was becoming guiltily transfixed by her beauty, dressed as she was in a tantalising green silk dress. She had only recently, on Kate's instigation, abandoned her obsession with wearing black. *It is time,* Kate had said*, to let go,* encouraging her to look to the future and, at the same time, reminding her that Rosie and Jimmy were soon to be married with the prospect of grandchildren.

Despite Kate's insistence, Lizzie was no nearer to fulfilling Marcus's wishes. His letter encouraged her to remarry. Admittedly, she had become closer to Daniel since Georgina's death, probably because they both lost their partners, but she still felt lonely. Looking after Victoria had helped and so had the people who loved her. Victoria was an inspiration having lost her mother. She gave Lizzie a reason to make the most of each day.

However, despite regular hints from Kate, Lizzie seemed reticent to encourage Daniel into believing they might be anything other than good friends. Maybe one day, but not now...she was not ready and, neither was he. After all, it was only four months since Georgina had died.

***

At this juncture, Lizzie glanced in his direction and perceived a broken man. Her heart went out to him, but her desires were still deeply buried. She was indeed sceptical they would ever resurface. She failed to realise that her feeling of betrayal of Marcus, could be the subconscious reason she was denying her innermost feelings, which went much deeper than she cared to admit.

Embarrassed, she looked away realizing Daniel's attention was still focussed on her. She was surprised, under the circumstances, to see an unexpected look in his eyes she had not witnessed previously. It conveyed desire, not friendship. She wondered how long he had felt that way. *Could it have been when he found her at the Goose Fair, over ten years ago?* At that time, she briefly entertained the idea of their love resurrecting, but all that changed with Marcus. Since then she viewed Daniel with a fondness, reflected in past memories, but nothing more, save that he was responsible for her recovering her memory, for which she would be eternally grateful. At that time, she had made it perfectly clear to him that Marcus was the man she loved and they could only ever be friends. He seemed to have accepted her decision, but now she had doubts, because his attention was unmistakeable. She had no idea what she should do.

Daniel continued to gaze upon her. He did not see a woman of thirty-nine, but a young girl of twenty-two, whom he had hoped to marry. He had known from the moment they were reacquainted, that his deep love for her had not diminished and regretted not trying to find her sooner. Realisation dawned, the present situation could not continue indefinitely. He was grateful to Lizzie for playing a significant part in Victoria's recovery after Georgina's death and, so far, she had not asked them to leave. He secretly hoped she might turn to him again and love him as she once did, although he struggled with the guilt. His realised his love for her was as strong as ever, despite his recent promise to devote himself to Georgina prior to her death.

Daniel's thoughts were abruptly interrupted when Kate suggested they all try some of the buffet food. Reluctantly and not wanting to offend their hostess, Lizzie and Daniel made their way to the buffet table. This gave Kate the opportunity to sit in the newly vacated chair next to Robert and left the small sofa vacant. Daniel returned with a plate of food followed by Lizzie who sat next to him, albeit uncomfortably.

Kate smiled to herself, her plan was coming together. 'Have you any idea when Rosie and Jimmy plan to marry?' she asked, addressing Lizzie. 'Rosie was a little guarded when I spoke to her last.'

Lizzie, nervous that Daniel was sitting in such close proximity, hesitated. She felt him turn his head toward her, but ignored the sudden quickening of her heartbeat and focussed on Kate's question. 'I'm not too sure, Kate. Jimmy feels they should wait until Rosie turns eighteen. He wants to save sufficient money for the wedding, securing another passage on the Australian run. Irrespective of the fact that Rosie has been left quite a substantial sum in Marcus's will and could easily fund the entire cost of the wedding, Jimmy is insistent that he should pay for it. He is very proud and would not hear of Rosie contributing. Actually, that dismays her, as she envisaged wearing an expensive dress and holding the reception in some grand venue. I imagine you and Robert also wanted to contribute, along with myself, but Jimmy's adamant. Has she mentioned anything to you about a venue?'

'She did mention it when they became engaged,' replied Kate, 'but Jimmy was very quick to point out that he would be paying the whole amount himself and that would be reflected in their choice. However, I have since thought of a wonderful compromise that would ensure Jimmy's pride remained intact.

'We could have the wedding feast in the grounds of *'The Chestnuts'*. I have spoken to James and he is in agreement. We could hire a marquee and make it a spectacular and wonderful occasion. Jimmy wouldn't have to compromise on such a lovely location for a summer wedding when the roses are in bloom. I see Rosie walking through the pergola down the steps from the terrace to the main lawn at the rear in the dress I wore for my wedding to James, if she agrees of course. It is really beautiful and it would not cost anything. I'll drop a subtle hint to Rosie soon. What do you think Lizzie?' asked an enthusiastic Kate.

Lizzie, mulling over her own thoughts, only heard the last part of the conversation and felt rather embarrassed when all eyes turned to hear her views. 'I'—she faltered, distracted once again by the warm feeling she was experiencing as she felt Daniel's shoulder brush against her own. She quickly recovered her poise—'I think that is a wonderful idea Kate. I am sure Rosie would be only too happy to wear your dress,' she agreed.

Kate realised that her suggestion regarding the venue had almost gone unnoticed by Lizzie. Her preoccupation with Daniel's closeness and her blushing hesitation confirmed Kate's obvious delight in her strategy.

To detract from her embarrassment, Lizzie foolishly requested another glass of 'Sherry Cobbler', which amused Kate and also Daniel. Robert replenished her glass. He smiled, recognising Kate's mischievous ongoing strategy.

Lizzie was still trying to make sense of her sudden desire and completely forgot that one glass of alcohol at Christmas and other formal occasions, was her usual quota, but already the first potent 'Cobbler' was having an effect. Cosseting the second glass in both hands, she began to relax in the comfort of her surroundings and in the midst of her family.

❧

As the evening wore on, Daniel noticed a change in Lizzie. She appeared to have turned a corner. He was looking forward to tomorrow's horse ride. If they rode together, he would orchestrate some time alone with her.

Lizzie, always familiar with horses had rode Barney on the odd occasion her father allowed, although it was several years later when she became an accomplished rider. She wondered how experienced the others' were. 'Do you know how competent Jimmy, Jack and Helen are in the saddle Kate?' she queried.

'Oh, according to Rosie, Jack and Helen are fairly confident, but Jimmy less so. Rosie has ridden on several occasions this past year and gained confidence, but Jimmy is not a natural rider. We should proceed slowly. Robert and I will head our group, so we can judge the route. For the most part it is fairly flat, although narrow, but if you and Daniel want to ride in front at your own pace, I am sure no one will mind. We'll lunch at the *Star Inn,* so if you two arrive early, you can secure a table. I expect the inn will be busy, as it is a popular place for visitors and it's expected to be sunny tomorrow.'

Daniel took the hint gratefully. 'That sounds like a good idea Kate, it is easier for riders to split into smaller groups. Some bridle paths are quite narrow. Are you happy with that Lizzie?' Daniel queried.

Lizzie, who was by now totally relaxed and comfortable with the arrangements, agreed.

Kate yawned deliberately, suggesting she and Robert retire, secretly pleased by her initial success.

༺༻

Left alone with Daniel so close, Lizzie was unsure of herself. The effect of the 'Cobbler' was rendering her too sleepy to move, unlike Daniel who now felt more confident about talking. 'So much has happened this last year Lizzie, but I do feel more optimistic for the future. I realise it will take longer than I imagined to come to terms with Georgina's death. Do you feel the same about Marcus?'

'Well Daniel, it might take some time. Of course, we'll never really forget, but maybe we will eventually come to terms with our loss. I seem to take one step forward and two back, despite the promises I make to myself. I've spent many nights asking why it happened to us and never really come up with any answers. I think the best approach is to keep your memories locked in your heart but allow yourself occasional moments to reminisce. I still talk to Marcus and tell him about my day, but I am trying to move on. Hopefully, those times will be less sad and intense. One day I'll look back on our life together and celebrate the good times we had. Some people will never know true love, so I already consider myself lucky to have experienced it twice in my life'—she paused to ask herself if this admission might give Daniel the idea they could resurrect their love for one another, although she was not sure it was what she actually wanted.

Daniel interrupted hesitantly—'Lizzie, your thoughts mirror my own. I also wish to be in a place where I can conjure up a memory and smile, rather than feeling sad. However, I have only experienced true love once. It's obvious who stole my heart on that occasion'—he paused, as he noticed Lizzie blush, but continued, to spare her embarrassment—'Please don't think I am suggesting anything right now, because I know our lives are fragile. I am just being honest. I want you to know that, if in the future, you feel we may have a chance of a life together, I will be here waiting for you. I've enjoyed being with you at your home and even if we remain just good friends, I will be a lucky man indeed. I know Victoria is coping better than she would have been had we returned to Ardwick and I am very grateful for the time you spend with her. A girl needs a mother figure and you have provided that, so thank you.' He smiled, hoping Lizzie reciprocated his feelings.

'Victoria is a pleasure to be around Daniel and she has actually helped me to focus on someone else. Rosie spends a good deal of time with Jimmy and soon he will be returning to sea'—she paused to wonder how Rosie would cope in his absence—'I'll admit to enjoying your company too Daniel. We always got on well, but should consider Victoria. She may be resentful if we decide to renew our relationship. She might imagine I am trying to replace her mother and that may turn her against me. I am not ruling anything out, but for now, we should just remain friends,' she tailed off, still unsure whether or not she was in denial of her feelings.

Despite Lizzie's desire, Daniel remained more optimistic than ever. One day he felt sure they would be lovers, or even, he dared to hope, man and wife.

CHAPTER THIRTY-NINE

Mixed Fortunes
December 1856

Kate's 'get together', resumed the following morning. A champagne breakfast greeted everyone, who'd arrived early, eager to participate in the day's events. Rosie was in good spirits, Jimmy was home again and had agreed to hold their wedding in the grounds of *The Chestnuts*, after Kate had excitedly told them of her plans. It meant they could marry earlier than expected and she couldn't wait for Jimmy to announce their proposal.

With breakfast complete, Jimmy stood up, chinking his champagne glass with a spoon to gain everyone's attention. An air of expectancy loomed around the table. He coughed presumptively, hoping his nerves would hold as he began. 'Thank you everyone,' he said, acknowledging their respectful silence. 'I want yer all ta know that me and Rosie have decided on a date ta marry'—he paused, conscious that under pressure, his Nottingham accent had resurfaced, but realised from the smiles of delight that no one even noticed, so, unabashed, he continued—'The date will be Friday, the 22nd January 1858, that's just over a year from now. Rosie will be almost seventeen and a half. Initially, we were go-an to wait until she wah eighteen, but the kind offer from her mamma, father and James ta hold the ceremony at *The Chestnuts* has enabled us ta bring it forward eight months,' he stated. Pausing again to accept the congratulations, he eventually continued, 'One more thing, I want ta ask me good friend, Jack, if he would be me best man...What da ya say Jack?' he challenged, not for an instant expecting a refusal and so it turned out.

Jack raised his glass. 'Nothing would give me greater pleasure,' he acknowledged, smiling and winking at Rosie, who responded with a knowing smile of her own, as understanding passed between them. Gently, she placed her hand on Jimmy's arm as a reminder she too wished to speak. 'Erm, I believe Rosie would also like ta say something, but first, I want ta thank Jack for being a very good friend ta me through good times and bad; thank you Jack, you taught me a lot and your friendship means everything ta me,' he said genuinely, seating himself as Jack acknowledged his grateful thanks, with a nod and a wink. Rosie looked on, proud of the men who had played a big part in her life.

Now it was her turn to contribute to the occasion. 'Thank you everyone. As Jimmy said, it will take place a little over a year from now, which is why I would like to share a story with you all about our preferred choice. On that day in 1847, when I was just over five years old, Jimmy told me he would marry me one day. I believe his words were, *'One day Rosie Merchant, I'm going ta marry yer and that's a fact'*, to which I replied, *'I know you are Jimmy. I knew you would marry me that day in the quarry, when my shoe got stuck between the boulders. I said to myself then, when I grow up, I'm going to marry Jimmy Mitchell!'* quoted Rosie amid cheers and laughter. 'A lot of water has flowed under the bridge since then and there were times when I thought this promise would not come true, significantly, when he was reported missing. After Jimmy's possible demise, Jack came into my life and became a very good friend to me'—she stated positively, pausing to turn her attention to Jack—'I will always love you Jack, but now Jimmy and I are delighted you found someone who will make you happy too...perhaps a double wedding could be in the offing?' she queried jokingly, grinning in satisfaction as she watched Helen blushing, before grasping Jack's hand.

'There's a big possibility of that happening, if she'll have me,' was Jack's audacious reply, instigating another buzz of excitement and whispered speculation.

Rosie continued, 'The other thing I wish to say is that I would be honoured to have Victoria and my two sisters' Harriett and Beatrice as my bridesmaids, if they agree of course?'

All three girls were overjoyed at the prospect, especially Beatrice who contemplated fulfilling the role of chief bridesmaid. However, she prudently refrained from asking the question at that moment and instead, joined Harriett and Victoria in accepting.

※

After breakfast, the eight adults gathered together for the ride across the beautiful countryside near Stone. Aunt Jayne was babysitting the three younger girls, as only Beatrice could ride and the terrain was considered too taxing for her. Daniel took the lead, alongside Lizzie, followed by Robert and Kate, Helen and Jack and Rosie and Jimmy. The intention was to head in the direction of the nearby canal and its pretty setting, then, as agreed, stop for lunch at the *Star Inn*.

Initially, they'd encounter a rough bridle path with its twists and turns, situated between an avenue of trees, before it gave way to open grassy fields and eventually, a steep path through a wood. Rosie and Jimmy watched the others go, as they fell behind. Sadly Jimmy was not a confident rider, although Rosie would seek to rectify that when they were married. The other riders needed to have their wits about them, up until the terrain plateaued, following a descent from the wood. They negotiated a country lane, then an old stone bridge, which joined a narrow tow-path at the side of the Trent and Mersey canal. Rosie, Jimmy, Helen and Jack, also lagging behind, dismounted to allow Jimmy, to adjust his stirrups. By now, they were some distance behind Kate and Robert and Lizzie and Daniel, so Rosie shouted for them to continue on to the *Star*. They would catch up with them later.

Lizzie and Daniel, galloping ahead at an exhilarating pace, eventually put a good distance between themselves and Kate and Robert. Some while later, Lizzie sighted the inn. In that instant, frightened by the galloping hooves, two swans suddenly took flight, spooking Daniel's horse, which reared up, ejecting him and throwing him on to the edge of the lock wall, then into the lock. He lost consciousness immediately, sinking below the surface. Shocked and distraught, Lizzie threw herself off her own horse and ran to his aid, but not before the lock keeper, quick on the scene, descended the lock ladder, grabbing Daniel's arm just as he resurfaced. Tom, an extremely strong lock keeper hauled Daniel over his shoulder and climbed the ladder effortlessly, before laying Daniel inert and seemingly lifeless on the tow-path.

Tom barked instructions to Lizzie. 'Fetch help from the inn, this man needs immediate medical assistance,' he implored.

Lizzie ran panic stricken to the *Star*, which was packed with people taking advantage of the good weather. 'Is there anyone here with medical training?' she shouted frantically while desperately scanning the faces of those standing at the bar.

One man immediately stepped forward. 'I have some medical knowledge,' he said, guiding Lizzie by the arm in the direction of the lock side and Daniel's prone form. To the man's astonishment, he recognised the bedraggled figure. 'Good God, it's Daniel Lorimer, as I live and breathe,' he exclaimed, but then wasted no time as he pumped his chest before turning him on his side. Daniel foamed, then spluttered water, groaning loudly. 'That's the worst over,' stated the man. 'Now let's deal with this broken leg!' Which until then had gone unnoticed by Lizzie. He covered Daniel with his coat then hastily fabricated a rudimentary splint from a small branch, finally securing it with his own belt. He pulled it tight, which made Daniel groan in pain, then addressed Lizzie. 'Lizzie Cameron, isn't it?' he stated somewhat unconvincingly, astounded by the circumstances of such an opportune meeting.

'Why yes, yes it is,' confessed a bemused Lizzie, unable to recall just who the Good Samaritan was. However, the urgency of Daniel's predicament curtailed further conversation.

'I need to locate a doctor,' stated the man. Make sure you keep him talking and reassure him until I return.'

'Of course,' agreed a worried Lizzie, cradling Daniel's head in her arms.

༄

It was a while before a doctor arrived. In the meantime, Daniel had lapsed in and out of consciousness, a few times, despite Lizzie's attentions. It was while she was waiting, she realised who the man was…Finlay McEwan…an old friend of them both, but for now, Daniel needed her whole attention. She whispered in his ear, which was inaudible to the small crowd that had gathered. At that moment, she realised how much he meant to her, but it wasn't long before Daniel was being secured to a stretcher on the back of a carriage on a journey to the hospital with Lizzie.

Robert and Kate arrived shortly after, followed by the rest of the riding party, just as the carriage was leaving the scene. They reacted to the news imparted by Finlay, with some disbelief, deciding to leave their horses at the inn before making their way to the hospital, located several miles away.

Two hours later, Daniel, lying in a hospital bed and surrounded by his friends, opened his eyes. He tried to focus on the sea of faces, but his gaze rested on one in particular. He was astonished and somewhat incredulous. His best friend, from Glasgow, Finlay McEwan, was smiling at him. 'Finlay…Finlay is it really you?' he managed.

Finlay placed his hand on Daniel's arm. 'Yes Daniel and believe me I was just as surprised when I discovered *you* lying on the tow-path. It's nigh on fifteen years since we've seen each other. I see you finally married your first love,' he said referring to Lizzie, wrongly assuming she was his wife.

Embarrassed, Daniel attempted a feeble explanation. 'Unfortunately, Lizzie's not my wife Finlay…it's a long story, but I hope I'll be well enough soon to catch up on the many years since we lost touch…Oh, and thank you Finlay, it appears you may have just saved my life,' he muttered, closing his eyes again, as exhaustion from his ordeal overcame him.

Several weeks passed before Daniel was discharged from the hospital into Lizzie's care. He and Victoria would live at her home in Southwell indefinitely while he recuperated. Her whispered words would remain foremost in his mind when he later recalled that fateful day at the lock.

CHAPTER FORTY

Circle of Destiny
December 1857

It hardly seemed credible that a year had passed since Daniel's riding accident. Lizzie insisted on nursing him at her home in Southwell, through this difficult time, ably assisted by Victoria. Now fully recovered, he felt able to embark on a new life, but first he needed an answer to the question which had haunted him for the last sixteen years.

That fateful Tuesday, in the September of '41, was burned in his memory. He'd arrived with a delivery of fresh fish and meat for Low Wood Hall. To his astonishment, Lizzie had taken flight. Unbeknown to Daniel his twenty-two year old lover, was already boarding the 'Royal George' on the first leg of her epic journey. He was distraught that the opportunity of asking her to be his wife, had fatalistically passed him by. Tragically, he was unaware that it would be five years before he would next see her at Nottingham's Goose Fair.

In those five years, Lizzie met Marcus, lost her memory and then regained it thanks to his intervention. Ten more years rapidly disappeared as he watched her life with Marcus unfold, while he silently suppressed his feelings for her.

But now, convalescing in Lizzie's home, he felt the wind of change. The validity of him returning to his home in Ardwick Green, Manchester had not been mentioned. Lizzie seemed keen on him staying. He was acutely aware that she occasionally glanced in his direction to share a look of tenderness usually reserved between lovers. Was this for friendship or pity, or more? He hoped beyond hope that it could be.

However, he wasn't prepared to wait any longer. He intended to remind her of this very day a year ago, at Kate's 'get together'. He had been thrown unceremoniously from his horse and into the lock water, after it was startled by swans taking flight. Lizzie's intervention in attracting the attention of the quick thinking of lock-keeper, Tom and Finlay, who efficiently applied a tourniquet to his leg, probably saving his life, he'd now made a full recovery, but it was a day Lizzie and himself would never forget.

༄

He watched her intently as she entered the sitting room, carrying a tea tray. Summoning his courage and acutely aware of her closeness, bade her sit beside him. He deliberately placed his arm on hers. 'Leave the tea Lizzie, I have something to say that can't wait,' he said, his heart pounding. He drew a deep breath. 'Do you remember the day of my riding accident last December?'

Lizzie, bemused, smiled wryly. 'Why of course Daniel, how could I forget, we thought we might lose you, until, fortuitously, Tom and Finlay's actions saved the day.'

Daniel focussed his innermost being on Lizzie's eyes. 'Yes, lucky indeed'—he agreed wholeheartedly—'I remember falling in and out of consciousness and honestly thought I wouldn't make it. It might sound unreal, but I recall seeing a bright light, which drew me towards it and I felt I was floating upwards, surrounded by love, but deep in my soul, I knew I had to return.

'However, in the midst of these hallucinations, if indeed they were just that, I heard a voice—yours Lizzie! Whereby I gradually regained consciousness. I was confused and disorientated, in fact, everything was a blur; but I recall one defining moment when you held me in your arms and whispered, 'I love you Daniel'. You pleaded with me not to leave you. Was it true Lizzie, or did I imagine everything?' Daniel asked anxiously, with an intensity that reached into her soul.

Lizzie averted her eyes, struggling with her emotions. Since that day, she had been fighting an ever increasing sexual desire for Daniel, her first love, tempered only by an overwhelming feeling of betrayal for Marcus. At that moment, she instantly remembered the words in his letter— *'I am, with all my heart, looking forward to a long and happy life together...Just like Perseus and Andromeda...I still remember our romantic night when we stood at the hotel window looking out at the stars. Of course, if you are reading this, you will know wherever I am, I will watch over you. If this be the case, I want you to lead a full and happy life, albeit without me in the physical sense. I know that will be difficult. Don't be afraid to remarry in the future. You have my blessing—*

She stopped her recollection dramatically, accepting the implication of the letter. His message was irrefutable; Marcus had given her his blessing. She turned to Daniel, anxiously waiting a reply. She must release his emotional turmoil. 'Oh Daniel, I *have* fallen in love with you again and I can no longer deny my feelings. Yes it is true, I did say I love you,' she admitted.

Relieved and ecstatically happy beyond his wildest dreams, Daniel took her in his arms and kissed her softly and sensuously. Their true love, dormant for many years, resurfaced, until a moment later he reluctantly broke away.

There was one more question he desperately needed to ask—'Will you marry me Lizzie Cameron?'

Without hesitation and with a contentment that promised eternal love, she answered—'Yes of course I will Daniel. I would have married you all those years ago, but fate intervened and the moment was gone. Maybe...just maybe, despite what has seemed a lifetime apart, our destinies will be forever intertwined.'

THE END